Peter Crowther lives in Harrogate ...
and two sons. His articles, reviews and interviews appear regularly on both sides of the Atlantic, and he has sold short stories to numerous magazines and anthologies.

In addition to editing the *Narrow Houses* series, he is co-author (with James Lovegrove) of *Escardy Gap*, and has recently completed *Heaven Sent*, an anthology of angel stories, and *Tombs*, a collection of tales involving incarceration. One of his stories is shortly to be produced for Yorkshire Television's *Chillers* series.

'A glittering showcase of contemporary horror and fantasy'

Stan Nicholls, *The Dark Side*, on *Touch Wood*

Also edited by Peter Crowther

NARROW HOUSES
BLUE MOTEL: Narrow Houses Volume 3

TOUCH WOOD

NARROW HOUSES VOLUME 2

Edited by Peter Crowther

WARNER BOOKS

A *Warner* Book

First published in Great Britain by Little, Brown and Company 1993
This edition published by Warner Books 1994

A CIP catalogue record for this book
is available from the British Library.

ISBN 0 7515 0698 2

Photoset in North Wales by
Derek Doyle & Associates, Mold, Clwyd.
Printed in England by Clays Ltd, St Ives plc

Warner Books
A Division of
Little, Brown and Company (UK)
Brettenham House
Lancaster Place
London WC2E 7EN

CONTENTS

Dedication

This one's for Muriel and Philip Hassam, for the best present I ever received.
And for Molly, in whose silent canine company so many ideas have been formulated.
Plus, of course, for Oliver and Timothy . . . always.

Acknowledgements

Ed Gorman and Martin Greenberg, for making things happen.
John Hanlon and Norman Thompson, for support while they were happening.

Special Thanks

David Borrowdale and Raymond Crow: for financial assistance and figure juggling.
Colin Murray and Andrew Wille: for continued belief and editorial management.
Phil Garnett and Keith Sorsby: for knowing where the bodies are buried . . . and how to get them there in the first place.
Simon Conway and Nigel Whiteley: for always being there when the phone rings.

FOREWORD

The real reward of doing an anthology, I now know, is in the critical judgement of one's peers. Inevitably, the exercise is a personal – almost narcissistic – affair with the beleaguered editor holding up the end result and saying 'Hey, this is what *I* like . . . how about *you?*'

Despite the fact that, with a collection of 29 stories, you're unlikely to please everyone with everything, last year's *Narrow Houses: Volume One* received plaudits aplenty from both sides of the Atlantic. Particularly encouraging were Gardner Dozois's inclusion of Pat Cadigan's 'Naming Names' in his *Year's Best Science Fiction*, and Ellen Datlow's and Terri Windling's decision to take Steve Gallagher's 'The Sluice' and Nick Royle's 'Glory' for their *Year's Best Fantasy and Horror* collection. Ellen and Terri even went on to list a further ten of that first volume's stories in their 'Honourable Mentions' section. So I guess it's safe to say the series kicked off well. So well, that work has already started on a third volume. *House of Omens: Narrow Houses III* will be available in December 1994.

Meanwhile, here's another batch of stories covering the whole spectrum of the weird and wonderful worlds of the macabre and the strange, each containing a small talismanic belief that ventures beyond what we have been taught is possible or even reasonable. This time, though, there seems to be even more of a link between the tales: I think the word that best sums up that link is 'optimism'.

Maybe it's to do with the sociological environment in which the stories were conceived and written. You don't need me to tell you that the past couple of years have been punishing, both here and in the United States, with few people escaping at least a small dose of pain or misfortune. People are looking for hope, they're looking for understanding and they're looking for escape. That's also true of the people in the stories you are about to read – sometimes they find it, sometimes they don't, and sometimes . . . well, then it's anyone's guess what happens.

Enjoy – I think you will . . . touch wood!

Peter Crowther
Harrogate
July 1993

INTRODUCTION

It might seem that the last thing the world needs is more superstition, or perhaps any at all. As we swarm towards the millennium, which may be the most fertile breeding ground just now for the dangerously irrational, aren't we most in need of some healthy jolts of reason? Won't books such as this one and its predecessor plant seeds in the minds of at least their more susceptible readers – seeds of paranoia and of the kinds of belief people cling to rather than examine? What are we – you, the reader as well as us, the writers – doing in this book?

Perhaps we are acknowledging the irrational, because even more dangerous than its most extreme manifestations is the idea that reason will or should destroy it once and for all. If a superstition is a belief adhered to in the face of reason, mustn't it be one for any of us to believe ourselves wholly rational? The unacknowledged and repressed invariably erupts in some worse form (which, incidentally, strikes me as the strongest argument against censorship). But I venture to believe that none of the contributors to this book would deny the importance of the imagination, and what is the imagination if not the harnessing of the irrational? That makes the notion of a world illuminated by nothing except reason begin to seem rather horrible to me. The only place without shadows I can think of is an interrogation cell.

Which is not to say that our writers fail to interrogate the superstitions they present. I would rather say that most train their imaginations on them. So Charles L. Grant shows us a folk belief becoming an obsession, and John Brunner demonstrates how religion and a phobia can aggravate each other and destroy a life, while Stella Hargreaves takes a preoccupation no bigger than a speck of dust and makes us watch it grow. Colin Greenland gets behind eyes which see religion as a superstition, and Kristine Kathryn Rusch gives her narrator a deeply personal belief to overcome.

Some of the stories take place in locales which might seem comfortably remote from most of us, but there's nothing reassuring about how Garry Kilworth takes tribal beliefs to their conclusion, or the tradition William Relling revives which it would be perilous to think had died, or the nightmare Bentley Little brings out of the backwoods, or the fears and prejudices of which Steve Lockley reminds us. The traditions in the tales by Paul Lewis and Yvonne Navarro sound eerily authentic to me, as does Bill Pronzini's symbol of a terror which we will all have to face.

Am I being too sombre? It must be the shadow of the millennium. Let me not suggest there is no fun to be had herein. Karl Edward Wagner finds a use for a mediaeval tradition which would not have been out of place in the classic horror comics, and, in the same spirit, Thomas Monteleone gives a new meaning to an everyday invocation of good luck. Spider Robinson amuses those who know, and do I spy a sexual pun underlying Adam Corbin Fusco's riff on a folk tradition? Stanley Wiater's version of an urban myth may seem to be about censoriousness as a form of superstition, and there are illustrations by Gahan Wilson to add to the uneasy laughs.

Superstition can be a way of evading reality or a delusory means of controlling it, but this book seldom offers so much reassurance, though Charles de Lint does put a traditional belief on the streets. Christopher Evans takes us to the future roots of paganism, and Simon Ings shows us the underside of tomorrow, but Stan Nicholls's contribution may be the most disturbing of all, distilling as it does a new myth from, alas, the everyday. Neil Gaiman leaves his material in our minds to make us . . . surely not superstitious. As for D.F. Lewis, it would take as long for me to come up with a summary of his tale as for the reader to read it.

What else have I to say on our subject? Nothing that wasn't said better by Douglas Winter in his introduction to the first volume. If you don't own both, do yourself a favour and improve your luck by buying them. Now *there*'s a superstition I endorse.

Ramsey Campbell
Wallasey, Merseyside, March 1993

TOUCH WOOD

t. Winter-Damon

A resident of the wide-open spaces of Tucson, Arizona,
t. Winter-Damon has had work appear in more than 250 magazines and anthologies around the world – including five outings
in *Year's Best Horror* volumes as well as every small press 'zine
that ever drew an excited breath. His most recent sales – and
there are many between each of our exchanges of correspondence – include the story 'Heretics' to Paul Sammon's *Elvis is Dead*
anthology, where Damon (his preferred soubriquet) will stand
alongside Joyce Carol Oates, ex-*Tonight Show* host Steve Allen
and troubadour Lou Reed.

He has been called 'the leading contemporary poet of surreal
mysticism and horror', but still speaks to the reviewer responsible
– clearly Damon is as generous as he's talented. And he's *very*
talented. He's also very superstitious, 'as seems the case with a
number of horror writers of my acquaintance,' he adds in his
defence. 'I was the type of child terrified by all manner of
imagined horrors . . . the dark shadows, the thing beneath my
bed, the boogieman – my parents still have a good laugh at how I
used to whistle hymns as I moved up and down the darkened
stairs.'

Not surprisingly, Damon is a fanatic about touching wood and
also about the number twenty-two, his lucky number. 'Actually,
I am far too influenced by numerological foreshadowings and
suspected omens . . . I even practice the little-known art of

1

'cookiemancy', cracking open a fresh fortune cookie when I write to people and including the fortune in the envelope.' (It's true!)

Damon used Zolar's *Encylopedia of Omens, Signs and Superstitions* in the drafting of his poem with the result that each line or image is, of itself, a highly compressed version of a superstition . . .

TOUCH WOOD

Hark! Somber toll the midnight strokes
Down past the graves at blackthorn abbey.
Moon's corpse-rind hides 'hind skyfire-shattered tree.
The ghost wind moans. A bullfrog croaks.
Veils haze the low-hung stars and willow boles
And swirl 'midst clumps of river reed.
'Ware 'cross those narrow plots of rustling weed,
Trod gentle lest you rouse their drowsing souls.
Now, you strive to hum, you muse old jokes . . .
No good! That shan't make those shadows flee,
Nor chase away the lich grown shabby.
Echoes raise of Saviour's elder-spokes –

Touch Wood!

Hark! Old screech owl shrieks out his knell.
Pass with chill the darkened church built
Where ancient grove once stood. By day,
Hoodies gyre 'bout its tower bell,
By night, 'tis batwings rise and swoop. Wilt
Thou venture here, beg tree-souls' good, and pray –

Touch wood! Touch wood!

Pale bone-whispers wail this aged charm,
To one another, taunting, half-understood.
Dust to dust, words warding mortal clay from harm –

Touch wood! Touch wood! Touch wood!

HOLDING HANDS

Charles L. Grant

Three-time winner of the World Fantasy Award, twice winner of the Nebula Award and recipient of the British Fantasy Society's Life Achievement Award, Charles Grant surely needs little in the way of introduction.

A string of quietly unsettling short stories and novels – including his 1982 epic *The Nestling* – spanning two decades culminated this year in *Raven*, from NEL, while his *Greystone Bay* and *Shadows* books, along with Tom Monteleone's *Borderlands* and J.N. Williamson's *Masques* collections, remain glaring examples of how to put together a good anthology series.

Grant lives with his wife-and-fellow-writer Kathryn Ptacek – whose monthly writers' guide to the markets, *Gila Queen*, is virtually de rigueur for serious wannabes – in a century-old haunted house in New Jersey where, he insists, he likes to think he's not superstitious. However . . .

Although black cats and Friday the thirteenth don't particularly bother him, he does admit to wearing a tiger's eye stone (on a chain around his neck) and his college ring with fanatical devotion. The one time he removed the ring – maybe to work on the car; he doesn't remember – he got drafted and ended up in Viet Nam. 'I've never taken it off since,' he says, adding, 'and I've never been back in the army!'

And yet, amazingly, there are people who still say there's to this superstition stuff . . .

4

I didn't want to stay, you know.

Honest to God, I really didn't.

But sometimes you say things you don't really mean, sometimes you give looks you don't realize say too much, sometimes you walk away when you really want to stay and it's so damn hard trying to get back.

It's so damn hard trying to find the way.

I guess that's what happened between you and me.

So be patient and listen to me, hon. Listen just a little while longer, stop your crying, and I'll tell you how it was. How it is.

Stop your fussing, girl.

It won't take all that long.

The first thing you have to know is the how it was.

And how it was, it was raining.

You remember that storm that summer? Hot days for a week beforehand, humidity fogging the trees, every night all those flashes on the horizon promising thunder and not giving us a thing. The afternoon before, that guy came out from the bank. Barrows, as I recall; Anthony Barrows. Nice-looking fella, a little young for my taste for all that responsibility, but then, I suppose the whole world was too young in those days for any of my tastes.

Mr Schoolman, he said, standing there on the steps, me in my chair on the porch. Mr Schoolman, you're not making this very easy on any of us, you know.

Yes, yes, I know, hon, I know you agreed with him for most of it. But that's the way I was. I'd worked all my life, or damn near most of it, and I couldn't help feeling both angry at him, and a little sorry for myself. I tried to tell him where it had gone, all that money, all those years, the new mortgage to pay Momma's hospital bills the insurance didn't cover, but he only smiled without any of it getting much past those skinny lips, and handed me the paper.

I tore it up.

He said, it doesn't matter, Mr Schoolman. You can tear up a hundred of them, it doesn't matter a bit.

Thank God, he had the sense to go away then.

If he had stayed, talking to me like that, like I had to be coddled and pampered and treated like a child, I would have killed him where he stood.

You came back from seeing Momma just as he drove away, and I do believe I took it out on you. Just about all of it. Damn, if you didn't start crying and hollering right out there on the porch, calling me all kinds of names, using words I didn't even know you knew, your face redder than a lobster fresh out of the pot. I knew it was wrong, dumping my anger on you like that, but you sure didn't like me then; you really didn't. Then off you went, storming down the walk like you were heading for a gunfight and God help the other guy.

I know; I didn't say anything.

I couldn't.

Part of it was that you looked so much like your mother, it would have been like yelling at her, and not once in all those years did I ever raise my voice to her, not once.

The rest of it, though, it's the house. You live in a place long enough – and I guess forty-some years was plenty long enough – and there are some things it just won't let you do. It gets to fit you, it gets to know you, and when it gets to when you can get around at midnight without turning on a light, without barking your shins ten to the dozen, you've become as much a part of it as it is of you.

The house wouldn't let me say what I really wanted.

So when you had your say and left, hands waving, head shaking like that, all I could do was sit there and try to calm down, try to keep my heart from blowing up. Staring at the lawn. Tapping my foot. Thinking about . . . things. Pretty soon feeling the weight of the air, the way it didn't move right, knowing there was a storm coming and wishing, right then, it would set itself off right over my head. Burn the house down. Serve the little bastard right.

It didn't, though, remember?

Flashes on the horizon once the sun had gone down.

Flashes on the horizon.

I remember – now don't move around so much, hon, you know what the doctor said, you have to rest, take it easy, don't get all excited. You just lie there and let me have my say. I mean, I have a right, don't you think? After all these years, don't you think I have a right?

That's good; that's fine.

You don't want to make it worse.

So anyway, I guess I thought so much I fell asleep, because the next thing I knew, my back was paining, my knees felt cramped, and I had the world's champion headache working an anvil on the back of my skull. You hadn't come back, all the lights were out, and when I finally managed to get to my feet without feeling like I was going to fall on my face and break a few bones, I got inside and to the kitchen, made myself a quick cup of coffee. But it tasted like hell, and I couldn't think of anything else to do, so I figured I'd best get to bed before you changed your mind, came in, and gave me what for.

You always did.

Ever since Momma left, you always told me what I should do, what I shouldn't.

I drank too much coffee, spent too much time in the Brass Ring, wasted too much money over at the Regency, watching all them movies. Far as you are concerned, I'd forgotten how to shave right when I was fifty, couldn't dress after I hit sixty, and probably didn't even breathe right when I rounded seventy at something a little less than a brisk walk.

Oh, for God's sake, Lizzy, it was a joke, stop your crying.

Jesus.

So I went to bed, but I didn't sleep.

The house knew, and it wouldn't let me.

It talked to me, hon, most of the night, the way houses do when they have something to say. The boards, the sills, the eaves, the cellar – it talked to me, reminded me, and when I got up the next day, I knew that Mr Anthony Barrows and that damn bank weren't going to do it.

You take my house, your momma's house, you do more than tear out my heart; you go much deeper, down where it's dark and light all at the same time.

Down where there are things we've forgotten all about.

No, of course, you don't get it. Hell, you never lived in one place more than ten, fifteen years at a time that I can remember; you or your brother. Always moving, just like everybody else. Always finding a better bedroom, a larger lawn, a prettier street, a safer town, a better God-knows-what but it sure isn't a better house.

Not one like mine, anyway.

I called Mr Barrows that very afternoon, told him he'd have to drag me out.

You know what he said?

He said, Your choice, Mr Schoolman.

Then he hung up on me.

I couldn't believe it; the little prick hung up on me.

That's when I went up into Momma's room for a while. First time I'd been there in weeks, but I needed a little peace and quiet, some place to think without the world butting in. It still smelled of her. Still does. Powder, that awful stuff she splashed on after she took a bath because she thought I liked it, and . . . her. Just . . . her. Hair, skin, breath, everything. Used to be, I'd go in, sit on the bed, talk to her a little when things got confusing.

She never liked being old, you know.

Old, she always said, was something dogs and horses got.

People, she said, just got worn out.

Well, I was about as worn as I could get that day, and you had gone back to your place, temper all in a knot, and I needed someone, hon. I needed someone who wouldn't look at me like I was just a crazy old man who could be taken care of with a pat on the head, a cheery smile, one of them stupid 'And how are we today?' things nurses always say when they know damn well that 'we' feel like hell.

I needed someone to tell me it was okay to go on.

Because, I tell you the truth, Lizzy, all of a sudden, after what you said to me, after Barrows hung up on me, the whole time I was sitting in there by myself, thinking about her, smelling her, hearing her humming while she did her hair before she slept, I wasn't real sure.

For the life of me, just then, I couldn't think of one good reason why.

Until after an hour or so I looked around, that is. Looked around and saw all those years in all those things I'd kept, things that don't mean anything to anyone else but me. That's when I started going through the place. Every room. Every closet. Attic to cellar. Every room, every closet, breathing it all in, remembering it all. Every damn thing. It took me all day, most of the night, but there isn't an inch of that old place I didn't stop to visit for a while.

There isn't an inch of my life I didn't remember, good and bad.

Good and bad.

Lizzy, you've got to stop that squirming, all right? You're only going to hurt yourself, and if you're to understand, you've got to listen.

Of course, you don't have to understand, not if you don't want to.

It'd just make it easier, that's all.

But I guess you – and your brother, too, rest his soul – you never got it.

Nobody does.

Nobody believes they're going to get old.

Sunset years, golden years, senior citizens, distinguished elderly . . . it's all lies, Liz, it's all lies. A spring coat to pretend that winter isn't coming.

Next morning it was cloudy.

The storm had come after all.

Flashes on the horizon were flashes now out over the old farm across Mainland Road, and the wind was getting itself ready to blow, and you could smell the rain in the air; by God, you could smell all that sweet waiting rain.

Which was why I was pretty surprised when Barrows came out that afternoon, for what he called one last appeal to reason – which meant he had a guilty conscience and wanted to shut the damn thing up. He was soaked, rain dripping off him left and right, so I took him into the kitchen, made him a cup of coffee, listened to him gab on for God knows how long about places they have for folks like me where I could be with folks like me, where I'd have things in common with the people I lived with. Retirement villages, retirement communities, but they're all the same . . . they're all the same.

The storm got worse, wind and lightning, and the lights danced a little.

Mr Schoolman, he said at last, looking like he was going to cry, why are you so damn stubborn? Why you making it so hard on yourself?

I asked him, I said, why should I have to go to some place where folks have given up? I told him I liked the kids in the neighborhood; they made me mad sometimes with their noise and stuff, but they made me smile and they never laughed at me. Hell, they called me 'Pops' sometimes, but what the hell, they weren't like their parents. The kids figured I was good for a laugh now and then; their folks didn't like me because it was like looking in a mirror.

Rain hit the window, sounding like ice.

He shook his head and said I was an awfully bitter man, afraid of dying, lying to myself, and I needed help before something happened to me.

I said, I'm my own help, Mr Barrows.

Then I shot him.

Hit him in the place where he used to have a heart.

The house didn't even flinch.

Then I quick made sure he was dead, put on my raincoat, and dragged him out to the back, dug myself a new garden – the ground was pretty soft by that time – and when I rolled him in, lightning showed me his face.

There was nothing there, Liz.

There was nothing there.

That's when I really decided I didn't want to go.

That's how it was.

Questions, the police, me being what they all thought I was –
a poor old widower who wouldn't harm a fly. I damn near
laughed myself to sleep every night until they stopped coming
and I saw in the *Herald* that Barrows had probably skipped town,
run off with some woman.

But even when I laughed, I saw his face, Liz.

Nothing there.

Nothing there at all.

That's how it was; and how it is.

That's easy.

When your brother was born, a little nurse – she wasn't very
young – she came in to Momma's room for the first feeding, in
case Momma needed help. When she saw the baby there, so
damn chubby and all cleaned up and wailing for the food, that
woman, she was from someplace down South, she told Momma
some kind of saying they have down there, that the hand, the
baby's hand we were holding, all soft and wiggly and just
scrubbed, is the one that'll take hold of us when it's our time.

When we have to go.

Momma never forgot that.

She didn't want to go, either; she just knew it sooner than me.

So she held his hand when he was in the hospital that time,
after that heart operation he had over to Boston. Pretty much
the same one you just had, darlin', except he wasn't so awake
after it was done.

She held his hand, Liz, and she kissed his brow, and if it
hadn't been for that stupid sonofabitch in that pickup, that
drunken goddamn bastard, she'd be right here with you now,
looking young as ever. She really would.

And so, when she went after all, especially like that, I
honestly wasn't sure I wanted to stay.

But there was the house, and Mr Barrows, and you called me
all kinds of ugly names, hon, and I don't think it's right to talk
that way to your father. I thought we'd brought you up better, I
really thought we had.

The house knew.

The house knew you'd torn out my heart.

So give me your hand, baby.

Give me your hand, my darling daughter.

It won't take very long.

Your brother was gone in just a few minutes.

Give me your hand, dear.

Give your daddy a kiss.

And when you see Momma, tell her I love her, and I'll be along one of these days.

Just don't ask why, Lizzy, don't ask why.

I don't want to go; it's as simple as that.

I don't want to go.

And I won't.

LODGINGS

Colin Greenland

Colin Greenland's novel *Take Back Plenty* (1990) won three awards and his latest book – *Harm's Way* – is a space-faring yarn of tall ships of the aether.

But despite the fact that his longer works have been science fiction or fantasy, there's a 'peculiar cannibalistic revenant' – in the author's own words – in *Other Voices* (1988), and his short stories tend more towards horror . . . especially the ones in Charles L. Grant's *Final Shadows* and the *Midnight Rose* shared world anthologies.

Not surprisingly, perhaps, Greenland admits to being very superstitious. 'I'm prone to much compulsive and irrational behaviour intended to placate invisible powers and bring about magical results,' he says. 'Thus I vote in elections; take medicine prescribed by doctors; and never cross a road without looking both ways first.'

Yes, but does it *work*?

I remember the first time I came to this house. It was the afternoon of a dark day in November, with the sky closed like a zinc lid over the town. There was no sign of life anywhere: cars parked all up both sides of Mount Street, but no one in any of them. There wasn't even a cat prowling. It looked as if everyone who had ever lived here had gone away long ago and forgotten about it.

I was a young thing then, striking out for the first time on my own. I had gone for a place at the Commercial College just to get away from home, and I'd got it. Now I was looking for the address they'd given me at the accommodation office. I took it out of my bag and read it again, though I knew perfectly well what it said. 37 Winterbrook Gardens. Miss Selby.

I saw the sign, to the right at the top of the hill. I crossed the road, passed the block of garages on the corner, then a bomb-site behind a fence. Halfway along the street I saw a row of tall old houses that nobody wanted any more. I supposed they were Victorian. I thought they looked shocked at their fate, their empty windows like black mouths gaping at the twentieth century. One of them was being used to store carpets. Most of the rest already had their front doors boarded up.

Number 37 still had curtains at the windows. They were all closed, upstairs and down. There was a black iron rod hanging beside the door. I noticed the paint on it was worn and parts of it were quite rusty. I pulled it. Far inside, a bell jangled.

For a long time, nothing happened. I waited. I had to. She had to be in. The accommodation people said she never went anywhere. They said she was very old.

Eventually the doorknob turned, and the door opened a bit, pushing against a curtain that hung behind it.

The old lady stood back in the shadows of the hall, squinting at the daylight, what little there was of it. She was tall and stooped. She was wearing a long dress of velvet the colour of seaweed, and a brown shawl. I could hardly believe people still dressed like that, even old ladies way out here.

'Miss Selby?' I said.

'Yes?' she said. Her voice was stronger than you'd have thought, though the hand she lifted to her face was as wrinkled as an old envelope.

'The college sent me,' I said. 'They said you had a room.'

'Oh yes,' said Miss Selby. 'There's always a room.'

Shading her eyes, she opened the door wider.

'Come in, then,' she said. As I stepped inside, she said, 'It's cold today,' sounding as if she were blaming me for it, or at least for keeping her waiting on the doorstep. It wasn't much warmer inside than out; but she pulled the curtain to again and showed me into the front room.

The front room was dark and shut away, very much as it is now, in fact. Miss Selby didn't make any effort to open the curtains. She switched on the light, a weak bulb in a brown paper shade, and knelt down stiffly to fiddle with the old gas fire. Blue flames popped and jiggled. It didn't make any difference to the temperature that I could feel. The room was as cold as any larder.

'You young people don't feel the cold,' Miss Selby said, rubbing her hands together. 'I'm afraid I do.' I could barely see her, but I could hear her rubbing her hands. It made a noise like mice on sandpaper.

'Yes, it's cold,' I said, hoping that was enough about the weather. I was looking at an ornament she had on the mantelpiece, a china soldier talking to a woman with a parasol. I remember thinking that it looked valuable.

Slowly Miss Selby got to her feet, holding on to the carving on the fireplace. She looked like a folded clothes-horse trying to stand up on its own. 'Well, sit down, now,' she said. 'I could make a cup of tea, if you'd like one.'

She managed to make it sound as if making a cup of tea were some distant, very difficult task that she'd accomplished once, when she was a girl, and supposed she might attempt again if I demanded it. 'You needn't bother,' I said.

She stood there sizing me up, inspecting me. I tried to guess how old she was. Eighty? More? Her eyes were bright, glittering deep in her head. I thought they looked like little varnished snailshells. I thought of my gran, and the torture of Sunday afternoon visits. She had always wanted to know everything about me. There was no telling whether this one was the same, or what she was capable of taking in, if anything.

I've never liked old people. I hate the way they turn into sticks and string inside their skins. Our skins, I suppose I should say, having come some way along that same road myself.

Miss Selby asked me my name.

'Mary Gillespie,' I said. 'I'm at the college,' I added. 'I've just started.' None of this made any impression. There seemed to be a funny smile twitching in the ruins of her cheeks. I hoped she wasn't the other sort, that would want you to listen to her life story. 'They said you wanted a lodger,' I said loudly.

'Oh yes,' said Miss Selby in a happy little whisper. 'I'm always glad to have a lodger.'

We sat and looked at each other in the cold yellow light.

'Could I see the room, then?' I said.

She took me up. There were no lights on the stairs. I made out a huge grandfather clock on the landing. As we went by I could see it had a brass face with bits of mother-of-pearl. I remember I liked the look of that, too.

I saw the stairs went on up, but Miss Selby opened a door on the first floor at the back. She turned her back to it, holding on to the handle. 'Here it is,' she said.

Inside it was all in darkness. She was making no attempt to go in, but stood right there in the doorway, in my way. She seemed to be exhausted. I could hear her breathing hard from the climb. I remember I wondered then, if I took the room, whether she'd last the year out.

I was tired of waiting for her to move so I pushed past and went in. I went over to the window and opened the curtains, which were thick, and full of dust. The heavy light seemed to come in slowly, as if it had not been in here for some time and had forgotten the way.

I looked around. I saw it was a big room, full of antique furniture. The dust was thick on it all. There were three different chairs and a table with an empty candlestick on it, and a chest of drawers. There was a drab olive green bedspread on the bed, with strange stains on it, and the wallpaper had been green too, with curly ferns all over. Now it was grey. The air smelled of stale carpet.

'It's very nice,' I said. 'How much?'

Miss Selby was still standing in the same spot, half in, half out, as if the door were shielding her from something in the room she didn't like. I wondered if it was something I had let in. 'How much is usual?' she said. 'I'm afraid I really don't know.'

The woman had told me at the office how much it would be. In my head I halved it. 'I haven't got much money,' I added.

Miss Selby nodded. 'Very well, Mary. That will be sufficient.' Whatever it was that had made her grin downstairs, it hadn't been the prospect of money. 'I had another young woman in here until quite recently,' she told me. I doubted it. There was no sign that anyone had set foot in there for years. 'I believe she was a student too,' Miss Selby said.

She was fiddling with the door. 'There isn't a lock, Mary, I'm afraid,' she said.

'It doesn't matter,' I said. 'I haven't got anything anybody would want to steal.'

For some reason, at that moment I started to open my coat. I suppose I must have been thinking about the crucifix around my neck; though if I was I don't know why, it's not worth anything now and it certainly wasn't then. It was just jewellery, it didn't mean anything; but I'd always had it, and I wore it all the time.

Perhaps I wasn't thinking about it. I never did. I would forget about it from the moment I put it on to the moment I took it off. I think about it all the time now, lying in there, in the back of the drawer, all coiled up like a silver snake.

Miss Selby was standing stock still. 'I'm afraid you'll have to get rid of that,' she said, in her whispering voice; and I thought I saw her shiver.

'What?' I said, fingering the chain.

'That,' she said, pointing. 'I can't have one of them in my house.' She was looking away as if the very sight offended her: as if it were a human penis I was wearing on a chain around my neck. 'Superstitious things, I can't abide them,' she said, but she was giving little gasps, obviously quite upset, turning away and pulling her shawl up over her head.

I was annoyed. I thought, *It's you that's superstitious, you stupid old cow.* I said nothing, but did my coat up, and we went back downstairs.

Miss Selby went back in the sitting room. Beside the gas fire she recovered herself. 'I was a student myself once, Mary,' she told me. 'In my day!'

'Oh yes?' I said. I didn't sit down. I'd got what I wanted; now it was my turn to stand in the doorway.

Miss Selby took no notice. 'I studied the piano with Mr Bulstrode,' she said. It seemed to occur to her then that I might not have known that gentleman. 'He was the organist at St Margaret's Church, you know,' she said.

She gestured, one thin white finger in the gloom, twitching in the direction of the window.

'On the corner there, Mary, as you came.'

I stared at her. There was no church on the corner of Mount Street, only the concrete garages, and then the bomb-site behind its fence made of corrugated iron and scarred old doors with the paint burned off. There were weeds growing all round it.

In a flash I understood about the crucifix. Mr Bulstrode had tried to put his hand up her skirt in the organ loft. She had hated all manifestations of religion ever since. I nodded. 'Oh, yes,' I said. 'St Margaret's.'

Miss Selby wouldn't let me go. She seemed to have perked up quite a lot since I had said I'd take the room. 'And I had to find my own lodgings, just like you young women nowadays,' she said. 'People considered it very daring of me then, to do any such thing on my own! Though I had Mr Bulstrode's letter of recommendation, of course.'

Her voice went relentlessly on in the gloom.

'I had been advised to apply to Mrs Leach. A policeman directed me to the house. It was this house, this very one. The district was very different then, really rather grand. I rang the bell, and a maid came to the door. She asked me who I was, and what I wanted, and then she left me standing on the steps while she carried my letter in to her mistress. Mrs Leach. She was an invalid, poor thing. She never left her bed. But she would interview me, to see if I were suitable. I had to go upstairs with the maid, all the way to the top and into the bedroom. There was an old-fashioned four-poster bed in there, with purple curtains all round. They were closed. The maid drew them back and there was Mrs Leach inside. She was wearing a cap, you know, and black lace gloves. She was terribly aged. I thought she was the ugliest thing I had ever seen! She had a long jaw like Mr Punch, and purple stains around her eyes. She asked me about my appetite and then she pinched me on the arm with her fingers, just like that, to see if I was fat! Then the maid brought us tea, and arrowroot biscuits.'

I scuffed my feet against the doorpost. I had stopped listening some time before. She was obviously the talkative kind, just as I'd suspected. Probably she had told this same story to all her lodgers, one by one, over the years. Probably I'd hear it again, if I didn't stay out of her way.

It was after four; the day had given up even pretending it was light. I heard some children going past on their way home from school, their piping voices sounding like creatures from another planet, insignificant, remote.

Miss Selby smiled faintly. 'You mustn't disturb me during the day,' she said. I was relieved to hear that. 'I have to rest,' she said. 'When you reach my age, you have to take great care of yourself, you see.'

Privately I hoped when I was Miss Selby's age I'd be decently dead and buried, but I didn't say so. Instead I asked her, 'Haven't you got any family, then?'

Miss Selby shook her head. 'They've all gone,' she said. 'All gone, long ago. I know you'll be happy here, Mary,' she said, keen suddenly. 'You'll fit right in. Come as soon as you like. I'll give you a key to the front door, shall I?'

I moved in the next morning, before Miss Selby could change her mind about the rent. I had a bag of books, a small case of clothes; there wasn't much to put away. Dust blew around me as I worked, as if the room were angry at being disturbed. There was no sign of the girl who'd had the room before me: no lost stocking behind the chest of drawers; not even a hair grip under the bed. Nor was there any sign of Miss Selby. I decided it would be all right living in her house if I never had to see her.

I hadn't had any breakfast, and I wondered if there were any food in the house. I remembered Miss Selby had said, 'I hardly eat a thing. You'll have to fend for yourself, I'm afraid. You won't mind, Mary, will you? I'm sure you'll soon get used to it.'

I clumped downstairs and poked around in the kitchen. It was empty. There was dust on the crockery and in the pans. There was even dust in the sink. I wasn't that bothered. I could always eat at the Union, where it was cheap. I turned the tap on. It wheezed and shuddered and spat out a twisted stream of brown water. There was nothing in the cupboards but an ancient wizened mop, and some old brushes with cobwebs in the bristles. I found the tea, in a yellowed paper packet on a shelf with half a dozen others, most of them opened and abandoned. I made myself a cup, with no milk because there wasn't any or, if there was, I never found it. I thought Miss Selby wasn't going to put in an appearance at all, but she came in then and said good morning. I wondered if I had to offer her a cup of tea. But she looked uncomfortable. She stood keeping the corner of the table between us, and she said: 'I did ask you, Mary.'

'What?' I said.

She nodded, eyes averted. The crucifix. I'd forgotten. I took it off and stuffed it in my pocket, thinking I would put it on when I got to college. But then I thought that meant I would have to take it off every day when I came home, and I'd be continually forgetting to, so when I went back up to my room I opened the top drawer and threw the crucifix in it, at the back, behind the underwear. It is not in that drawer now, it's in another one, one I never open. One of these days, when I'm feeling strong, I shall have it out of there and get rid of it once and for all.

I slept badly on my first night in that room. I always used to whenever I had to sleep in a new place. I'm glad I never have to do that any more. I had a dream that first night, I remember. I dreamed I was running along the top of a wall with broken glass on it. It was very high, and extremely narrow, with cracked grey tarmac one side, like a school playground, and a dead garden the other, dead brown bushes and brambles everywhere. I knew the ground was dangerous on both sides, and I knew I was bound to fall off, but I didn't care. In my dream, I was full of confidence.

Then I saw Miss Selby. She was sitting on the wall in front of me like Humpty Dumpty, swinging her legs, not caring a bit how high up we were. When I came up to her, she turned and grabbed hold of me. I think she grabbed me by the ankles. I pitched forward and fell on the sharp glass. I was still on top of the wall, looking at the blood on my hands. I saw Miss Selby's face come nearer and nearer. She opened her mouth and let loose a great shriek.

It was my alarm clock. I reached out and groped for the switch. I didn't know where I was for a minute. I felt horrible, as though I hadn't slept at all. The covers were all untucked and tangled. I lay there stupidly, staring at the spidery ferns on the wallpaper. I wondered if it was that wallpaper that made me dream about the garden.

I got dressed and went downstairs. My dirty teacup was still sitting on the draining board. I rinsed it out and made myself a cup of tea. It was spitting with rain outside, and looked likely to go on for a while. I felt weak after my rotten night, and I thought I ought to eat something before I went in, but I hadn't been shopping yet. I couldn't have faced eating anything anyway.

On the Monday, I went to the accommodation office and told them Miss Selby had died and the house was empty, but I said I'd found somewhere else. I didn't give anyone my address. I had said I'd let my parents know, but I didn't. I thought the fewer people who knew about this place, the better. If anyone heard about it there would be bound to be somebody else wanting to move in; or I thought somebody might tell the old girl the rent was twenty years out of date. Not that that room is anything to write home about. The bed is one of those big old iron ones that squeak with every move you make, and the mattress is as hard as iron itself. Every night I used to think something was biting me; I was sure there were fleas in the horsehair.

I always slept badly in that room. I never got through the night without waking up, confused and sweating, or chilled to the bone. I thought it must be the bed, or the dirt everywhere, and I knew I ought to do something about it, but I never seemed to have any energy. I could never get properly to sleep until it was almost light enough to see the shapes of the stains on the bedspread; and then I was useless the next day. I started sleeping in, skipping morning classes, sitting dozing in the library and coming home late at night. There was nothing to come home for anyway, not even a gramophone, and nothing to read but my textbooks and the letter my mother had written to me care of the college. I hardly ever saw Miss Selby, though once or twice that first winter when I came in I was surprised to find her up and dressed, sitting in the kitchen reading a huge black book. The smell of her ropy shawl filled the room with old grease and damp wool.

She looked up to see me with her bright, hard little eyes. 'Ah, Mary,' she'd say, as if just that moment remembering I existed. 'How are you getting on, my dear? You look as if you're settling in nicely.'

In fact I was looking ghastly. There were black circles round my eyes, and my skin was pale and white as something that lived under a stone. The bites were itching on my legs and on my shoulders and I was worn out and weary. I mumbled something, saying I was very tired, and that I wanted to go to bed.

Miss Selby took a slim pencil from the table and wrote something in the margins of her big black book. I supposed it was a bible; but then I remembered Mr Bulstrode and crucifixes. I didn't want to know what was in her book, or what she was writing in it. I was simply too tired to be bothered. 'I hope you'll be here for a nice long time, dear,' Miss Selby said. 'Are you going to be able to manage? I wish I could provide for you, but I'm really not up to it any more, you see.'

I wondered who was providing for her. It was obvious she was nowhere near as weak as she let on with her invalid impersonation, having to rest all day and not be disturbed for anything. Sundays, when I was trapped in the house, she would come wandering into the kitchen and sit down at the table, waiting for me to put the kettle on, though I never gave her a cup of tea and she never asked. Sometimes, on my worst days when I hadn't slept a wink and felt dead on my feet, she would be at her liveliest. She would tell me odd things, scraps of stories about the young women she'd had lodging there before me. There were dozens of them, by the sound of it. I could never remember them apart. Years ago, according to Miss Selby, they had had wonderful, wonderful parties, with guests from far and wide. 'They came up Mount Street, the little children running after their carriages!'

It was obvious her memory was playing tricks on her. She was confusing her memories with something her mother had told her, or her grandmother, just as likely. What had happened to Mrs Leach I never ascertained. While Miss Selby sat slowly turning the whispering pages of her black book, I'd look at her sparse hair like dandelion fluff, the bone yellow skin stretched over her skull. I still had no idea how old she really was. She was so wrinkled she looked like something that had completely dried out, and I never saw her eat a thing. There was something keeping her going, though. She seemed to have more energy than me.

I dreamed about a ball. Miss Selby was there somewhere, of course. I didn't see her, but I knew she was there, handing out pieces of white card to everybody. The floor was full of women of all ages in white gowns. I even had one on myself, though I'd never in my life worn such a thing. All the other women had white, flawless skin, and withered flowers wound in their hair. One had a pink and white parasol; she was holding it up in the air and twirling it round and round. There was music playing, scratchy and hissing like an ancient gramophone. We were supposed to be dancing, all the younger women, but really we were just milling around as if we were all new there and none of us knew properly what to do. I saw the soldier from the mantelpiece, in his red coat and bearskin. He was standing to attention, staring stiffly into space. There was a woman kissing him. She was opening his collar.

I suddenly woke up. I was in bed. My bedroom door was open, there was a light. Miss Selby was walking away from my bedside.

I tried to speak, but my throat was numb. I remember only a sort of croaking noise came out.

Hearing me, Miss Selby turned. She had an oil lamp in her hand. She held it up. In the shadow of their deep sockets her eyes looked completely black, all pupil and no iris. She stared at me and scrubbed at her chin with her hand. Then without a word she turned and went out, shutting the door behind her.

I knew I should get up. I knew I should go and talk to her, and find out what she meant by sneaking in and out of my room all the time; but I was paralysed. Sleep swallowed me again, like a great black whale.

When I woke up there was sunlight shining feebly between the curtains, shining right in my eyes. I turned my head away. I was feeling dreadful, but I made myself get up then, before I could change my mind.

I dragged myself out of bed, opened one of the curtains and stood there leaning on the window-sill. More than that was beyond me. It was a lovely sunny day. I stood there blinking stupidly at it. The sun glared down, scouring out all the empty, barren gardens. It hurt to see. I pulled out a drawer, meaning to get out clean clothes and put them on; but instead I pulled the drawer all the way out as far as it would go and found the crucifix.

I thought what a hateful thing it was, that figure of a tiny starving man stretched out on a torture machine. It was no wonder Miss Selby detested it. I picked it up. It felt sticky in my hands, as though it had had food spilt on it. The chain caught in my hair as I pulled it on, the cross caressing my cheek with the cold slither of silver.

I put my slippers on and went out of the room, along the landing, then upstairs to the top of the house, to the door of the room where Miss Selby lay, sleeping peacefully. I knew which it was. I'd been up there once, one night when she was downstairs with her book, just to find out where she slept.

I opened the door and went in.

The room was in darkness, but I knew she was there, lying in her four-poster bed, with the purple curtains closed all round. I went across the carpet of powdery dust that seemed to be nothing other than flakes of skin, and screwing up my eyes with dread I opened the curtains at the window. They came apart with a tumbling of dust and a ripping of cobwebs. The sun came in and lit up the room, and I saw that the dust lay everywhere, thick on the mantelpiece and heaped in the fireplace, covering the chairs like cushions of soft grey fur. There were ancient cobwebs thick as stalactites hanging from the ceiling.

I was holding my breath. I did not want to smell the air in that room, that had been so long shut in upon itself. I did not want to breathe the dust. I went straight to the bed, took hold of the purple curtains one in each hand, and hauled them apart.

Miss Selby lay tucked up in bed with her hands folded on the rotten sheet, like a forgotten corpse. She had a mob-cap on, and a pair of black lace gloves.

There was a scent coming off her like lavender and sweet, rotting meat. I felt dizzy. I stood there a moment hanging on to the bed-curtains and looking in at her. It was the first time I'd seen her by the full light of day. There was a stain around her mouth and on her chin like the bloodstain that kept appearing on the neck of my nightdress, deep red turning to brown.

Suddenly, she woke up. Her eyes opened, flared wide.

I stood up straight, holding the curtains apart. I looked her in the eye, then in terror looked away. I held my chin up for her to see my crucifix, that I had put on specially in her honour.

I believe I heard Miss Selby try to speak; then she started to choke. She bared her long yellow teeth and made a strange hissing sound, like a balloon collapsing. Suddenly my nerve broke. I tore off the crucifix and threw it at her, and bolted from the room, slamming the door behind me. I stumbled down the stairs, back to my own room, where I banged the door shut and stood with my back to it. I leaned there with my eyes closed, panting. My head was spinning. I couldn't move another step. I slid slowly down the door and sat on the floor.

I sat there with my eyes closed, wondering if I were going to be sick. Then I opened them and found it easier. I sat on, staring at my feet, wiping my hands slowly back and forth on my dress. Nobody would know. Nobody would come. Miss Selby's house was all mine now, to do whatever I wanted.

I don't know how long I sat there, straining my ears, expecting each minute to hear something come slithering and thumping downstairs after me. Nothing did. Nothing moved in the ancient house.

Eventually I clambered to my feet and weakly went downstairs. I fetched a dustpan and brush from the cupboard in the kitchen and trudged all the way back up to Miss Selby's bedroom. There was no sign of her. I scooped up the crucifix in the dustpan and buried it away at the back of Miss Selby's bottom drawer where no one would ever find it. There was a lot of dust on the bed, though no more than anywhere else. I started to sweep it up, but it was so fine and dry it was hard to gather; and the window was closed, of course, and filthy; so there was nowhere to put it but on the floor. I dropped the pan, drew the curtains over the window again, then collapsed right there on top of the mouldering sheets and fell fast asleep.

That was the first decent sleep I ever had in this place. Hours I slept, and if I dreamed anything, I don't remember a scrap of it. When I woke up, it was almost midnight, and I had a raging thirst.

I got up and felt my way downstairs in the dark. My house, I thought. This is my house. It felt good, all around me, secure, and absolutely still. I needed a drink. I meant to go to the kitchen and make some tea, but instead I found myself opening the front door and going outside to stand at the top of the steps.

Under the acid streetlights, Winterbrook Gardens was an empty, frozen waste. All the way down Mount Street and every street I could see the houses in their bleached lines. They looked like the abandoned skeleton of some unknown giant animal, its flesh and features long since eaten away. I knew there was life there, though. Soon it would be stirring, moving around behind those whitened walls, going about its daily business. People lived there, ordinary people; tame and without suspicions, without any imagination at all.

I started down the hill, walking quickly, and faster and faster as the thirst got a grip on me. I knew that night I should have to

make do with what I could find. Before long, though, I would
have to get somebody in, as Miss Selby herself had done, and
Mrs Leach before her. A lodger. It is much the best plan.

There have been several here, since then. In fact it is high
time I took a new one. I must write to the college and remind
them. But first I must open that drawer and get rid of that
crucifix. Not that it makes any difference, but it annoys me,
lying there always where I cannot see it. I wonder if I took out
the drawer, and carried it out in the garden and set fire to it,
would the vile thing melt? Would it melt and lose its shape?

BREATH

Adam Corbin Fusco

'I'm glad to have sold this to a superstition anthology,' Adam Fusco writes, 'because the story was completed on Friday the thirteenth.'

That may be, but trying to get details of his own superstitions from the author is like pulling teeth. 'Maybe I'm superstitious about revealing them,' he says. 'I know that a clipping of ivy taken from a graveyard and grown in a jar preserves life, and that a string around your finger is to remind you not of an errand but to avoid the hangman's rope. Singing in an empty house makes ghosts appear – to listen – and you must always tell the bees your troubles . . . for obvious reasons.'

Obvious?

Adam works in the film and television industry in Maryland. His work has appeared in *Cemetery Dance*, *Young Blood* and *Expanse*. The story which follows – like one or two others in this volume – demonstrates a burgeoning attitude of optimism among practitioners in the fields of fantastic fiction.

Dale Cunningham woke to find the cat standing on his chest, sucking the breath right out of him.

He jerked; he shoved; he flung the cat off him and wiped his mouth to rid himself of the stink of fish and the feel of that furry muzzle.

My God, it's happening again.

Golden flecks blinked at him, then disappeared. Dale sat up, breathing hard. Blue light from the street lamps glowed in the louvered blinds. Daney remained asleep, thank goodness. A fall of frizzled hair hid her face. He saw by the clock that it was five fifteen. He wouldn't be getting any more sleep tonight.

It had happened before, yes. A number of times. He remembered his sister Jessica sitting at the green-lacquered kitchen table when he was seven as she snapped peanut shells and, after scolding him for chewing with his mouth open, told him that when he was a baby they had found Mr Smits, their silver tabby, in the crib with him, sucking on his mouth. 'That's not true,' he had said. 'Mmm-hmmm. It is,' said Jessica. 'I saw it. I saw it three times. But it was okay. We swatted him away just in time.' She teased him with it whenever she wanted to be mean. He knew she had made it up – until he was eight.

Just in time for what?

Dale peeled the sheet away from his body. His legs were sweaty with shock. He looked toward the doorway to see if the cat had returned. The cat was black with white paws; maybe he'd be able to see the paws as they approached.

He had been living with Daney for half a year, and this was the second time the cat had jumped on him. He never told her about the first time. She'd scold him for being crazy; she'd accuse him of hating the cat. She knew he hated cats. He wouldn't tell her, no, but tonight was one of the worst. Every time it had happened it was the edge of a nightmare that lingered into waking – lingered because the cat was still there. He wanted to wake Daney and tell her; maybe they could make love.

He floundered in the bed, lying on one side to gaze at Daney's sweet form and then on the other to watch the floor and wait for the cat to return. Was it the second time or the third? In six months? Numbers, numbers, too many numbers. The cat must have left the room by now. What the hell time was it anyway? Seven thirty. He got up to shower and shave.

After he had dressed in his uniform he went into the kitchen. Daney was already awake. Though definitely not a morning person she was an early riser. She sat at the kitchen table in the pair of his flannel pajamas she had heisted early in their relationship. In the mornings, with eyes puffy and dry lips slack, he found her irresistible. She poured milk over a bowl of Peanut Butter Captain Crunch. The cat sat in his seat eating peanut butter nuggets Daney had laid out for it.

'Morning,' he said.

'Howdy.'

He slid the pan on to the stove. He broke a couple of eggs into a bowl, whisked them with a fork. He didn't want to look at the cat; its nonchalant attitude made him shiver. Maybe it didn't remember, but he did. And this habit of having the cat sit at breakfast infuriated him. But no, the morning was the last place to confront Daney about something.

He threw pepper and cheddar cheese into the bowl. 'That sugar stuff is bad for it.'

'Oh?' Holding the spoon with her fist, she shoveled a heap of Crunch into her mouth. 'He likes it. It's his favorite.' She fished a piece from her bowl, held it aloft. 'Here, Snowshoes. Munchies.' The cat snatched it.

She must have seen the look on his face because her eyebrows meshed as if to say, 'What the hell's the matter with you?'

The eggs sizzled in the pan. 'It's not good for you either.'

'Well, thank you for your diagnosis, Dr Cunningham, Mr Clogged-Artery of the Week.'

'I'm just looking out for you.'

'I can look out for myself.' Not mean, just a statement of fact.

Dale approached the table with his cooked eggs. Daney scooped the cat into her lap so he could sit.

'He says it's bad for you, but it isn't, is it, precious?' she cooed at the cat, scratching its ears. 'You like the milk, that's all.' She let the cat dip its muzzle into the bowl. Dale cringed. 'I want to paint the apartment, 'kay?' she said brightly.

'Paint the apartment?'

'Yeah. I think we should. How about Robin's Egg Blue?'

'Robin's Egg?'

'Blue. You know what blue is.'

'You want to paint the apartment? What's wrong with what we have?'

'What's *wrong*? Don't you see how dingy it is? Oh, c'mon. I feel like it. You *like* blue.'

'I like blue.'

'Great. I can get the paint for free.' She tickled the cat under its chin. 'Oh, don't be sour, Dale. You'll like it. It'll be fun.'

'Yeah, I know, but—'

'*Gawd*, you're so sour in the morning.'

The eggs turned to silvery mush in his mouth. 'No, I'm not. Yes, it'll be fun. I'm just tired right now.'

'Will you help me paint? Snowshoes will help too.'

Dale didn't want to finish his eggs. He wasn't good with decisions in the morning, like this painting thing, and his brain was still addled by the encounter with the cat. She had sprung it on him so suddenly. He didn't notice things like blank walls. Theirs were laundry white; maybe they did need some color. He felt bad for being such a bump on a log. Now he had got Daney mad at him, and if he had wanted to say that he liked blue but not 'Robin's Egg' blue, he had missed his chance.

To put a smile on things, he said, 'All right, I'll paint. But you have to wear your tool belt.'

'I always wear my tool belt.'

'Nah. I mean, *only* your tool belt.'

She rested her chin in her hand and winked. 'Well, we'll just have to see about that.'

All done. Fixed. No more argument. Relieved, he rinsed off his plate in the sink and deposited it in the dishwasher. 'Time to hit the coal mines.'

'Dig me a diamond.'

He turned and she was there behind him, holding one of the cat's white paws and waving with it. 'Have a nice day,' she said with irony; she had always hated that phrase.

He wanted to kiss her goodbye but that meant getting near the cat. Instead, he brushed her hair off her forehead. 'I'll have a day at least,' he said.

She smiled sweetly. 'See ya.'

Rain speckled the windshield as he pulled out of the parking lot. He would call it love, if pressed. He had met her on his lunch hour outside the post office where he worked. She was pacing frantically in front of the mailboxes. She had just popped in a scathing letter to a former boyfriend and now that it was irretrievable she wanted to retrieve it. He said that it wouldn't be right to meddle with the mail that way. She pouted. He was lost. He got the keys and nabbed the letter. His invitation for a cup of coffee was met with an askance look and a why-not nod. The coffee warmed a place in him that needed warming; they were living together four weeks later.

He had to flick the wipers on by the time he turned on to Frederick Road. Daney was a painter. Not the artist type but the industrial type. She did houses, both outside and inside, and a school once in a while. She worked at ABC Painting and hoped one day to add her name to continue the alphabet. Her real hope was to be an artist type but she despised the tiny brushes; Daney liked big strokes.

What he couldn't figure was why she was attracted to him. He was sure attracted to her. He had always liked 'dangerous' women. Daney was dangerous; she had an edge: fickle, indeterminate, ambiguous. She was fiery and fiercely attractive, especially when swaying that tool belt and peeking through a bundle of straw hair under a painter's cap. Maybe it was the opposites thing: he had an affection for stasis, which marooned him in a postal clerk job, and she didn't.

When he learned that she owned a cat it didn't bother him. He had to weigh the advantages and disadvantages anyway, and Daney was a big advantage. Besides, Snowshoes wasn't one of *those* cats, wasn't one of his family cats. He figured it would be different. He should have known better. But it had been months since Snowshoes had leapt on him. Maybe it wasn't the same thing; maybe it was a mistake.

Rain spat at him as he crossed the parking lot. Big Ed opened the door into the sorting room.

'Bingo!'

R & B burbled from the radio on top of the bins. Dale eased on to a stool and shuffled his feet in the dust coating the checkerboard floor. Big Ed always made the back room a bastion of rhythm and laughter, but that didn't take away the government green walls or the dingy yellow lights.

Big Ed balanced a stack of mail on his pot belly, launch pad into the bins. 'You okay, Dale-man? Somethin' got you down?'

'Nah,' Dale said. 'Just one of those days.'

'Bingo!'

Dale sorted mail. Maybe Ed was somebody he could confide in, tell about the cats. Maybe he would have some advice, or know just how to solve it, have a cousin with the same problem. Or maybe he would listen, sucking on his beard, and call out 'Bingo!' – the solution to everything. Dale had never told anyone.

When he was eight and they had moved to the Baltimore backwater, Mr Smits was thirteen years old and mangy. It couldn't keep its fur ruffled; it was, instead, matted and damp. It prowled the rowhouse with wide chocolate eyes as if the new territory were a personal indignity visited upon it. Jessica had graduated from pigtails to ponytails which she fastened from a drawerful of dayglo barrettes that she accused her little brother of stealing to make catapults every time one was missing. It was a cottony August night when Dale opened the window and lay atop his sheets – the air conditioning never seemed to pump into his room – and fell into a fitful sleep only to realize the cat was on top of him. Snuzzling. Sucking. He pushed it to the floor, catching his breath. The cat stared at him a moment, accusing Dale of being mean. Dale shuddered. What his sister told him about what happened in his crib was true. A tendril of nightmare gloomed the walls. The sensation of cat paws on his chest, the wet muzzle, the sucking sound were familiar, like a dream you know you've had before while dreaming it, then upon waking aren't quite sure. When Mr Smits was pounded by a Good Humor truck in late autumn Dale celebrated.

'Gotta take a leak,' said Big Ed. 'Hold down the fort, McHenry.'

'Okay.'

When he was thirteen his sister was well into teasing other boys in other ways. They had a new cat, a red Persian longhair, that Jessica had cajoled their parents into purchasing. She named it 'Mr Bits' but occasionally called it 'Mr Shits' in deference to the dead one. It was a summer marked by the giant rock piles at Patapsco State Park. A guy could make the best forts there. He and his friends would gather discarded wood and metal slats and make a fort, one on each pile, and have mud fights. As the leaves turned they would find the detritus left by the night-time visits of the older kids: cigarette butts, smashed cans of Bud, paper bags with gobs of glue, all charred by some bonfire. And bits of dirty magazines. They came in pockets of five or ten pages, torn, moist from the earth, burned on their edges, and a few would have some amber-colored nudey lady torn just below her stomach, the mystery beneath forever hidden by a line of black ash. Dale would feel his face flush when he found one of those pictures. His loins would tingle with the thrill of unearthing a secret, knowing that he wanted something but not knowing what. He hid the pictures in the rocks. He wouldn't take them to his room for fear of them being discovered by his parents, or worse, by his sister; but he would think about them at night, and on a few of those nights he would be caught in a fever of sweat half-asleep, dreaming of red soft flesh, and reaching up would encounter the brittle fur of Mr Bits as it stood on his chest. Disgusted, he would shove the animal away. It was a maelstrom of feelings that summer, of tantalizing ladies hiding their most tantalizing parts, and that blasted cat secretly flicking its tongue between his lips.

Dale shuddered. The mail piled into the bins, was carted away, piled some more. Big Ed twisted the dial to classical in the downslope of the day. Four o'clock. Dale headed home.

When he opened the door he saw a pyramid of paint cans atop

a splattered canvas. The sides of the cans were streaked with blue. Leftovers.

Jeez, she really means it.

He thought of the work involved in painting the apartment and groaned. Why did she always have to have these little projects, and why did they always have to involve him? The cans squatted in front of him like a dare, expecting him to pop their tops and dip in a brush and start that disruptive chore that people try to make fun but always turns into aggravation. Moving furniture, covering things up, getting paint in your hair, cleaning the brushes, the smell – he didn't want those things to be happening now; he just didn't want his spare time eaten up.

The cat was nowhere to be found, thankfully. Fuming with frustration, exhausted from the boredom of work, he turned toward the bedroom. The door opened and Daney stepped out.

'Howdy,' she said, smiling. She was wearing the tool belt. Nothing else. He smiled back.

The frustration and exhaustion drained from his spine. They had a marvelous time.

The paint cans lay dormant for two days. On the third day one wall had been turned into a canvas. A huge face in Robin's Egg Blue had been painted there, a woman's face with Picasso nose, with doves and porpoises dancing around her.

A painter's cap slouched on Daney's head. She stood with hip cocked and paint roller dripping. 'Do you like it?'

She was being her artist self, and now expected him to accept a painting of hers to cover one of their walls. 'Well, how long do you want to have it up there?'

'Oh, forever.' She mashed the roller into the paint can, then looked at him. 'I'm just *kidding.* Gawd. I just wanted to see what I could do. It's not permanent.' She proceeded to cover her painting with the roller.

Irritable, Dale noticed that his stereo was only half covered by a tarp. He bent to see if any paint had splattered on it. 'Daney, my stereo—'

'I'm not painting over there yet.'

'But you still have to protect it from—'

'Jezuz, Dale, I'm not gonna wreck it. All you can think about is yourself.'

Selfish? Him? With the place all disoriented, covered in plastic and canvas, the furniture piled in the middle of the room, just so she can entertain herself with painting? He *hated* that damned color.

She puffed a lank of hair from her forehead. A patch of Robin's Egg had smudged her nose. 'I thought you were gonna help me,' she said softly. 'You tired from work and all?' As if she didn't expect him to be.

He was being selfish. He wanted her to be an artist, to let herself go free. Was he holding her back? If he were a drag on her she'd just leave and fly away, wouldn't she. He wished he could give her the self-esteem to get some canvas and do *real* paintings. Maybe this was the first step for her, doing the apartment walls. Guilt fluttered his stomach.

'I'm sorry,' he said. 'Just tired. Got another cap somewheres?'

She whipped one out from her back pocket and tossed it. 'Betcha I do.'

Snowshoes ignored the proceedings. The cat pranced daintily over the canvas, careful not to step in any wet spots, sidling up to Daney's legs to rub them. Dale eyed the creature with contempt, hoping it would think the pan of paint was filled with water and drink its filthy muzzle full of poison.

Teeny darts pricking his nipple. *Suck, suck, slurp.* Silent elfin weight on his chest. Wet nose on his tongue, dipping . . .

He shot upright. The cat rolled on to the floor. It swished its tail, gleamed golden eyes into his, waiting.

Dale stretched his lungs with air. His head felt stuffed with cotton. His temples throbbed.

Goddamned cat.

Paint fumes stuck needles up his nose. He couldn't get comfortable, lay on his side instead. His legs were wet with sweat, quivering. He must still be half asleep to feel so muzzy. He was glad Daney was still asleep; he didn't want her to think he was freaking out.

He leaned his head over the side of the bed to feel the cooler air. The blue pearl-light from the window cast no illumination on the objects of the room, simply made their indistinct outlines throb. A balled outline near the door moved. Or had he imagined it? He could work up quite an imagination, he knew. If he concentrated hard enough he could imagine that ball pacing back and forth. Phosphenes in his eyes made it dance with amber pinpoints.

He mustn't play this kind of game with himself. He'd scare himself to death. The cat had left, certainly. Imagining things moving in the room wasn't like counting sheep; if he kept trying to see something moving he'd never get to sleep.

The outline's white paw took a step nearer.

My God, the thing's stalking me.

He eased back into the pillows and held himself still. Soft *plomp* as a weight landed on the bed. The bedspread crimped along his calves, his thigh. It was getting nearer.

Dale sat up and the form disappeared. Was he never to get to sleep? Was it not going to let him lie down? The thing was relentless tonight.

Anger and fear roiled in his belly. What did it want? Where was it now? He searched the shadows but saw nothing. As an experiment he lay flat on his back. *I'm not going to move,* he thought. *Let's wait and see.*

He didn't know how many minutes it took. Did it see that his eyes were open? What was it *doing*? If he had to stay up all night—

Sleet, sleet, slip, the brush of claws on the bedspread. The fabric indented between him and Daney. He held his arms at his sides. He didn't move. It paused at his hand. There was a shift in weight. *It must have one paw raised,* he thought. *It's deciding. I don't dare close my eyes. I don't dare.*

Light white footfall, closer. Dale flung the bedspread and heard a plop as the cat landed on the floor. *Goddamn.* This was downright frustrating. It was going to keep coming after him.

Raging, he flopped back on to the bed. *I'm going to go to sleep, goddammit,* he thought. *To* hell *with that cat.* He scrunched over on his side and closed his eyes.

Paw pads making tracks along his legs.

Dale arched his back, kicked, flung his arm through the air. It connected with something soft. The cat screeched and plummeted to the floor.

'Wha?' Daney raised her head from the pillow.

'Oh, jeez, go back to sleep.' Dale shivered.

'What happened? Was that Snowy?'

Irritable, Dale said, 'That cat keeps jumping on me.'

'Jumping on you.'

'It jumped on me while I was asleep.' He couldn't tell her all of it.

'So?'

'Daney, it won't get off the bed.'

She hunched herself on to an elbow and switched on the light. 'He likes you.'

Snowshoes stood by the doorway, back ruffled.

'What did you do to him?' asked Daney.

'What did I—?'

'Oh, come here, precious.' Daney scrabbled her finger on the covers. Snowshoes leapt to gnaw playfully at it. Dale gulped back a shudder.

'It's what it did to me.'

'Oh, come on.' Daney gathered the cat in her arms and rocked it. 'Poor baby,' she said to it. 'What did the mean man do to you?' She rubbed her cheek against the cat's head. 'Did he hurt my precious boy?' She smiled at Dale. 'He just wants to snuggle. You're a big Daddy Cat to him.'

'I'm not his Daddy Cat.'

'Oooh, yes you are.' Daney lifted the cat's paws and walked them towards Dale. 'Aren't you a Daddy Cat?' she said in a little girl voice. She stroked the cat affectionately.

Dale lay down. Daney turned out the light and turned her back to him, curling up with the cat. He looked at the clock. Five thirty. Might as well stay up all night.

*

The next evening they finished the walls of the living room and started the trim. Dale wore the painter's hat like a dunce cap. Snowshoes padded over the room and Dale did his best to avoid it, and did his best to hide his fear of the cat from Daney.

Drained from too little sleep and the toil of meticulous painting, he prepared for bed gratefully. As he was slipping under the sheets Daney entered the bedroom dragging behind her the paisley pillow that was Snowshoes' bedding.

'What's that?'

'What do you think? I can't have Snowy sleeping in the fumes. He'll sleep with us tonight. Cozy, huh?'

'Cozy.'

Snowshoes stretched, pounced on the pillow. Daney closed the door. He couldn't believe it. He was hoping to close the door against the fumes *and* the cat tonight, something he'd missed the night before, but now he was trapped. His eyes were wide open. Daney looked at him for an extra second. He wasn't going to say a word, not against the cat. He had been getting on her nerves for days and if he started complaining about something as simple as letting the cat sleep in the bedroom she would rail at him for sure. Then she might leave him. She would just pack up and leave and then where would he be? That would be the worst. He wouldn't be able to stand the loss. *It's only for one night*, he told himself. *Do it for her. Just don't fall asleep.*

He smiled and nodded. He watched as she slunk into her pajamas. She winked at him, scrunched under the covers, planted a goodnight kiss on his cheek, then buried her face in the pillow after turning out the light.

He lay still. And waited. Maybe it wasn't going to do it tonight. Maybe it was all random, just a fluke. He settled his shoulders into the mattress, tried to relax. The paint fumes made his breath catch in his lungs; he could only manage shallow breaths. He fidgeted, fixated by the light vibrating in the blinds.

Soft pad near his feet. *Jesus, here it comes.*

He waited. He felt something press his thigh. A whiteness pressed his stomach.

He pushed the cat off the bed, exasperated. He wasn't going to sleep tonight. He wasn't going to sleep *ever*.

So let it come, he thought. *Come on, you. I'm going to give you what you want. If I just lie still and close my eyes it will come to me, and if I let it get to my mouth and let it do* whatever the hell it wants, *if I wait long enough I'll find out what it's about after all these years.*

Buoyed by the strength of desperation he lay down and closed his eyes. *It'll come if I lie still. It'll come if I close my eyes.* He wished he could look at the clock; its numbers would be a beacon of sanity as he waited. But he kept his eyes closed.

Footfall. Paw pad. Near his shin. *Come on and get me.* At his knee, a hesitation. *It's looking me over, looking into my eyes with those slits, those unblinking wide slits, to see if my eyes are closed, to see if I might be asleep. It comes when I'm asleep.*

Sleety-slit, slip, along his thigh. Pause. Pounce to his chest. A paw flexed on his sternum, gaining purchase.

Dale's feet sweated. An awful tingling began in his loins. The horrid anticipation. If the tingling didn't stop he was going to shudder uncontrollably.

A susurrant slip of paws echoed along his ribs and jangled nerve endings at the base of his stomach. *Hurry up. Just get it over with. My heart's pounding; I can hear it in my ears. It's going to know. It's going to know I'm awake 'cause it can feel my heartbeat through its claws.*

He wanted to look. He wanted to open his eyes. Where was it? His breath came in and out. With a sixth sense he could feel the cat's face angling toward his own. His shoulders wanted to tense. His legs wanted to kick. His back wanted to arch and fling the thing off his chest.

Snuffling. The cat muzzled into his mouth. He could hear its rapid breathing. The cold, wet nose touched his teeth. Whiskers burred his lips. The tongue—

Oh God, no, stop it. Just stop it!

It sucked on him. A fishy bite to the air mingled with acrid fumes of paint. The cat nuzzled into his mouth, its movements quickening, becoming desperate. It wanted to get deeper. It drew in its breath to take the breath out of him. The claws tensed.

I can't stand it, what the hell do you want—

He could feel the heat of its fur. The snout snuzzled deeper. The cat clung to him like a child, cloying, needful.

In quick breaths it sucked. And its breaths became fuller. The fuller they became the less air he had to breathe. He was suffocating. The cat drew the air out of his lungs until they throbbed.

He lay paralyzed. Such a sense of loss. He was empty. His lungs were flat. The breath of life had left him, stolen. The ache that began in his lungs leapt to his heart.

Don't take it away. Don't take it away from me.

His spine arched. Dizzy, he spun back to the other times he had been assaulted in this way, back to his sister telling him about the cat in his crib. *We swatted him away just in time.*

Just in time?

It came back to him then: *We swatted him away just in time, before you started to cry.*

His stomach muscles bunched. His back whipcracked him upright. The cat fell away. And drawing a deep breath he felt such an aching loneliness that a sob escaped his lips, then choking. Tears formed in his eyes. His lungs hurt. They hurt bad. He cried from the hurt. He couldn't remember crying before.

Great choking sobs struck his chest. Loss. And anger.

Daney stirred awake. 'What is it?'

Dale drove his fist into his thigh. 'I don't like that goddamned color.'

'What the—'

'I hate it. Can't you see? Haven't you noticed?'

'Noticed?'

'I don't *want* to paint the apartment. It's a *stupid* color. It's *ugly*. Why don't you *know* that?'

'Know what?'

'I *hate* it. And all of your *teasing*. You're so condescending to me.'

Her voice whispered. 'No, I'm not.'

'To *me* you are. God*damn*.'

'Dale, Dale, what's the matter?'

'If you don't like me what the hell are you doing here?'

'Why would – but I do—'

He held his knees to his chest, rocking. 'And why, why do you love that goddamned *fucking* cat more than me?'

She was fully awake now, brushing her hair out of her eyes. 'I don't love the fucking cat more than you.' She put her hand on his back, rubbed it gently. 'What brought all this on? You *idiot*, I love you.'

His gasps eased. He looked her in the eye. Oh, irresistible, as always.

'Why didn't you tell me you didn't like the color?' she said. 'Or painting?'

'It isn't just that.'

'Obviously not.'

'I'm just really upset.'

'I can see that. You have to tell me these things.'

'I know.'

'Why didn't you?'

His breathing slowed. His nose was running. 'I was afraid you'd – you'd get mad. Leave me. I don't know. Find some guy painter who did like it.'

'I don't want some guy painter. Jesus, Dale, I *like* you, okay? I'm stuck on you. Get it?'

'I get it.' He was shocked at all that had poured out of him. His eyes hurt from the pressure that was behind them. He wiped the tears from his face and took a deep breath, filling his lungs. He put his arms around her, kissed her.

The cat swished its tail and curled into its bed. It seemed content to leave him alone.

HEART FLESH

Kristine Kathryn Rusch

Kristine Kathryn Rusch is the editor of the *Magazine of Fantasy and Science Fiction*. She has sold ten novels and more than a hundred short stories, receiving five Hugo nominations and three World Fantasy Award nominations. Her work with Dean Wesley Smith on Pulphouse Publishing won them the World Fantasy Award, and Kristine received the John W. Campbell Award for Best New Writer.

'Heart Flesh' is one in a series of heart stories, including 'Hearts', a mainstream story which appeared in a women's magazine in the United States, and her recent novel *Heart Readers*.

Kristine was a very superstitious child and, as a result, is a very superstitious adult. 'As a child,' she says, 'I believed that my stuffed animals could talk, that crossing my eyes would make them stick in that position, and that stepping on a crack would indeed break my mother's back. There were days when I would avoid those cracks, and days when I would jump on them with all of my strength. Mom's back is still fine. For years I believed I needed to go to Albuquerque, New Mexico, and told many friends that. When I finally went, I met Dean Wesley Smith (who also knew that Albuquerque was important) and we haven't been apart since. Perhaps someday I'll find out why I'm afraid of moths and why I avoid California whenever possible.'

✳

In those weeks, I had trouble getting out of bed. Sleep brought me dreams of Tim – laughing, taking my hand, his fingers firm and warm in mine. Sometimes he would kiss me and I would relish those dreams more than others. Then I would wake and lie there on the faded sheets, sheets I didn't wash until three weeks after the funeral, hoping to preserve Tim's scent as long as possible.

But dreams were dreams, memories were memories, and Tim was dead at thirty-four. He had a brain aneurism while driving to the grocery store at three a.m. on 18 August 1992. He lost consciousness at thirty miles per hour and the car drifted straight, even after the road turned, hitting an electric pole and knocking out the power to half the city. At three-thirty, I knew something was wrong. By four, I was pacing. At five, the police officer arrived, hat in hand, to take me to the hospital.

After that, everything blurred into a jumble of noise and images. Occasional unattributed sentences stuck in my memory: *You're lucky he died, Sarah. If he lived, he would have been a vegetable. At least it was quick. Now you have to get on with your life.* Clichés, maybe, but clichés and dreams were all I had.

I cherished the dreams. I thought Tim lived in them. I wished I did.

By December, things appeared normal. I cleaned my place again, showed up on time for work, and bought cats to keep the apartment from being so lonely. By December, I realized that the heaviness in my chest would slowly ease, and an hour could go by without thinking about Tim.

December. The dark month between Thanksgiving and Christmas. The month the dreams changed. The month *he* arrived.

I reached across the table and grabbed the bill. Paul pulled the slip away from me. 'Nope,' he said. Behind him, the jukebox rattled to Buddy Holly's stammering love for P-P-Peggy Soo-o-ooo. Dishes clattered in the kitchen and the diner smelled of eggs and bacon. 'I love having someone to bounce off again, instead of another voice dutifully reading the news before getting off the air.'

'And for that you're buying me breakfast?'

'Brunch, my dear,' he said in his stentorian I-am-performing voice. 'Every day we eat this meal, and every day I remind you that it is too late for breakfast, too early for lunch, hence, brrrrunch.'

I laughed and settled back in the booth. Tim would have – I stopped the thought. Tim wouldn't have done anything. Tim never accompanied us on these jaunts. This was the morning crew's daily ritual. On air at six, off by ten with clean-up and tomorrow's prep, and then food. The morning drive-time team had the highest listenership of any radio period, and rapport with each other and with the audience was essential. Somehow the morning meal added to our feeling of camaraderie. Without this group, I probably wouldn't have made it through the fall.

'All right,' I said. 'If you let me buy tomorrow.'

'No deal.' Paul glanced up. Hank, the engineer, and Eve, the receptionist, waited at the cash register. 'I was serious. I'm glad you're back, Sarah.'

'I never left,' I said. My tone might have been a little sullen. I didn't want any more reminders of the way things had been.

'No,' he said, 'but you faded out for a while.' He grabbed my hand, squeezed it, and slid out of the booth. The heaviness had returned to my chest. I took a deep breath, and let the pain subside a little before standing. Faded out, like a microphone manipulated by a half-crazed engineer. A person could keep talking, voice fading, until nothing went over the airwaves. I felt like that without Tim: a woman sitting alone in a sound-proofed room, speaking into a microphone that someone had shut off a long, long time ago.

'Coming?' Paul called.

I turned. I had left my car at the station. I had to ride back with these folks. I grabbed my coat, slung it over my shoulder, and followed the crew out the door.

The winter chill hit like the blast of an air conditioner. An outside speaker positioned above the door made the Big Bopper sound small and scratchy. I pulled my coat closed.

The street was empty and slush-covered. An icicle beside me dripped water to the pavement below, pavement the diner kept liberally sprinkled with salt. The crew had already gone around the corner of the building to the parking lot. Eve's laughter filtered through the morning air.

'Miss Dobson?'

I whirled. A man stood beside me. His voice was as deep as Paul's, only without the professional edge. The man had large dark eyes covered by wire-rim glasses, and he wore his hair past his shoulders, making no attempt to hide the bald spot on the back of his skull. He was at least forty, small and solid in a heavy winter jacket.

I swallowed. People often recognized me by my voice. Perhaps he had been listening inside the diner. 'Yes?'

He shook his head, as if rejecting sentences before he actually spoke. 'I just wanted to meet you. I've enjoyed your show for a long time.'

'Thank you,' I said. 'I appreciate hearing that.'

He smiled a little and I got the sense he wanted to say more. Instead, he leaned back toward the warmth of the diner door.

'Hey, Sarah! Are you coming?' Paul's voice boomed across the parking lot.

'My ride,' I said by way of apology and hurried away.

The others were already in the car. I opened the door and climbed in, settling next to Hank on the plush seats. The heater whistled as it blasted cold air inside the small space. Paul pulled out. I glanced at the diner door. The serious little man was gone.

The day I met Tim, I wore a navy blue suit and a blouse with a Peter Pan collar. I had my long hair conservatively bound in a topknot, with litte wisps framing my face. I looked young, and cute, and harmless, just like I intended. I was out to become the next Woodward and Bernstein all by myself, and I figured the way to do it was to hide my toughness behind a soft voice and a little girl facade.

I was sitting in the offices at Hutchinson, Anderson, McGillicudy and Quick, making final notes on the interview I had just finished. Old Man Hutchinson had purpled and almost destroyed client confidentiality in addition to his political career before he threw me out. I planned to write the interview out for the monthly city magazine as well as broadcast Hutchinson's damning words over the air. I checked the recorder, heard his voice and mine, then proceeded to make notes about the wood-lined walls, the pretty secretary sitting behind the large oak desk, the phone that rang incessantly. I was career-making at twenty-one, visions of National Public Radio and the *Washington Post* dancing in my head. Then he walked into the room.

At first, I thought he was an attorney or a legal assistant. He wore expensive gray pants, a white shirt and a topcoat draped casually over his shoulders. His hair was an inch too long, curling slightly over his collar, and his gray eyes sparkled with intelligence. He stopped at the receptionist's desk and placed his hands on the oak surface.

'I'm Tim Reston,' he said. 'I'm here to fix your copier.'

I did a doubletake. Expensive clothes, nicely tailored. Cavalier attitude of a man who believed in himself. And he fixed copiers?

'Good,' the receptionist said. 'Let me clear everything out of the copy room and then you can have a go at it.'

She got up and walked down the hall. He watched her swish, and then he turned to me.

'You don't look like a man who repairs copiers.'

He grinned. His smile carved a line in his left cheek. 'And you don't look like a girl who can run all that equipment.'

I glanced at my air-quality portable cassette recorder, and the heavy microphone I had yet to detach from it. I couldn't tell if he wanted me to be defensive or if he. wanted me to bat my eyelashes at him. I did neither. 'People aren't always what they seem.'

'Ah,' he said and this time I heard the sarcasm. 'A truism.'

'So?'

'Would-be reporters should never use clichés.'

'Rules.' I wrapped the mike cord around the steel base. 'I bet you can't talk for ten minutes without using a cliché.'

'I'm not a would-be reporter.'

'No, you're an overdressed man who fixes copiers.'

He laughed then, and the sound had a warmth that made the wood paneling seem chill. 'Tell you what. This job will only take me about half an hour, if they were right about the problem. I'll meet you in the café across the street when I'm done.'

He didn't wait for my answer. The receptionist had come back and he turned to her. I picked up my equipment, filed my notebook in my oversized purse, and left the office.

I hesitated before going into the café. Then I decided I could use a cup of tea and a little more time to expand my notes. Forty-five minutes later, Tim joined me, and we stayed together until the day he died.

I let myself into the apartment and found three cats waiting by the door. Usually, they stared at me from various sleep spots around the living-room. This time, something had awakened them.

I took off my coat and hung it in the small hallway. Then I kicked off my boots and let them rest on the mat in front of the door. The apartment was warm in the mid-afternoon sun. The furniture that Tim and I had purchased, the long floral couch, the easy chair and the rocker, seemed more mine now that they were covered with cat fur and newspapers. I had never been comfortable in a place that looked as if it were about to be photographed for *Home Beautiful*.

My mail sat on the coffee table. Louisa, my landlady, usually brought the mail in when it arrived, about nine a.m. I didn't mind. It gave the cats an extra visitor during the day, and saved me from wrestling with the post office box in the lobby of the building.

I shoved a newspaper aside and sat on the couch, ignoring my own exhaustion. I slept during the day so that I had my nights free until I started work at five a.m. I had gotten into the habit when Tim was alive, and had seen no need to change it.

The cats crowded beside me, purring and butting their heads on my arms. I set aside a small package, obviously a book, and opened the letter. It was from my friend Brenda at National Public Radio. Brenda and I got our start in radio together nearly ten years ago. She went on to the national news when I got married.

The letter was chatty, filled with gossip and the news of a position opening in the production department. Low-level, sure, but a foot in the door at NPR was better than nothing. I set the letter down. Sweetheart, my big gray tom, rubbed his face against my chin. I ran my hands along his soft fur. A job in D.C. meant moving. It meant leaving everything that Tim and I had built here, slowly, over seven years. It meant leaving the morning team and brrrunches at the diner.

I didn't want to think about it. Not yet. I picked up the package and hefted it. My name was written in block letters across the brown bag surface. I saw no return address, but I had been right. The package felt like a book.

I ripped off the wrapping, and found myself holding a collection of short stories. A note, written in the same block letters, had been paperclipped to the dust jacket: PLEASE SEE PAGE 15. No signature. No dedication on the inside flyleaf. I turned the book over in my hands. I usually got things like this at work, not at home. Time to remind the station receptionists yet again not to give out my real last name. Either that, or go unlisted in the phone book.

I leaned back and opened the book to page fifteen. Across the top of the page, above the story, someone had written: FOR SARAH, WITH THANKS. Again, no signature. The cats cuddled next to me, convinced that I would not sleep yet. The book itself was a collection of fantasy stories by various authors, some of whom I had heard of, others I hadn't. I hadn't heard of the author of the story I was to read. The piece was short, only ten pages, and I read quickly.

The story told of a woman whose husband had died suddenly. He had been an organ donor, as Tim had, and another man, an executive, had received the husband's heart. The executive found himself obsessed with the woman. He followed her around, spied on her, and fell in love with her. Gradually they both realized that because he had her husband's heart, he was becoming her husband. They all lived happily ever after.

I slammed the book closed and tossed it across the room. Sweetheart chased the book, then when it landed, lay down beside it because he couldn't play with it. My hands were shaking. What a sick, sick thing to do to me. And the wacko knew where I lived.

I got up, closed the blinds and double-checked the lock on the door. Then I turned on my answering machine. I didn't want to talk to anyone. Not if someone would do this so soon after Tim died.

For the next three days, I dreamed of Tim.

He sat at our kitchen table, staring out the window at the snow. The cats' bowls were empty – silly detail because we had had no cats then – and I clutched Brenda's letter in my left hand. *What will I do in Washington?* he asked. *Why can't we stay here?* The words echoed through my memory to the first year of our marriage, snuggling on the couch, watching old movies in the dark of a Sunday afternoon. *All we need is each other, Sarah,* he would whisper. *You don't know how much I love you.* Then he sat up, unzipped his chest, and removed his heart. *It's yours, forever.* I took the heart. It was soft and moist, and felt as if I squeezed too hard, it would burst. I didn't want it, I didn't want the responsibility, but when I turned to tell him, he was gone. Only his heart remained, thudding softly against my palms.

The mall was filled with harried shoppers. I clutched three bags to my chest, already tired and I had only been at it for a half an hour. Children lined the walkway between stores, waiting to sit in the sleigh with a too-skinny Santa. Muzak Christmas carols coming from various stores warred each other for ascendancy. I was wondering if I really wanted to fight the crowd in one of the shoe stores to find a pair of pumps to match my new holiday dress, or if I wanted to go in the knick-knack shop to look for something for my great-aunt, when the kid ran in front of me.

I saw it all in slow motion: the small child cutting across foot traffic, hand on his crotch, probably following a minor emergency of his own. My legs collided with his, and we both went sprawling. The floor was white tile, covered with scuff marks, and I had been lying on it for nearly thirty seconds before I realized that I had scuff marks too and they burned. My packages had scattered, the child was screaming, and all I wanted to do was join him.

Hands grabbed my shoulders and eased me into a sitting position. 'You okay, Miss Dobson?'

The man from the diner. His brown eyes were creased with worry, and his hair had fallen forward against his face. Not a bad face either, I thought. Rather quiet, and shy.

He grabbed my packages, then helped me to my feet. Someone had moved the child, and the traffic continued, as if the accident had never happened.

'Let me buy you a cup of coffee,' he said. 'You look a little shaken.'

I was shaken. I let him lead me into the coffee shop next to J.C. Penney's. We sat at a booth near the window, and he ordered coffee and Danish for both of us.

'I seem to be seeing you a lot lately,' I said.

He shrugged. 'The only mall in town is not such an unusual place to be on a Saturday.'

I felt a twinge of guilt. Ever since that book arrived, I had been feeling suspicious of everyone. So suspicious, in fact, that I had called the hospital to find out what organs Tim had donated. The woman I spoke to said such information made things hard for the survivors, so the hospital never gave it out. 'You're being very kind,' I said.

'It's not often I get to sit with a celebrity.' His smile softened his words, and added a certain fey charm to his face.

'I'm not a celebrity,' I said.

'Locally, a little. But I bet you could really be big if you tried.'

The waitress set the coffees down. I put my hands around the steaming cup. The china felt hot against my skin, warming me all the way through. 'I think it's too late for that.'

He shook his head. 'It's never too late to do what you want.'

'And what do you do when you're not rescuing women in malls? Ghost for Ann Landers?'

He chuckled. The sound resonated through him and I wondered how long it would take me to teach him to speak before a mike. 'No. I teach school. High school kids. Some of them think it's too late too.'

'Jesus.' I took a sip of my coffee. It was bitter and potent, the way I liked it. 'You know, we haven't been formally introduced.'

'Ooops.' He extended his hand. 'Gregory Fenner. Greg.'

'I'm Sarah.'

We smiled at each other idiotically, as if we had just signed a joint agreement to rid the world of nuclear weapons. I decided then that I liked him.

'So,' I said, as I cut the Danish in half. 'Out shopping for the wife and kids?'

'Parents and grandparents. Wife and kids never materialized.'

'Never?'

He shook his head. 'First I got too busy trying to stop a stupid war. Then, somehow, I got socialized. And now I try to socialize others.'

'And they let you teach with such long hair?'

'If I tie it back.' He took a sip of his own coffee. 'This is the strangest conversation. I feel as if I've known you forever, and you don't know anything about me.'

'You don't really know anything about me,' I said. 'Most of the stuff that goes over the air is superficial and some of it is just lies.'

'Your husband did die, though.' His quiet words were a statement, not a question. 'Your personality disappeared through the entire fall.'

'I didn't realize that people listened that closely.'

'Some of us do,' he said.

Three times in the next week, we met for unbuttered popcorn, Coke, and the latest season blockbuster. We sat next to each other in the theater, gabbed during the trailers, watched in silence, and shredded the movie while standing in the lobby. Then we went to our separate cars and drove home.

I learned that Greg liked teaching, although he had been on an 'enforced sabbatical' this last semester, and that he was an incisive and witty critic. I think he learned as little about me.

It was after the third movie he asked for a real date. 'You know,' he said. 'Dinner, wine, the works.'

My smile was faint. 'I've been married for seven years. I'm not so sure I'm ready for the works.'

A slow flush crept across his cheeks. 'That wasn't really what I meant. I just meant I would wine and dine you, do something special.'

'I would like that,' I said.

And I did. He took me to a Mexican restaurant on State Street. We ate, and laughed, and talked. By the time he was ready to take me home, I had decided that the works might be rather fun.

'Would you like to come up?' I asked when his car stopped in front of my apartment building. The look on his face was part surprise, part longing and part something else.

He shut off the ignition and took my hand. 'I'd love to,' he said.

We walked through the door, past Louisa's apartment, and went up the stairs. Greg studied the brown decor as if he had never seen late-seventies clone apartments before. When I unlocked my apartment door, Sweetheart was there, waiting for us.

'A cat?' Greg laughed. 'Let me guess. How many others? Three?'

I smiled. 'Two. When Tim died, I sort of went overboard. I didn't want to be lonely and I didn't want my cat to be lonely, so I got three, figuring that at least two of them would be together at all times.'

Greg put an arm around my shoulder. I leaned into the hug. It felt good to have someone hold me. 'You must have loved Tim a lot.'

'I don't know.' I pulled out of his arms and turned on a table lamp. The other two cats were glaring at us from the couch. I closed the blinds and turned on another lamp. 'Six months ago, I would have said yes. Now I'm beginning to realize how free I feel without him.'

Greg said nothing. I turned. He was standing in the middle of the room, staring at the strange book. 'Free?' he asked, his voice oddly hollow.

'Last week, I sent a resumé and demo to National Public Radio. I never could have done that with Tim.'

Greg looked up at me. 'He didn't want you to?'

'He never said that. It was the things he didn't say. So I never tried before. I didn't want to lose him. I used to call that love. But I'm beginning to wonder if it was just fear.'

I cleared the newspapers off the couch and sat down. One of the cats jumped on to the coffee table. Greg sat down beside me and picked up the strange book.

'Have you read this?' he asked.

'Just the second story,' I said. 'Someone sent it to me as a prank. It's about—'

'I've read it,' Greg said. He leaned over, put a hand on my shoulder and kissed me. His kiss was soft, exploring my mouth instead of possessing it. When he pulled away, he tucked a strand of hair behind my ear and kissed my earlobe. 'You're beautiful, Sarah.'

He got up, walked around the coffee table, and let himself out the door. I sat on the couch for a moment. I thought he was going to come back. Finally, I got up and went to the stairway in time to see his car pulling away from the curb.

That morning, I dreamed that I held a heart in both hands. I squeezed and squeezed and squeezed until the heart burst. Warm blood and flesh spattered me, the walls, the cats and the sofa. I knew that I should glue the heart back together, but there were too many pieces. Someone else had to do it, not me. I didn't want the responsibility any more.

A ringing echoed in the room, making the heart-flesh quiver. I concentrated until I realized I heard the phone beside my bed. I opened my eyes and reached, clearing my throat so that I sounded awake when I answered.

I was glad I did. On the other end, a woman from National Public Radio asked me to interview three days before Christmas.

*

I called Greg and asked him to an early dinner. We met at the Blue Iris, a trendy Cajun restaurant that seated fifty on a good day. Flower paintings covered the walls, and a stained-glass blue iris decorated the front door. I liked the decor, the friendly ease of the wait staff, and the short walk from my apartment building across the street.

Greg arrived, hair pulled back, cheeks flushed with cold. I was sipping poor California chardonnay with an acidic aftertaste. He looked at the glass with longing.

'Sorry,' he said as he sat at the table and pulled off his jacket. 'Meeting. I might go back for the second half of the year.'

I pushed the glass aside. 'You don't look too pleased about it.'

He shrugged. 'I guess I've gotten used to the slower days. It would be nice to be paid for doing nothing, don't you think?'

'No. I like working.'

A waitress came by and set a plate of hot bread on the table. She handed Greg a menu, and left.

He smiled. 'I suspected that of you. It comes through over the air. You love the news. You have a passion for it.'

'You must have a passion for something.'

The flush hadn't left his cheeks. He looked at the door, at the iris with its ripply blue petals. 'Sometimes, when a person has too much time on his hands, he makes things up. You know?'

I didn't understand the segue. 'I thought you liked the free time.'

'Now.' He pushed his menu aside, then clasped his hands and leaned toward me. 'People make up their own superstitions, most of them about death and exchange of souls. As a boy, I used to think that people shared dreams – that if I dreamed about you, you were also dreaming about me. I never believed that people had their own dreams separate from mine.'

His words made me shiver. They were too close to the feelings I had had shortly after Tim died. I grabbed a piece of bread. It burned my fingers. 'I don't understand, Greg.'

The waitress glanced at us, but didn't come by. She seemed to sense we were in deep conversation. Greg's knuckles had turned white. 'You don't have to understand. What I'm talking about isn't rational. It's like that story in the book – the story that upset you so badly. What if people actually believed that? What if part of a person's body carried his soul?'

I buttered the bread on my plate, not looking at Greg. 'That story really frightened me.'

'Because you believed it could be true?'

I shook my head. 'Because someone knew enough about me to send it to me, to send it to my home.'

Greg let out a small sigh. 'Harassment?'

'Of the most bizarre kind.' I willed my fingers to stop shaking, and popped a piece of bread into my mouth. 'What does this have to do with passion?'

'It has to do with dreams. I sit at home, and I read, and I write a little, and I listen to the radio, and I prepare for my classes next spring. But at night, Sarah, I dream about you.'

I started. The piece of bread caught in my throat, and I had to swallow twice. 'And you want to know if I dream about you?'

He smiled. The expression warmed his face. 'I obsess about it.'

I pushed my plate aside. 'I dream about Tim, but I think about you. I wonder what your skin feels like, or if your hair is as soft as it looks.'

'Really?' This time, his cheeks were not flushed with cold but with pleasure.

'Really.' I took his hand. His eyes were shining. 'I'm not hungry, are you?'

He shook his head. We stood together, and I left money on the table for the wine and bread. We held hands as we walked past the iris to the cold, the chill unable to dampen the warmth between us. The dash across the street into my apartment took less than a minute, but felt like an hour. Once inside, Greg pushed my hair from my face and kissed me.

The kiss was tentative, gentle, not insistent but full of desire. His arms held me loosely. I knew I could pull away at any minute, and he wouldn't stop me. He would wait until I was ready.

I had never been kissed like that. No one had ever given me

permission to change my mind once I had already said yes. No one had ever respected me that much.

I slipped his jacket off him, and then unfastened the top two buttons on his shirt. He took my hands and kissed them, studying my face. Then he set my hands free, and I continued to undo the buttons. Then I pushed his shirt back and kissed him.

His skin was as soft as I had imagined – not hard and muscled as Tim's had been. I teased his right nipple, then slid to the left. My fingers brushed against a ridge of flesh that shouldn't have been there and I pulled back.

A scar ran along his chest, red and garish, shiny with newness. Greg watched me, eyes bright, strands of hair loose from his ponytail. Heart. They had operated on his heart. That's why he wasn't working. Because he couldn't.

I took a step back.

'I've been meaning to tell you,' he said. 'That's what I started to say at dinner.'

'You sent that book.' The terror of that morning was back. Shudders ran though my entire body. I had been touching him. I had been making love to him. 'You sent me that book.'

'Yes,' he said. 'But not for the reason you think. I had the surgery at midnight on 17 August, and the nurses were talking about you being in the hospital that night, and how sad it was and then when I met you—'

I picked up his jacket. The heavy material repelled me. 'Get out.'

He didn't move. I flung the jacket at him. 'Get out.'

'Sarah, it's not like that—'

'Get out, or I'll call the police.'

He clasped his jacket to his chest, bowed his head, and let himself out the door. I turned all the locks and leaned against the frame, listening as his steps diappeared out the front. Then I picked up the book and slowly, mechanically, tore it apart.

I didn't dream after that, until the night before my interview in D.C. Tim sat at the edge of the oak dresser, next to the hotel's fancy television. He stared at the king-sized bed. *We slept in a double on our honeymoon*, he said.

I pushed a pillow behind me, and leaned against it. He looked perfect there, as if the plush decor suited him. *We were young then. We couldn't afford much.*

Still can't on my salary, he said. Then he opened his shirt. His chest gaped open, and his heart was missing. *I sold it for you, Sarah. So you can have everything you want.*

So that was what had gone wrong. He never understood. I got up and took his hand. His fingers were cold. *I don't want money*, I told him. *I just want someone to love me. Me, Tim. Not some perfect wife.*

You'll never be a perfect wife. His voice sounded sad.

No, I told him. *I won't.*

On 24 December, a taxi dropped me off at my apartment. The building looked quiet. Most of the residents were gone for the holidays and Louisa always went to Hawaii until New Year's.

The trip had gone well, but I was tired. I passed the production tests and the interview seemed positive. Brenda was convinced I would get the job, but I wasn't. I was ten years older than most of their production assistants and had, according to one of the engineers, learned some bad habits. Everyone I spoke to wanted to know why it had taken so long for a woman with my credentials to follow her dreams. Fear? Low self-esteem?

Marriage, I had told them, and they had all nodded as if they understood. But I wondered if they weren't right. In my dreams I had held a heart. But I had always assumed the heart was Tim's. What if it were mine? And what if I had been afraid to let it go?

The hall smelled of pine trees and Christmas. I trudged up the stairs, my leather duffel heavy against my back. I had planned so hard for the interview that I had forgotten the holiday. My first without Tim – and I was going to spend it alone.

Something moved in the shadows near my door. I stopped. Greg stood up. He had deep circles under his eyes and his skin was pale.

'What do you want?' I hadn't thought about Greg – I hadn't let myself think about Greg – since I last saw him.

'To apologize,' he said. 'I went a little crazy.'

'I guess.' I gripped the banister for support. I could push away from it if I needed to run.

'No, you don't understand.' He stepped into the light. It reflected off the bald spot on the top of his head. He didn't look like a violent person. He didn't even look crazy. Just lonely. And sad. 'You saved me.'

'When I met you, you were well.'

He shook his head. 'Not you, really.' He sighed. 'I always do this wrong. First the book, then in the Blue Iris – I know you think I'm weird, but just listen to it all, okay?'

I almost left then, but something in his voice stopped me. I had been attacked by two men during my reporting career, and they never had that calm, pleading, self-effacing tone. Not even the groupies had that. I had liked Greg, respected him, until the last time we saw each other. I owed him a few minutes.

I waited.

He swallowed. The sound echoed in the narrow hall. 'I nearly died in August, all by myself in a hospital room. No family. Close friends, but at moments like that, you want someone more. I used to listen to your radio show before – and when the nurses told me you were there for your husband, I pretended you were there for me. And then I heard how he died, and read the obit, and found out about the organ donating, and I figured that I had a new heart and it had to be his. I sent the book as a thank you. I wasn't even sure you would understand. I didn't realize how you would take it – and I didn't want to marry you. I didn't know you. I wanted to thank you outside the diner, but I couldn't without sounding stupid, you know? So I didn't. I just pretended that I did.'

'So you followed me around, to the mall, and then here?'

He shook his head. 'That was an accident. I saw you when the kid hit you. I never planned to see you again. That's why I left when you told me about the book. I got scared that you would realize it was me and you would hate me—'

'But you tried to tell me at the Blue Iris.'

'Because you were opening up, and I didn't want any secrets.'

He ducked his head – a nervous gesture – and backed away from the stairs. 'That's all. I made a mistake. Then I thought you had left because of me. I pounded on your door the next day, and your landlady told me where you went. I hope I didn't interfere with the interview. I know how much it meant to you. I never wanted to be in your way.'

I stared at him for a moment. He wasn't handsome. He was an overweight middle-aged man who wore his loneliness like a shield. He had a gentleness I had never found before, and he made me laugh more than anyone else. He had a vivid imagination, but then so did I. I dreamed about bursting hearts and a man months dead. And I had turned a shy admirer into a villain who wanted to usurp my husband's place on the basis of an odd gesture.

'You don't have Tim's heart,' I said. 'He didn't die until three a.m.'

'I know,' Greg said. 'But sometimes, it's better to hold on to what you believe than to listen to the truth.'

'You think so?' I picked up my duffel and climbed the remaining stairs. 'Because if I agreed, I wouldn't let you inside.'

'I didn't mean to hurt you.'

'That's truth.'

'But not what you believe?'

'Believed.' I unlocked the door. Sweetheart paced in front of it, tail waving. I petted him. 'What are you and your friends doing for Christmas?'

'Small turkey, dressing, lots of pie, of which I will eat just one piece.' Greg stood just outside the frame.

'Tonight?'

'Tomorrow. You want to come with me?'

'Maybe.' I held the door open. 'Come on in before Sweetheart gets out.'

Greg slipped inside and I let the door click shut. Sweetheart rubbed against my bag, and the other two cats emerged from the bedroom, looking sleepy.

I took Greg's hand. It was as soft as I remembered. 'What happens if I go to Washington?'

He looked startled by the question. 'Depends. I'll drive you to the plane if you want me to. Anything else we can discuss.'

He would let me go. He would let me go no questions asked. My heart gave a little leap. I felt it move for the first time in forever. 'Christmas Eve is a night for belief and truth,' I said. 'Those are things we have to work out. Would you like to have dinner with me?'

As he smiled, his entire body relaxed. His face took on a kind of beauty I had only seen once before – the night we left the Blue Iris, the night we were going to make love. 'Thank you,' he said with a formality his joy belied. 'I would like nothing better.'

THE TEN O'CLOCK HORSES

Paul Lewis

Paul Lewis, a journalist on the *South Wales Evening Post*, is thirty-one and was born in Port Talbot. 'The Ten O'Clock Horses' is his first foray into the fantasy/horror field – Paul has already produced comedy scripts for the *Spitting Image*, *Davro* and *Hale and Pace* television shows – and it's an auspicous debut.

The tale only came about when, stuck for comedy ideas – and already in contact with some other young writers working in the genre – he thought he would 'have a crack . . . just for a change of scene'. The basis of the story was told to him as a child by a babysitting uncle.

'I never used to think of myself as being superstitious,' he says, 'but I suppose I must be. I don't go as far as throwing salt over my shoulder . . . but I do think I'm due for some good luck if a black cat crosses my path.'

Are you sitting comfortably? Then we'll begin . . .

✳

Summer in Bethesda, the air alive with the lazy drone of insects, heavy with earthy smells from the farms nearby.

The village dozed in the August sunlight, the fields surrounding it pale and parched. The houses were scattered around, dating from a time long before planning regulations, while above them rose the Beacons themselves, solemn and solid, like grass-and-granite sentries.

Jenny Wilson felt settled in, at ease in her new home after just a week. With the moving and unpacking behind her, she could relax.

The cottage was small and easy to manage, and her acquiring it had been a stroke of luck. The estate agent in Brecon, twenty miles away, was divorced herself. The two women had chatted for some time about the pain of separation, the difficulties of bringing up children alone. Perhaps she felt sorry for Jenny, perhaps she was just kind, but she had agreed to rent out the cottage until a buyer was found. And if Jenny decided she liked her new school, she had first option on the sale. It was a perfect arrangement. To Jenny, after months of acrimony between herself and her ex-husband while the divorce went through, it seemed like a good omen at last.

She sat in the garden, flicking through the pages of a magazine. There were still things to be done, she knew, but they could wait. Here the pace of life was slow; in Bethesda, nothing was hurried.

Jenny tilted back her head, let her face soak in the sunlight. Craig would be gone a few more hours at least. Idris Phillips, who owned the fields which adjoined the cottage's back garden, had taken a shine to the boy, letting him help out on the farm whenever Craig felt like it – which was often. A rumbustious eight-year-old would most likely get in the way rather than help. But Mr Phillips didn't seem to mind.

Quite the reverse; he and his wife Gwen appeared to love the boy's company. They had no children of their own and perhaps saw him as a kind of surrogate grandson. Craig, for his part, was discovering a whole new world, one denied him during his city upbringing. He would come home dirty and tired, but breathless as he related how this pig had done that, or that horse had done this. Any fears Jenny might have held about the effects of the move to Bethesda had vanished.

For the first time in a year she felt good about life.

*

Later, with Craig long asleep, Jenny lay on her bed in the darkness and listened to the sounds of the night.

The stone walls of the cottage soaked up the heat of the day, releasing it when darkness fell. Even with the windows open, the bedroom felt stifling; Jenny was naked, her body slick with perspiration. The warmth was lulling, soporific, and her cares and worries faded and disappeared. She drifted into sleep.

The last thing she heard was the sound of horses.

Bethesda Primary School served a number of villages in the area, as well as the isolated farms. It dated back to the last century, and looked weather-worn and defeated. The children were divided by age into four small classes, with Jenny supervising the youngest, the seven-year-olds who had just moved up from the neighbouring infant school.

She knew from experience that a new teacher combined with a new class – and some of the children looked to be from pretty rough families – could add up to trouble. She expected misbehaviour, backchat, even the odd tantrum; these were, after all, young children. With their talk of computers and turtles and the latest high-tech footwear, it was sometimes easy to forget that.

There was no trouble. If anything, Jenny's class was strangely subdued. If she asked them to read, they would not simply flick through the pages. They would give the books their full attention, almost as if they were studying individual words for the first time, trying to fathom their meaning. When Jenny took them out for games, she would be amazed at the apparently endless reserves of energy they possessed. It went beyond the normal child's vitality; these youngsters played like professionals, like their lives depended on it.

They did not squabble. They never started any half-hearted fights, as was sometimes the case in Jenny's last school. They were such *perfect* pupils. They were too good to be true.

*

'I've never known anything like it,' Jenny admitted. 'I mean, I've had good classes before now, but never anything like *this*.'

Miss Parker, the headmistress, tapped a pen against her false teeth and nodded. 'I know,' she said. 'But don't worry about it. Things are different here, as I'm sure you've found. It's just the way they're brought up – most of their parents are used to hard work and I suppose it must rub off.'

Jenny frowned. The explanation sounded glib, rehearsed. Regardless of what Miss Parker said, the children's behaviour – the total lack of *bad* behaviour – was simply not normal. The headmistress was close to retirement and had spent her entire career in this school; it may be a simple case of her being too close to a problem to realise it existed.

'You're not worried, are you?' Miss Parker continued. 'There's no signs of hyperactivity, or anything like that?'

'No, no. Nothing I could pin down,' Jenny said. 'It's just that . . .' She let the sentence trail off. It was hard to put her finger on what was wrong with her class, if indeed there was anything wrong.

Maybe she had spent too many years in the city, where life was harder and the kids tougher. Although only an hour's drive from Cardiff, Bethesda felt as if it belonged in a distant place, a long-ago time.

'They seemed *obsessed*,' she said.

That earned her a half-smile which Jenny found vaguely irritating, condescending. She felt as if Miss Parker was treating her like a child.

'Obsessed?' the headmistress asked. 'In what way?'

Jenny almost mentioned the paintings, decided against it. One wet morning, with the weather too bad for games, she had told the children they could paint. She expected enthusiasm – the prospect of mess always an exciting one for children – and got merely nods. They went about their artwork with the same utter devotion they applied to any other activity. There was no joy in what they did, no giggling and paint-flicking, almost as if they were being punished for something.

From their pictures, it seemed they were obsessed with horses.

Crudely drawn equine shapes featured in each child's painting. Sometimes prominent, sometimes in the background, but always there. The figures were not always immediately recognisable as horses. Some were twisted, misshapen, mouths crammed with curved teeth. Others had wings and flew Pegasus-like above the land. One was obviously inspired by the Loch Ness Monster, its body that of a serpent, a fish clenched in its jaws. At least, Jenny assumed it was a fish; for one unsettling moment it looked more human than piscine.

How could she tell Miss Parker this? The old woman wanted nothing to upset her last two years before retirement, that much was obvious. So when the headmistress asked in what way the children were obsessed, Jenny merely shook her head. 'Forget it,' she said. 'I suppose I'm still not used to all this peace and quiet.'

The subject was dropped, and never raised again.

Jenny stood at her classroom window, watching the children as they ran breathlessly around the playground during mid-morning break.

Craig was running with them, ostensibly playing football. His face was bright red and sweaty in spite of the bitter November cold.

His little legs pistoned as he raced from one end of the yard to the other, sometimes with the ball, sometimes without. There appeared to be no pattern to the game.

Jenny leaned forward as two older boys waved Craig over. With his mother a teacher there was a danger he would be an obvious target for bullies, even though he was a year above the class she taught. But now she could see him standing silently before the two boys as they spoke. Occasionally he would nod.

The conversation lasted perhaps a minute. When it was over, Craig stared at the sky as if searching. Then he said something back to the boys and dashed at breakneck pace across the yard.

The next morning, as Jenny leaned close to the mirror to apply her eye make-up, Craig wandered into her bedroom. He paused at the window.

'What's that in the sky?'

Jenny turned and looked, but her son's face was a blur and the sky an uninterrupted blue haze. She picked up her glasses from where she had placed them on the dressing table and put them on; the sky was empty.

'What did you think was there?'

Craig shrugged. 'Nothing,' he said. 'Can I go out to play now?'

'Finished your breakfast?'

'Ages ago. If I don't hurry, the boys'll be gone.'

'All right, off you go. But don't be late – and don't get into any trouble.'

Jenny turned her face for Craig to kiss her cheek; he was already heading out of the bedroom. 'And be careful!' she called after his rapidly retreating back. Moments later she heard the door slam. She shook her head slowly, contemplating the change that had come over him since the move to Bethesda three months ago.

Back in the city it was all she could do to drag him out of bed every morning, help him get dressed, pester him into eating breakfast in time to be away for school.

Now he was up before her, wolfing down his food like there was no tomorrow, out playing before she'd even dressed. And not only because this was the half-term break. He'd been the same for weeks. Jenny had given up worrying about the change; the boy had simply settled into his new school, his new home, and for once had plenty of friends his own age to play with. And if none of those friends was available, he'd simply stroll to the farm and help out Idris Phillips. Craig was fit and active. His mother had never seen him look healthier.

Jenny wished she could say the same about herself. As she looked into the mirror she saw a too-thin, mid-thirtyish woman whose grey hairs seemingly grew in number by the day. Since the divorce, she had resigned herself to single status – no chance of finding Mr Right in Bethesda. At least she had Craig to grow old with.

Something disturbed her in the early hours of the following

morning. Still half asleep, Jenny imagined she had heard a cry. She lay in the darkness, heart thumping, waiting for a repeat of the sound. Through the wall she could hear Craig shifting in his bed. Jenny wondered if he was having a nightmare. He rarely suffered from them, but bad dreams were something every child experienced once in a while.

She briefly considered looking in on him. After a moment, though, he had settled. Reassured, Jenny wrapped the duvet tightly around herself, and within minutes was asleep again.

Craig stopped visiting the farm. Jenny thought nothing of it at first; her son seemed to have found too many other things to occupy his time. He wanted to play with the other kids. He needed to catch up on some homework. Idris Phillips seemed to take it personally.

The old farmer telephoned Jenny one night, to ask if he or his wife had somehow upset the boy. They would never do anything like that intentionally, of course, but you never knew what children that age might be thinking.

Jenny assured Mr Phillips that, whatever the problem with Craig was, it was nothing to do with him or his wife.

'Glad to hear it,' Mr Phillips said, the relief evident in his voice. 'You can tell him from me, he's welcome up here any time he feels like paying a visit.'

But Craig never went back. He seemed happy enough the way things were, and Jenny did not push it.

Autumn drifted into winter; soon it would be Christmas. The school atmosphere changed almost imperceptibly, as if everyone in the building felt the excitement but was determined not to let it show. It was early December, less than three weeks until end of term, but as far as the children were concerned this was no time for slacking off.

They studied as diligently as before, played their games with the same relentless determination, and occasionally drew pictures with horses in them. To Jenny, their behaviour was no longer a cause for concern.

There was very little sickness; the youngsters seemed in better-than-average health. Literacy and numerical skills matched those of children two years older. Clean air, the more sedate pace of country life . . . who knew, or even cared, why?

Jenny began to think seriously about how to spend Christmas. Her first inclination was to stay with her parents, but the more she thought about it, the less a good idea it seemed. Since the divorce, they had treated her like some kind of cripple, an emotional cripple who needed their constant support and attention. Their hearts were in the right place, she told herself, but they could not grasp the fact that she needed to come to terms with her life in her own way.

So. She would celebrate her first Christmas as a divorcee in Bethesda. Craig would not mind. After all, the village was where all his friends, his new friends, were. On Christmas Day, families were fine up to a point, but, for a youngster, the best fun was to be had from going off with other youngsters, riding new bikes, showing off the currently in brand of trainers, swapping tales of who had been treated to what presents.

Jenny had still not decided what to buy Craig this year. His father would send money, as no doubt would the boy's grandparents, now they would not be seeing him in person. But money was not the same as presents you could sit down and open. Jenny was not exactly flush, but she had put enough away over the past few months to afford a reasonably good range of gifts.

It was Friday tomorrow, the last day of term. On Saturday she would make the hour-long trip to Cardiff and let Craig decide what he wanted. It would not be a problem to stash a few extra surprises away. They could make a day of it, maybe take time out from shopping to catch the latest Disney cartoon at the Odeon. Craig would be thrilled.

By four o'clock, laden with bags and exhausted by the crowds, Jenny wondered if her promise of a visit to the cinema had been such a good idea after all.

Craig was getting fidgety himself. 'What time is it?' he asked. They had managed to find a seat in a McDonald's, Craig attacking a cheeseburger as if he hadn't eaten for days. Jenny could only pick at her food. The stores had been badly overheated by a combination of warm air blowers and the crush of human bodies; she felt slightly sick.

'You should have asked for a watch for Christmas,' she said. 'I've lost *count* how often you've asked me the time today.' He was simply excited, she knew, overawed by the lights strung across the main streets, the throngs of people, the buzz of excitement in the air. There was a Salvation Army band playing carols just outside the restaurant. Jenny, feeling the onset of a headache, wished they'd play elsewhere.

'Can we go home now?' Craig said.

'Go home? I thought we were going to the pictures.'

'I want to go home.'

'There's no rush. We can—'

'I want to go *home!*'

Jenny felt a hundred pairs of eyes on her. She felt embarrassed and slightly angry. At Craig. *Don't be so damned ungrateful*, she felt like snapping back.

She forced herself to calm down; if she was tired and irritable after hours of being bumped and jostled by careless shoppers, God alone knew how an eight-year-old would feel.

The day out was part of Jenny's plan to ensure her son had the best possible Christmas under the circumstances, and within the restraints of her budget. Perhaps she had been trying too hard to please. It wasn't Craig's fault his father was gone.

'All right,' she said, giving him a weary smile. 'Finish your food and we'll go get the car.'

He seemed happier after that, but subdued during the drive back to Bethesda. He did not ask for the time again, but on several occasions Jenny noticed him study the clock on the dashboard. She assumed he wanted to see his friends; if so, he was going to be disappointed. The city had been congested, the car park clogged. It would be seven at least by the time they got home, too late to go out to play. She'd get him to help put up the decorations. His job for the last few years had been to arrange tinsel and baubles on the tree; that would cheer him up.

But when they got home, Craig wanted to go straight to bed. He seemed edgy, and Jenny wondered if he was coming down with something before dismissing the notion. It was probably nothing more worrying than a simple case of doing too much in one day.

Jenny spent an hour on her own putting up the decorations. When she went to check on Craig, he was sound asleep. His hands were clasped together on the pillow next to his head, as if he prayed while he dreamt.

Christmas Eve. Jenny spent the day wrapping Craig's presents while he was out playing. She peeled and sliced vegetables, leaving them to soak in bowls of water in the fridge. She telephoned her friends back home, exchanging last-minute festive greetings. Her family she would contact tomorrow morning, while the turkey was cooking.

She called at the village stores, picking up extra milk, and bread to put in the freezer. A few neighbours came out to talk as she walked back, invited her in for drinks. She declined, wanting to get home. Christmas Eve she allowed Craig to stay up late, until midnight. Then he was permitted to open one present before going to bed. It was their own little tradition, and this year would be no different.

She couldn't believe it. 'You what?'

'I want to go to bed,' Craig said. 'I'm tired.'

'But it's not even half past nine yet! Don't you want to stay up and open a present?'

Craig shook his head. He'd been pretty listless all evening. Not even the Bond film on the television had appeared to interest him. He picked at his food, moped around the house as if bored. This was not like Craig, not like him at all. Jenny sighed. Was he missing his father? Missing his old house, his old friends? She didn't think so. He seemed to have settled into their life in Bethesda better than she had hoped. And yet . . .

She put her hand gently on Craig's shoulder. 'Craig, I want you to tell me what's wrong.'

'Nothing,' he said, looking down.

'Yes there is,' Jenny said. 'I know there is. I want you to tell me what before you go to bed. This is getting ridiculous.'

He jerked his shoulder, and Jenny took her hand away. 'I mean it,' she said, more firmly. 'I've had just about enough of this. If you're not going to tell me what the problem is now, you can just sit there and think about it until you *are* ready to.'

'I've got to go to bed!' he screamed, startling her. He jumped up from the settee, glaring, his little fists clenched at his side. 'You can't stop me! I want to go to *bed*!'

'Sit down,' Jenny ordered. Craig did not move. 'Sit down,' she repeated, 'and tell me why. Then you can go to bed.'

Craig swallowed audibly. 'Horses,' he murmured.

'Horses? What horses?'

Jenny was immediately reminded of the pictures her class had drawn, the strange renditions which made the animals look more like creatures of nightmare. 'Why are you scared of horses, Craig?'

'The ten o'clock horses!' he blurted, crying now. 'They ride in the night, and if you're not asleep by ten o'clock, they take you away!'

Jenny drew breath sharply. What the hell kind of story was that? It was like the bogeyman tale her older cousin would tell her when she was a kid, the kind of childish fantasy designed purely to scare impressionable youngsters. And Craig, at eight, was not yet old enough to recognise the story for what it was.

'Craig, there's nothing to be afraid of, honestly,' she said. She moved forward and held him; he was trembling. 'It's just a story—'

'No it isn't!'

'Yes it is, I promise. I bet the older boys told you that story. Didn't they?' No response.

'That's the sort of things boys do, Craig. They tell scary stories to younger children because it makes them feel good. It makes them feel good because they can have a good laugh about it.'

'It's true!'

'No, Craig, it's not true.' It did, however, explain much. No wonder the kids were so active; they were probably so terrified by the idea of the ten o'clock horses they would – probably without even thinking – go to any lengths to make sure they were tired enough to be asleep early. It explained those horribly twisted paintings. And perhaps why Craig had stopped wanting to visit Idris Phillips and his wife. There were horses on the farm.

'When I was about your age,' she continued, 'my cousin Elaine used to come and stay over most weekends. She was five years older than me and I used to worship her. If she told me something, I believed her.

'One night – we used to share the same bedroom – she told me about the monster in the cupboard where all my toys were. The bogeyman who would sneak out when I was asleep and strangle me if I hadn't been good. I was so scared it used to keep me awake for hours.'

Craig looked at her, interested. 'What happened?'

'Nothing,' she said. 'Nothing happened. After a while I forgot about it, and as I got older I realised Elaine was just scaring me. For the sake of it. That's what older children do, Craig. That's what they have always done, and I suppose what they'll always do.'

'The ten o'clock horses aren't real?' There was eagerness in his tone now, as if he wanted to believe her and needed persuading.

'Of course not,' Jenny said. 'Think about it. Horses flying around at night, taking children away . . : Have you ever seen a flying horse? And how do they get into bedrooms? Down the chimney, like Santa?'

Craig began giggling. 'Like Santa . . .'

Jenny hugged him. When term started she would have a word with Miss Parker, and with some of the older boys. A few names sprung to mind. But for now everything was fine.

She made him sandwiches, gave him a glass of milk. They sat on the settee together and watched television, the fire turned up high while rain hammered at the windows. It felt cosy.

At midnight, Craig opened one present – a video of cartoons –

and went to bed. Jenny tucked him in, kissed him goodnight, promised to wake him early. She went into her room, took Craig's wrapped presents from their hiding place in the wardrobe, and carried them downstairs. Then she spent a few minutes arranging them around the small pine tree – their first 'real' tree, Craig had dubbed it.

The storm had not let up; there was thunder in the distance. Before going to bed herself, Jenny pulled back the curtain and looked out.

Wind-driven clouds swirled over the Beacons, and there was a flicker of lightning. She knew if she stared long enough, she would begin to see imaginary shapes in the clouds. She wondered if she would see horses.

She awoke early on Christmas morning. Even with the central heating on for two hours, the house felt cold. Jenny glanced at her watch; nearly seven-thirty. She got out of bed, pulled on her dressing-gown, went to get her son. He was little more than a bump beneath the heavy quilt. Jenny smiled. For a moment she debated leaving him to sleep on, but knew he would want to be up as early as possible.

She pulled back the quilt.

Craig's eyes were closed, but his mouth was open. A glistening thread of saliva had run down his chin, spilling on to his pyjamas. Jenny could see his hands clasped together tightly. His flesh was blue. She reached out to touch him, but his skin was cold, lifeless.

Her recollection of what happened after that was fragmentary. Even now, ten months later, she could barely recall the ambulance, the hospital, the doctors and their failed attempts to revive her son. A jumbled series of images replaced memory; in some ways that was a blessing.

Jenny glanced at the window. Low, grey clouds glared down, threatening rain, and frequent gusts of wind rattled the window frames. It would snow before Christmas. Here it always did.

She did not want to think about Christmas. There was

nothing to celebrate any more. But neither was there anything to distract her. The children, as usual, were behaving impeccably. The only sound to disturb the silence was the occassional rustle of a page being turned.

Even the twins, the beautiful Ellis girls, were concentrating on their reading, fitting in perfectly even though they had only joined the school two weeks ago. She wondered if she should tell them about the horses. It may not be a good idea. She could scare them, and if they repeated her words to their parents, she may find herself in more trouble than she could cope with. But what if she did *not* tell them, and something happened? How would she feel about that? She would feel as guilty as hell.

She asked them to stay behind after class.

Now they sat, waiting patiently. Jenny knew what she wanted to tell them, but could not find the right words. She only had a few minutes before their mother, who usually waited in her car outside the school gates, would start to worry.

Rebecca and Gemma were virtually identical. With their blonde hair, blue eyes, and elfin features, they looked as fragile as china dolls. Jenny would watch them as they played in the yard. They seemed healthy enough; but then, so had Craig.

The doctors could not explain his death. His heart had simply stopped sometime during the night. They told her not to blame herself. There could have been no way of knowing, no tell-tale signs she should have picked up on. It was something that simply happened. Jenny wondered. She wondered about the ten o'clock horses. They did not – *could* not – exist. Not in the real world. But in the mind of a child? Perhaps she had not convinced Craig after all.

Jenny still did not know what to say. She had to make a start, hope something would suggest itself. 'Well, girls,' she said. 'I just wanted to ask how you're settling in here.'

'Fine, thank you, Miss Wilson,' said Rebecca. Gemma nodded.

'Good. No problems at all?'

'No, Miss Wilson,' said Rebecca. Gemma shook her head.

'If ever you *do* have any problems, or something you want to talk about, you know you can come to me any time. Okay?'

This time the two girls nodded their response.

'That's good,' Jenny said. *Tell them*! She wanted to, but her feelings refused to frame themselves into words. She shook her head, defeated, and forced a smile for the twins. 'Your schoolwork is fine, girls,' she finished. 'Better run along now, before your mummy starts wondering where you've got to.'

Rebecca and Gemma stood and walked to the door. They paused, and exchanged a quick, almost furtive, glance before looking back at her. 'Don't worry, Miss Wilson,' Rebecca said. 'We know about the horses.'

Jenny could only watch in silence as the girls clasped hands and walked out of the room, out to where their mother was waiting.

FUNNY WEATHER

Steve Lockley

I met Steve Lockley – along with his friend Paul Lewis – at last
year's Fantasycon in Birmingham (this was after I had accepted
both of their stories, thank goodness!), and spent an enjoyable
hour or so talking about the horror field and Writing in general.

Since then, Steve's bank job has gone the way of so many
others and he now finds himself with time on his hands. On the
strength of 'Funny Weather', he should be able to put it to good
use. Indeed, he's recently completed (with Paul Lewis) the
impressive *Cold Cuts*, an anthology of original horrors,
predominantly penned by Welsh writers (plus the ubiquitous
Ramsey Campbell) and available from Alun Books. On the plus
side, he and his wife Elaine produced Rebecca Louise last year
and now he can't remember what life was like without her.
(Give it time, Steve, give it time . . .)

Steve has been writing for about ten years, with sales to a
handful of small press magazines. He doesn't remember any
superstitions as a child but was well aware, particularly among
other children, of a sense of unease when gypsies were talked
about. 'At the time,' he says, 'I felt unable to reveal that,
according to my grandfather, there were gypsies in our own
family.'

There are some here, too . . . and they've brought the
damnedest weather with them.

77

It had been a strange summer all round. The weather had changed dramatically several times, with heavy thunderstorms in the evenings and rain that seemed to hit the windows in sheets. During the day the air was full of the scratching grasshoppers, clouds of midges and glorious sunshine. My sister had been born on the last day of July and shortly before that I had been packed off to stay with my grandmother to keep me out of the way. I was ten at the time, and while I had stayed with Gran numerous times before, it took me quite a while to make friends with any of the other boys in the village.

Gran had sent me out one morning to the common, knowing that that was where the village boys tended to congregate to play cricket and football. They were in the middle of a game of cricket when I arrived, using sticks for wickets and a heavy-looking bat which bore the scars of years of use. After I had been watching them for a few minutes the batsman skied the ball over the head of the last fielder and in my direction. It seemed to hang in the air around me and I was almost oblivious to the calls of 'Catch it! Catch it!' I took two steps forward and caught it, two hands together and clutched the ball to my chest. The boy who had been batting stepped through the huddle of players which had gathered around me, patted me on the back, and said, 'Want to play?'

I nodded and he handed me the bat. 'You're in then,' he said, then proceeded to introduce the other boys. He was Kev while the others had names like Brains, Croc, Spider, Smiffy, Nige and Gannet. Each name was accompanied by a nod of the head from the boy in question and the list continued until each of the fourteen or fifteen boys had been called. I only managed to put two or three of the names to faces but it was obvious from Kev's demeanour that this was his gang, but I was being asked to join, even if it would only be on a temporary basis.

'What do they call you then?' asked Kev as we walked to the crease.

'Tim.'

'No nickname?'

'No.' I lied. I had been given a nickname and it had stuck with me for so long that I hated it. This was a fresh start for a while at least. Why should it be tainted with experiences from my normal life?

The game continued but only lasted for twenty minutes or so. The peace was shattered by the arrival of a gaudily painted caravan pulled by a horse that appeared to be on its last legs.

I had never come across gypsies before and didn't really understand what all the fuss was about but, when the caravan pulled on to the common, the other kids ran, and I ran with them. It was 1963, long before the tinkers had taken over with their mobile homes and reputations for dishonesty. These were real gypsies and the other boys seemed genuinely afraid, although the driver of the horse, a young man with a wide-brimmed hat, acted with total disinterest. On the roof of the van, swaying with the rocking and rolling progress of the horse, sat a bird which was taking far more interest. In the split second that we took to register its presence it cawed and took to the air.

'Gypos,' Kev shouted. 'Don't let them put the Evil Eye on you. You'd better come with us, Tim,' he called.

I had no idea what this Evil Eye was, but I ran all the same, albeit slower than the rest who seemed to be running for their lives, barely stopping long enough to snatch out the pieces of cane that we had been using as stumps.

The common lay on one edge of the village and we ran almost the length of Church Street, taking us almost to its other side, before we stopped for breath.

'What's all the fuss about?' one old man called out as we passed his house.

'Gypos,' shouted Kev. 'On the common.'

The old man had disappeared inside his house before I could see what sort of response he made, but by that time my lungs were hurting like mad and the sound of blood pumping past my eardrums meant that I would not have heard anything less than a shout.

We stopped at the church wall and all of us fell against it, gasping and wheezing. One kid who was called Brains in deference to the National Health glasses that he sported threw up into the churchyard. Kev patted him on the back but I was unsure as to whether this was in commiseration or congratulation. Whichever it was, it was a sure sign of the camaraderie which bonded us together that day.

It was late afternoon by the time that we had all recovered from our flight, and dark storm clouds appeared from nowhere and drew across the sky. We arranged to meet again the following morning, but it was agreed that we would have to keep away from the common, at least for a few days. Kev suggested that we meet at some derelict house; there were still a few windows to smash, or we could stick some hardboard at the broken windows to use for practice. I had shrugged at the suggestion but had agreed even though I had no idea where it was. Thankfully Kev offered to call round for me. I knew instinctively that if I chickened out from this enterprise I would run the risk of exclusion when the common was ours again.

Tea with Gran was always a quiet affair, but that day she noticed that I was more subdued than normal. 'Something wrong?' she asked.

I shrugged and although reticent about telling her what had happened that day, I needed to ask someone what was going on. There was no way that I could ask the other boys; it would just make me more of an outsider than I was. I needed to find out why they were frightened.

'There are gypsies on the common.'

'Oh,' she said. 'That explains a lot.'

'What do you mean?'

'Gypsies. They always bring funny weather with them. Should have known. Were you playing on the common today?'

'Yeah. Or at least we were until they arrived, then the others got scared and everyone ran away. What are they frightened of, Gran?'

'It's hard to say really. A lot of people are just frightened of things that they don't understand.'

I didn't understand, but I wasn't frightened. What I did know was that the storm clouds had suddenly passed and the sky had brightened again. It looked like we would miss out on a storm that night.

'They'll probably be round soon,' Gran said after a few minutes broken only by the sound of eating and the heavy tick of her large wall clock.

'Who will?' I asked.

'The gypsies.'

'Here?' I asked, sensing a sort of contagious panic rising in me. 'Why would they want to come here? Besides, it will be getting late soon.'

'They'll be round with their pegs and scraps of tatty lace, and offers of fortune telling. They always come in the early evening to make sure that they get as many people at home as they can. There would be no point in calling at people's houses if they were all out at work or doing the shopping, would there?'

'I guess not.' I thought about this for a moment, still uneasy at the thought of them coming to the door, bringing their Evil Eye with them. I wondered what that could be. Would it be some sort of animal's eye, or like a glass paperweight? Something like a huge marble, yes that could be it. A huge glass marble with the green swirl in the middle. That would look like an eye. But why was it evil, what could it do to you?

'Have you ever had your fortune told, Gran?'

'Not on your life. There are things I would rather not know. I buy a few pegs to keep them happy, 'cos it doesn't do to cross them, but I don't go in for this magic stuff that they do.'

Gran's house was set in the middle of a block of four houses, and the back entrance to all four was through a gate at the side of the furthest house. The gate had always creaked for as long as I could remember, and on that clear summer's evening it seemed to creak louder than it had ever done before. In a matter-of-fact way Gran said, 'That'll be them now.'

'At the back? Don't they use the front door?'

'Oh no, they always come around the back. It's harder for you to say no when they come around the back, and they know it.'

'Would it hurt to say no to them? Tell them that you don't want any of their pegs or stuff?'

'To be honest, Tim, I don't really know, but I'm just not prepared to take a chance when peace of mind means buying a few pegs once a year.'

I could hear voices outside, and when Gran went into the kitchen to find her purse I ran upstairs to the back bedroom to watch what was going on. I had to press my face to the glass to see the gypsy but there was no way that I was going to open the window and attract her attention. She was standing at the back door of old Mr Daniels who had acepted the offer of a piece of lace and mumbled something about his granddaughter. When she moved away from his door to the end of his yard before coming around to Gran's, I got a better look at her, or at least what she was wearing; it was difficult to see her face at that angle. A bright red headscarf seemed totally at odds with the rest of her clothes. An old grey cardigan over a shabby dress of indeterminate colour made her seem very plain, but oddest of all was her boots. She was wearing men's working boots which sparked as she walked across the paving stones. At first I thought that this was magic, but then remembered the metal segs that dad put in his own boots to make them last longer.

Gran barely said a word to the woman as she handed over the money and accepted the bundle of wooden pegs tied up with string. As soon as the transaction was completed she closed the door without a thank you, or goodbye. I still didn't really understand. Maybe Gran was afraid of the Evil Eye just like the rest.

I shifted my position so that I could watch as she went next door to Mrs Granville's house. She was old and looked more like a witch than this gypsy did. It was a strange thought, like when you suddenly understand something for the first time, something that has eluded you no matter how hard you think about it. That was the first time I had ever considered that gypsies and witches could all be the same sort of people.

Mrs Granville lived with her daughter who also seemed to be ancient and yet I knew that she was a schoolteacher. The gypsy seemed to be taking her time, fiddling with something in the wicker basket, and I was distracted for a moment by something moving at the top of the garden. Marmalade, Gran's fat cat, was sitting on the coalshed roof watching two starlings that were

perched on Mrs Granville's washing line, their breasts reflecting
a turquoise sheen in the late sunshine.

'Get away with you,' said the unmistakable voice of Mrs
Granville. 'We don't want any of your rubbish around here. Just
clear off.'

The gypsy didn't move at this first retort, but slowly walked
away as a tirade of abuse sprang from the old woman's lips.
Somehow I found the scene so funny that I could not help but
laugh. The only person I knew that I was frightened of had
managed to beat the woman that everyone else seemed to be
hiding from. Somehow I felt that I had been part of a small
victory. The feeling lasted only for a moment or two because the
witch looked up at my bedroom and I felt her eyes burning at me.
I hid behind the curtains, afraid that she might produce the Eye.

When I dared look again, she had gone, but the storm clouds
had returned. Marmalade was still on the coalshed roof, but he
had made his way along the ridge and was now on that section of
outhouses which belonged to Mrs Granville. Even from where I
was standing I could see that his gaze was fixed on the starlings
whose very chirping seemed to be a source of annoyance to him.
In an instant he leapt from his crouched position and launched
himself at the birds on the washing line. Despite the speed with
which he had travelled, he was too slow to catch the birds which
had taken flight at almost the same point at which the cat had
made his attack. Vainly he clawed at the line which twanged
under the pull of his weight, then snapped. He was on his feet in
an instant and ran away into the gooseberry bushes.

Within seconds of him having found cover in which to lick his
wounded pride, the storm clouds returned. A flash of lightning
heralded thunder and the heavens opened. Gran was right, it
was funny weather. It was only then that I noticed that Mrs
Granville had some washing on the broken line which was now
sticking to the mud that her garden had become.

Kev called for me the following morning at around ten o'clock.
Dad had already been over on his motorbike to let me know that
Mum was coming home that afternoon but asked if I minded

staying on until the weekend. It was Wednesday already and staying on with Gran for a few more days wasn't too much of a hardship. I knew that I was missing out on seeing a few of my own mates but they would wait. As I walked away with Kev, Gran called out something about red sky in the morning, and to keep an eye on the sky but it meant nothing to me. Perhaps I didn't want to know.

Kev already knew about Mrs Granville's argument with the gypsy but had only seen the devastation caused by the broken washing line that morning.

'Looks like she got the Evil Eye all right. Still she should think herself lucky that it's only a broken line and a bit of washing that needs doing again.'

'The gypsy didn't do that,' I said. 'Gran's cat did it.' I pointed to Marmalade who had resumed his position on the coalshed roof, basking in the sunshine without the harassment of the two starlings. In a way, his efforts the previous day had been a success.

'What do you mean, the cat did it?'

'He jumped off the roof after a couple of birds. He broke the line just before it rained.'

'You don't understand how gypos work do you? She would have made the cat do that.'

'Oh,' I said, not convinced by this argument, and followed him back out on to the street and down to the house that he had been talking about.

Some of the other boys were already there by the time that we had crossed the rough waste ground.

'Watch out,' cried a slightly muffled voice from the upstairs window as stones hailed in its general direction. A face made itself plain for an instant – Brains – only to be replaced by a battered piece of cardboard.

'Wait until he gets out,' said Kev. 'He deserves the first shot after he's climbed up that deathtrap.' In a lower voice he said to me, 'No stairs in there. Brains is the only one light enough and daft enough to climb up just so we have a target to aim at. You got places like this were you live?'

'Nah. People live in all the houses near us, but there's an old chimney left from when the pottery closed down. We try to throw stones into the top.'

'Now that sounds like it needs skill. You any good?'

'Did it once. Either that, or I threw it so far that nobody heard it fall.'

After less than an hour, signs of boredom began to set in. The piece of cardboard had been forced in by a battery of stones within ten minutes and even the last few fragments of glass jammed into the corners of the window frames had been chipped away. Various suggestions were made about what we could do, but no one could really come up with anything that inspired the majority.

'Why don't we just go and play cricket on the common?' I said.

'Are you stupid or just forgetful,' said one of the others. 'The gypos are still there, aren't they.'

'So what? What are they going to do to us, all of us?'

'The Evil Eye. We've all heard that Mrs Granville's had a run-in with them already. Not that I'm particularly sorry about that but there you go.'

The others all sniggered. Most of them were taught, or had been taught, by Miss Granville and there seemed to be only minor argument over whether the mother or the daughter was in league with the devil.

'I know what happened to Mrs Granville's washing, and I don't believe that the gypsy had anything to do with it. I saw what happened and, if you like, I'll go and tell the gypsies that. You all let them come and take over. You just ran away from that common yesterday without a fight.'

There was silence, then whispers. I didn't know why I had made such a rash statement but the feeling seemed to be growing that it would be good sport to watch me make a prat of myself.

The only person not egging me on was Kev. In a way I had challenged the leadership of the gang by proclaiming myself to be braver than any of the others; braver even than Kev and he was the oldest in the group. He was the leader and he couldn't be seen to be running away from the confrontation.

'Let's see you do it then,' he said. 'You think you're better than us, so prove it.'

It was strange how his attitude to me had changed so quickly. One minute I was being treated like he was taking me under his wing, the next he was almost turning against me, daring me to challenge the gypsies. To risk the Evil Eye.

The walk down Church Street seemed to go on forever. I had set off ahead of the others and a few of the boys seemed reticent about following but gradually they had begun to trail in my wake. Along the way a group of girls playing a skipping game shouted out to ask what was happening but I ignored their questions, determined not to let doubt enter my mind. Someone else answered them and I heard the clatter of skipping rope handles falling to the ground and the chatter of the girls as they joined the growing throng. A fear was growing inside me, a fear of the unknown Evil Eye. All I could do was to hope that perhaps the gypsies had already moved away. To try and calm myself I tried to look at the sky above the horizon but it only served to unnerve me further as clouds were racing across the sky without there being a breath of a breeze on my face.

By the time we reached the end of Church Street and the start of the common, I was sweating. When I turned to face the following group, led by Kev, I saw that there must have been over twenty faces looking back at me in silence. I would not back out. No, I could not back out now. I had to go through with it.

The caravan was still there, despite my secret wish, but in full sunlight the colours which had at first sight seemed bright and gaudy now looked drab. The horse was being hooked up by the man that had been driving when they had arrived and as I slowly approached he kept his back to me.

'You the one called Tim?' he called out, startling me.

I swallowed hard before I could reply, my mouth dry. 'Yes. How did you know?'

He shrugged. 'You live next door to Annie Granville?'

How could he have known my name, how could he know that I was staying there? The bird was back on the top of the caravan as it had been the day before, and again I heard its shrill cawing.

The old woman appeared from the far side of the caravan. 'I told him that you would be coming.'

'But how did you know?' I said, for an instant not knowing if she was referring to the man, or maybe the bird.

'There are things I know that are not to be explained. You've come to tell me something.'

I hesitated, my mouth dry again, unable to answer. The crowd behind me jeered, asking if I would rather run away but they only gave me renewed courage. 'It's about Mrs Granville. I know that you didn't make her line break. The cat did it, I saw it happen.'

'You saw it all, did you?' she said with strange laughter in her voice as she displayed the decay inside her mouth, a hotch-potch of brown and broken teeth. 'You saw it did you, from behind the curtains in your grandmother's bedroom? Like a peeping Tom afraid to let himself be seen. Just like you watched me. Is that how you saw it? Like a dirty little sneak?'

I felt the heat rising to my cheeks. I knew that she had seen me at the bedroom window, but how could she know so much about me. The jeering started again. They could not have heard what the gypsy had said to me, they had all stayed far enough back.

'Give him the Evil Eye,' one of them shouted, and I knew that it had to be Kev. I had challenged the leadership and now they had rejected me. I had tried to stand up against something they were afraid of, and yet they had now all turned against me. I wanted to run but my legs felt like jelly. Worst of all, I wanted to hide and cry. It was a trick, it had to be. They were all against me, they must have told the gypsy about me, just so that they could tease me. I felt the venom rise in me and it burst out in a flash of anger. 'You're a fake, all of you are. There is no Evil Eye, it's just a game you're trying to play with me. Well, it won't work.'

I tried to turn, to run, but she managed to trap me with her stare. It was the same piercing look that she had given me the day before but she was looking deeper. I was sure that she knew everything about me and I was finally convinced. There was no glass bauble; this was the Evil Eye. I could not look away or close my eyes. I was trapped until the man laughed and and took my gaze as I stared at him. His eyes had always been in the shade of the brim of his hat, but then I saw them in their full glory. White. Soft white, like hard-boiled eggs fresh from their shells, and with no iris.

'There are things that children should not meddle with. Particularly children who still wet their beds some nights.'

He said this loud enough to ensure that the others could hear and their laughter rang out behind me.

'I don't wet the bed,' I said, or at least tried to say, but the lie choked in my throat.

'Never lie to travellers, Tim. We always know the truth and can make sure that everyone knows it. Perhaps you need a reminder.'

For an instant I felt a sense of relief as if he had released me from that eyeless gaze. It took a few seconds before I realised that my shorts were warm and damp, and that hot piss was running down the inside of my leg.

He laughed again and the bird cawed at me but I ran, bursting through the crowd of tormentors. I ran faster than I had ever done in my life, faster even than when I had joined in the flight with the other boys. This time I ran as if my life depended on it. Even though it felt as if my lungs were about to burst I ran and did not stop until I reached the safety of Gran's house.

I spent the rest of the day in my bedroom, intent on keeping out of the way of the others until the weekend, when Dad would come and take me home. In the evening Gran asked me to fetch in her washing as the clouds had begun to develop again. This time the clouds were so black and menacing that I felt that it would get to be too dark to see by the time that seven o'clock came around. Where sunlight managed to break through a thinner patch of cloud it seemed to shine down in a shaft against the black backdrop, like a torch aimed at nowhere in particular. I was sure that as soon as the gypsies moved on the weather would change back to a normal pattern, even if it meant the end of summer. It could not come soon enough for me.

The starlings were back, this time perched on the top of the coalshed but Marmalade was nowhere in sight. At least I didn't see him until I had put the last piece of washing in the basket. He was lying at the edge of the patch of gooseberry bushes and ignored all of my calls to him.

There was something wrong, there had to be for him to ignore me all together, and so I made my way gingerly between rose bushes in order to reach him. He was stiff and the fur around his face was caked with blood. Birds had pecked out his eyes.

FOR LOVE OF MOTHER

Yvonne Navarro

Yvonne Navarro lives in Illinois but dreams of relocating to Arizona. Her mother's side of the family comes from Kentucky where old timers and youngsters alike swear that the superstition in 'For Love Of Mother' is true.

By day she works in a law office and by night writes tales like 'Memories' (which appeared in *Pulphouse #7*, was reprinted in *Quick Chills II* and honourably mentioned in Datlow's and Windling's *Years Best Fantasy and Horror*), 'Zachary's Glass Shoppe' (*Deathrealm #10*, also mentioned in *Year's Best Fantasy and Horror*), and 'I know What To Do' (*Women of Darkness II*). Her first novel, *After Age*, was published by Bantam Books in September. Rare spare time is taken up with the occasional article and a whole slew of macabre illustrations for small press magazines.

'I'm embarrassed to admit that I probably wouldn't wall up a doorway,' she says, giving readers some indication of what is to follow. 'Also, I don't write in my cheque book in red, I cook black-eyed peas for luck and spinach for wealth on New Year's Day, and I never carry a wallet or purse that doesn't have a penny tucked into it somewhere. My mother's family believes in cauls – midnight suppers held after an engagement to see if the marriage will work – and that the unexpected smell of flowers means an unexpected funeral. I could list dozens more . . . life was always interesting in Brownsville, Kentucky!'

Better put the kettle on – I think we have guests . . .

'I knew he was going to die,' my cousin told me smugly. My mind's eye could see Diane in her little apartment, crouched over the telephone and wearing a tank top and a pair of too-tight pink stretch pants, a well-thumbed pile of scandal papers on the floor beside her chair with a sweating glass of iced tea balanced precariously atop it all. 'Just as sure as the sun rises in the east, and I told Cornell, point blank, they shouldn't be closing it off like that, somebody'd die for sure. But that old shit, he thinks he knows everything. Mr Burton was a good man—'

'Mama's got dinner ready,' I interrupted. 'I have to go.'

'All right, Rosie.' Diane's tone of voice made it clear she didn't like me cutting her off but she didn't push it. God, I hated it when she called me Rosie. 'But you have your mother call me after you all eat. All that talk about redecorating and such, I want to tell her about this—'

'You'll do no such thing,' I snapped. I could feel my fingernails dig sudden crescents into my palms. 'It's taken me a long time to get the money to have this house redone, and a longer time for her to believe I could afford it. I am *not* going to let some of your superstitious bullshit screw things up. Do you hear me?'

'But Mr Burton had a stroke only two days later! Don't you realize that! It happens every time a door is walled over – *every time!*'

'Burton was an *old* man,' I said firmly. 'It was his time, that's *all*. Don't you know how many people renovate every day? Thousands – hundreds of thousands!' The smell of Mama's meatloaf, the summer recipe with fresh tomatoes and green peppers from the garden, swirled around me from the two doors joining the kitchen and living room. 'Now I really do have to go, and remember what I said. You don't say a word, not even that he died, you understand?' Silence greeted me from Diane's end, and I continued. 'She didn't know him anyway, and it'll only upset her. You just stick to your papers and gossip to someone else.' I frowned when she still said nothing, anger making the next words grind their way through my teeth. 'Dammit, Diane, are you listening to me?'

'Yes, Rosie,' she finally answered in a small voice. 'All right. But I still think—'

'And don't call me Rosie!' I hissed before hanging up.

'What did Diane have to say?' my mother asked. Her eyes were bright with interest as she chewed her bite of meatloaf. Vitality just about *sparkled* around her; for being close to seventy, she still turned a few heads at the grocery.

'Nothing important, Mama. You know how she is – stirring the shit just to keep the flies moving.'

She lowered her eyes to her plate and speared a forkful of mashed potatoes. 'It breaks my heart that you think of people in your family like that.'

My family . . . my *mother*. Instinctively picking up the pieces of my shattered life and reguiding them, dragging me back up when I would have wallowed in my own idiocy.

At fifteen, I'd gotten pregnant and gotten married.

At sixteen, I'd come home with nothing in my arms but the ghost of a tiny, morning-stiffened corpse and a load of threadbare clothes.

Seventeen years later, she could still make me feel small. Loyalty makes an eternal debt.

'I don't know about this,' I said doubtfully as I eyed the southernmost door. 'What if it cuts off the air circulation?' Diane's words, sharp and confidential, floated in the nether regions of my thoughts. *Mr Burton was a good man . . . died of a stroke. I told that Cornell, point blank, that they shouldn't wall up that doorway. But that old shit, he thinks he knows everything . . .*

'Don't be silly, Rose. I thought we had this all decided, now you go into one of your decision crises.' Mama studied me, her face frank. 'Is there something you're not telling me? Is this going to be too much money?'

I opened my mouth, Diane's gossip trembling on the edge of my tongue. All those years intervened, shards of memory – me as a pancake waitress, then as a thin, frightened clerk teaching myself to type and really *think*, finally the long climb from white trash to The World of Middle Class – forming my past into its complex, hard-won lifeweb.

Superstition is not so much an odd thing as a *prideful* thing: almost everyone is at least a bit superstitious, but nearly no one will admit to it. My mother's side of the family is Old South Kentucky, steeped in folklore and a so-called southern hospitality that never seems to extend itself comfortably towards me, a girl the old folks at first considered too wild, then too smart for my own good. Besides, I'd been transplanted to the city as a baby and had made it clear from the first time I was able to voice my own coherent opinion that nothing more than occasional, strict obligation bound me to that group of aging, spooky relatives.

Countless struggles, won and lost; there was simply no room in this web for the unexplainable, much less those things which could not be acknowledged.

'Now look who's being silly,' I said mildly. I squelched the thought that my voice sounded too smooth, almost oily. 'You said it yourself – sometimes I just need someone to push me in the right direction. So you think we should go ahead with it?' I tried to keep my tone light, conversational, unconcerned. There was a sudden, sick ferocity to the hope that she would say *No, to be honest, I never liked the idea.*

'Of course!' Her face was bright with anticipation. 'We talked about it – a double bonus, remember? More wall space in both the kitchen and living room, but still plenty of light from the windows. Should I call the contractor and confirm it?'

I nodded cheerily, afraid my throat would strangle any words of agreement. 'When – ?' was all I could finally manage.

'Tuesday morning.' My mother clapped her hands, delight an unmistakable imprint on her features. 'Oh, I can't wait!'

*

'Tell me,' I said slowly, not knowing how to phrase this without starting Diane on yet another one of her verbal rolls. 'What if you brick up the doorway, then . . . change your mind or something?'

'You just tear it down,' Diane said promptly. 'No harm done – provided, of course, that you did it in time.'

'And what if you didn't?' I persisted.

'Didn't what?'

'Do it – tear it back down – in time?'

'Well then, you're shit out of luck, ain'tcha? *Pop!*' Her gum smacked sharply in my ear; I winced and bit back the urge to complain. '"Course, *Pop!* you would always open it up again right quick and see if they come back.' She cackled, and for a horrified instant my mental image of her, revolting as it was, was replaced by a much more frightening picture. 'But I was only kiddin',' she added quickly.

'That's probably how these damned superstitions start,' I muttered.

'What?'

'Nothing,' I said. From the other room, I heard Mama's footsteps and the sound of running water. In the next instant the front doorbell rang, causing my stomach to give a single, sick twist. 'I have to go. Call you tomorrow.' I hung up before she could protest, though I knew my future penance would be Diane's ten-minute speech about how nobody ever had time to listen to her and people were always cutting her off in conversations.

Mama was already at the door, her face all smiles as she stood aside and motioned someone in. In a quaint, old-fashioned move, the man, who looked like an over-stretched version of a colorless Gumby doll, tipped his cap towards me. When he spoke, his voice was thick with down-home accent.

'Mornin', ma'am. I come to fix up that doorway.'

*

'Looks nice, doesn't it?' My mother came and stood by the recliner, where I'd been sitting with an untouched glass of Kahlúa and cream at my side and contemplating the smooth expanse that now represented most of the east wall of the living room. The darkness outside the picture window spilled in and stopped, as if walling up the doorway had trapped it.

'Yeah, great.' Mama glanced at me in surprise and I realized how surly my voice had been. Instead of apologizing, I lifted the glass and drank, letting the sweet coffee taste soothe my throat.

'Well, I like it,' she said. For a second her expression was half-dreamy, half-frightened. 'You know, when I was a girl in Brownsville, everybody thought that if you closed up a doorway someone would die.' Now it was my turn to look sharply at her, but she only laughed, the sound oddly girlish. 'I don't know how many of those foolish women down there probably tried it to get rid of their husbands!'

'Did it ever work?' I had to ask.

'I wouldn't know,' she said lightly. 'I think I'll go to bed now. It's been a hectic day.' But I thought I saw her frail, vein-mapped hand tremble as it skimmed the stair banister.

It's the booze, I told myself. That's all.

Three more drinks, each more generous with the rich, dark Kahlúa, before I could sleep; still I rose every hour to listen for the gentle sound of her breathing.

'What're you doing?' I peered at Mama through the steam rising from my coffee mug. My eyes felt sticky, as though Kahlúa was oozing from their corners, while my mouth was thick with the taste of last night's alcohol. I decided I didn't like the looming feel of the kitchen's new wall at my back.

'Going out in the garden,' she said cheerfully. 'Do a little weeding, pick some more of the tomatoes and peppers that're ready. Some of the cucumbers are ripe, too.' Her movements were slow but efficient, like an old, well-trained animal.

I set the mug down, ignoring the coffee that sloshed over its side. 'It's going to be hot today,' I reminded her. 'Why don't you let me do it for you later?' Careful, I told myself. Don't make her feel like she can't do it herself.

'It'll be even hotter then, Rose.' She frowned at me as she set her gardening gloves on the small table next to the door and slipped an apron over her head. The words *It's Time To Mother Nature* were sprayed across the apron's front in a profusion of intertwined flowers and vegetables. 'You ought to go back to bed, you know. You look tired.'

'I'm fine,' I said shortly. She opened her mouth, then shrugged and pulled the small metal bucket filled with gardening tools from beneath the sink cabinet. I felt a pang of sadness as I realized she had to use both hands to bring it to waist level now.

She balanced the bucket precariously in the crook of one elbow and pushed open the screen door with her other arm. 'Well,' she said brightly, raising her voice above the racket of the door spring, 'maybe a nice hot shower would make you feel better. I'll be back in a little while.' I winced as the door slammed shut, spilling yet another minor wave of coffee on to the tabletop that I made no move to clean up.

A few minutes later my eyes registered the gardening gloves still lying on the small table and I pushed my reluctant body up and went to the door. I thought about going out, then remembered I was still in my baggy pajamas, not even wearing a robe. 'Hey!' I yelled out the door instead. 'You forgot your gloves!'

It sounded like she started to answer, it really did. Whatever words her mouth had planned to form were twisted at the second syllable into something incomprehensible and full of pain. I heard the bell-like singing of the gardening tools as they clattered among themselves within the bucket when it dropped to the ground.

I ran outside, tripping gracelessly across the lawn and my mother's bucket, knowing that it was too late and that my presence with her in this place of green and growing things would make no difference. She was face down, legs splayed and broken-looking, like some fragile puppet dropped and forgotten.

In the end, searching through the storage shed where fragmented pieces of my father's short, long-ago life still lingered, my clumsy hands grasping at unaccustomed tools, I realized that I hadn't even closed her eyes.

I try not to imagine her fingers pulling free of the earth, nails grimed and brown as they brush the ants and flies – opportunistic little scavengers – from her skin and pluck them from the softer, moister parts of her face. Remembering becomes unbearable: the sun, hot and summer high, hardening the blood-flecked foam leaking from her lips, one hand resting palm up beside her denim-clad thigh as the other clutched the earth, nails sunk deep into the ground next to one gentle cheek.

I hear the *screeeetch* of the spring on the outside door as it's pulled open, the slam as it closes behind a footfall that is at first unsteady, then stronger as it moves into the familiar kitchen territory. Always a fastidious woman, lately age has gentled her once sharp mind; still I stay where I am, ignoring the thready, fearful *ping* of my own pulse and wondering instead if she will think to wash her hands.

The sun slides a little lower, its beam finding an angle between the blinds to splatter across the pile of cracked mortar and shattered chunks of plaster, finally glinting dully on the sledgehammer. I watch from the doubtful comfort of the recliner as the light inches across my ragged re-creation of the doorway to spill once more into our cheerful kitchen. I should clean up the floor, I remember, before the mess gets ground into the carpet or . . . something. But I am tired and achy and unsure about how to do this: should I vacuum, or try to sweep first? Perhaps it would be best simply to drop to my knees and pick up the larger pieces by hand. My mind spins indecisively.

From the kitchen, the noise once more unimpeded, I hear the soft, persistent thumping of cookie dough being mixed and flattened by hand, then the clattering of a baking sheet being lifted from the counter, followed finally by the unoiled squeal of the oven door opening and closing. I am silent, waiting, telling my cowardly pulse to calm itself, safe in the knowledge that Mama will still be there to help with the really difficult decisions.

In a few minutes I breathe deeply as the good smells of baking cookies and hot soil fill the air.

EIGHT LIMBS

John Brunner

Born in 1934 in Oxfordshire, John Brunner wrote and sold his first novel while he was still at school. 'Mercifully it appeared under a pseudonym,' he says, 'but it did at least pay for a typewriter of my own.'

The investment turned out to be money well spent.

His interest in the field of science fiction began when he was six years old with a copy of Wells's *The War of the Worlds* but, something of a slow starter, he didn't collect his first rejection slip until he was thirteen. Between leaving school and being drafted into the RAF, he made his first magazine sale – 'Thou Good and Faithful' under the pen name John Loxmith – which appeared in the March 1953 *Astounding*.

Since then, of course, we've had nearly one hundred novels, novellas and story collections – including the ground-breaking (literally) *Stand on Zanzibar* and his pre-emptive ecological masterpiece (it was published in 1972) *The Sheep Look Up* – in virtually every genre imaginable.

Out of his many shorter works, Brunner's imaginatively inventive 'posthumous collaborations' and his recent series of 'Mr Secrett' stories in *Fantasy and Science Fiction* – which culminates in the splendidly wistful 'The Man Who Lost The Game Of Life' (*F&SF* January 1992) – are essential reading.

Never much given to superstitions, Brunner nevertheless remembers being convinced – aged five or six – that he had a lucky number. 'It was eight,' he recalls, 'so I took to doing whatever I could by eights – steps, mouthfuls and no doubt other things I've forgotten. And when that wasn't possible I tried at least for an even number. Thank goodness I grew out of it before boarding school!'

Talking of eight . . .

✳

There had been one yesterday, the day before, the day before that. It was too much to hope that the invasion of his bathroom had stopped. Bracing himself, Alec Miller lifted down the shower-head on its flexible pipe.

No sign of movement caught his eye. He began to relax. However, for safety's sake he turned on the water and played it first along the bottom of the tub, then down the sides. Still no spider. Muttering thanks to the Lord, he closed the tap and made to replace the spray. With his elbow he disturbed the shower curtain.

And jumped back, gasping, as a brownish many-legged horror fell into view, frantically scrabbling back and forth on the wet plastic.

'Oh, *damn!*' he exploded. Sweat burst out all over his body; nausea rose in the back of his throat. He hated spiders. He hated using bad language, too, knowing it was offensive to the Lord, but spiders . . .

Drawing a deep breath, he forced himself to advance, turn the water back on, broom the tub again from end to end. Writhing madly, the creature contrived to postpone its doom by catching the rim of the drain-hole, and for a dreadful moment Alec feared he would have to reach down and – and *touch* it . . . But at that point the water started to run hot, and the spider disappeared.

Also the telephone rang.

Wiping his face with the sleeve of his towelling robe, he went reluctantly to the kitchen. As he unhooked the receiver from the wall, he saw a movement in the sink: something darting across a pile of unwashed dishes.

Not in here as well!

'Good morning!' said a sonorous and authoritative voice in his ear.

Alec swallowed hard. 'Oh – morning, Dad.'

'Well, I must say you don't sound like someone off to spend a whole month with his best girl!' After thirty years in his profession Doug Miller could no longer talk even on the phone without sounding like the preacher he was. This time his delivery combined mild reproof with amused sympathy. 'Didn't sleep much, hm?' he added. 'Too excited?'

Had it been another spider he had spotted in the sink, or was he imagining things? Distracted, Alec could think of nothing else to say except the truth.

'No – uh – actually I slept pretty well. It's just that I found a spider in the tub when I was just about to take my shower.'

'Never tell me you're still scared of spiders!' His father's tone modulated to a blend of incredulity and contempt. 'I thought you'd grown out of that.'

You mean you thought you'd whipped it out of me!

The memories still burned. He had been seven. Finding him whimpering in the cellar, afraid even to duck under a cobweb that hung down in front of him, his father had first demanded why he found spiders so terrifying. Alec couldn't answer – he knew only that there was something dreadful about eight limbs, something unspeakably and indescribably appalling. Next his father mocked him; then tried persuasion, saying how useful spiders were, killing flies that carried germs; then caught one and forced him to let it walk across his palm, claiming that it was beautifully designed and a marvel of the Lord's creation; then, when Alec shrieked and flung it from him, took off his leather belt . . .

'No son of mine is going to be afraid of anything less than twice his size – and in the end, not even that!'

It was a spider in the sink. He could see it clearly now, casting around on an upside-down saucepan for a route to the adjacent worktop. Was he in reach of a newspaper or something else he could swat it with? Even if he did hit it, though, he risked knocking down the stack of dishes, breaking a plate or cup . . .

Heaven help me! I'm going to be away a solid month! If even one of the horrible things comes in every night I'm away, let alone two, my home is going to be uninhabitable when I return!

'Boy, aren't you listening?' his father demanded.

'Sorry,' he mumbled. 'No, I'm not scared of spiders, not like when I was a kid. But you know how I hate killing any of God's creatures, and I had to drown the poor thing. I have a plague of them right now. I find them every morning in the tub, the washbasin; now there's one in the sink. I don't know how they get in!'

'Up the wastepipe, of course,' his father declared. 'All you have to do is leave the plug in the hole.'

'I've done that, of course,' Alec countered irritably.

'Then through the overflow –'

'But they're too big!'

'If you block the drain and they still get in then they must come through the overflow,' his father insisted. 'You do like I tell you – you've got time before catching the plane. Put all the plugs in, tight, and cover the overflow holes with tape. That'll keep 'em out. When you get back you'll find I'm right.'

As usual . . .

'Yes, I'll do that,' Alec muttered. 'I should have thought of it myself. I guess I am a bit overexcited.'

'So you should be! You're going to some of the most famous places in the world to view some of the greatest creations men have ever made to magnify the Lord! When I think of those great cathedrals I've only seen in pictures, especially in France – Rouen and Chartres and Notre-Dame – I can't help wishing I were going along. Not, of course, that I don't wish even more you and Ruth were making a pilgrimage to the Holy Land itself, the way your dear mother and I did when we were engaged.'

'Dad, we've been over that. You know how much I'd have liked to follow in your footsteps. But with the political situation like it is out there, no matter how glad I'd have been to go, I

couldn't possibly expose Ruth to that kind of risk, could I?' Alec
was never going to be a preacher like his father, but he hadn't
been able to avoid picking up some of the tricks of the trade, and
his words sounded convincingly heartfelt.

'No, of course not.' Firm approval now, swiftly evolving into
man-to-man confidentiality. 'Speaking of Ruth, young man, you
know how I feel about her, don't you? She's an admirable person
– sensible, devout, just the sort of girl I look forward to being the
mother of my grandchildren.'

'Oh, I admire her too!' – fervently.

'I know you do,' his father soothed. 'None the less I'm going to
have to give you a bit of parental advice. You do realise, don't
you, that you're about to face the greatest test of your manhood
that you've undergone so far?'

Alec blinked, half his mind still on the spider, wishing cold
sweat would stop crawling down his spine. What was all this
supposed to be about?

'Oh, I know the temptations that face a young man in foreign
parts for the first time. Believe me, I felt my share of that
temptation when I travelled with your dear mother, rest her soul.
But I fought it, and I won, and when we came home she
graciously agreed to be my helpmeet. Had I yielded, she would
have scorned me, and justly.'

'I promise, Dad, I shall do my utmost to live up to your
example,' Alec choked out. The spider was turning its attention
the other way. Could spiders jump? He seemed to remember
reading somewhere . . .

'You do that!' Doug Miller boomed. 'I have every confidence
in Ruth, of course. She's a well-brought-up Christian girl, and
even constant proximity to her intended will, I'm sure, never
encourage her to waver from the straight and narrow path.
Young men, on the other hand, even a young man like you who
I'm so proud of—'

'Excuse me just a second,' Alec cut in. With the phone still in
his other hand, he snatched at yesterday's newspaper and smote
the spider as it reached the edge of the sink. Barely in time. Had
it managed to scuttle into hiding under one of the cupboards, he

would never have had time to search for it before the cab arrived to take him to the airport. Indeed, thinking of the time; 'Dad, will you please forgive me? I only have an hour.'

'I told you to pack your bags well ahead of time—'

'I did, I did! But I need to shower and shave and dress and eat something and —' Inspiration dawned. 'And take your advice about keeping spiders out while I'm away!'

'Ah. Well. Yes, of course. Okay, then.' He sounded appropriately miffed, but prepared to exhibit Christian forgiveness. 'Bear one thing in mind, though, all the time you're away. Remember, son: I love you.'

'And I love you, Dad,' Alec returned. 'I'll write you every time I can, even if it's only a postcard.'

'You do that! And when people ask after you I'll be able to show them photos of all these great and glorious buildings in Spain and Italy and France, that you will have seen with your own eyes and your poor old father will go to his grave never having seen except in pictures.'

'Oh, Dad! In the days God still has to grant you, I hope with all my heart that you'll find time to go there too!'

'Ah, perhaps when I've grown old in the Lord's service he may allow me a sufficient stay of execution . . . ' With a sigh. 'Meantime, I'll make the trip by proxy. Take my blessing with you, boy.'

'I'll remember you every day in my prayers!'

'And I you! Safe journey!'

Still not having breakfasted, Alec stared at himself in the bedroom mirror, conducting a head-to-toe inspection. His brown hair was short and neatly combed. His grey suit, white shirt and plain blue tie identified him as one who belonged to the respectable majority. His thin, rather pallid face – well, he could never decide whether he was in any sense handsome, but at least when he donned his heavy-rimmed bifocals they loaned him an air of studiousness. He felt he'd earned it, having been among the top five in every class at his theological college. He nodded, content with his turnout, and with a glance at his watch headed towards the kitchen. He had time for a bowl of cereal . . .

Kitchen.

Spiders!

Seal those holes!

Frantically he dug out the roll of plastic tape he kept for emergency electrical repairs. The bath was still wet from his shower, the washbasin from shaving and cleaning his teeth, so it took ages to make the tape stick across the overflow holes. The sink, miraculously, was easier (though he knew he was going to feel ashamed throughout his trip by the dishes he was leaving to soak in it) but even when he had dealt with that he felt haunted by the apparent ability of these damned spiders to creep through gaps far smaller than themselves . . .

His father's stern voice spoke in memory, rebuking him for the swearword. At the same moment a car-horn blasted outside, announcing the arrival of his cab. Tape in one hand, newspaper in the other for fear of finding another spider unexpectedly, Alec uttered another curse at the prospect of having to start his journey on an empty belly.

Furious at his inability to govern his tongue, he ran to the window and shouted that he was on his way. Then, grabbing his bags, hoping desperately he wouldn't be embarrassed by finding that he'd left something important behind, he shut the door and hurried down the stairs.

His driver was accelerating away from the kerb when he realised he had indeed forgotten something: the Bible his mother had given him on the day of his confirmation, which he had promised to keep with him always.

But he knew most of Scripture by heart, anyway.

He was later than the rest of the tour party at the airport, but even though he had never met them before it was easy to identify them among the swirl and bustle of other travellers at the departure gate. All bar one were a good twenty years his senior, some perhaps forty. The men were in sober suits and ties like his, the women in calf-length dresses with hats and white or grey gloves: Sunday morning garb. The exception, naturally, was

Ruth, who had chosen a biscuit-coloured pants suit. Reverend Miller had never entirely approved of women wearing trousers and had forbidden his wife to do so. Dutiful, Alec echoed his views – like, plainly, the majority of their companions-to-be – but one had to admit such clothes were practical for travelling.

He hurried up, full of apologies, and Ruth turned her head to permit the chaste peck on her cheek appropriate to an engaged couple. Drawing back, he did his best to adopt the role of the devoted swain, smiled, nodded, said, 'How lovely you're looking!' Her straight brown hair was cut in a pageboy bob; on her square, large-mouthed face she wore only the merest trace of makeup, as usual; and if he caught a whiff of unfamiliar perfume it was doubtless in honour of this very special occasion.

'Good morning! You must be Alec Miller!'

A beaming, dark-haired man in his mid-thirties, deeply tanned, taller than Alec, with a wide white smile and a clipboard under one arm, approached and offered his hand. 'I'm Peter Dale, your courier and guide. Do feel free to call me Peter. I already made the acquaintance of your charming friend Ruth. Glad you made it – we were starting to worry.'

Alec mumbled something, feeling a pang of envy at this man's good looks and obvious sophistication. On his lapel he wore a silver cross; was he an ordained minister? The brochure hadn't indicated that one would be in charge.

'Now we're all here at last,' Peter went on, raising his voice in a way Alec recognised as one of his father's techniques, not shouting but simply commanding attention, 'I feel you may wish to draw aside and invoke heaven's blessing on our enterprise . . .?'

There were nods. The group moved a little apart and stood with bowed heads as Peter recited a brief prayer. While he was speaking, however, Alec could not concentrate. His eyes kept being distracted by those around: middle-aged businessmen laughing, no doubt, at bawdy jokes; tourists in comfortable-looking outfits, tracksuits and thick-soled canvas trainers; young men and girls identically clad in flimsy tee-shirts and cut-off jeans, holding hands or even with their arms around each other's waists, their fingers innocent of marriage-rings . . .

*I wonder whether Ruth will let me walk like that with her while
we're away. I wonder whether some hot evening in Spain or Italy
she'll let me—*

*Stop! Stop! 'Who so looketh on a woman to lust after her – !' I must
not dishonour in my mind the woman who one day will be my wife!*

The prayer concluded, he moved to rejoin Ruth, intending to
say something, anything, about Europe. He had been reading it
up extensively, and though he might have forgotten his Bible he
had several travel guides in his carry-on bag. But he was too
slow. By the time he made up his mind what his opening remark
should be, she was listening with fascination to Peter. In a
resonant baritone (yes, he might well be an ordained minister, for
that voice would echo round a church without amplification,
and if not then he had missed his vocation) he was recounting
personal experiences in all the countries that to the rest were
terra incognita, describing strange delicious foods, traditional
music and dances, exotic costumes, in such vivid terms one
could almost visualise them, almost smell and taste the spices.
One of the oldest members of the group – probably, Alec
diagnosed, a widow – coughed when he mentioned wine, and he
glanced brightly at her.

'You refer very casually to strong drink,' she said in a
suspicious tone.

'Ah, but not to distilled liquors,' Peter answered earnestly.
'Only to what Jesus did not disdain to provide for the wedding
guests in Cana. Does not the Good Book praise "wine that
maketh glad the heart of man"? Like all the gifts of heaven we
infirm mortals sometimes abuse it, but iron can as easily become
a ploughshare as a sword. Everything is in the intention!'

The widow retired in confusion, and Ruth said, laying her
hand on Peter's arm in a way she never did to Alec, 'Do tell us
more about Rome!'

Looking back later, Alec felt that was the moment when the
disaster began. At the time he couldn't be sure. He thought the
ice cream might have been the turning-point, or the lipstick, or
the Spanish jeans, or the Italian dress exposing half her thighs,

thighs he before had barely more than glimpsed as Ruth was getting out of a car. Once, daringly, visiting her family, he had suggested they go swimming together, but she had divined his ulterior motive and assured him she never wore anything as immodest as a bathing suit. Her parents, nodding, smiled . . .

Yes: that touch on Peter's arm. That was where the rot originally set in.

Of course, the ice cream too was a sign, but that was in Rome, their first destination, and it was too early for him to have caught on to what was happening. The tour being a full month in length, their schedule was a leisurely one: they would gather after breakfast for a few prayers – none of them felt sufficiently ecumenical to attend a Catholic mass, though facilities were arranged for Sunday worship in more familiar contexts – and then visit a church or cathedral. A prolonged lunch would be followed by a museum or art gallery, with special emphasis on religious art, and in the evenings they were offered concert or theatre tickets, or directed to unusual and interesting restaurants. Several times Alec said to Ruth what excellent value they were getting, and she agreed. But somehow she never seemed to be paying him full attention. When he repeated carefully memorised passages from his travel guide she grew abstracted, even though his information was nearly as detailed as what Peter was imparting, and as often as not moved away from him so as to be able to hear more clearly.

Alec's heart began to sink. The episode of the ice cream loaded it with extra ballast.

After two days in Italy Ruth discarded the church-going hat and gloves she had worn since arrival, substituting a scarf if obliged to cover her head in a church. When Alec remonstrated, she tossed her head and said she felt like a laughing-stock in such old-womanish gear. In the street she kept dawdling to look in shop windows. At mealtimes she astonished him by sampling foods for which he felt instinctive revulsion; she ate octopus and squid and curious fungi and announced they were delicious, earning the disapprobation of the rest of the group . . . but more and more approval from Peter. On the third (or was it fourth?)

evening she declined to attend the choral concert that was on
the programme, and dutifully – though he had been told the
choir was exceptional – Alec yielded to her preference, telling
himself that in marriage the husband must allow his wife some
leeway, especially in minor matters.

So what else to do? Peter, inevitably, supplied the answer.
Himself dismissing the concert on the grounds that he attended
more than enough every time he brought a group to Europe, he
stated that the best ice cream in the world was to be found in
Italy, and offered to prove it. Tempted by the offer of something
at once familiar and exotic, three of the others agreed to join an
expedition down endless winding alleys to a café where, Peter
said, they sold the most delicious ices he had ever eaten.

And indeed they were superb. They were so good Alec found
himself saying they made it hard to believe that greed was
genuinely a sin. Their more formal companions took umbrage at
this risqué joke, but Peter smoothed it over, and for once Ruth
looked at him with a speculative expression that he interpreted
as: *Can this young fogey have a sense of humour after all?*

It had never crossed his mind that that might be among the
things she was looking for in a lifetime partner. He resolved to
devise more witticisms. In this atmosphere it felt as though it
ought to be far easier than at home.

The last ice they sampled was a blackcurrant sorbet,
wonderfully aromatic but incredibly purple. Ruth adored it and
told Alec to order her a second helping, regardless of the fact
that her wide mouth was stained with it from corner to corner.
Turning back from catching the waiter's eye, Alec saw Peter
bending close to whisper something in her ear. Grinning, she
blushed . . . he thought. But he couldn't be sure in the dim
light. All he could think of was that he had never managed to
make Ruth grin that way.

It was next morning that she appeared in lipstick, a colour
redder than the blackcurrant ice, but no less vivid. Horrified, he
tried to reason with her, but she simply grinned again – not for
him, but at him.

She bought the too-short dress that afternoon. Moreover it

was sleeveless and exposed her shoulders.

And he was virtually certain she could not be wearing proper undergarments with it.

Rome – Florence – Ravenna – he was losing track of where they were taken, and there were Spain and France to follow. The older members of the tour group began to condole with him. Finding their sympathy unbearable, he brushed aside their professions of concern, forcing a smile, saying, 'When in Rome . . . ! She's entitled to her little fling.'

Yet knew he was deceiving himself, was uttering a falsehood when he had been brought up always to tell the truth.

Had been whipped into telling it, by his father's belt that had also hurt him into hiding his arachnophobia.

Was not that too a form of dishonesty? And he beat me until I agreed to tell the lies he wanted . . .

In Spain, in the fabulous city of Granada, they went to a flamenco club. Sitting around a small table, drinking Coke when everybody else was drinking sherry, Alec saw how Ruth leaned forward, her bright eyes fixed on the dancers as they whirled their skirts and petticoats, exposing their legs clear to the crotch. He felt he ought to have a showdown with her, confront her when they returned to their hotel and make it clear this was no way for someone to behave who was destined to bear Reverend Doug Miller's grandchildren . . . But he couldn't find the words.

Next day she bought a pair of extremely tight jeans. Alec was horrified. His dismay redoubled when several of their companions complimented him on her figure.

Something's corrupting us! What? Can it be Peter? I haven't seen that cross on his lapel since Italy . . . !

Contriving to inquire why, he was met with a casual shrug.

'Oh, one takes the colour of the group one's with. You all know me by now. I don't have to wear a label, do I?'

'You don't – uh – specialise in tours like this?' Alec forced out of a dry mouth.

'Goodness, no!' Peter smiled, displaying his superbly cared-for teeth. 'I just happen to love Europe. I'm a professional courier because it's the only job I know that will bring me over here six times a year. But I'm not bad at it, am I?'

In all honesty Alec was forced to shake his head. This man – he was beginning to think of him in terms like *sleek* and even *offensively sleek* – had one redeeming feature: it was obvious that he did love what he was doing. He was a fountain of recherché information, could talk as freely about Islamic religious art as about Christian, seemed to be as welcome and well known in Spanish tapas bars as in the ice-cream parlours of Italy, and doubtless when they crossed the frontier to France would prove to be as knowledgeable about the schismatic popes at Avignon, the gargoyles of Notre Dame, as about everything else so far.

Also he spoke Italian, Spanish and presumably French with dismaying fluency.

Alec said something to that effect over lunch with Ruth, making a vast effort not to comment on her jeans. She interrupted him.

'Yes, aren't we lucky? We could so easily have had some dry old stick reading aloud from a guidebook.'

Alec tensed. Was that a dig at him? He had given up quoting his own guidebooks in Ravenna, but even so . . .

She was still talking.

'Tomorrow's a free day. Peter suggests we might take a bus to Fastosa.'

'Where's Fastosa?'

'Oh' – a dismissive wave. 'Some place he knows. By the sea. No museums or castles or anything. But a taste of the real life of the country. Right off the tourist beat. You can sit in the shade of pine trees and eat octopus cooked in sherry with piñon nuts—'

Octopus.

Maybe it was something he had eaten today or yesterday, maybe it was some infection that had been lying in ambush for days. Maybe it was just that word. Alec rose blindly, muttering apologies, and dashed to the men's room.

Apparently he was not the only member of the group to have experimented unwisely with the local tapas. A clear majority of them were denied the opportunity of enjoying the free day.

Ruth – 'salted', perhaps; the old term came to Alec from his childhood reading in his father's, that had been his grandfather's, library – felt fine, and waved him a cheerful goodbye as she and Peter caught a bus oppposite the terrace of the hotel they were staying in. She was carrying a canvas shoulder-bag slung from a thick white cotton rope. He wondered what it might contain. He didn't remember seeing it before. But then, he didn't remember seeing Ruth before. Not like this, at any rate: laughing, bare-armed, showing off her body in those so-tight jeans and a skimpy tee-shirt under which . . .

How can she be doing this to me? We've had an understanding for a year!

He looked around guiltily. Apparently he was the only member of the party afflicted with the bowel disorder who wasn't confined to his room. He caught a waiter's eye. In another of his father's books he had read that certain herbal drinks, albeit alcoholic, did serve a medicinal purpose.

The waiter understood his need at once, and brought something syrupy and blackish green, horribly bitter but incredibly restoring. After three glasses Alec made his way back to bed, and slept on and off for eighteen hours. By morning he felt weak but normal. And resolved to have that long-postponed showdown with Ruth.

As she told him over breakfast, Fastosa had proved so delightful that she and Peter had come back only on the very last bus, by which time he must again have been asleep. She had on a new top today, flimsy pink cotton with straps no wider than spaghetti-strands, and when they slipped aside – as they did repeatedly – he sought in vain for pale breaks in the redness of her sunburned shoulders.

Also, this time, it was impossible to believe that she was wearing a bra. A question sniggered demonically in the corner of his brain: *Was she wearing one on the beach yesterday? What was in her canvas bag? A bikini? Less than that?*

But he didn't want to face the possibility. He didn't want to believe that the future mother of his children, who had told him in her parents' presence that she never wore a bathing suit, could have been so shameless, so indecent.

Yet he must speak out about her behaviour! This could not be tolerated any longer! He drew in breath, he framed harsh words—

'Ten minutes!' Peter called from the doorway of the breakfast room. 'Everyone at the bus with all your baggage please! Ten more minutes – Hello, Ruth! Morning, Alec! Enjoy yourself yesterday?'

Alec's resentment threatened to boil over into words – *Don't you know I was sick? How the hell do you think I could enjoy myself?* But the question wasn't aimed at him. Ruth's wide, brightly lipsticked mouth was beaming the answer even before she uttered the words.

'Oh, Peter, it was absolutely wonderful!'

After that, on buses and trains and planes, Peter made sure Ruth had a seat close to him – with Alec beside her, of course. He struggled to keep up polite appearances, and when, urged on by the scandalised elderly widow, the group proposed nominating a delegation to chide Peter about his behaviour, he talked them out of it. Yet every smile she bestowed on the other man was like a dagger in his heart.

What had become of the Ruth he had known at home, the devout, respectable, above all modest girl he had so looked forward to marrying?

Or – had he?

Did he not in fact prefer this version of her?

He felt giddy, as though he were looking at the world with his glasses on upside-down. A myriad locker-room jokes that he had striven to erase from memory returned to haunt him. For the first time he began to consider the possibility that some of them might enshrine constructive advice. In a moment of rare confidentiality his father had once boasted that he had never seen his wife naked, not even after marriage – that the doctor who delivered Alec had seen more of her body in the light than her husband.

Resentful, brooding, he stared at Ruth's sun-red shoulders and wondered how many strangers at Fastosa might have seen more of her than her husband-to-be was allowed.

I don't want to visit any more cathedrals! I want to go to Riviera beaches! I want to ogle pretty girls with practically nothing on! I want to be – I want to be normal, and ordinary, and happy! I don't want to be singled out by God for misery and boredom and hypocrisy!

Maybe if I tried to act more like Peter . . .?

Their route in France was to take them from Avignon and Orange northward to the western cathedrals, then back to Paris, whence they would fly home. At their next en-route stopover he made a great effort to be agreeable to Ruth, displayed more affection to her than for days past, contrived a few jokes that made even Peter chuckle. The opinion of their companions was obvious; one could read on their faces, plain as words: 'They must have had a lovers' tiff, but things are back the way they should be.'

As they left the dining-room they smiled and said good night with more than usual conviction. Even Peter rose before Alec and Ruth, clapped Alec on the shoulder and murmured, 'Sweet dreams! See you in the morning!'

Yet even that dismayed Alec, who now felt he was adrift, not simply in a foreign country but on a different planet. If this sleek courier had had designs on Ruth, how was it he was – well – surrendering so readily? A fit of conscience? Did someone who could as cheerfully take in hand a bunch of atheists as this group of Christians, even to leading them in daily prayer, possess a conscience? It was no use; he was bemused.

At least he had the chance to escort Ruth to her room, arm in arm. Taking her key to insert it in the lock, he risked kissing her instead. She permitted that. But the instant he dared to touch her breasts she pulled away, snatched back the key and retreated behind the door.

He registered little of France, keeping track only by the lying postcards he sent home. All his messages were basically the same: 'Rouen/Chartres/whatever even more amazing in reality than pictures. Ruth and I both well' – he'd said that even on the day he was ill and she went to Fastosa – 'and we send our love.'

Considering the latest of the cards, stamping it for posting in the morning, he wondered whether subconsciously he was hoping that his false pretensions would be penetrated, so he wouldn't have to explain when he returned what had gone wrong, how he had betrayed the father who so much hoped his son had met the woman who would afford him his third and maybe fourth generation.

Finally: Paris.

Yes, the ascent to the Sacré Coeur was magnificent, and the view from the top. But when they returned to the foot of the hill they paused for refreshment in a bistro selling Norman cider. Peter recommended it. The instant the first drop passed his lips Alec realised it was hard. He reached for Ruth's glass, intending to prevent her even sipping.

But she jerked it away. Her large dark eyes glared an unspoken question: *Are you going to humiliate me in public?*

Had those eyes truly become larger and darker during the trip? Her mouth seemed to have done so; she had bought more lipsticks and today's was almost orange, as though she had wiped her face with a neon sign. They were in a big city, yet she was wearing another of the brazen bare-armed tops she seemed to be acquiring by subterfuge, for he had never seen her come out of a shop with one . . .

Maybe she hadn't. Maybe Peter had.

Alec was so taken aback by this alarming insight, he forgot about seizing the cider from her, and she drank it with relish and suggested a second round. The rest of the party, not having noticed what Alec had, chorused agreement. By the time they left even the old widow was ignorantly tipsy and extremely cheerful. Alec, leaving his drink untouched, was the reverse – yet, he thought, a stranger might have concluded otherwise, at least in comparison with Peter. Despite three large glassfuls he was his usual urbane and charming self (*damn him!*) and while they were waiting for the bus back to their hotel regaled them with fluent anecdotes about the history and legends of the city, to such effect that when the bus at last drew up he was accorded a rattle of applause.

Alec had not tasted cider, only bitter gall.

Next day was Notre Dame in the morning, and an afternoon for shopping, and dinner in high style at the restaurant of their hotel, prior to an early departure for their plane. At the conclusion of the meal Ruth rose, holding up her wine glass – she had drunk wine this evening, disregarding Alec's reproachful looks, and what was more she had taken full advantage of her last chance to go shopping, and had on a green satin dress, long-skirted, but bare-backed and slit nearly to the hip! – called for silence, and proposed a vote of thanks to Peter. Suave, in perfect possession of himself (and Ruth?), he rose to reply, addressed every member of the party by name, quoted some episode from the tour involving each of them (except Ruth), singled out Alec as having been the only one he knew the name of before they met because he was the sole person not yet checked off on his clipboard list (Alec cringed and wished he were a thousand miles away, but the rest were chuckling), and at last, with a lightning shift of emphasis worthy of a preacher like Reverend Doug Miller, invited them all to close their eyes and offer silent thanks for the success of their tour, before raising their glasses in a mutual toast and wishing all their temporary friends long life, good health and future happiness.

Alec was stunned. He knew this man was a phoney, for he had admitted as much. Yet he, even he, had been briefly moved by the skill with which Peter played on his listeners' emotions.

Dad, I think you just got showed up.

He was still sitting there, desperately confused, having been unable to find anything else to say, when the party started to disperse.

'Alec? Alec, are you okay?'

He hoped for a second it might be Ruth who was displaying solicitude toward him, but it was Peter's voice.

'You do know we leave at seven for the airport?'

'Yes – yes, of course.' With an effort Alec looked up. 'Ruth?'

The bare arms, bare back, that had been so red in Spain, had turned to a pale delicious brown like lightly done toast. Alec ached with the need to touch that skin, to inhale its scent, to taste it with his tongue, to . . .

To do all the shameful things that Dad forbids.

For a second he imagined he could read a question in Ruth's gaze: *Are you or are you not coming upstairs?*

But he had tried to kiss her, and had been rebuffed. He said with effort, 'Good night. See you at breakfast.'

What passed across her face, which had become so much more beautiful since leaving home – not just because of makeup, though she now wore it expertly, nor because of the high-fashion dress that showed off her shapely figure? Was it disappointment? Was it anger? But it was brief, at all events. Shrugging, she turned away. After a pause (but that was because he was such a good tour-guide, ever concerned lest one of his party fail to make the bus or the train or the plane), Peter did the same.

From here it was possible to watch the lobby in front of the elevators. Waiting, Ruth took Peter's arm, and smiled.

Some time later, when the restaurant was closing, Alec approached the front desk. A drowsy clerk raised his head.

'The number of our courier's room, please.'

'Ah, you're with Monsieur Dale's group, *n'est-ce pas?* Just a moment . . . *Voilà!*'

He passed him a slip of paper. Alec tucked it in his pocket and moved away. So Peter's room was next to Ruth's, whose number he had noted when they checked in. He had done so as a matter of course since the start, thinking that sooner or later she might forget which room was hers this time, and he could make a good impression by reminding her.

So what? The group was always accommodated together; this was a very well-organised tour. His own room was the other side of Peter's.

Not next to Ruth's.

Suspicions clamoured for attention in his mind. He battled with all his might and failed to conquer them. How far he felt from home! How remote he felt even from his own body! For as he entered the elevator, confirming that his key was where it should be in his jacket pocket, he began to move without volition, exactly as though he had been taken over by a higher power.

For the first time he understood the term *possession*.

It was not by deliberate intention that he found his knuckles rapping on Ruth's door; indeed, had she opened to him he would have had no notion what to say. Yet he did it. Waited; knocked again; and then, still under the control of something other than his conscious will, took the few steps that brought him to Peter's room. His ear bent to the door, even as he told himself: *But this is shameful! This is spying! This is another of the childhood crimes that – leather belt . . .*

He heard laughter. He heard what could only be the chink of glasses. He heard more laughter, and then moans he could not comprehend. They didn't sound like suffering, that was all he could deduce. Unless there was some kind of suffering that was also joyful. (Christ in agony? He slapped down loathsome blasphemy.)

Then there was a word, a name, in a voice he recognised. Her voice. It said, 'Oh – *Peter!*'

What I would not have given for it to be: 'Oh, Alec!'

He was still there, leaning against the opposite wall, dry-mouthed, dry-eyed, when the door opened in the greyish light of dawn. She was wearing her green dress and carrying her purse, but she was also holding in the same hand what presumably had been her only other garment. Yawning as the lock clicked behind her, for a moment she didn't realise he was there.

When she did, the transformation was instant. Her words were not so much spoken as spat out.

'So you've been spying on me! Oh, you stinking bastard! You revolting creep!'

He had been drowsing upright. With a start he pulled himself together.

'Ruth —!'

She stared at him levelly. Her makeup was all gone; her tanned face glistened, as though she had washed it moments past. Yet she looked beautiful in a way he would never have credited at home.

This is more like the woman that I really wanted. Why did I not find out about her until now?

'Shut up,' she said, her voice low but intense. 'Even if you want the world to know what a wimp you are, I don't. When I think how deluded I was – ach, I feel disgusted! I gave in at every turn, didn't I? Held my tongue like a good little girl, let myself be pushed and shoved at you when if I'd had a normal upbringing I could have had a bit of fun out of life! I thought coming to Europe would make all the difference! But here or there, Alexander Maxton Miller: you are still a wimp! Hear me? A feeble plastic imitation of a real man!'

His tongue was too dry to lick his lips; still, he tried it.

Inanely: 'Are you going to marry Peter?' It was all he could think of to say.

'Marry him?' She drew back, on the verge of laughter. 'You *are* nuts, aren't you?'

'But you gave yourself to him!' He stepped forward, clenching his fists.

'Sure I did! As I would have done to you, if you'd had half his honesty and guts!' She was grasping her purse in both hands as though she might need it for defence, and the silken rag of her panties – green to match her dress – hung across it like an ensign of defiance. 'I set out on this trip determined to lose my virginity! Are you shocked? I guess you are! But it could have been to you! If you'd acted like a man, I would probably have married you and raised your kids. After all, that's the kind of life I've been educated to expect. As it turned out, I couldn't even make you jealous!'

Alec felt as though his very heart were curling up and trying to hide.

'But – but *Peter!*' he forced out. 'He's such a hypocrite! He told me he —'

'And he told me he told you!' she snapped. 'He's not a hypocrite. He's an honest man. He picks up a pretty girl from each of his tour groups, or else a middle-aged lady, a divorcée or a widow, if that's all there is, and has a pleasant little affair and sends her on her way contented. And he's totally up front about it. He's not the hypocrite! You are!'

'But I —!'

'Oh, don't deny it.' She turned towards her own room, suddenly weary, fumbling in her purse for the key. 'You wanted to take me to bed, didn't you? We were as good as engaged, weren't we? So why the hell didn't you try?'

'But when I kissed you the other night—'

'It was too damned late!' The key was in the lock, the door ajar. She glanced back, scornful-faced. 'We had a whole goddamned month to find out whether we liked screwing each other enough to get married. You didn't make one single goddamned move until you'd wasted more than half the trip. In any case, thank God I didn't have my first experience with you, or I'd never have realised how much fun sex can be . . . Oh, go to bed! They'll be calling us to breakfast in an hour. And when you find another girl, try acting like a proper man!'

Remember, son: you're facing a test of your manhood . . .

Her door closed quietly. Even now Ruth was considerate enough not to make noises that might wake her neighbour on the other side. Strangled by sobs, Alec let himself into his own room, flung himself down fully clad on the bed, and wept away the time until the phone shrilled with a warning that their tour group had a plane to catch.

During the homeward flight Alec spoke to nobody, but tried to sleep, albeit with small success. When he did doze off he kept dreaming of the naked body he had never seen, but Peter had, that stranger handsome and seductive as the devil. Images of him and Ruth swarmed in his brain, intertwined in ways he could not make clear. Muzzily he realised that between them two lovers mustered eight limbs. That wasn't human. No wonder, then. Eight limbs . . .

Why, though, he found himself wondering when he was roused for the final descent, did their faces keep on merging into one, and that his father's?

It was more than his overburdened mind could stand. Giddy with fatigue, he let himself into his apartment. It smelt stale and the dishes in the sink had grown a mould. The hell with it. All he could think of was undressing and washing his hands and face and brushing his teeth and falling into bed without even changing from underwear into pyjamas. He had unhooked his phone to make sure Dad could not disturb him. Tomorrow he was going to have a showdown after all, only it would not be with Ruth, but Reverend Doug Miller . . .

He was asleep.

And suddenly awake again. There was a rustling noise. Nervous, Alec glanced at his bedside clock. He had slept only a few minutes. What was happening?

Abruptly, fearfully, alert, he sat up and switched on the light.

And understood.

He had pulled out the plug in the bathroom washbasin and forgotten to replace it. Worse yet, he had left his face-cloth where it could serve as an arachnid ladder. Pent for a month behind the barriers his dad had told him to create, here came the invaders whose patient waiting was finally at an end. The door was closed, but they could easily creep under it: one, after another, after another . . . How many per day? Two, three? A dozen?

He froze, watching long fragile legs scutter across the floor. In due time they scaled the foot of his bed, cast about as though in search of prey, reached a decision, set out determinedly in his direction. He tried to move, and could not. Those eight limbs moving in such organised conjunction: they no longer signified inexplicable terror, but something infinitely worse. At last he had remembered why he so feared any creature with eight limbs.

How old was I? Four, I must have been. When I caught Dad with the lady who played organ for the choir. When he whipped me till I fainted for being a dirty little spy, swearing to kill me if I ever breathed a word.

Then he told Mother he had beaten me to drive the devil out.

In horrid fascination Alec waited for the intruders to fumble their polypodal way towards the lax hand he had left exposed on the coverlet. Eventually – out of how many? By now, scores, maybe hundreds, pouring under the door like a rippling brown rug – the first made contact. It stung.

That released him. He started to think again. What he thought was:

Damn you, Dad. You lied to me about spiders, too.

After that he was able to scream.

LITTLE LESSONS IN GARDENING

Karl Edward Wagner

A former psychiatrist now turned professional writer, Karl Edward Wagner was born in Knoxville, Tennessee, in 1945.

Since the publication of his first book – *Darkness Weaves* – in 1970, Wagner has written or edited some 45 more . . . including the Kane series, the annual *Year's Best Horror Stories* and two volumes of contemporary horror stories (*In A Lonely Place* and *Why Not You And I?*).

He has also written screenplays – including the unproduced *Conan III* and *The Twist* – and a graphic novel for DC comics entitled *Tell Me, Dark* which, he says, bears little resemblance to his original concept (the title refers to a novel he is working on) although he is 'given grudging credit'. Other current projects include the novels *The Fourth Seal, Satan's Gun* and *At First Just Ghostly*.

'I can't really recall any childhood superstitions,' he says, before adding, in his customary deadpan delivery, 'although I was convinced by older kids that if you swallowed a watermelon seed it would sprout and the vines would grow out of your ears and nose. They actually put me up to asking a pregnant woman if she had swallowed a watermelon seed. She was not amused.'

The benefits of discovering the hanged man were not immediately apparent to Darren Grover.

Shocked, then suspecting a prank, Grover cautiously approached the hanging object. It was not a prank, and Grover was doubly shocked.

Sunlight pierced the wooded glade and dappled the pallid body. It was that of a young man – possibly a student from the nearby university campus. He was quite naked except for some sort of black latex hood stretched tightly over his head, and Grover was relieved that he was spared seeing his face. A length of cotton rope was affixed to a padded leather collar, looped over the outreaching limb of a large oak, and tied to one gnarled root. Beneath the trunk lay a neat pile of clothes, and inches beneath the dangling toes lay the stained grassy earth. Some distance away a short section of log had rolled.

Although badly shaken, Darren Grover quickly hiked the half-mile trail through the woods to his house and phoned the police.

In the end, the death was ruled accidental – some small consolation to the student's parents. A search of his discarded clothing revealed no suicide note, but did discover a small quantity of crack and attendant paraphernalia. Publications of dubious and pornographic nature were found in his dormitory room, and an alcohol level of ·2 was found in his blood. The forest was a short walk from campus and traditionally was an area favored for clandestine and often questionable activities. Whether others had been present at the time of the student's death was never determined.

However, on the basis of the evidence and the absence of other physical restraint, it was concluded that the unfortunate young man had hanged himself accidentally while engaging in a bizarre sexual experience under the heavy influence of drugs and alcohol, either by himself or in conjunction with unknown participants who had fled.

Case closed.

Regardless, it had been an unnerving experience for Darren

Grover, a solitary man who enjoyed his salutary walks through the woods. Pine Hill was itself a quiet university town – 'a bastion of learning amidst the untroubled fields and forests of the rural South' in the words of William Jennings Bryan at a graduation ceremony. This had been said well before Grover's day, and before the town and university had begun to sprawl across the untroubled fields and forests, but much of this ambiance persevered, and it was entirely suited to Grover's tastes.

Darren Grover was professor emeritus of medieval history at the university. Coronary bypass surgery had prompted his early retirement; his health became robust again subsequent to recovery, owing to regulated diet, exercise, medication, and his less stressful schedule. He was a regular at faculty teas, a frequent guest lecturer, and often at work on some scholarly treatise for the journals. Still in his middle sixties, he appeared rather younger: a bit over six feet tall with no trace yet of a stoop, thin and quite wiry now, with much grey in his once bright black hair and beard. His face was long of jaw and nose – the latter capped with bifocals assisting bright brown eyes. He was a temperate man, and after his second and final glass of sherry he would tell the history majors at the faculty smokers about when he and his students had occupied the dean's office in 1968. Until now, this had been his greatest adventure.

A bachelor of the old school, Grover lived in a cluttered and book-laden cottage in a wooded glen, only a brisk walk to the campus where he had spent some thirty years instructing students in the fascinating history of medieval and early modern Europe. Forbidden now his pipe, he still enjoyed his constitutional, weather permitting, in his baggy tweed jacket and shapeless hat, to chat with former colleagues and putter about the university library. Darren Grover was fondly liked by both students and peers, and he was a man at peace with himself and with life. Except for one thorn.

One terrible thorn.

Her name was Clara Perth, and some ten years before she had buried her husband in Passaic, New Jersey and moved south to enjoy the untroubled fields and forests of Pine Hill. Bryan's florid comments had been preserved in real estate ads in *The New Yorker*, and Pine Hill was rapidly becoming a retirement community for acidulous yankees who wanted a climatic compromise between Northeastern winters and Florida summers. Mrs Perth used her late husband's insurance money to purchase the cottage next door to Grover's.

The grounds of both properties were small. Both landowners liked to garden – Grover was himself quite the amateur botanist. All should have gone well . . .

Their war began over the English ivy.

Now then: Hargrove Terrace was a wooded cul-de-sac. The street itself ran along the bottom of the glen up to its head, where there was a small turnaround. Some two dozen small houses perched along either slope – most of them two-bedroom brick cottages of similar pattern and built cheaply just after the War. By now most of the houses along Hargrove Terrace were held as investment properties and rented to students and young couples. Groundskeeping was therefore not a high priority, and tenants changed from year to year, and the forest was reclaiming much of its former range.

When Clara Perth purchased her house, its former landlord had bothered with its upkeep about as little as had a succession of student tenants. The grounds were a tangle, the small lawn weed-grown, and the various plantings of shrubbery in a dismal state.

So it was that Darren Grover noted with approval when Mrs Perth began directing workmen to clear her yard. His own grounds would never make the cover of *Country Living*, but he had a fine mass of shade-loving plants and flowering shrubs that melded pleasantly with the returning forest, and he was delighted to have a fellow gardener as neighbor. True, his several attempts at introduction had been greeted stonily, but he shrugged this off as typical New York manners.

And one bright morning, there she stood on his doorstep, rapping at the glass pane.

She said, 'I want to know what you're going to do about all that ivy.'

Clara Perth was a lumpish, stoop-shouldered thing of sixty-some winters, clad just now in a shapeless grey warm-up suit. Blued curls framed a pinched face set in a perpetual scowl. Her beady eyes, behind thick glasses, radiated suspicious hostility – on the rare occasions when she did make eye contact, and this was one such occasion.

'The ivy?' Grover had just started to ask her in.

'That English ivy you've got growing all across my yard.' Mrs Perth turned and led him to the offending vine.

Where their lot lines converged, Grover's side garden was at a higher level by a few feet, owing to excavation at the time their houses were constructed. A lush cover of English ivy grew over the bank and extended into his neighbor's yard. Grover had planted it on his bank years ago to stop erosion. Little else would grow in the poor soil and dense shade. He was quite pleased with its success.

'What's the problem with my ivy?'

'It's full of snakes, and I won't have it growing in my yard.'

'All right, then. Have your workmen clear it away.'

'Why should I pay to clear away your ivy?'

'Because it's *your* ivy in *your* yard.'

'I want it all cleared away.' She had that abrasive nasal accent that set his teeth on edge.

'You mean mine as well?'

'Of course! I don't want it growing back into my yard.'

'Look,' said Grover firmly, thinking of his morning coffee now growing cold. 'You do what you like with whatever's in your yard. I'll do as I like with mine.'

They did not part wishing one another a good morning. Later workmen ran a string along the property stakes that marked their mutual boundary, and by evening there was only bare earth on Mrs Perth's side of the string.

And so the war began.

The English ivy was not the only innocent martyr. Mrs Perth's gardening was, in fact, a massacre – a bare-earth policy. Granted that some of the shrubbery wanted trimming, the iris and day lilies should be thinned, the roses and azaleas needed feeding . . . But everything went: chopped down, uprooted, carried away by the harassed workmen – until at last there remained only barren soil and a few fatally overpruned ornamental evergreens.

Grover watched the destruction in horror. On pleasant days he liked to sit out in his side yard listening to his stereo, and over the years he had grown fond of the haphazard gardening efforts of previous tenants, had come to rely upon the late-blooming azalea set out by a newly-wed couple (Mick and Nora, was it?) a dozen years back, had marked the advent of spring by the naturalized bed of yellow daffodils that had been there since before he had moved to Hargrove Terrace, had admired the tangle of wild rose that sprawled almost into the street. Eradicated. All.

As Grover mourned the murder of old friends, he consoled himself with the thought that his new neighbor was indeed a serious gardener. No sooner was the earth laid bare, than she began to replant. Workmen under her sharp-tongued direction planted dozens of flowering trees and ornamental shrubs, bulbs and perennials were set out everywhere, flagstone walks and concrete bird baths appeared, patches of river gravel and clusters of native stone transformed the former unkempt lawn into a sprawling rock garden, tufts of periwinkle and liriope replaced grass and weeds. It was a total transformation, mounted at great expense and considerable energy.

Grover decided that he had misjudged Mrs Perth and that his behavior toward her had been churlish. Quite clearly her intentions were good, albeit she was planting too much and too closely together. Six flowering cherry trees in a ten-foot row would never do. When she began work on her rose garden, Grover felt it only neighborly to give her the advantage of his good advice.

The workmen were at lunch. Mrs Perth, in a shapeless dress and pulled-down straw hat, was regarding their work with disapproval at their progress. She was preparing a bed of tea roses along their mutual property line.

'You've certainly put in a lot of good work here, Mrs Perth,' Grover observed. Since the English ivy matter, they had barely spoken.

Mrs Perth favored him with her habitual lowering expression. 'I'm paying enough for it.'

Undaunted, Grover persisted. 'I'm sure you are. That's why I thought I might suggest that you consider a sunnier location for your rose bed. You see, it's dense shade along here. Shame to put all this work into . . .'

'I'll plant my roses where I please, thank you.' Mrs Perth straightened her lumpy body and glared at him. 'When you do something about your jungle of a yard, then perhaps I'll ask your advice.'

Grover retreated, and the chill set in to stay.

After that, it was an unending series of skirmishes.

The roses, of course, did abysmally in the deep shade. Mrs Perth fed and sprayed and pruned them mercilessly, but by end of season the roses appeared more sickly than when they were unpacked as sticks and roots from the nursery.

A letter to Darren Grover, placed (stampless) in his mailbox: 'Will you please remove that thicket of trees at the edge of my lot. It is shading out my rose garden.'

Grover had a row of dogwoods, taken from the wild, which he had planted along their lot line. They were now handsome small trees: graceful drooping branches, large white flowers in the spring, bright red berries in the winter. True, their branches overhung Mrs Perth's property. Grover ignored her letter.

Not long after, workmen came and pruned away every branch that violated his neighbor's airspace. It was, after all, the law.

Next season, the roses did equally poorly. In a mass execution, Mrs Perth had them all uprooted and flung into the rubbish heap to be carted away.

She then began work on a dahlia bed. Grover was past explaining to her about shade and drainage, and the dahlias died horribly. Somehow it weighed upon his conscience.

The flowering cherries were too crowded to do well, and they soon shaded out her peonies. Mrs Perth had the lot cut down and uprooted, replacing them with a bed of iris and a great mass of forsythia. The forsythia struggled gamely to please her, but after a few seasons they were ripped up and replaced by flowering quince. The surviving iris gave place to day lilies. The dahlia bed became a tulip bed, which became a row of clematis vines along the newly erected rail fence, which became a rose garden once again.

The shorn evergreens had died that first year.

And so the years passed.

Darren Grover no longer enjoyed sitting out in his side garden, face to face with the glowering lump as she prowled about her grounds wreaking slaughter. He began to think of her as the Wicked Witch of Hargrove Terrace – a malevolent creature constantly setting out innocent vegetation, then summarily executing it. Of course, weeds were her special prey, and she roamed her grounds daily, peering nearsightedly for anything that might be a weed, pulling it up and placing it in her basket. Leaves were also a target. No leaf fell into her yard that Mrs Perth did not hear and find and remove.

It would have been a brilliant garden, if the old witch had any clue as to *how* to garden. Instead she flung plant after plant into the soil, only to cast it forth once it failed to meet her expectations. Grover thought of a bad general hurling his troops against impossible odds, then executing the survivors for cowardice.

All of this leads into the matter of the deaf dog.

The acquisition of the deaf dog came about not long after the murder of the maple.

The tree that Grover prized above all others on his grounds was a large and aged maple, probably well settled in at about the time the American colonials were sniping at British redcoats from behind fencerows here. It was gnarled, sprawling and ungainly, and it had the most wondrous red and gold autumn foliage of any maple in Pine Hill. Of course, Clara Perth hated it. Hated it for the shade it cast upon her garden. Hated it for the leaves it shed across her well-picked yard. Hated it because it was wild and unfettered.

There had been many notes in the mailbox and surly conversations, all to the point that Grover should do something about that half-dead tree. Grover ignored her dire warnings of lawsuit, should the tree topple on to her house, as he ignored the witch in all other matters – having by now forsaken his quiet interludes in his side garden.

When a large branch blew down in a storm and crushed a

birdfeeder and a despairing magnolia in her yard, Grover agreed in the out-of-court settlement to pay damages and have the tree removed. The tree fought gallantly for two days, but it had never faced chainsaws before. Mrs Perth watched its dismemberment from a lawn chair.

A stranger in his own yard, Darren Grover sought refuge in his daily walks through the forest. It had been close to a year now since he had encountered the hanged student, and Grover usually avoided that particular wooded glade. On this day his steps were aimless and automatic, and the westering sun found him wandering along his once-familiar path.

As he crossed the glade, Grover paused to study an unfamiliar plant – unusual, in that he could readily recognize most of the local flora. The short-stemmed plant had ovate leaves and bore attractive solitary flowers with a purple bell-shaped corolla. It grew lushly in the loose forest loam and dappled sunlight of the clearing, and it was only after he straightened up from his examination that Grover realized he was standing beneath the oak limb where the unfortunate student had hanged himself.

In some agitation, Grover hurried back to his house and began to search through his various reference works. While he was a fair amateur botanist, he *was* a noted medieval scholar, and it required only a short time to interface legend with scientific observation.

The mystery plant was clearly a mandrake – *Mandragora officinarum* – found in southern Europe and northern Africa, not to be confused with the May apple, native to the United States and also called mandrake. No matter: exotic plants often adapted to other climes, and this could easily be a stray from the university's botanical gardens or someone's flower bed.

On the other hand – and this fascinated Grover – according to legend, mandrake was commonly found beneath a gallows – supposedly grown from a hanged man's final ejaculation as the rope wrenched out his breath. A plant spawned of the earth and a dead man's seed. A plant whose root was shaped like a human – legs, torso, arms, its head hidden beneath its foliage. A plant said to hold all manner of magical properties. A plant that uttered a human-like scream when pulled from the earth.

A deafening scream that brought stark madness and death to those who heard its cry.

Darren Grover paged through his books throughout the evening, learning more. Formulating a plan.

It took rather less time than Grover had anticipated. The workers at the local animal shelter were curious as to why Grover wished to adopt a deaf dog. Grover explained that his recently deceased dog had grown deaf during its final years, and that this was a blessing of sorts in that the dog then no longer barked at every odd noise. This kept the neighbors from making complaints and made for a more pleasant companion. Besides, he had grieved so over his pet's passing that he wanted a dog of familiar habits and behavior to replace that loss.

The animal control officers had been prepared to put down the aged bulldog immediately after she was brought to them, but someone remembered the eccentric professor and phoned him. And so Grover acquired a deaf dog.

Her name was Precious, and she was a white English bulldog. Her elderly owners were moving to a retirement condo in Florida (no pets or children allowed), and they had tearfully left her for adoption, not realizing that euthanasia was the usual policy of the local APS. Grover prided himself on her rescue from her politically correct executioners.

Although aged and deaf, Precious retained the ungainly strength of her breed, and the years seemed only to have increased an already voracious appetite. Grover found that his new pet would readily eat anything he offered her, from expensive dogfood to leftovers of any sort. Beef bones or boiled carrots – their fate was certain once dumped in to her bowl. Precious quickly took to her new master and made it a point of honor that the cushions of his favorite chair should not grow cold during his absences. When not eating, the dog usually plopped down and slept close to where her master might be. Grover formed the opinion that Precious's snoring was the cause of her deafness.

More to the point, the bulldog was incredibly strong. On their walks, Grover was virtually dragged along by the panting bulldog as she strained at her leash. Grover was by no means a small man.

Once again, fate seemed to have provided him with the proper tool.

And on one moonlit night . . .

Darren Grover had already soaked the earth about the mandrake. Gingerly he made fast a nylon cord to the base of the plant, scraping away as much loam as he dared. He had not fed Precious all day, and this bothered his conscience.

The bulldog regarded him with curiosity, as he fastened the nylon cord to her leash. Was she meant to stay here? Then why had Master placed her food dish several feet out of reach? That mixture of barbecued chicken and cat food – her very favorites – smelled awfully good. Precious barked loudly as her careless master hurried away. Perhaps he also was growing deaf?

Well, clearly the food was intended for Precious. She dug in her stubby legs, hunched her massive shoulders, and kicked some eighty-five pounds of bulldog into gear. At first there was some resistance. Paws scraped at earth. Muscles strained. Then the leash pulled free. Precious experienced a sudden twinge, but this did nothing to put her off her feed as she plunged into her dish.

Almost home, Grover suddenly felt . . . *something*. He stumbled and fell, crouched upon the trail for breath – wondering whether this might be the predicted final heart attack. He supposed he lost consciousness for a moment, as his next clear memory was that of Precious anxiously licking his face. Her breath stank of catfood, and the bulldog was dragging an uprooted plant at the end of her lead.

Grover gathered up lead and bare root, and he and Precious fumbled homeward through the dark.

The mandrake root *did* look like a tiny man. Small arms hung down beside a fleshy torso, and the tap root was closely bifurcated. A knobby bit at the bifurcation caused Grover to think of the root as male. A broad tuft of foliage crowned its head.

Grover quickly wrapped the mandrake root in wet towels. Next he selected a gardener's trowel from his shed, and crept with the mandrake root into the bottom of Clara Perth's garden. There, by light of the moon, he replanted the mandrake, taking care that it blended in with an anemic patch of hosta lilies. Undetected, he returned home to a snoring Precious.

Darren Grover might have relented. It was, after all, just a malicious prank: a harmless experiment, no doubt, based upon foolish legend. Catharsis. It wasn't as though he had laid land mines about her garden – although this thought, too, was pleasant.

A day or so after he had transplanted the mandrake, Grover was accosted by Mrs Perth as he carried letters to his mailbox. He smiled. She returned her fixed querulous grimace.

Clara Perth said, 'It's time you did something about all this mess in your yard.'

Grover looked quickly about, saw nothing. 'Mess?'

'Weeds. Overgrown shrubbery. Ivy everywhere.' Mrs Perth pointed in agitation. 'Your lot is an eyesore.'

'Thank you, but I consider it a naturalized wooded slope with native trees and shrubs pleasingly intermingled with chosen plantings.' Grover had used such language before, but always with sympathetic admirers of his grounds.

'Well, it's a jungle of weeds, and it breeds rats. I've already spoken to my lawyers. There's a town ordinance that requires property owners to clean up their premises, in case you didn't know. I can give you the number of the firm that keeps my grounds clean, if you like.'

'Thank you, but I can use the exercise,' said Grover with studied calmness.

'Just don't be too long about it.' Mrs Perth next turned her scowl toward Precious. 'And keep that dog away from my yard. She's been fouling it every night. We have a leash law here, you know. I'll phone the animal control people next time I find a pile in my yard.'

Grover protested. 'But I walk her myself. She's never in your yard. After all, there are a dozen other dogs in this neighborhood.'

'One thing more,' Mrs Perth had bent the ear of her lawyers that day. 'Turn down that stereo of yours. There's a noise ordinance, you know. I moved here expecting a clean, quiet neighborhood, and that's what I'll have.'

After that, Grover made a token effort at trimming back some wild roses and a row of boxwood. He kept Precious on her lead, and he always walked her on the other side of the street – feeling the baleful weight of Mrs Perth's glare. As the autumn turned the leaves, he returned to his side garden – silently lounging with a book, a tethered Precious snoring contentedly beside his lawn chair.

It took about a week more to happen.

Grover rather wished for a dark and stormy night, or at least a gathering tempest with looming black clouds and the approaching growl of thunder. It was, however, about four on a pleasant, sunny autumn afternoon.

From above the pages of his book, Grover watched. Mrs Perth: shapeless smock, horrid hat, death basket, shears and trowel, on the prowl. He thought suddenly of *A Tale of Two Cities*. Her malignant eyes stabbed each square inch of her yard, as she remorselessly approached the bottom of her garden – snipping and uprooting all that offended her. Another aristocrat's head rolls. And another. Snick, stab, clip, rip.

Grover held his breath as Mrs Perth zeroed in on the mandrake. It had recovered nicely from its uprooting and was clearly at ease amidst the hosta lilies. None the less, it was a weed.

Clara Perth grasped the short tuft of leaves with both hands, braced her stubby legs, and heaved with all of her lumpy strength.

The mandrake easily tore free from its freshly dug planting.

Precious twitched in her sleep.

Clara Perth clapped her hands to her ears, evidently screaming. Bright blood gushed slowly between her clutched fingers and jetted from her mouth. She spun about dizzily – her eyes wide and unseeing. Grover would never forget her face: total horror expressed upon a lifetime wrinkled mass of disapproval.

Mrs Perth staggered several more steps – clawing at the air and mouthing shrieks, as she careened through her garden of martyred plants. She tumbled into the street. For a moment she clutched at the barren asphalt.

A van rounded the curve, honked futilely, and tried to brake in time.

There was an impact, but the coroner's ruling was death by

massive cerebral hemorrhage previous to the accident. After all, an elderly lady, straining at the task of her gardening. Moreover, the esteemed Professor Grover has witnessed the attack.

That verdict came later. Just now Darren Grover did two things quickly.

He switched off the Walkman that had plugged his ears. No loud stereo to annoy Mrs Perth. He hated rap music, but it really was deafening.

Then Grover replanted the mandrake in his own garden, patting down the soil with a loving touch.

HIS OWN PETARD

Spider Robinson

Spider Robinson was born, he says, in the Bronx in late 1948 on three successive days (they had to handle him in sections).

Since he began writing professionally in 1972 he has been awarded three Hugos, a Nebula, the John W. Campbell Award for Best New Writer, the E.E. ('Doc') Smith Memorial Award (Skylark), the Pat Terry Memorial Award for Humorous Science Fiction, and Locus Awards for Best Novella and Best Critic. Sixteen of his twenty books are still in print – in ten languages – and his short work has appeared in magazines around the planet and in numerous anthologies.

His most recent published novel is *Lady Slings the Booze,* ('It opens with the words, "It was noon before they finished scraping Uncle Louie off the dining-room table," and gets sillier from there.') and he has recently completed *The Callahan Touch*, a continuation (of sorts) of his much-loved Callahan's Crosstime Saloon, a small tavern which, over the course of some fifteen years and eighteen wondrous stories, has played host to time travellers, ethical vampires, talking dogs, little green men . . . and the most agonising pun-contests in the western world. It even has a role-playing game modelled on it!

Spider lives with his wife – the writer and modern dance choreographer, Jeanne – in Vancouver, British Columbia. The pair have produced two novels in collaboration (*Stardance* and *Starseed*) and a third – tentatively titled *Starmind* – is scheduled for 1994.

Superstitions? Not a one. But lots of opinions.

'I have never liked Elvis, seen the movies *Batman* or *Dick Tracy*, or used the word "Not" as a sentence, and it's too late to start now. I do not believe that we're all doomed and good riddance, or that nothing happened back in the sixties, or that housing development despoils nature any more than a beaver dam, or that anything of any sort should ever be censored for any reason whatsoever. I own every recording Ray Charles ever released, and some he doesn't know about. I know a coffee almost as good as Blue Mountain at a third of the price, and I won't tell you what it is. I also know where the best coffee plantation in Australia is located, and I will tell you that if you'll promise to score me a couple of pounds when you go. (Geb won't go near a post office. Interesting man.)'

'Steven, can you come over right away?' Ann's uncharacteristically flat, hollow voice asked.

Some people find it odd that a science fiction writer, in this day and age, should choose to live without a modem, a pager, or a fax machine. I'm of the opinion that modern technology has made it *too* easy for people to get in touch with each other. But you *have* to have a phone – at least, if you want to make a living. Damn it.

Well, that's why God made answering machines. It was a cold night outside, and I had been hard at work when the phone rang. Ann was a friend; she knew I often turned off the speaker on the machine so I could concentrate on writing without interruption. She was a friend, she wouldn't be too disappointed if I didn't pick up the call.

She was a *good* friend, and she sounded like she needed help badly . . .

I hesitated with my hand an inch from the phone, thinking that the definition of 'friend' should be 'someone you don't have to make excuses to'.

'Rubin's dead,' her voice said. 'I was there.'

Well, that would have been more than enough to fetch me –
at any time of day or night, in any weather. But then she
clinched it . . . by bursting into tears.

I picked up the handset, said, 'Fifteen minutes,' and hung up.

'Well,' I said to my wife as I pulled on my shoes, 'that was the
most amazing call of the month.'

'Who was it?' Mariko asked obligingly.

'Ann. She says Rubin is down.'

Her jaw dropped. 'Billy Rubin? Dead?'

'Brown bread,' I agreed. 'She says she saw it happen.'

'Wow. That *is* amazing.'

I shook my head. 'That's not the amazing part. Get this: *she
didn't sound happy about it.*'

I left Mariko looking as puzzled as I was, and drove to Ann's
place.

Ann is a science fiction writer too, just starting out. Tall,
willowy, blonde, pleasant-faced and good-natured, in her late
twenties. She's had a few short stories in small-press anthologies
and fanzines, one real sale to *Analog*, and has had a novel
ostensibly sold to Charnel House for the last eighteen months,
although they still haven't given her a firm pub date yet. She's
pretty good – good enough that if she has incredible luck, and
lives long enough, one day she might be as poor as I am. I like
her as a person, too. More important, my wife, a very subtly
calibrated Jerk Detector, also likes her.

She was in rotten shape when I arrived at her flat.
Tear-tracked, half in the bag, spattered with blood – Rubin's
blood! – an uncapped half-empty bottle of vodka next to an open
bag of grass on the coffee table. Her eyes were dangerously
bright, and her voice was higher in pitch than usual. I sat beside
her on her sprung and faded couch while she told me the story.

'I know I shouldn't have,' she said, 'but I was desperate.
Charnel House has had *The Cosmic Cabal* for almost three years

now, and I haven't even been able to get that rat bastard down
there to return a phone call or answer a query since he bought it
– a year after I sent it to him. And my agent says there's no point
even trying to sell another book until the first one's been out
long enough to have some kind of track record to judge by . . .
Jesus, who'd have guessed you could bring your whole career to a
shuddering halt by selling a book? I'm maxed out at Visa, the
bank, and the credit union; even my parents are starting to
tighten up. So I called Rubin.'

'Jesus,' I said, 'that is desperate.'

If you're new to science fiction, Billy Rubin was almost
certainly the most influential critic in sf history, with a regular
column in *Alternities*. He was also, in the nearly unanimous
opinion of the membership of SFWA, a direct descendant of the
Marquis de Sade. Any critic will pull the wings off a crippled fly,
of course – it's part of the job description – but Rubin was the
kind of guy who would stake out a pregnant female fly, slice her
open without anesthesia, and pull the winglets off all her little fly
feti in front of her eyes. Elegantly. It was he who called Pournelle
'The King of the Cyber Rifles', accused Gibson of 'reasoning
incorrectly from data which he does not possess', dubbed
Shepard 'The Sultan of SWAT', summed up *The Jaws That Bite,
The Claws That Catch* with 'Beware the dub-dub book, and shun
the three-and-a-quarter snatch', and reviewed a nonexistent
book by Bradley called *Dragon Harass*. He's the one who created
that whole resonant-sounding, ultimately meaningless and
divisive dichotomy between the 'anti-science' fiction writers and
the 'Aunty Science' fiction writers, which has had the whole
field at each other's throats for a couple of years now. No matter
how new to sf you are, this ought to convey something: *Harlan
Ellison was polite to Rubin.*

In short, Rubin was to science fiction writers what Geraldo
Rivera is to people of alternate lifesyles. No, worse, for the slimy
bastard had a modicum of genuine wit, used a surgical scalpel
rather than a clumsy bladder full of dung. He evinced a special
fondness for flensing beginners. First novels were his favorite
victims-of-choice; since few of his readers had actually read

them, he was relieved of that onerous necessity himself, and the tyros had no cliques of friends to fight back for them. In a few famous cases he had actually succeeded in single-handedly aborting the publication of a first novel, by panning the galley proofs so savagely that the publisher changed his mind and decided to eat the advance.

In corollary, Rubin could also get a first novel published with a phone call, if he chose. Or hurry one along the pipeline. And he lived here in town . . .

'So I invited him out to dinner,' Ann said.

'Ann, Ann,' I said, shaking my head.

'Dammit, I was desperate! Don and Ev told me about a new restaurant in Chinatown where the owner was so green he hadn't learned to confirm plastic before accepting it yet, so I had Rubin meet me there and stuffed him full of Szechuan. He was actually pleasant, for Rubin. Ordered the most expensive stuff, naturally, and of course he eats twice as much as a human —' She tripped over the present tense. 'Well, he did, anyway. And had five rye and gingers. So I played it very cool, didn't say a word about the book or the business, just kept the talk general. I charmed the shit out of him, Steven.'

'Sure you did,' I said soothingly.

'So I wait until we're outside the restaurant, walking toward where I'm parked so I can drive him home, and then I casually mention that I've got this novel in the pipe at Charnel House. . .' Her face went to pieces.

I took her hand and held it until she could continue.

'It sounds like something out of a cheap porno movie,' she said finally, 'but I swear to God the moment I said that sentence, he got an erection. Wham, like that. I thought his pants were going to rip. And he gave me this *look* —' She began crying again.

I hugged her with some awkwardness. 'He certainly lived up to his pen name,' I said savagely.

Even through her tears, her puzzlement was plain.

'It's got to be a pseudonym,' I explained. 'He probably thought nobody else was smart enough to get it. Medical students are usually too busy to read sf. Bilirubin is a primary component of bile.'

She snorted, but was still too upset to giggle, so I went on. 'It has special relevance here. All bilirubin is, really, is red blood cells that died and decomposed. Dark brown goo. The liver skims it out of the blood, and passes it on to the intestines for disposal. It's why shit is brown . . . and part of why it smells bad. Pretty appropriate name for him, huh?'

This time she did giggle – but only for a second, and then the giggle segued back into tears again. I gave up and held her. She would tell the rest of it when she was ready.

She had passed the point where further tears could be any help: the only thing that might make the nut now would be to get her to laugh somehow. And I couldn't see any angle of approach. I tried constructing something about 'Rubin on rye . . . cut the mustard,' but before it would jell she was speaking again and it was too late. Her voice was harsh, strident, full of self-disgust.

'I was going to do it. I knew what he was going to say, and I was just making up my mind to say yes. Can you understand that? I had time enough to know that I was going to say yes, and he had time to see it in my eyes. And then we saw them.'

I already had a rough idea where she was going. 'A gang.'

'Yeah.'

'What colors?'

She shook her head. 'The cops wanted to know that too. All I saw was eyes – and blades. Generic Asian streetgang, that's all I can tell you. Lots of eyes. Lots of blades. All sharp. You know about the swords?'

I nodded grimly. This year the streetgangs all seemed to realize at once that fighting with guns uses up troops too fast, and has no element of skill. But fighting with knives requires *too much* skill, gets in too close and nasty and personal, and also violates the 'concealed weapon' statutes. So they began using swords. It started with Japanese kids wearing ceremonial blades, for show – but the idea made so much sense from the streetgang point of view that before long, puzzled fencing supply outlets were sold out. It'll take the establishment at least another year to get the laws changed. Meanwhile the streetgangs all give each other

Heidelberg scars – not that they'd understand the reference.

'Let me guess,' I said. 'Rubin ran away so fast his heart exploded.'

She grimaced, as though she wanted to smile but was not entitled. 'You know, that's *exactly* what I was expecting. I'm like: well, I better make sure I'm not in his way, wouldn't want to get trampled to death before I get a shot at being raped and cut. Or the other way around. You know: thinking how stupid I'd been to come to Chinatown without a man with me. And then he did it – or I guess I mean he was already doing it.'

'Did what?'

'Nothing.'

I sighed. 'I see,' I lied politely.

'No, I mean, he did nothing whatsoever to acknowledge their existence. He just kept right on walking. Like they weren't there. We're walking along, and these guys materialize in front of us, and I stop in my tracks so I can get mugged and killed like a decent citizen – and Rubin just keeps right on walking, and since he's just taken my arm, now I'm walking again too, and we walk right into the middle of them.'

Making people laugh is a large part of what I do for a living . . . but I sure didn't have much to work with, here. 'Jesus.'

'So this real little guy is right smack in front of us, like, small, but the moment you see his eyes you know he's the meanest guy in the gang, okay? And he waves that big shiny sword, and he goes, You can motor, Fatty, if you leave the girl. And the rest close in from both sides . . .'

She trailed off as the memory looped on her. After a time, still hoping against hope for a way to get her laughing, I prompted, 'So Billy died of happiness?'

She didn't even crack a smile. 'He stopped, and he let go of my arm, and he walked right at that little snake. He just walked right at him, with his hand out like he was going to push the guy out of his way, and he walked right on to the sword. He just kept walking until it c . . . came out his b-b-back, and . . . and then he just stood there, locking eyes with the little guy, squirting blood all over him, looking sort of puzzled, until finally he . . .

he fell down and died. And the little guy just looked down at him – and then he walked away. Like, in tribute to his courage! Do you see? I owe my life to the heroism of *Billy Rubin*! I've lost even the luxury of hating him.'

I began to laugh.

I couldn't help myself. Maybe it was the worst thing I could have done at that particular moment, as wrong as laughing can ever be – I knew I should be comforting my shocked and traumatized friend – but that just made it funnier. Unable to stop, unable to explain, I roared until the tears came.

Ann was nearly crying herself again by then – tears of anger this time, at me. And I couldn't blame her. But finally I got enough control to explain.

'Don't you get it?' I honked. 'Jesus Christ, it's perfect! The son of a bitch was done in by the most ironic weapon imaginable: his own narrow mind. Woo ha hoo! What an appropriate fate for a critic: he died of his own preconceptions! Oh, haw haw haw . . .'

'What the hell are you talking about?' Ann demanded.

'Don't you see? Heroism, my left kidney! He literally didn't see that sword. Billy Rubin was a *science fiction critic*. He said it himself a dozen times in his column: he was fundamentally, constitutionally incapable of believing in a world that has *both* laser beams *and* swordfights!'

Her eyes widened . . . and at long last, thank God, she began to laugh too.

SPOIL

Stan Nicholls

Chances are that, if you've ever read a book review or interview concerning one or more of the many branches of fantasy/horror fiction, you're already acquainted with Stan Nicholls's work. It's appeared everywhere . . . from the national daily newspapers, women's magazines and comics magazines to *Time Out, Locus* and *Interzone*.

Stan first became involved with the book business in 1965 as assistant manager of the London office of Washington's Library of Congress. Since then he's been editor of a trio of award-winning small press magazines, co-founder of the Gothique Film Society – twice winner of The Federation of Film Societies' Excellence Award – co-owner of a specialist SF/comics shop in West London, proof reader, research editor for Dennis Wheatley's *Library of the Occult* series, an assistant editor of *Fortean Times*, course lecturer in Creative Writing and Journalism, advertising copywriter (for the likes of Saatchi and Saatchi among others), manager and company secretary of the old Dark They Were And Golden Eyed comics shop in the West End, and Forbidden Planet's first manager. He also helped to establish and run FP's New York store and has subsequently acted as a consultant for the group.

Stan went full-time freelance in 1981 . . . presumably to get his breath back.

His short stories are thin on the ground – not surprisingly – but

his graphic novel adaptation of David Gemmell's *Legend* is due
out from Random House any time now and Stan has signed up to
adapt another Gemmell novel (*Wolf in Shadow*) as the second in
the series. His book of interviews – *Wordsmiths of Wonder* – is
now available, also from Little, Brown, featuring Stan's
discussions with fifty writers in the fantasy, horror and science
fiction fields. He also has several other projects coming to the
boil but he doesn't want to tempt fate by mentioning them!

In fact, that's one half of Stan's superstition problem. The
other is his belief that talking about things – 'positive thinking'
he calls it – can actually make them happen. 'It's a bit of a
dichotomy,' he says. 'On the one hand I'm wanting to keep
things under wraps until they're signed up and on the other I'm
wanting to talk about them in case they aren't.'

Sounds like a classic no-win situation.

Which brings us nicely around to *SPOIL* . . .

If it's true what they say about AIDS being a disease for the
ungodly . . . here's one for the righteous.

✳

> And ye shall know the truth. And the truth
> shall set you free.
>
> *Gospel of St John*

At precisely 3.15 p.m. Cardinal Paolo Fabrizzi kept his
appointment to kill the Pope.

Vatican protocol required he be escorted to the pontiff's
chambers. The aide carrying out this task wore the usual air of
stiff formality, yet Fabrizzi was aware of envious, sidelong glances
from the man. Given the vivid red scabs covering the Cardinal's
face this was hardly surprising, and as they walked he used a
corner of his lace handkerchief to dab at a trickle of yellowish pus
weeping from one of them.

In the welcoming cool of the private meditation room His

Holiness the Bishop of Rome rose from prayer and embraced his assassin.

They crossed to a sofa facing a low table, laid with an exquisite bone china tea set, and sat together in silence until the aide discreetly exited.

'It ill suits to ask if you are well, Paolo.' The Pope's tone betrayed a weariness belying his years.

'I am well enough, Holy Father.'

'And you are prepared for your . . . undertaking?'

'With the help and guidance of the Almighty, yes, Holy Father.'

God's Shepherd sighed. 'At least He has not forsaken *you*, old friend.'

'Your Holiness, I—'

The response was waved aside. 'This is not bitterness, Paolo. Certainly I feel none toward you. I have examined my conscience, and while at a loss to understand how I have failed our Lord, I know Him to be just.'

He smiled weakly. 'Since our days in the seminary I have devoted myself to a life of piety. Apparently that has not been enough. But whatever error I may have committed I will not compound it with the ultimate affront. That would surely condemn my immortal soul.'

'Have all avenues been explored, Father? After all, who are we to interpret the will of God?'

'You clutch at straws.' He toyed with the crucifix at his chest, regretting the tetchiness of his response. 'I do not presume to know God's purpose, Paolo, but I cannot believe He would wish the True Faith harmed because of the failings of His servant. You act for the good of the Church, do not trouble yourself on that score. Your salvation is doubly assured.'

'And you?'

'I commend myself to His infinite mercy.'

Fabrizzi moved to kneel before the Pope, taking his hand and kissing it. 'Forgive me for what I must do, Holy Father.' He stifled two watery coughs and swallowed. 'Give me your blessing.'

The Vicar of Christ glanced at the sores speckling the

Cardinal's bald pate and steeled himself against thoughts of jealousy. 'Under the circumstances,' he said, 'I may not be the most appropriate person to do that.'

'ENVY!' the Reverend Mason Dexter yelled, punching the air. The crowd echoed him with a roar. Six more times he led, and they answered, each return louder than before.

'PRIDE! COVETOUSNESS! LUST! GLUTTONY! ANGER! SLOTH!'

The stadium, filled to capacity, rocked with applause, shouts and whoops as the litany was completed. A tiny figure standing on the edge of the podium, his image enlarged to gigantic proportions by three massive telecast screens high above, Dexter raised his arms for silence.

'Mortal sins, brothers and sisters! Mortal sins!'

A rumble of agreement swept the mass.

'Who can say they have not transgressed in the eyes of the Lord? But now – *now*, brethren – our store of past wrongs is about to be weighed against us!'

Hallelujahs rang out as one of the cameras zoomed in on the rangy Texan. For a fraction of a second the screens blurred, then refocused and filled with a close-up of Dexter's sweat-sheened face, the angry scarlet weals strangely incongruous under his neatly coiffured silver-grey hair.

'For all things there is a season, brothers and sisters! A time to keep and a time to cast away! A time to be born . . . and a time to *die*!'

A chorus of amens.

At the back of the podium an organ struck up 'Nearer My God to Thee' as two lines of people of varying ages began to file on stage, women and children from the left, men from the right. Some rode wheelchairs or shuffled on crutches. Each was accompanied by a young male or female attendant, dressed identically in dark blue blazers, with white trousers for the men, pleated white skirts for the women. Unlike any of their charges, about half had their faces, and in some cases hands, peppered with sores.

'I carry my burden happily,' Dexter continued, 'and thank

God for my tribulations! For the cross I bear assures my everlasting reward! And I want to share that blissful burden with every one of you here tonight!'

The crowd thundered its approval.

A girl of about eight, steered by a smiling helper, arrived at his side. Dexter pointed the microphone at her.

'What's your name, honey?'

The child, red-faced, studied her feet. 'Amy,' she mumbled.

'And do you believe in the everlasting grace of our Lord Jesus Christ, Amy?'

Staring up at him wide-eyed, right thumb seeking the comfort of her mouth, she could only nod. Dexter passed the mike to an attendant, relying on the cordless pinned to his lapel, and placed a hand on each of her temples. He brought his face close to hers and she blinked rapidly, seemed on the verge of tears.

'No need to be frightened, darling.' On his knees now, still cradling her, he threw back his head and addressed a point on the distant ceiling.

'Oh Lord, whose compassion passeth all understanding, look kindly upon this child, that she may bask in the radiance of Your love for all eternity! With the laying-on of hands I pray that the gift You have seen fit to bless me with will pass to her! Allow this innocent to join the band of the select and let her deliverance be assured! Thank You, Lord! Amen!'

The girl looked bewildered and took an uncertain step back as Dexter stood again. A ripple of applause and more hallelujahs broke out as she was led away.

Reverend Dexter's attention passed to the next in line, an overweight middle-aged man, who seemed even more perplexed than the child. A nervous tic spasmed the corner of his mouth as the evangelist laid a hand on his shoulder. 'Repeat after me, brother. I abhor and reject the Devil and all his—'

Sheila Harvey killed the picture and tossed the remote aside. Reaching for the mirror again she studied herself. She pulled and stretched the skin on her cheeks, examined the whites of her eyes, checked her tongue.

Nothing.

For at least the tenth time that day she pushed away the increasingly familiar mixture of relief and disappointment. Determined to concentrate on the job at hand, she turned back to the screen and re-read what she had written.

Dr Preston Geddes of the Institute for Genetic Research today called on the government to make more funds available for the study of SPOIL.

Dr Geddes adds his voice to many in the scientific community who maintain research is being hampered by lack of finance. Expressing alarm at the speed with which the disease is spreading, and the failure to make any significant progress in understanding its nature or origin, Dr Geddes also hinted that pressure groups may be influencing government policy.

'Its peculiarly selective character, unparalleled in the history of epidemiology, makes SPOIL a particularly tough nut to crack,' he said. 'Since the first reported case, some eight months ago, there has not been one documented instance of an infected person surviving. That should be of grave concern to the authorities.'

He added that all attempts to arrest or even postpone the advance of the disease had failed. 'The prognosis never varies. This thing gets a hold and runs its course irrespective of our efforts. There is no apparent vector. Indeed, transmission remains as much a mystery now as when we first became aware of the condition.'

What significance did he see in the fact that so far the only factor that seemed to link the victims was

She was holding a cigarette and didn't even remember lighting it. Stubbing it out, she consulted her notes. What *was* the common factor? Or rather, how to put it? She bent to the keyboard.

Social rather than medical? Social wasn't quite the right word, but would do for now. She carried on typing. *'As a scientist,' Dr Geddes responded, 'I find that aspect both fascinating and an affront to logic. There must be another element the infectees share which we simply haven't discovered yet.'*

He was less forthcoming on allegations that powerful lobbies are frustrating the medical profession's ability to combat the disease. Choosing his words with care, Dr Geddes would only comment that,

'Certain groups, purporting to act in the best interests of the people they represent, may be placing obstacles in the way of research. Encouraging their followers to refuse treatment, as they have in some cases, is an act of gross irresponsibility.'

He added, 'The unique properties of SPOIL, and the extraordinary way it manifests in its terminal stage, presents us all with a tremendous challenge. Potentially, SPOIL makes AIDS pale into insignificance. It is a major risk to an as yet unknown percentage of the global population.'

An unknown percentage of the population. That, Sheila thought, was the point. We think we know who is most at risk, but the evidence makes no sense. And how do you fight a disease people want to catch?

Once more, she stretched for the mirror.

In the slums of Delhi she was known simply as Little Mother. Diminutive in stature she certainly was, but her calling had precluded Sister Kathleen from achieving the status of true motherhood. To the starving and dispossessed to whom she devoted her life, however, Little Mother was an object of reverence.

She was vomiting into an orange plastic bucket.

Doctor Miller handed her a Kleenex. She wiped her mouth with it and dropped the soiled tissue into a bin, then allowed him to take her arm as they returned to his desk.

They seated themselves, and without preamble the doctor delivered his verdict.

'Insofar as I can be sure, your suspicions are confirmed. You have SPOIL.'

Contradictory emotions flooded her. Joy mingled with concern for the two hundred and eleven souls she currently ministered to. What would become of them? Would many follow her?

'How long?'

'If it takes its usual path, and we have no reason to believe otherwise, six to eight weeks.'

Kathleen closed her eyes. The heat, which she had learned to tolerate years before, suddenly returned with an oppressiveness she recalled from her early days in India. The ceaseless racket from the street outside, also long ignored, washed over her.

'Sister?'

She found herself back in the doctor's makeshift surgery, the hub of her mission. 'I am sorry, Edward. I was thinking that there is much to do and so little time. We have seen few cases here so far. What can I expect?'

'The nausea you are experienceing marks the onset. It will pass in a few days. You will begin to develop sores, accompanied by occasional headaches and sporadic rigidity in your limbs. There may well be a constriction of your vocal chords. You are aware of how it ends, of course.' He paused. 'There is nothing I can do to alleviate any of these symptoms.'

'Nor would I want you to.'

'Naturally.'

A realisation struck her. 'Oh dear, Edward. Please forgive my selfishness. I am so preoccupied with my own position I was forgetting that you—'

He raised a hand. 'No matter. We all await God's judgment now, and I trust to His wisdom. There is time for me yet.'

She made to leave. 'I will be in the chapel giving thanks, should I be needed. I will pray for your deliverance.'

Her martyrdom, he knew, was just a matter of time. But there would be many martyrs, and who would be left to revere them?

'Sister Kathleen.'

At the door, she stopped and turned to him. 'Yes?'

'Congratulations.'

They both smiled.

'Forgive me, Father, for I have—'

'I think we can drop the formalities, Bernard.' Father O'Halloran shifted uneasily in his half of the confession booth. 'Did you bring it?'

'I have it here, Father.'

'Keep your voice down, man!'

The priest slid closer to the grill separating them. 'Are you absolutely sure it's the . . . genuine article?' The rasping whisper only emphasised his edginess.

'I am, Father.'

'And where did it—'

'Be assured that the source, shall we say, met requirements.'

Father O'Halloran shuddered. He relegated thoughts of 'the source', and how he or she may have been persuaded to cooperate, to the back of his mind. Best stick to the business at hand.

'Pass it to me as we leave the confessional, but be sure no one sees us.'

'As you say, Father. And you have the, er, wherewithal?'

'Yes.'

'It's only to cover my expenses, as I explained, Father.'

'Yes, *I understand*, Bernard. Let's get this over with.'

They emerged from the booths to find only two other people in the church, a pair of elderly women sitting to the left of the altar, engrossed in conversation. Neither paid them any attention.

Bernard dragged a small package, a sticky-taped newspaper bulk, from his overcoat pocket. The priest produced a thick brown envelope. Following a surreptitious glance in the direction of the old ladies, they were exchanged.

'You know what you have to do?'

'Yes, yes. Good day to you.' He hurried off.

Locking the study door behind him he swept away the debris that littered his desk and tore at the parcel. A small glass vial of darkly red liquid, a plastic hypodermic and a shrink-wrapped needle tumbled out.

Father O'Halloran sank into a chair and rolled up his sleeve.

Outside, Bernard Harris finished counting the notes and slipped them into a trouser pocket. Probably from the parishioners anyway, he thought. Plenty of that flowing in these days. People trying to buy their way into paradise, the hypocrites. Like the old fool back there.

Easing himself into his car, he looked over at the church. St Helen's, was it? You had to laugh. St Jude, patron saint of hopeless cases, would be more to the point.

He turned the ignition and engaged gear. Obviously the priest was too stupid to know you couldn't deliberately catch SPOIL. Bernard could attest to that aspect of the disease personally.

The thought of Father O'Halloran trying to curry favour with God by injecting pig's blood brought a bitter grin as he gunned the engine and took off down the street.

After four hours of reverse healing Dexter was exhausted.

There were more and more of them every night, seeking an intermediary with the Creator, a conduit to redemption.

It was sweet. Dexter took the credit for those who got SPOIL, publicly paraded them and encouraged others to come forward. As for those who didn't catch it – well, they only had themselves to blame. Or God. In any event chance was on his side. Some were bound to develop the disease, the law of averages saw to that.

But none of this relieved his apprehension.

He acknowledged the audience's ear-splitting farewell with a wave, and as he left the stage ushers were starting to pass along the aisles, many of their donation pails already brimming.

To get to his dressing room he had to pass through the area where tonight's meeting was being relayed nationwide via satellite. He reciprocated a nod from the linkman who was cueing in SALVATION TV's next offering with a voice-over.

'That's all from the Reverend Mason Dexter's ministry for tonight, folks. And remember, pledges can be phoned in on any of our toll-free numbers.

'In a few minutes you can see another edition of Bell, Book and Buzzer, the *fastest-moving* religious quiz show with the *biggest* prizes! But first, more zany, uplifting adventures featuring that lovable cartoon character Magnificat!'

Dexter slammed the door behind him and was met by a personal assistant waving her clipboard. 'One hundred and forty-two thousand last night,' she intoned crisply, 'getting on for three times that amount promised. It's up again.'

'Thanks, Rebecca. Send June in here right away, would you? And see we're not disturbed.'

Shortly, June Bridges, carrying a small valise, entered without knocking. It was the sort of privilege allowed only to the most trusted of his inner circle.

'Lock it.'

She secured the door, then joined him in front of the mirror, flipping the switch to the neon strip above it.

'Seems like a good take again tonight.'

'Yeah.' He looked preoccupied.

'And?'

'And I don't know how much longer I can get away with it.'

'You should worry, Dex. The way the money's rolling in we can—'

'Do you know what those people would do if they found out?' He inclined his head in the direction of the muted clamour from outside. 'They'd tear me to pieces.'

'What's really eating you?'

'Never could keep anything from you, June. I keep thinking why I've been passed over.'

'You're starting to believe it!'

'Aren't *you?*'

She ignored the question, countered with one of her own. 'So it really bugs you, does it? Not having SPOIL, I mean.'

He caught her eye in the mirror. 'Suppose everything they say about this plague is true?'

'Dex—'

'No, listen. I've seen it. I've seen the way it is at the end, when it takes them. It's not . . . *natural,* June. There's no disease ever known could do that to a person.'

'They'll sort it out, find some kind of cure. Meanwhile we clean up.'

'You can't think that. Not now.'

Tight-lipped, she hefted the case, slamming it on the dressing table. 'We should get you seen to.'

He knew her well enough to realise there was no point arguing, even though he suspected she was just as troubled. Anyway, what was the use? Events were overtaking them all, and he had never felt in less control of his life.

'All right.' He expelled a breath. 'It was real hot out there tonight. You're going to have to fix it stronger this time.'

With thumb and index finger he took hold of a scab above his upper lip and pulled. The latex elongated and snapped like a piece of old chewing gum.

'Get this shit off me.'

'Good evening. I'm John Whitestone and this is *Forum*, your weekly guide to current affairs.'

As the opening music swelled the camera pulled back to take in his guests, occupying a semicircle of swivel chairs, then cut back to him.

'Tonight we address what may be the most important crisis facing the world in living memory, a crisis many contend is the profoundest humanity has *ever* faced.

'According to the World Health Organisation, Spontaneous Poly-Organic Idiopathic Lupus Erythematosus, commonly known as SPOIL, is now officially designated a pandemic. Estimates of the number of fatalities resulting from the disease vary, but are conservatively put at fifteen million. At least twenty times that number are said to have contracted it.

'Catching SPOIL means dying. There is not a single case of anyone recovering from it.

'More remarkable even than the figures are the nature of its victims and the manner of their passing. It's these aspects we shall be discussing here.

'I'm joined by Archbishop Alan Beaumont, himself a SPOIL sufferer; *The Times*'s medical correspondent, Sheila Harvey, and Gerald Sterling, Chairman of the Rationalist Alliance.

'If we can turn to you first, Archbishop. You were diagnosed as having SPOIL several weeks ago. Tell me . . .'

Sheila Harvey hoped Whitestone would manage to avoid saying it.

'. . . how did you feel?'

He didn't, and she squirmed inwardly at the cliché.

The Archbishop, just beginning to display the characteristic facial eruptions, seemed oblivious to Whitestone's crassness.

'Well, John, certainly not like a sufferer, as you stated in your introduction. In common with believers worldwide, I accept SPOIL as a benediction, the culmination of God's plan.'

'You have no doubt about that?'

'None whatsoever.'

'I'll return to you in a moment, Archbishop, but I would like to bring in Sheila Harvey here. Miss Harvey, you have written extensively on SPOIL. What conclusions have you reached?'

She suppressed a smile. 'That's a big question, bearing in mind some of the finest scientific intellects admit to being baffled by it. But what Archbishop Beaumont had to say sums up what must be the majority view.'

'The majority view,' Whitestone interjected, 'but not the only view. Are you saying you subscribe to it?'

'The honest answer would be that I don't know. However, it should now be apparent to the most sceptical observer that SPOIL represents something more than just a public health risk.'

'We were talking before going on air and you mentioned that you had a fairly traditional religious upbringing.'

Sheila resented the breach of confidence but resolved not to show it. She merely nodded in agreement.

'I understand you were brought up in a convent, in fact, and subsequently moved away from religion. So your feelings about the present situation are presumably mixed?'

'I have, let's say, reservations about organised religion. But it was the Church I rejected, not necessarily belief.'

'Do you regret that decision now?'

'No. It seems to me that what you're implying is based on a misconception about SPOIL. Membership of a church, sect or cult isn't in itself any kind of a guarantee. It seems to go much deeper than that, to the core of faith. All those people rushing to join up, if I can put it that way, miss the point.'

Whitestone turned from her. 'Of course it's not only the churches that are seeing their attendances swell, is it, Gerald Sterling? There's been a large increase in the ranks of non-believers too, hasn't there?'

'There has. Many people who see SPOIL as a purely medical

problem resent the religious establishment hijacking it for their own purposes. But, to be honest, we've had nearly as many defections as new recruits.'

'Yes,' the Archbishop put in, 'this must present you with a dilemma. I am satisfied that SPOIL is divinely inspired. When you too come to this realisation, as you must, your position will be untenable.'

'Perhaps,' Sterling responded. 'I think it represents more of a quandary for other groups. For the sake of argument let's accept that SPOIL exclusively afflicts the religious. How do you define religious? There are cases of atheists and agnostics dying from it. Do we assume they were secret believers? Muslims seem widely affected, but what about Hindus, Taoists, Sufis and the various cultists? Individuals in all these groups have gone down with it, even if the groups themselves, en masse, don't seem to.'

'I've given this some thought as well,' Sheila said. 'Statistics are a mess at the moment because nobody can deal with the sheer volume, but I've yet to come across more than a handful of cases involving Buddhists or Rastafarians, for example. So perhaps the atheists you mentioned really were closet believers, even if they didn't acknowledge it to themselves.'

'What do we think this means?' Whitestone asked.

'Maybe that the factor uniting the victims is not religious belief alone,' Sheila stated, 'but, specifically, belief in a *monotheistic* deity.'

' "You shall have no other gods before me." '

The Archbishop's quote silenced them all until Gerald Sterling broke the impasse.

'That's going to make life a bit uncomfortable for Satanists.'

'I beg your pardon?' The clergyman looked puzzled.

'Well, when you think about it, Satan-worshippers must by definition be believers in God. They can hardly accept one without the other, can they? It might be interesting to see how *they're* faring with SPOIL. Anyway, this is all academic until someone proves SPOIL really is God-given. Needless to say, I use the word God advisedly.'

'Quite.' Whitestone could see the discussion slipping out of his control. 'I think what we're saying is that there are no pat answers.'

Just pat statements, Sheila reflected.

'But it is the final stages of SPOIL,' their host went on, direct to camera, 'that presents the biggest challenge to believers and non-believers alike. And, despite the high number of deaths, thus far comparatively few of us have witnessed that terminal stage.

'Death, except in exceptional circumstances, is an intensely private occurrence. All the more so with SPOIL because of the religious connotations so many people attach to it.

'At this point we want to run a piece of film *Forum* has obtained showing the final moments of a SPOIL victim. We believe this is the first time such scenes have been shown on British television, and would like to stress that we do it with the full consent of the family concerned.

'What you are about to see was shot by an amateur cameraman – so the quality may not be up to our usual standard – in a small hospice in a suburb of Lima, Peru. Viewers are advised that they may find it disturbing.'

Sheila was not expecting this. No one had said anything about it, and from the expression on Gerald Sterling's face he was equally surprised. The Archbishop seemed unmoved, however, and she guessed he had been forewarned. At least they had had that much sensitivity. The monitor beside them began its five-four-three-two-one lead-in.

It had all the hallmarks of being filmed with a hand-held camcorder. A man, probably in his mid-forties, eyes closed, lay propped up against pillows in a hospital bed. Every inch of his exposed flesh was scabrous. Mostly out of shot, someone sat to his right. As the camera approached, the man in the bed opened his eyes, something like a smile lighting his face.

The picture swayed and briefly showed the person sitting by him. A grey-haired woman, in her late sixties perhaps. His mother? She was twisting a rosary in her hands. The camera moved back to the man and steadied. He seemed to be trying to rise.

Sheila sneaked a look at the others. Archbishop Beaumont was completely still, entranced by the flickering screen. Sterling, beyond him, sat with his mouth hanging open. In other circumstances she would have laughed.

She turned her attention back to the screen in time to see the final act. Even softened by the medium of film she found it too intense, and during the last seconds had to look away. They all did.

Oh God, she thought. *Oh God.*

Veronica Flint speculated on the unreliability of au pairs. Maria, the current one, was proving no better than any of her predecessors; only interested in boyfriends, wanting to go out all the time, forever bringing unsuitable people to the house . . . Now the wretched girl had been half an hour behind with supper and had made Veronica late for the public meeting at St Helen's.

As a leading light in the burgeoning Morality Now movement, Mrs Flint felt it beholden upon her to set an example, and lax punctuality went against the grain. She put her foot down and the speedometer nudged sixty.

It was bad enough having to wait with such patience for God to give her SPOIL. She had no fear He would not, of course, but wished He would hurry up and get around to her. Needing to worry about feckless, lazy – and doubtless *promiscuous* – little madams taking advantage of her generosity was an additional millstone she could well do without, thank you very much.

Heaven knows it wasn't as though Mrs Flint was unreasonable in what she asked the girl to do. Looking after the children, doing the housework, shopping, running errands, some light chores in the garden, washing the car, a little redecorating – nothing a young woman should find too taxing. All this talk about hearing someone in her family back in Argentina, or whereever it was, had SPOIL was just a way of getting at her employers, Mrs Flint was sure of that. Well, she would have to go, that's all there was to it.

She selected a middle-of-the-road music station on the car

radio, and had barely begun to relax into its soothing string versions of popular classics when a strident voice replaced them.

We interrupt this programme to bring you a newsflash. The Vatican has just announced that His Holiness the Pope has passed away as a result of contracting SPOIL.

Trust the Catholics to get in first, Mrs Flint thought.

Rumours that His Holiness had been suffering from the disease, fuelled by his recent absence from the public eye, have been circulating for several months.

In a brief statement, the Vatican referred to the Pope's significant contribution to world harmony, and his much-publicised initiative to bring the Catholic Church to a closer understanding with other major Christian denominations.

God obviously wanted to put a stop to *that*, she felt sure.

'His Holiness has been taken by the Almighty to sit at His right-hand,' a spokesman said. *'In keeping with the traditions and law governing these matters, the pontiff's final moments were witnessed by his personal physicians and a triumvirate of senior officials of the True Church, who bore witness to the dignity of his passing. All followers of the Faith are urged to pray for the deliverance of his immortal soul.'*

One of those thought to have been present was Cardinal Paolo Fabrizzi, a lifelong friend and colleague of the Pope, who is known to have SPOIL himself.

As Catholics fill St Peter's Square to overflowing tonight, speculation turns to the question of the Pope's successor. Many of the cardinals who will make the choice are already in Rome, and their decision will be taken against a background unprecedented in the Vatican's history. In light of SPOIL, the question being asked is . . .

Bernard Harris, having stopped off at a pub to down seven or eight large whiskies with Father O'Halloran's money, was resuming his journey homeward sans seat belt.

He had no recollection of turning on the radio, but the announcement of the Pope's death cut through his alcohol haze somewhat, if not enough to correct the way he was allowing the car to meander from one side of the road to the other.

. . . whether there is any point in selecting a successor at all.

Meanwhile, two additional items of news concerning the SPOIL crisis are coming in. Sister Kathleen of Delhi, who has won the admiration of the world for her work among the poor on the Indian sub-continent, has let it be known she has SPOIL. Her intention, she says, is to carry on working as long as possible.

And in the United States evangelist Mason Dexter has been reported missing. Indications are that a substantial sum of money, collected at mass rallies at which he claimed to pass on the SPOIL strain, may be unaccounted for. There are unconfirmed reports that a number of his associates are under arrest pending an inquiry by the FBI.

We will have more on these stories in our nine o'clock bulletin.

Harris burped loudly, accelerated, and strained to focus on the road ahead.

Sheila was in her local supermarket when it happened.

A woman, around thirty, a wire basket over one arm, was queuing at the delicatessen counter. The evidence of SPOIL marking her features, although an increasingly common sight on the streets, still drew the occasional stare. A small knot of shoppers, laden trolleys parked to one side of an aisle, punctuated their gossip with peeks in the woman's direction. But they quickly averted their gaze whenever it seemed she might notice them.

It was quite sudden and totally unexpected.

Sheila, rummaging in a deep-freeze compartment, was brought up short by a loud crash. Looking for the source, she saw the woman had dropped her basket and, absolutely still, was pressing her forehead against the glass top of the counter. Her breathing became a rapid pant, like a dog with sunstroke. People around her, obeying the peculiarly English impulse not to get involved, were edging away.

The tableau remained in place for what seemed like an eternity. Then the woman quivered, a heaving of her shoulders first, followed by waves of involuntary shivers running the length of her body.

Sheila approached, anxious to help; but also curious, if she were being honest. The small crowd moved further back. An assistant, sporting a badge that declared he was, irrespective of youth and acne, the deputy manager, appeared from the front of the store. But he held off too, looking uncertain as to how to handle the situation.

At the woman's back now, no one else within ten yards of them, Sheila gingerly reached out and lightly touched her shoulder. There was no immediate reaction. As she was about to try again, the woman turned.

The look on her face, while by no means grotesque or threatening – indeed as far from these as could be – nevertheless made Sheila involuntarily move back. If it was possible for a face to wear an expression of serenity so intense, so all-embracing and unmistakable, that was what her countenance conveyed.

Slowly, silently, and with what Sheila could only think of as *nobility*, despite the bizarre circumstances, the woman sank to her knees, her look of ecstasy unwavering.

Sheila knew what was about to come, but could not have moved away if her life depended on it. She wondered how many of the others present, most of them mute and rooted with fascination, had any idea of what the last stage involved.

It began.

The woman, slumped in a tangled approximation of the lotus position, started to sway back and forth, imperceptibly at first, then gathering momentum.

After a moment she stopped, arms flopping, the sound of her knuckles cracking the tiled floor clearly audible in the quiet expectancy.

The air above and around her head shimmered like heat over tarmac on a summer's day. Gradually, so gradually Sheila was at first doubtful it was actually occurring, a gentle bluish light appeared to pulse faintly along the woman's body. The look of rapture remained fixed upon her face as her skin took on an appearance of milky translucency.

There was no denying the throbbing light now, alternating white and electric blue, its intensity growing with each beat.

What looked like ghostly flames ringed the woman's figure. Momentarily, Sheila was reminded of those newsreels of Buddhists who burnt themselves to death in protest at the Vietnam war.

But it was a bad analogy. This was infinitely more awesome.

There were audible gasps – perhaps including Sheila's own, she couldn't tell – and a squeaky scream came from somewhere behind. The radiance built and built, pounding with an almost physical force, as a sparkling, multicoloured semicircle formed itself around the crown of the woman's head. The spaces between the rhythm of luminescence grew shorter.

Blinding glory. The burst of a thousand supernovas.

In the nano-second before, Sheila thought she could make out something in the heart of the throbbing inferno of light, something that seemed to rise and move away from the shell of the crumpled body.

It was beautiful.

Someone was laughing, semi-hysterically.

Sheila peered through the dazzle playing before her eyes. The dead woman was whole, complete, untouched. More: the stigmata of SPOIL, for that was how Sheila had come to regard it, was gone. Only the grimace of bliss remained.

For hours afterwards she had stinging floats on her retinas, as though she had been staring into the sun.

Mrs Veronica Flint, founder and director of the Morality Now organisation, was killed in a car crash this evening. Her Ford Fiesta was in collision with another car at a junction in Upper Sydenham, South East London. Mrs Flint died instantly. The other driver, who police say was well over the alcohol limit and not wearing a seat belt, died of his injuries later in hospital. Mrs Flint is survived by her husband, Andrew, and seven children.

She will be remembered for her work with the pro-life movement, and tireless campaigning against pornography, underage sex, and homosexual practices, which she regarded as essentially anti-Christian. Mrs Flint was forty-eight, and is believed not to have had SPOIL.

And now here is a SPOIL update. There were seven hundred and sixty-four notified deaths from the disease in the London area alone yesterday. The Department of Health reminds people that the crisis is stretching the medical and emergency services to the limit. In view of this, you are advised not to expect an immediate response from the emergency services. If a member of your family dies, the DoH says, wrap them in a blanket or sheet . . .

Sheila sat by the window in her flat at the Barbican, the lights out, a glass of white wine in her hand.

She remembered something Gerald Sterling said that had made her laugh, after the *Forum* broadcast. He was actually quite nice, and she warmed to his irreverent humour, despite their different world views.

They were talking about SPOIL, of course, and she got him to put his preconceptions aside and speculate on God's purpose. Gerald said he was born a Jew, and rejected the faith in his early twenties, but he frequently remembered something his grandmother used to say when he was a boy. Whenever he asked her why God didn't intervene in the world and put right its many injustices, she would always quote an old Hebrew adage. If God lived on Earth, she said, people would break his windows.

Sheila hadn't bothered to go into the office today, and wasn't surprised when nobody rang about it. Things were falling apart fast now. It was as though some kind of event horizon had been reached, with the number of SPOIL cases overwhelming the system.

As if on cue, far off in the darkened streets below an intense, lightning-like flash flickered and died. Almost immediately another caught her eye in one of the apartment blocks opposite, briefly illuminating the interior of someone's living room.

God's firework display. She giggled. They had been flaring up all over town ever since it got dark, and at first she toasted each one, before realising their quantity far out-numbered her capacity for drink.

It was funny how things like Gerald's quote came back to you. In her case it was something the nuns got her to memorize when she was a girl, a passage from Thessalonians – 'For the Lord himself will come down from heaven, with a loud command, with the voice of the archangel, and with the trumpet call of God, and the dead in Christ will rise first.'

Well, not much in the way of loud commands or trumpet calls so far, but things were certainly livening up down here on earth. About an hour ago she had seen a large mob of people milling around outside St Paul's. The cathedral had been locked and there was a thin line of policemen trying to stop them getting in. It was pretty ugly, with people shouting and waving sticks, but somehow it didn't frighten her the way it once would have.

Of course, things were different now. She lifted her wrist and looked at the sores developing there, knew there were several coming up nicely on her face too. When the bouts of sickness had hit her a couple of days ago she had hardly dare hope, but it looked as though she hadn't been forgotten.

She tried not to feel smug about it.

The Time of the Gathering, the Bible called it. She remembered that. The Harvest of the Earth. Although in the event God seemed to have come up with a slow Armageddon.

Gerald had said something else. What was it? Oh yes. He'd said, 'If SPOIL is God's doing, what's the Devil up to?' That was a funny thing to say. Still, theology wasn't his strong point, not surprisingly. Sheila felt quite sorry for him really.

She poured another drink and settled back to watch the churches burning.

DEAD MAN'S SHOES

Charles de Lint

Charles de Lint was born in the Netherlands and is presently a
citizen of Canada. While insisting he was not 'an army brat', his
father's job with a surveying company did allow him to grow up
in places as diverse as the Yukon, Turkey and Lebanon.

A professional musician for 14 years – in a band called
Wickentree – Charles is back to playing professionally in a new
band, Jump At The Sun, which specializes in traditional and
Celtic music. He is also the proprietor/editor of Triskell Press, a
small publishing house for fantasy chapbooks and magazines. His
work in the field of faerie and fantasy is well loved on both sides
of the Atlantic; the delightful (but sadly short) *Ghostwood*, *Our
Lady of the Harbour* and *Greenmantle* are particularly worthy of
attention.

Charles treats superstitions the same way he treats everything
else that we are unable to prove exists – he both believes and
disbelieves at the same time. 'But I do tend to pick up "lucky"
pennies and pebbles and avoid walking under ladders . . . and I
feel a vague nervousness when a black cat crosses my path.'

And dreams . . .?

There are people who take the heart out of you,
and there are people who put it back.

Elizabeth David

In her office, her head rests upon her arms, her arms upon the
desk. She is alone. The only sound is that of the clock on
the wall monotonously repeating its two-syllable vocabulary and
the faint noise of the street coming in through her closed
windows. Her next appointment isn't until nine p.m.

She meant merely to rest her eyes for a few moments; instead,
she has fallen asleep.

In her dream, the rain falls in a mist. It crouches thicker at
knee-level, twining across the street. The dead man approaches
her through the rain with a pantherish grace he never displayed
when alive. He is nothing like Hollywood's shambling portrayals
of animated corpses; confronted by the dead man, she is the one
whose movements are stuttered and slow.

Because she is trapped in flesh, she thinks.

Because in this dreamscape, he is pure spirit, unfettered by
gravity or body weight, while she still carries the burden of life.
The world beyond this night's dreams retains a firm grip,
shackling her own spirit's grace with the knowledge of its
existence and her place in it.

Not so the dead man.

The rain has pressed the unruly thicket of his hair flat against
his scalp. His features are expressionless, except for the need in
his eyes. He carries a somewhat bulky object in his arms, bundled
up in wet newspapers. She can't quite identify what it is. She
knows what he carries is roundish, about the size of a soccer ball,
but that is all. All other details have been swallowed in the play
of shadow that the rain has drawn from the neon signs overhead
and the streetlight on the corner.

She is not afraid of the dead man, only puzzled. Because she
knows him in life. Because she has seen him glowering from the
mouths of alleyways, sleeping in doorways. He has never been
truly dangerous, despite his appearance to the contrary.

What are you doing here? she wants to ask him. What do you

want from me? But her voice betrays her as much as her body and what issues forth are only sounds, unrecognizable as words.

She wakes just as he begins to hand her what he is carrying.

The dream was very much upon Angel's mind as she looked down at the pathetic bundle of rag-covered bones Everett Hoyle's corpse made at the back of the alley. But since she had always believed that the supernatural belonged only to the realm of fiction and film and the tabloids, she refused to allow it to take root.

Jilly would call what she had experienced prescience; she thought of it only as an unhappy coincidence and let it go no further. Instead she focused her attention on the latest addition to the city's murder victim statistics.

No one was going to miss Everett, she thought, least of all her. Still, she couldn't help but feel sorry for him. It was an alien reaction insofar as Everett was concerned.

The streets were filled with angry individuals, but the reasons behind their anger usually made sense: lost homes, lost jobs, lost families. Drink, or drugs. Institutions turning out their chronic psychiatric patients because the government couldn't afford their care. Victims of neglect or abuse who discovered too late that escaping to a life on the street wasn't the answer.

But Everett was simply mean-spirited.

He had a face that would make children cry. He wasn't deformed, he simply wore a perpetual look of rage that had frozen his features into a roadmap of constant fury. He stood a cadaverous six-four that was more than merely intimidating to those from whom he was trying to cadge spare change; it could be downright frightening. With that manner, with his matted shock of dirty grey hair and tattered clothing, he didn't seem so much a man down on his luck as some fearsome scarecrow that had ripped itself free from its support pole and gone out to make the world around him as unpleasant as he felt himself. Which put him about one step up from those men who had to kill their families before they put the gun in their own mouth and pulled the trigger.

No, Angel corrected herself. Think in the past tense now because Everett had terrorized his last passer-by.

Surprisingly, death had brought a certain calm to his features, smoothing away the worst of the anger that normally masked them. This must be what he looked like when he was sleeping, Angel thought. Except he wasn't asleep. The blood pooled around his body bore stark testimony to that. She'd already checked for a pulse and found none. Having called the police before she left the office, now it was simply a matter of waiting for them to arrive.

The scene laid out before her held an anomaly that wouldn't stop nagging her. She took a step closer and studied the body. It was like a puzzle with one piece missing and it took her a few minutes before she could finally pinpoint what was bothering her. She turned to the young white boy who'd come to her office twenty minutes ago and brought her back to where he'd found the body.

'What happened to his boots, Robbie?' she asked.

Everett's footwear had been distinctive: threadbare Oxfords transformed into boots by stitching the upper half of a pair of Wellingtons on to the leather of each of the shoes. Olive green with yellow trim on the left; black with red trim on the right. The Oxfords were so old and worn that they were devoid of any recognizable colour themselves.

'I guess Macaulay took 'em,' the boy replied.

'You never said Macaulay was here with you.'

Robbie shrugged.

She waited for him to elaborate, but Robbie simply stood beside her, face washed pale by the streetlight coming in from the mouth of the alley, thin shoulders stooped, one Doc Marten kicking at the trash underfoot. His dirty blond hair was so short it was no more than stubble. He wouldn't meet her gaze.

Angel sighed. 'All right,' she said. 'I'll bite. Why did Macaulay take the boots?'

'Well, you know what the homes are saying, Miz Angel. Man gets nined, you got to take away his shoes or he's gonna go walkin' after he's dead. He'll be lookin' for who took him down, usually, but Everett now – he's so mean I suppose anybody'd do.'

With all her years of working with street people, dealing with the myriad superstitions that ran rampant through the tenements and squats, Angel thought she'd heard it all. But this was a new one, even on her.

'You don't believe that, do you?' she asked.

'No, ma'am. But I'd say Macaulay surely do.'

Robbie spoke casually enough, but Angel could tell there was more to what had happened here tonight than he was letting on. He was upset – a natural enough reaction, considering the circumstances. Keeping Everett's corpse company until the police arrived had upset her as well. But the tension underlying Robbie's seeming composure spoke of more.

Before she could find just the right way to persuade him to open up to her, one of the sirens that could be heard at all hours of the day or night in this part of the city disengaged itself from the general hubbub of night sounds and became more distinct. Moments later, a cruiser pulled up, blocking the mouth of the alley. The cherry red lights of its beacons strobed inside the alley, turning the scene into a macabre funhouse. Backlit, the two officers who stepped out of the cruiser took on menacing shapes: shadows, devoid of features.

At Angel's side, Robbie began to tremble and she knew she wouldn't get anything from him now. Hands kept carefully in view, she went to meet the approaching officers.

Angelina Marceau ran a youth distress centre on Grasso Street, from which she got her nickname, the Grasso Street Angel. She looked like an angel as well: heart-shaped face surrounded by a cascade of dark curly hair, deep warm eyes, next to no make-up because she didn't need it with her clear complexion. Her trim figure didn't sport wings and she leaned more towards baggy pants, T-shirts and high tops than she did harps and white gowns, but that didn't matter to those living on the streets of Newford. So far as they were concerned, all she lacked was a visible halo.

Angel wasn't feeling particularly angelic by the time three a.m. rolled around that night. She sat wearily in her Grasso

Street office, gratefully nursing a mug of coffee liberally spiked with a shot of whiskey that Jilly had handed to her when she walked in the door.

'I appreciate your looking after the place while I was at the precinct,' she said.

'It wasn't a problem,' Jilly told her. 'No one showed up.'

Angel nodded. Word on the street moved fast. If the Grasso Street Angel was at the precinct, *no one* was going to keep their appointment and take the chance of running into one of the precinct bulls. The only one of her missed appointments that worried her was Patch. She'd spent weeks trying to convince him to at least look into the sponsorship program she administrated, only to have this happen when she'd finally gotten him to agree. Patch was so frail now that she didn't think the boy would survive another beating at the hands of his pimp.

'So how'd it go?' Jilly asked.

It took Angel a moment to focus on what she'd been asked. She took a sip of her coffee, relaxing as the warmth from the whiskey reached her stomach.

'We were lucky,' she said. 'It was Lou's shift. He made sure they went easy on Robbie when they took our statements. They've got an APB out on Macaulay.'

'Robbie. He's the skinny little peacenik that looks like a skinhead?'

Angel smiled. 'That's one way of putting it. There's no way he could have killed Everett.'

'How *did* Everett die?'

'He was stabbed to death – a half-dozen times at least.'

Jilly shivered. 'They didn't find the knife?'

'They didn't find the weapon and – I find this really odd – they didn't find Everett's boots either. Robbie says Macaulay took them so that Everett's ghost wouldn't be able to come after anyone.' She shook her head. 'I guess they just make them up when they haven't got anything better to do.'

'Actually, it's a fairly old belief,' Jilly said.

Angel took another sip of her whiskey-laced coffee to fortify herself against what was to come. For all her fine traits, and her unquestionable gift as as artist, Jilly had a head filled with what could only charitably be called whimsy. Probably it was *because* she was an artist and had such a fertile imagination, Angel had eventually decided. Still, whatever the source, Jilly was ready to espouse the oddest theories at the drop of a hat, everything from Victorian-styled fairies living in refuse dumps to Bigfoot wandering through the Tombs.

Angel had learned long ago that arguing against them was a fruitless endeavor, but sometimes she couldn't help herself.

'Old,' she said, 'and true as well, I suppose.

'It's possible,' Jilly said, plainly oblivious to Angel's lack of belief. 'I mean, there's a whole literature of superstition surrounding footwear. The one you're talking about dates back hundreds of years and is based on the idea that shoes were thought to be connected with the life-essence, the soul, of the person to whom they belonged. The shoes of murdered people were often buried separately to prevent hauntings. And sorcerers were known to try to persuade women to give them their left shoes. If the woman did, the sorcerer would have power over her.'

'Sorcerers?' Angel repeated with a cocked eyebrow.

'Think what you want,' Jilly told her, 'but it's been documented in old witch trials.'

'Really?'

'Well, it's been documented that they were accused of it,' Jilly admitted.

Which wasn't quite the same thing as being true, Angel thought, but she kept the comment to herself.

Jilly put her feet up on a corner of Angel's desk and started to pick at the paint that freckled her fingernails. There were always smudges of paint on her clothes, or in her tangled hair. Jilly looked up to find Angel watching her work at the paint and shrugged unselfconsciously, a smile waking sparks of humor in her pale blue eyes that made them seem as electric as sapphires.

'So what're you going to do?' Jilly asked.

'Do? I'm not going to do anything. I'm a counselor, not a cop.'

'But you could find Macaulay way quicker than the police could.'

Angel nodded in agreement. 'But what I do is based on trust – you know that. If I found Macaulay and turned him over to the police, even though it's just for questioning, who's going to trust me?'

'I guess.'

'What I am going to do is have another talk with Robbie,' Angel said. 'He's taken all of this very badly.'

'He actually liked Everett?'

Angel shook her head. 'I don't think anyone liked Everett. I think it's got to do with finding the body. He's probably never seen a dead man before. I have, and I'm still feeling a little queasy.'

She didn't mention that Robbie had seemed to be hiding something. That was Robbie's business and even if he did share it with her, it would still be up to him who could know about it and who could not. She just prayed that he hadn't been any more involved in Everett's death than having stumbled upon the body.

'Actually,' she said after a moment's hesitation, 'there was another weird thing that happened tonight.'

Although she knew she'd regret it, because it was putting a foot into the strange world Jilly inhabited where fact mixed equally with fantasy, she told Jilly about her dream. As Angel had expected, Jilly accepted what she was told as though it were an everyday occurrence.

'Has this ever happened to you before?' she asked.

Angel shook her head. 'And I hope it never happens again. It's a really creepy feeling.'

Jilly seemed to be only half listening to her. Her eyes had narrowed thoughtfully. Chewing at her lower lip, her head was cocked and she studied the ceiling. Angel didn't know what Jilly saw up there, but she doubted it was the cracked plaster that anybody else would see.

'I wonder what he wanted from you,' Jilly finally said. Her gaze dropped and focused on Angel's. 'There has to be a reason he sent his spirit to you.'

Angel shook her head. 'Haven't you ever dreamed that someone you know died?'

'Well, sure. But what's that—'

'And did they turn out to be dead when you woke?'

'No, but—'

'Coincidence,' Angel said. 'That's all it was. Plain and simple coincidence.'

Jilly looked as though she was ready to argue the point, but then she simply shrugged.

'Okay,' she said, swinging her feet down from the desk. 'But don't say you weren't warned when Everett's spirit comes back to haunt you again. He wants something from you and the thing with ghosts is they can be patient forever. He'll keep coming back until you figure out what he wants you to do for him and you do it.'

'Of course. Why didn't I think of that?'

'I'm serious, Angel.'

Angel smiled. 'I'll remember.'

'I just bet you will,' Jilly said, returning her smile. She stood up. 'Well, I've got to run. I was in the middle of a new canvas when you called.'

Angel rose to her feet as well. 'Thanks for filling in.'

'Like I said, it was no problem. The place was dead.' Jilly grimaced as the word came out of her mouth. 'Sorry about that. But at least a building doesn't have shoes to lose, right?'

After Jilly left, Angel returned to her desk with another spiked coffee. She stared out the window at Grasso Street where the first touch of dawn was turning the shadows to grey, unable to get Everett's stockinged feet out of her mind. Superimposed over it was an image of Everett in the rain, holding out a shadowed bundle towards her.

One real, one from a dream. Neither made sense, but at least the dream wasn't supposed to. When it came to Everett's boots, though . . .

She disliked the idea of someone believing superstitions almost as much as she did the superstitions themselves. Taking a dead man's shoes so he wouldn't come back seeking revenge. It was so patently ludicrous.

But Macaulay had believed enough to take them.

Angel considered Jim Macaulay. At nineteen, he was

positively ancient compared to the street kids such as Robbie whose company he kept, though he certainly didn't look it. His cherubic features made him seem much younger. He'd been in and out of foster homes and juvie hall since he was seven, but the experiences had done little to curb his minor criminal ways, or his good humor. Macaulay always had a smile, even when he was being arrested.

Was he good for Everett's murder? Nothing in Macaulay's record pointed to it. His crimes were always non-violent: B&Es, minor drug dealing, trafficking in stolen goods. Nothing to indicate that he'd suddenly upscaled to murder. And where was the motive? Everett had carried nothing of value on his person – probably never had – and everyone knew it. And while it was true he'd been a royal pain in the ass, the street people just ignored him when he got on a rant.

But then why take the boots?

If Macaulay believed the superstition, why would he be afraid of Everett coming after him unless he *had* killed him?

Too tired to go home, Angel put her head down on the desk and stared out the window. She dozed off, still worrying over the problem.

Nothing has changed in her dream.

The rain continues to mist. Everett approaches her again, no less graceful, while she remains trapped in the weight of her flesh. The need is still there in Everett's eyes, the mysterious bundle still cradled against his chest as he comes up to her. But this time she finds enough of her voice to question him.

Why is he here in her dream?

'For the children,' he says.

It seems such an odd thing for him to say: Everett who's never had a kind word for anyone, so far as Angel knows.

'What do you mean?' she asks him.

But then he tries to hand the bundle to her and she wakes up again.

Angel sat up with a start. She was disoriented for a long moment

– as much by her surroundings as from the dream – before she recognized the familiar confines of her office and remembered falling asleep at her desk.

She shook her head and rubbed at her tired eyes. Twice in the same night. She had to do something about these hours, but knew she never would.

The repetition of the dream was harder to set aside. She could almost hear Jilly's voice, I-told-you-so plain in its tone.

Don't say you weren't warned when Everett's spirit comes back to haunt you again.

But it had just been a dream.

He wants something from you and the thing with ghosts is they can be patient forever.

A disturbing dream. That shadowed bundle Everett kept trying to hand to her and his enigmatic reply, 'For the children.'

He'll keep coming back until you figure out what it is he wants you to do for him and you do it.

She didn't need this, Angel thought. She didn't want to become part of Jilly's world where the rules of logic were thrown out the door and nothing made sense anymore. But this dream . . . and Macaulay taking those damn boots . . .

She remembered Jilly asking her what she was going to do and what her own reply had been. She still didn't want to get involved. Her job was helping the kids, not playing cop. But the image of the dream Everett flashed in her mind, the need in his eyes and what he'd said when she'd asked him why he was there in her dream.

For the children.

Whether she wanted it or not, she realized that she was involved now. Not in any way that made sense, but indiscriminately, by pure blind chance, which seemed even less fair. It certainly wasn't because she and Everett had been friends. For God's sake, she'd never even *liked* Everett.

For the children.

Angel sighed. She picked up her mug and looked down at the cold mixture of whiskey and coffee. She started to call Jilly, but hung up before she'd finished dialing the number. She knew what Jilly would say.

Grimacing, she drank what was left in her mug, then left her office in search of an answer.

Macaulay had a squat in the same abandoned tenement where Robbie lived, just a few blocks north of Angel's office on the edge of the Tombs. Angel squinted at the building, then made her way across the rubble-strewn lot that sided the empty tenement. The front door was boarded shut, so she went around the side and climbed in through a window the way the building's inhabitants did. Taking a moment to let her eyes adjust to the dimmer light inside, she listened to the silence that surrounded her. Whoever was here today was obviously asleep.

She knew Macaulay's squat was on the top floor, so she found the stairwell by the boarded-up entrance and climbed the two flights to the third floor. She looked in through the doorways as she passed by the rooms, heart aching with what she saw. Squatters, mostly kids, were curled up in sleeping bags, under blankets or in nests of newspaper. What were they going to do when winter came and the coolness of late summer nights dropped below the freezing mark?

Macaulay's room was at the end of the hall, but he wasn't in. His squat had a door, unlike most of the other rooms, but it stood ajar. Inside it was tidier than Angel had expected. Clean, too. There was a mattress in one corner with a neatly folded sleeping bag and pillow on top. Beside it was an oil lamp, sitting on the wooden floor, and a tidy pile of spare clothes. Two crates by the door held a number of water-swelled paperbacks with their covers removed. On another crate stood a Coleman stove, a frying pan and some utensils. Inside the crate was a row of canned goods while a cardboard box beside it served to hold garbage.

And then there were the shoes.

Although Angel didn't know Macaulay's shoe size, she doubted that any of them would fit him. She counted fifteen pairs, in all shapes and sizes, from a toddler's tiny sneakers to a woman's spike-heeled pumps. They were lined up against the wall in a neat row, a miniature mountain range, rising and falling in height, with Everett's bizarre boots standing like paired peaks at the end closer to the door.

It was a perfectly innocent sight, but Angel felt sick to her stomach as she stood there looking at them. They were all the shoes of children and women – except for Everett's. Had Macaulay killed all of their—

'Angel.'

She turned to find him standing in the doorway. With the sun coming through the window, making his blond hair look like a halo, he might have been describing himself as much as calling her name. Her gaze shifted to the line of shoes along the wall, then back to his face. His blue eyes were guileless.

Angel forwent the amenities.

'These . . . these shoes . . .?' she began.

'Shoes carry the imprint of our souls upon their own,' he replied. He paused, then added, 'Get it?'

All she was getting was a severe case of the creeps. What had she been thinking to come here on her own? She hadn't told anyone where she was going. Her own hightops could be joining that line of shoes, set in place beside Everett's.

Get out while you can, she told herself, but all she could do was ask, 'Did you kill him?'

'Who? Everett?'

Angel nodded.

'Do I look like a killer to you?'

No, he looked as though he was on his way to mass – not to confess, but to sing in the choir. But the shoes, something about the way the shoes stood in their tidy, innocuous line, said different.

'Why did you take them?'

'You're thinking they're souvenirs?'

'I . . . I don't know what to think.'

'So don't,' he said with a shrug, then disconcertingly changed the subject. 'Well, it's a good thing you're here. I was just going out to look for you.'

'Why?'

'Something terrible's happened to Robbie.'

The flatness of his voice was completely at odds with his choir boy appearance. Angel's gaze dropped to his hands, but they were empty. She'd been expecting to see him holding Robbie's shoes.

'What . . .?'

'You'd better come see.'

He led the way down to the second floor, on the other side of the building, then stood aside at the open door to Robbie's room. It was as cluttered as Macaulay's was tidy, but Angel didn't notice that as she stepped inside. Her gaze was drawn and riveted to the small body hanging by a rope from the overhead light fixture. It turned slowly, as though Robbie's death throes were just moments past. On the floor under him, a chair lay on its side.

Angel turned to confront Macaulay, but he was gone. She stepped out into the hallway to find it empty. Part of her wanted to run him down, to shake the angelic smugness from his features, but she made herself go back into Robbie's room. She righted the chair and stood on it. Taking her penknife from the back pocket of her jeans, she held Robbie against her as she sawed away at the rope. When the rope finally gave, Robbie's dead weight proved to be too much for her and he slipped from her arms, landing with a thud on the floor.

She jumped down and straightened his limbs. Forcing a finger between the rope and his neck, she slowly managed to loosen the pressure and remove the rope. Then, though she knew it was too late, though his skin was already cooling, body temperature dropping, she attempted CPR. While silently counting between breaths, she called for help, but no one stirred in the building around her. Either they were sleeping too soundly, or they just didn't want to get involved. Or maybe, a macabre part of her mind suggested, Macaulay's already killed them all. Maybe she hadn't walked by sleeping runaways and street kids on her way to Macaulay's room, but by their corpses . . .

She forced the thought out of her mind, refusing to let it take hold.

She worked until she had no more strength left. Slumping against a nearby wall, she stared at the body, but couldn't see it for the tears in her eyes.

It was a long time before she could get to her feet. When she left Robbie's room, she didn't go downstairs and leave the building to call the police. She went upstairs, to Macaulay's room. Every room she passed was empty, the sleeping figures all woken and fled. Macaulay's room was empty as well. It looked the same as it had earlier, with one difference. The sleeping bag and the clothes were gone. The line of shoes remained.

Angel stared at them for a long time before she picked up Everett's boots. She carried them with her when she left the building and stopped at the nearest payphone to call the police.

There was no note and the coroner ruled it a suicide. But there was still an APB out on Macaulay and no longer only in connection with Everett's death. Two of the pairs of shoes found in his squat were identified as belonging to recent murder victims; they could only assume that the rest did as well. The police had never connected the various killings, Lou told Angel later, because the investigations were handled by so many different precincts and, other than the missing footwear, the M.O. in each case was completely different.

Behind his cherubic features, Macaulay proved to have been a monster.

What Angel didn't understand was Robbie's suicide. She wouldn't let it go and finally, after a week of tracking down and talking to various street kids, she began to put together another picture of Macaulay. He wasn't just a killer; he'd also made a habit of molesting the street kids with whom he kept company. Their sex made no difference – just the younger the better. Coming from his background, Macaulay was a classic case of 'today's victim becoming tomorrow's predator' – a theorem put forth by Andrew Vachss, a New York lawyer specializing in juvenile justice and child abuse with whom Angel had been in correspondence.

Even more startling was the realization that Macaulay

probably hadn't killed Everett for whatever his usual reasons were, but because Everett had tried to help Robbie stand up to Macaulay. In a number of recent conversations Angel had with runaways she discovered that Everett had often given them money he'd panhandled, or shown them safe places to flop for a night.

Why Everett had needed to hide this philanthropic side of himself, no one was ever going to find out, but Angel thought she now knew why Robbie had killed himself: it wasn't just the shame of being abused – a shame that kept too many victims silent – but because Everett had died trying to protect him. For the sweet soul that Robbie had been, Angel could see how he would be unable to live with himself after what had happened that night.

But the worst was that Macaulay was still free. Two weeks after Everett's death he still hadn't been apprehended. Lou didn't hold out much hope of finding him.

'A kid like that,' he told Angel over lunch the following Saturday, 'he can just disappear into the underbelly of any big city. Unless he gets picked up someplace and they run his sheet, we might never hear from him again.'

Angel couldn't face the idea of Macaulay in some other city, killing, sexually abusing the runaways on its streets, protected by his cherubic features, his easy smile, his guileless eyes.

'All we can hope,' Lou added, 'is that he picks himself the wrong victim next time – someone meaner than he is, someone quicker with a knife – so that when we do hear about him again, he'll be a number on an ID tag in some morgue.'

'But this business of his taking his victims' shoes,' Angel said.

'We've put it on the wire. By this time, every cop in the country has had their duty sergeant read it to them at roll call.'

And that was it. People were dead. Kids already feeling hopeless carried new scars. She had a dead man visiting her in her dreams, demanding she do she didn't know what. And Macaulay went free.

Angel couldn't let it go at that, but there didn't seem to be anything more that she could do.

*

All week long, as soon as she goes to sleep, Everett haunts her dreams.

'I know what you were really like,' she tells him. 'I know you were trying to help the kids in your own way.'

For the children.

'And I know why Macaulay killed you.'

He stands in the misting rain, the need still plain in his eyes, the curious bundle held against his chest. He doesn't try to approach her anymore. He just stands there, half swallowed in mist and shadow, watching her.

'What I don't know is what you want from me.'

The rain runs down his cheeks like tears.

'For God's sake, *talk* to me.'

But all he says is, 'Do it for the children. Not for me. For the children.'

'Do *what?*'

But then she wakes up.

Angel dropped by Jilly's studio on the Sunday night. Telling Jilly she just wanted some company, for a long time she simply sat on the Murphy bed and watched Jilly paint.

'It's driving me insane,' she finally said. 'And the worst thing is, I don't even believe in this crap.'

Jilly looked up from her work and pushed her hair back from her eyes, leaving a streak of Prussian blue on the errant locks.

'Even when you dream about him every night?' she asked.

Angel sighed. 'Who knows what I'm dreaming, or why.'

'Everett does,' Jilly said.

'Everett's dead.'

'True.'

'And he's not telling.'

Jilly laid down her brush and came over to the bed. Sitting down beside Angel, she put an arm around Angel's shoulders and gave her a comforting hug.

'This doesn't have to be scary,' she said.

'Easy for you to say. This is all old hat for you. You like the fact that it's real.'

'But—'

Angel turned to her. 'I don't want to be part of this other world. I don't *want* to be standing at the check-out counter and have seriously to consider which of the headlines are real and which aren't. I can't deal with that. I can barely deal with this . . . this haunting.'

'You don't have to deal with anything except for Everett,' Jilly told her. 'Most people have a very effective defensive system against paranormal experiences. Their minds just automatically find some rational explanation for the unexplainable that allows them to put it aside and carry on with their lives. You'll be able to do the same thing. Trust me on this.'

'But then I'll be just denying something that's real.'

Jilly shrugged. 'So?'

'I don't get it. You've been trying to convince me for years that stuff like this is real and now you say just forget it?'

'Not everybody's equipped to deal with it,' Jilly said. 'I just always thought you would be. But I was wrong to keep pushing at you about it.'

'That makes me feel inadequate.'

Jilly shook her head. 'Just normal.'

'There's something to be said for normal,' Angel said.

'It's comforting,' Jilly agreed. 'But you do have to deal with Everett, because it doesn't look like he's going to leave you alone until you do.'

Angel nodded slowly. 'But do what? He won't tell me what he wants.'

'It happens like that,' Jilly said. 'Most times spirits can't communicate in a straightforward manner, so they have to talk in riddles, or mime, or whatever. I think that's where all the obliqueness in fairy tales comes from: they're memories of dealing with real paranormal encounters.'

'That doesn't help.'

'I know it doesn't,' Jilly said. She smiled. 'Sometimes I think I just talk to hear my own voice.' She looked across her studio to where finished paintings lay stacked against the wall beside her easel, then added thoughtfully, 'I think I've got an idea.'

Angel gave her a hopeful look.

'When's the funeral?' Jilly asked.

'Tomorrow. I took up a collection and raised enough so that Everett won't have to be buried in a pauper's grave.'

'Well, just make sure Everett's buried with his boots on,' Jilly told her.

'That's *it*?'

Jilly shrugged. 'It scared Macauley enough to take them, didn't it?'

'I suppose. . . .'

For all she's learned about his hidden philanthropic nature, she still feels no warmth towards the dead man. Sympathy, yes. Even pity. But no warmth.

The need in his eyes merely replaces the anger they wore in life; it does nothing to negate it.

'You were buried today,' she says. 'With your boots on.'

The slow smile on the dead man's face doesn't fit well. It seems more a borrowed expression than one his features ever knew. For the first time in over a week, he approaches her again.

'A gift,' he says, offering up the newspaper-wrapped bundle. 'For the children.'

For the children.

He's turned into a broken record, she thinks, stuck on one phrase.

She watches him as he moves into the light. He peels away the soggy newspaper, then holds up Macaulay's severed head. He grips it by the haloing blond hair, a monstrous, bloody artifact that he thrusts into her face.

Angel woke screaming. She sat bolt upright, clutching the covers to her chest. She had no idea where she was. Nothing looked right. Furniture loomed up in unfamiliar shapes, the play of shadows was all wrong. When a hand touched her shoulder, she flinched and screamed again, but it was only Jilly.

She remembered then, sleeping over, going to bed, late, late on that Sunday night, each of them taking a side of the Murphy bed.

'It's okay,' Jilly was telling her. 'Everything's okay.'

Slowly, Angel felt the tension ease, the fear subside. She turned to Jilly and then had to smile. Jilly had been a street kid once – she was one of Angel's success stories. Now it seemed it was payback time, their roles reversed.

'What happened?' Jilly asked.

Angel trembled, remembering the awful image that had sent her screaming from her dream. Jilly couldn't suppress her own shivers as Angel told her about her dream.

'But at least it's over,' Jilly said.

'What do you mean?'

'Everett's paid Macaulay back.'

Angel sighed. 'How can you *know* that?'

'I don't know it for sure. It just feels right.'

'I wish everything was that simple,' Angel said.

The phone rang in Angel's office at mid-morning. It was Lou on the other end of the line.

'Got some good news for you,' he said.

Angel's pulse went into double-time.

'It's Macaulay,' she said. 'He's been found, hasn't he? He's dead.'

There was a long pause before Lou asked, 'Now how the hell did you know that?'

'I didn't,' Angel replied. 'I just hoped that was why you were calling me.'

It didn't really make anything better. It didn't bring Robbie back, or take away the pain that Macaulay had inflicted on God knew how many kids. But it helped.

Sometimes her dreams still take her to that street where the neon signs and streetlights turn a misting rain into a carnival of light and shadow.

But the dead man has never returned.

THE COFFIN TRIMMER

Bill Pronzini

A full-time writer since 1969, Bill Pronzini has published – alone
and in collaboration with others – more than forty novels,
including twenty in his popular 'Nameless Detective' series;
three non-fiction books; six collections of short stories; and some
275 uncollected stories, articles, essays and book reviews. He has
also edited or co-edited more than eighty anthologies of mystery,
detective, horror, science fiction, and western stories, and
received two Shamus Awards and the coveted Lifetime
Achievement Award – from the Private Eye Writers of America
– plus five nominations for the Mystery Writers of America's
Edgar Award.

'As for childhood superstitions,' Bill says, 'I was rank with
them. I couldn't walk under ladders, I avoided black cats, I
wouldn't step on sidewalk cracks, I stayed out of dark cellars . . .
and so on. I've outgrown most of them now, but I'm glad that I
had them. They helped develop an active imagination into an
overactive one and thus allowed me to become what I wanted to
be ever since I was twelve years old – a professional writer of
fiction.

'I wasn't afraid of coffin trimmers – or the Coffin Trimmer –
but that's only because I didn't know that particular superstition
then. Good thing, too.'

✳

I'm scared.

I have never been so scared.

No one in Little River shares my terror. They refuse to listen to me, to open their eyes to the terrible truth. They call me a superstitious fool. Or tetched, or downright deranged. One day they will realize how blind they've been – the ones that are left. But by then it will be too late.

Lord have mercy on us all.

It doesn't make sense that Little River was chosen. Ours is no worse nor different than any other small northern California town. Dairy and beef cattle is what supports us; agricultural crops such as alfalfa, too. We have six saloons, a gambling house, and a whorehouse, compared to only three churches, but that doesn't mean there is much sin or even much impiety. There isn't. We haven't had a killing or any other major crime in nearly twenty years. Rowdyism is confined to Independence Day and once in a while when a cowhand off one of the ranches gets liquored up of a Saturday night. We're a God-fearing town of thirteen hundred and sixty-eight souls, according to the 1892 census. Good souls, with no more than a bucketful destined for a handshake with Satan on their judgment day.

Doesn't make sense, either, that it would start when Abe Bedford put up his new undertaking building. But it did, and no mistake. I used to believe everything that happened in this life had its clear-cut purpose and meaning, and if you studied on it long enough, looked at it in just the right way, you'd come to know or at least suspect what it was. Not this, though. No one can figure out the cause or reason for this – no one mortal, anyhow. And perhaps that's a blessing. I know too much already; I'm too scared as it is. I reckon I couldn't stand to know the rest of it too.

Abe Bedford buys all his rough pine boxes and fancier coffins from a casketmaker in the county seat. He used to store them in the barn back of his house on Oak Street. Had the coffins trimmed there, as well, by his wife Maude before she passed away and then by the Widow Brantley; he buys them without lining because it's thriftier that way. His embalming room and viewing parlor were in a rented building down on lower Main, near the train depot. He'd been the only undertaker in town for some while, but Little River was growing and Abe took to fretting that before long some other mortician would move in and open a fancy establishment and take away a good portion of his business. He came to the idea that what he had to do was build his own fancy establishment first, in a better location than lower Main – a place that was big enough for embalming and viewing, and to show off and store his caskets and rough boxes.

So he had a new building put up on the other side of his Oak Street property, close to the street. It had a large plate glass window in front so folks walking or riding by could look in and see the trimmed display coffins with their satin linings and silk pillows and shiny brass fittings. Abe also laid in shrubbery and a lawn and a brick walk and a wide brick drive to accommodate his black hearse and team of four. When it was all done, everybody agreed the new undertaking parlor was a worthy addition to the community.

Abe had been open for business in the new place less than a week when the woman who called herself Grace Selkirk came to town.

No one knew where she came from, or even how she arrived in Little River. She simply appeared one day, and took a room overnight at the hotel where the drummers and railroad men always stayed; and the next day she was living in Abe Bedford's house, keeping it for him and working in the Widow Brantley's stead as his coffin trimmer.

Tongues started to wag right off. Gossip's a major industry in any small town, and in Little River the women and members of the Hot Stove League in Cranmer's General Merchandise Store work harder at it than most. I hear more gossip, I reckon, than just about anyone in town. Cranmer's General Merchandise Store is mine, inherited from my daddy when he passed on fifteen years ago. George Cranmer is my name.

Abe Bedford is a widower and reasonable handsome for a man in his late forties. Grace Selkirk looked to be about thirty-five and was not too hard on the eye, in a chilly sort of way. Before long, folks had Abe and the Selkirk woman sharing a bed. Some even went so far as to claim he had met her on one of his trips to San Francisco, where his son lived, and brought her back with him on the sly so they could live together in sin.

I didn't believe any of it. I've known Abe for four decades; there is no more moral and God-fearing man in this state. He'd heard the gossip, too, and it hurt him. He wouldn't have anything to do with Grace Selkirk, he said to me one night, not that way, not if she was the only woman in a thousand miles. She made him shiver just to look at her, he said.

I asked him why he hired her and he said he didn't rightly know. She'd showed up on his doorstep the morning after she arrived in town and asked him for the work; he was about to refuse her, for he'd had no trouble doing for himself since Maude died, but he couldn't seem to find the words. Couldn't bring himself to let her go since, either. She was a good cook and housekeeper, he said, and the fact was, she trimmed coffins better than Maude or the Widow Brantley ever had. Why, some of her finished caskets were funerary works of art.

Nobody liked Grace Selkirk much. She never made any effort to be neighborly and little enough to be civil. Stayed close to Abe's home and undertaking parlor, and on the few occasions she came down to Main Street and into my store, she hardly spoke a word. I could surely understand why she made Abe shiver. She was the coldest woman I'd ever laid eyes on. Ice and snow weren't any colder.

One blustery day when she walked into the store, old Mead Downey was occupying his usual stool by the white-bellied stove, and he tried to make conversation with her. She wouldn't have any of it. Went about her business and then walked out as if old Mead wasn't even there. He spit against the hot side of the stove, waited for it to sizzle, and allowed as how he'd never believed those rumors about her and Abe and now he knowed for a fact they weren't true.

'Why's that?' one of the other loafers asked him.

'He's still alive, ain't he?' Mead said. 'First time he stuck his pizzle in that woman, him and it would of froze solid.'

All the boys laughed fit to choke. I laughed too. I thought it was a pretty funny remark then.

It isn't funny now.

The one thing about Grace Selkirk that you couldn't fault was her coffin-trimming. As Abe had said, she was an artist with silk and satin, taking pains to get the folds in the lining and the fluff of the pillows just so. She did her work right there in the showroom, in plain sight behind the plate glass window. Most any time of day, and late some evenings, you'd see her at it. She spent twice as much time working in the undertaking building as she did keeping Abe's house for him.

It wasn't that she was readying caskets for future use. No, all the ones she trimmed were for fresh business. More folks than usual had commenced dying in Little River. Nobody worried about the increase in fatalities; births and deaths run that way, in high-low cycles. A feeble joke even got started that Abe had done such a bang-up job on his new establishment, people were dying to get into it.

Grace Selkirk had been in town about six weeks when Charley Bluegrass came rushing into my store one night. It was a chilly fall night with a touch of rain in the air. I'd stayed open late, as I often do, because I am a confirmed bachelor and I'd rather be in the store playing checkers and dominoes and shooting the breeze with members of the Hot Stove League than sitting alone in my dusty parlor.

Bluegrass wasn't Charley's true last name. Everyone called him that on account of he'd planted a Kentucky Bluegrass lawn for Miss Edna Tolliver a few years back and it had come up so rich and green, half the women in the county took after him to do the same job for them. Which he did. He'd given up his handyman chores and taken to working as a gardener full-time. Charley was a half-breed Miwok and liked his liquor more than most men. He'd been liking it pretty well on this night; you could smell it on him when he blew in.

He was all het up, his eyes sparkly with drink and excitement. 'That new woman, that Grace Selkirk – she's dead!'

The Hot Stove League and I all came to attention. I said, 'Dead? You sure, Charley?'

'I'm sure. I seen her through the window at the undertaker's. All laid out in one of them coffins, deader than a doornail.'

Frank McGee crossed himself. He was new in town and a freshman member of the League, a young clerk in the Argonaut Drugstore who drove his wagon all the way to the county seat of a Sunday so he and his wife could attend what he called Mass in the Catholic Church over there. Old Mead said, 'What killed her? Frostbite?' and commenced to cackling like a hen with a half-stuck egg. Nobody paid him any mind.

'I don't know what killed her,' Charley Bluegrass said. 'I didn't see no marks, no blood or nothing, but I didn't stop to look close.'

'Some of you gents better go on over to the undertaking parlor and have a look,' I said. 'And then tell Abe.'

Toby Harper and Evan Millhauser volunteered and hurried out. Charley Bluegrass stayed behind to warm himself at the stove and sneak another drink from the flask he carried in his hip pocket. I don't usually allow the imbibing of spirits on the premises – I don't drink nor smoke myself; chewing sassafras root is my only vice – but under the circumstances I figured Charley was entitled.

We all thought Toby and Evan would be gone a while, but they were back in ten minutes. And laughing when they walked in. 'False alarm,' Toby said. 'That Selkirk woman ain't dead. She's walking around over there livelier than any gent in this room.'

Charley Bluegrass jumped to his feet. 'That can't be. She's dead, I saw her laid out in that coffin.'

'Well, she just got resurrected,' Evan said. 'You better change the brand of panther piss you're drinking, Charley. It's making you see things that aren't there.'

Charley shook his head. 'I tell you, she was dead. The lamplight was real bright. Her face . . . it was all white and waxy. Something strange, too, like it wasn't—' He bit the last word off and swallowed the ones that would have come next. A shiver went through him; he reached for his flask.

'Like it wasn't what?' I asked him.

'No,' he said, 'no, I ain't going to say.'

Toby said, 'I'll bet she was lining the coffin and laid down in it to try it for a fit. You know how she is with her trimming. Everything's got to be just so.'

'Tired too, probably, hard as she works,' one of the others said. 'Felt so good, stretched out on all that silk and satin, she fell asleep. That's what you saw, Charley. Her sleeping in that box.'

'She wasn't sleeping,' Charley Bluegrass said, 'she was dead.' And nobody could convince him otherwise.

The next morning *he* was the one who was dead.

Heart failure, Doc Miller said. Charley Bluegrass had been thirty-seven years old and never sick a day in his life.

Citizens of Little River kept right on dying. Old folks, middle-aged, young; even kids and infants. More all the time, though not so many more than it was alarming. Wasn't like a plague or an epidemic. No, what they died of was the same ailments and frailties and carelessness as always. Pneumonia, whooping cough, diphtheria, coronary thrombosis, consumption, cancer, colic, heart failure, old age; accident and misadventure too. Only odd fact was that more deaths than usual seemed to be sudden, of people like Charley Bluegrass that hadn't been sick or frail. Old Mead was one who just up and died. The young Catholic clerk, Frank McGee, was another.

When I heard about Frank I took over to the undertaking parlor to pay my respects. Mrs McGee was there, grieving next to the casket. I told her how sorry I was, and she said, 'Thank you, Mr Cranmer. It was so sudden . . . I just don't understand it. Last night my Frank was fine. Why, he even laughed about dying before his time.'

'Laughed?'

'Well, you recollect what happened to that half-breed Indian, Charley Bluegrass? The night before *he* died?'

'I surely do.'

'Same curious thing happened to my Frank. He went out for a walk after supper and chanced over here to Oak Street. When he looked in through Mr Bedford's show window he saw the very same as Charley Bluegrass.'

'You mean Grace Selkirk lying in one of the coffins?'

'I do,' Mrs McGee said. 'Frank thought she was dead. There was something peculiar about her face, he said.'

'Peculiar how?'

'He wouldn't tell me. Whatever it was, it bothered him some.'

Charley Bluegrass, I recalled, had also remarked about Grace Selkirk's face. And he hadn't wanted to talk about what it was, either.

'Frank was solemn and quiet for a time. But not long; you know how cheerful he always was, Mr Cranmer. He rallied and said he must've been wrong and she was asleep. Either that, or he'd had a delusion – and him not even a drinking man. Then he laughed and said he hoped he wouldn't end up dead before his time like poor Charley Bluegrass . . .' She broke off weeping.

Right then, I began to get a glimmer of the truth.

Almost everyone in Little River visited my store of a week. Whenever a spouse or relative or close acquaintance of the recent deceased came in, I took the lady or gent aside and asked questions. Three told me the same as Frank McGee's widow: Their dead had also chanced by the undertaking parlor not long before they drew their last breaths, and through the show window saw Grace Selkirk lying in one of the coffins, dead or asleep. Two of the deceased had mentioned her face, too – something not quite right about it that had disturbed them but that they wouldn't discuss.

Five was too many for coincidence. If there was that many admitted what they'd seen, it was likely an equal number – and perhaps quite a few more than that – had kept it to themselves, taken it with them to their graves.

That was when I knew for certain.

My first impulse was to rush over and confront Grace Selkirk straight out. But it would have been pure folly and I came to my senses before I gave in to it. I went to see Abe Bedford instead. He was my best friend and I thought if anybody in town would listen to me, it was Abe.

I was wrong. He backed off from me same as if I'd just told him I was a leper. Why, it was the most ridiculous thing he'd ever heard, he said. I must be deranged to put stock in such an evil notion. Drive her out of town? Take a rope or a gun to her? 'You go around urging such violence against a poor spinster, George Cranmer,' he said, 'and *you'll* be the one driven out of town.'

He was nearly right, too. The ministers of our three churches wouldn't listen, nor would the mayor or the town council or anyone else in Little River. The truth was too dreadful for them to credit; they shut their minds to it. Folks stopped trading at my store, commenced to shunning me on the street. Wasn't anything I could do or say to turn even one person to my way of thinking.

Finally I quit trying and put pen to paper and wrote it all out here. I pray someone will read it later on, someone outside Little River, and believe it for the pure gospel truth it is. I have no other hope left than that.

She calls herself Grace Selkirk but that isn't her name. She has no name, Christian or otherwise. She isn't a mortal woman. And coffin trimming isn't just work she's good at – it's her true work, it's what she is. The Coffin Trimmer.

The Angel of Death.

I don't know if she's after the whole town, every last soul in Little River, but I suspect she is. Might get them too. One other fact I do know: This isn't the first town she's come to and it won't be the last. Makes a body tremble to think how many must have come before, all over the country, all over the world, and how many will come after.

But that is not the real reason I'm so scared. No, not even that. Last night I worked late and walked home by way of Oak Street. Couldn't help myself, any more than I could help glancing through Abe Bedford's show window. And there she was in a fresh-trimmed coffin, the silk and satin draped just so around her, face all pale and waxy and dead. But the face wasn't hers; I looked at it close to make sure.

It was mine. A shadow vision of my own fresh corpse waiting to be put into the ground.

I'm next.

STEPS

Stella Hargreaves

Stella Hargreaves was born in Shropshire and has lived in London for most of her life, with occasional escapes to Yorkshire and Sussex. She even lived, for nine years, in a lodging house which at one time housed all the Behans . . . which perhaps led to her qualifying as a creative writing tutor and adult literacy teacher.

She has had a go at most jobs, including a few unlikely ones such as singing in northern clubs wearing a red polyester frock and an ash blonde wig. She now sings in a blues band and wants to be Etta James.

Since January 1991 Stella has had more than twenty stories, mainly humorous, published in the United Kingdom and Scandinavia, and her reviews and articles appear regularly in *Albsu, The Writers Newsletter, Quartos* and many others. Two novels – *Good Girl Jane* and *Kickers* – are currently under consideration.

Most of Stella's superstitions are connected with family. 'I remember sitting outside the kitchen door as a child,' she says, 'wishing on my ruby ring out of a Christmas cracker that my balmy, disfunctional family would stop screaming at each other. And I recall baking a cake every Sunday night for years on end as a kind of charm against harm befalling my children on the way to school.

'Once, when I was a lonely single parent, my horoscope said

I'd find love and make friends. On the strength of this I embarked on a whirlwind romance, accepted a proposal of marriage and then was surprised and disappointed when the man suddenly disappeared without trace. And he never even returned my Levi's sweatshirt!'

✳

The doctor fixed up an appointment at the eye hospital, but by the time the appointment came round, she was worse. So then he said she'd better see a psychiatrist instead. The psychiatrist seemed bored and easy to deceive. Zoe wondered why he didn't wear a crisp white coat instead of a suit that had seen better days.

She said to herself, They're all getting at me, just because I don't want to live in dirt and filth; because I got on all right with Joyce and no one else did. That psychiatrist's the worst of the lot. Sits there in his nice office, drinking coffee out of a clean cup. Never thinks about the poor cow who keeps things up to scratch for him. Thinks the world goes round on jaw jaw, take these pills, see you next week and off down the golf course, the pillock. I'm never going to tell him about looking after Joyce's stone, or the steps or anything. He wouldn't believe me anyway.

What was it he said?

'Zoe, do you think that perhaps never knowing your mother made you vulnerable to Joyce? Perhaps you went overboard trying to win her approval, to the point where you threatened your marriage. And then you were forced to make a choice between her and your marriage, so that when you fell out over the steps it tipped her over the edge, so to speak. Now she's dead, you feel bereaved and guilty.'

Fat lot he knows. I'm not saying anything to any of them, not Gary, not him, not the doctor, not Sonia. I'll do what I have to do and they can go for a run.

It began with the flat. Sonia went with Zoe and Gary to the housing association to see a man called Jake with a perfectly bald head and earrings, who looked worried all the time.

Jake said, 'We can offer you a three-room flat in Nye's Road, near the common. It's been refurbished and it's a good area.' He laughed self-consciously. 'I wouldn't mind living there myself.'

Zoe thought, 'So what? You look a right scruff.'

Smiling sadly, Jake turned to Sonia. 'Did you tell them the snag?'

Gary said, 'Don't worry, we'll keep out of her way.'

Jake frowned. 'She's a difficult lady, the sitting tenant. Ultra-houseproud. They've lived in the ground floor flat for a long time – she thinks of the house as hers. She's already scared off two lots of prospective tenants. Here's the key, go and have a look. But it's no use taking it, then coming back in a while to say you can't stand her and you want a transfer.'

Gary said, 'All me and Zoe want is to get married and get out of the hostel and be together. That right, Zoe?'

Zoe had PMS and ached all over. Too weary to move, she smiled at Gary and nodded. She thought, Sonia was right, it's a mistake. Only you kept on at me, you rotten pest.

It was true, Gary had kept on at her to marry him. Sonia said, 'You're both just eighteen, Zoe. I know it feels good to have someone special when you've both grown up in care, but you haven't had any life yet, you've only seen homes and this hostel. Can't you live together?'

Zoe said, 'I'm not living sticky with any bloke – what d'you take me for?'

In her indignation, she forgot how Gary irritated her, that he'd pestered her ever since they'd arrived at the hostel from their separate children's homes two years earlier. She wanted to be married and have a proper home where she could do things her own way.

Sonia said, 'Okay, we'd better try and get you a decent flat. No good going to the council, you'll be lucky if they offer a hard to let. I'll get some application forms from housing associations – you might be lucky.'

They were lucky. They had the key to a three-room flat in a tree-lined road, and the only snag was Joyce. When the three of them went to view the flat, Joyce was scrubbing the fourteen stone steps that led from the front door to the short path. She didn't move to let them past and they left footmarks on the steps. Joyce looked at their backs with hatred in her sad, slightly protruding eyes. Gary whistled as he took the stairs two at a time. Gary often whistled when he was annoyed. Zoe loved the flat.

Gary settled to married life as though trained for it. He was halfway through his City and Guilds, and worked in a motor repair shop in Edmonton, miles from Nye's road. On Friday nights, he went out with his workmates. On Saturdays, he went to football. On Sundays he played football on the common, then went to the pub till closing time, then came home, ate his dinner and napped until teatime. After tea, he took Zoe for a drive.

Zoe got a job at a building society close by. She did the shopping in her lunch hour, got home two hours before Gary and cooked their evening meal. She spent Saturdays cleaning the flat and shopping. She spent her Sundays waiting for Gary to go back to work. She didn't mind cleaning the flat, it was rewarding. She loved Friday nights, when Gary stayed out and she had the place to herself.

The women at the building society were all married too. They all shopped in their lunch hours and all hurried home to cook meals. In repose, they looked as depressed as Zoe, and never had time to talk to one another. Not really talk, the way the girls at the hostel had.

They'd been in the flat for six months without being bothered by Joyce, and then one Saturday she knocked on the front door. She was carrying a homemade cheesecake in a biscuit tin. She stood looking at Zoe with her sad, protruding eyes, smiling and at the same time trying to hide her bad teeth. Zoe felt obliged to invite her in. Joyce accepted tea, but refused a piece of cheesecake. She said, 'I never touch solids. I have that invalid food in a jar. Sometimes I put honey in it.'

'Oh,' Zoe said. She looked at Joyce from under her eyelids. Perhaps Joyce couldn't eat solids. Perhaps her teeth were too far gone.

'My heart,' Joyce volunteered.

'Oh,' Zoe said again.

'It never stops me, mind. You've got this place lovely. I couldn't do much better myself.' She drew a finger along the edge of the self-build sideboard, inspecting it for dust.

'Thanks,' Zoe said, without sarcasm.

'Does he make much mess?' Joyce looked at Gary in the wedding picture on the television.

'Gary? No. He doesn't move much.'

'That's good,' Joyce said. 'Husbands can be a drawback in a place. They're not attuned. It's taken years to get my Ted up to the mark.'

Zoe went to make tea. When she came back, Joyce was on her hands and knees, peering under the settee. She pulled herself up and sat down again. 'Lovely. Not a speck of dust.'

Zoe smiled gratefully. 'I always do the cleaning Saturdays.'

'Only Saturdays? You're never finished, not in a house you're not. It's a filthy, dirty World, that's the trouble. We've all got to do our bit, Zoe. It's a pity people don't. Thanks for the tea, dear. I'll see you Monday – your Gary never gets in till seven, does he? Be nice for you, a bit of company.'

'I have to cook,' Zoe said doubtfully.

'Half an hour won't hurt.' She saw herself out.

After this, Joyce popped up to see Zoe every evening when she came in from work. She helped to unpack the shopping (taking the chance to vet Zoe's cupboards and fridge for cleanliness) and then made them both a cup of tea. She always brought Zoe a piece of cake or a sandwich, but never asked about her day at the building society. Joyce's interest in Zoe seemed not to go beyond her relationship to the flat. Just the same there was comfort in the cake and tea. Zoe wondered if this was how it felt to have a mother.

If she saw a fingermark on a door or a smear on the furniture, Joyce would pull a duster from her overall pocket and wipe away the offending smear or mark. She showed Zoe how to polish wood, using only a duster and two fingers. When she came up one evening and saw the new armchairs, she said, 'Lovely.'

Zoe said, 'They're second-hand, really. Out of the paper.'

Joyce looked frightened. 'You don't know who's been in those chairs. Good job they're linen covers – we can give them a scrub.'

She went for her scrubbing brush because Zoe didn't have one. Zoe filled a bucket with water and disinfectant. 'I'll do this,' said Joyce. She eyed the chairs vengefully.

Zoe watched Joyce scrubbing the armchairs. As she worked, her large eyes grew larger. She bit her lower lip with her wobbly teeth and her sallow face flushed.

'There. We'll blow them dry with the fan heater,' Joyce said. 'Tomorrow I'll buy you a scrubbing brush.'

Gary was furious when he sat in one of the damp armchairs. 'Keep her out of here. It's not her effing flat.'

When Joyce knocked the next evening, Zoe said, 'Gary was angry about the chairs. He says you can't come in.'

For a moment, Joyce looked wounded. Then she said in her hollow voice, 'Come down to me then. I've made a Battenburg.'

Joyce's flat made Zoe gasp in admiration. There was a lot to admire, because Joyce had the ground floor and the basement rooms filled with dralon sofas, velvet pile carpets, pink ruched blinds and ornaments for every shining surface. She let Zoe play with the blinds, explaining how she sent them for cleaning every six weeks; she showed her the spare ones she kept for a change. She invited Zoe to look under her bed, behind her fridge and in her understairs cupboard, defying her to find one speck of dirt. She said again. 'You're never finished in a house, Zoe.'

Gary wasn't pleased about Zoe visiting Joyce. 'We're supposed to be keeping our distance.'

Zoe stared at Gary's fingernails, each with a wadge of engine oil behind it. She looked at the fresh ketchup stain on the front of his shirt. She thought, At least Joyce is clean. And she's kind to me.

Joyce poured tea, made Zoe put her shoes behind the front door, then let her put her feet on a velvet pouffe. She advised Zoe about cleaning. 'Vinegar and water and elbowgrease is best for windows and mirrors, then polish them up with old newpaper. If you do them every couple of days, the dirt can't get a hold. And don't use that varnish on your cork tiles, Zoe. It looks nice at first, but after a bit it goes like tar. Get it all up now, with some white spirit and wire wool. You can't beat homemade polish and elbowgrease – all these fancy creams and polishes and sprays in the supermarket, they're for sluts and pub cleaners.'

Zoe took to doing some cleaning every night. Taking care of the flat was more interesting than television; Joyce had opened Zoe's eyes to the true test of a good cleaner, paying scrupulous attention to the places that nobody sees. The pipes in the under-sink cupboard, the top of the wardrobe, those little cups you put under the legs of settees and chairs to save the carpet. Besides, sitting with Gary wasn't nice for Zoe; he looked grubbier each day. He smelled of his work.

When Gary found Zoe putting paper on top of the wardrobe to catch the dust, and then changing this paper and the drawer linings every week, he called Sonia.

Sonia said carefully, 'How are you getting on with Joyce?'

Zoe bit her lip. 'I see. Gary got you here.'

'You're turning funny,' Gary said plaintively. 'Honest to God, Sonia, she never comes to bed before one. You'd think we lived in the middle of a bleeding factory, the way she goes at it. Look at her, Sonia – that Joyce and her'll end up like twins.'

'What's wrong with being clean?' Zoe said angrily. 'It's a dirty filthy world – we've all got to do our bit.'

She got her broom and told Gary and Sonia that she was going to clear some leaves from the front path. Gary stood against the door. He said, 'Look at yourself in the mirror, Zoe. Look at that Joyce. Yellow skin, teeth falling out, hair like a bunch of cobwebs stuck on her head. She's sick in her mind. Her Ted told me she hasn't been out, only to Sainsbury's, for twelve years. Won't eat anything except invalid food because she's scared of germs. You needn't look surprised, Zo. I see Ted over the pub all the time – he can't stand being in the house with her. You've got to pull yourself together. Tell her, Sonia.'

There was a tiny mark on the front of Sonia's jumper, where her baby had dribbled. Sonia said gently, 'I think you're over-doing it, Zoe love.'

'I don't care,' Zoe shouted. 'I like Joyce and I hate dirt! Fancy Gary sending for the bloody social worker, just because I want a nice home.'

She pushed past Gary and went to sweep the leaves. When the path was clear, she looked at the tree overhanging the path and decided she might as well shake it and bring down as many leaves as she could, to clear the lot in one go. It was almost midnight before she stopped shaking and sweeping.

Zoe was so angry with Gary, she invited Joyce to view the new curtains. It's my place too, she thought. It's more my place, because I take care of it. I know every little crack and corner and nail and splinter. I know it better than I know myself.

Joyce said, 'Lovely bit of Sanderson's, Zoe. Class, that is.' Then her face clouded. 'Shame about that plastic curtain rail, it lets you down. Let me buy a nice stained mahogany one from Woolworth's. I'll send Ted.'

Zoe said sadly, 'Better not, Joyce. You know, Gary . . .'

'Well, let's wash this one. It does look a tad dirty, don't you think so?'

Zoe had already washed the curtain rail. She bowed to Joyce's superior eye. They took the curtains down again, washed the rail with disinfectant, dried it and put the curtains back.

Afterwards, Joyce dug into her overall pocket and brought out a colour picture from a magazine. She said, 'Look at this, Zoe. Looks like a shrimp or something, doesn't it? It's not though – it's a house-dust mite, magnified a few million times.'

Zoe shuddered gratifyingly. 'They live in our houses, Zoe. They eat dust and dirt and dead skin. They're in your bed, up your nose, all over. Any place you can think of, there's a few hundred of these things, some dead, some alive and wiggling around and chewing. That's what we're fighting. That and all the dirt the dirty people make, and the smoke from cars, and bits of ash from crematorium chimneys. The dirty people can't see the fluff and dust whizzing through the air, and the nasty microbes, and these things. But I see them, Zoe. I see them as plain as that mite sitting on your nose.'

She brushed her hand over Zoe's nose.

Zoe put her cup down. 'I never see them.'

Joyce looked grim. 'You will. I'm doing my kitchen cabinet, come and look.'

They went downstairs. Joyce had up-ended her cabinet and was about to scrub its backside with bleach and water.

'You must do this. This spiders come round and spin little webs on the underneath, then lay eggs. Ted found a spider in his Weetabix when we were first married. It'd hatched and climbed in the cabinet and run in the box.'

She closed her eyes against this vile memory. 'Got to get on. I'll tell you what – I don't know how you manage to work full time with the flat to look after. You can't let up, dear.'

It was a Sunday. Gary came back from playing football to find Zoe scrubbing the underside of the kitchen cabinet. She said without looking up, 'I'm going to ask at work if I can go part time. There's too much to do in this place.'

Gary picked up Zoe's bucket of bleach and water and tipped it down the sink. He prised the scrubbing brush out of her hand and threw it into a corner. Then he pushed Zoe into a chair. 'Listen, stupid mare; you're losing your marbles. We're going to stay at Reen's. When we come back, you'll start acting normal or else. I'll pack up football, we'll go out, I'll even take you down the Locarno. We'll buy a video, go to bed at the same time at night. Start having sex again, instead of you doing a cleaning loony every night till I'm asleep. You're gonna keep away from that nut job downstairs. Can't you see what she's doing to you? Ted tried to get her to the doctor years ago, but she locked herself in the bathroom. Her own daughter won't have nothing to do with her. Now get packed.'

Zoe pulled a duster from her overall pocket and started to two-finger polish the kitchen table.

Gary grabbed the duster and dragged her to the car. He pushed her in, then ran to the driver's side and started the engine.

Zoe said, 'This car's filthy. You're filthy too, Gary.' There was a carpet of dandruff on the side of Gary's collar. A small herd of house-dust mites was grazing on it.

'Shut your beak,' said Gary viciously. 'I can get you put away.'

Zoe decided to be quiet. Gary's aunt was pleased to see them; she was fond of Gary, although she hadn't been able to look after him when his parents died, because of her job. She said, 'You look tired to death, Zoe.'

Reen had dogs and no interest in housework. Unable to face Reen's grubby décor, Zoe stayed in bed. Gary tried to be kind; he even phoned the building society to say she was sick.

But when they returned to the flat, she could see black and grey flecks and specks of dirt, grit and fluff in the air. Crowds of house-dust mites rushed over and began to greedily gnaw at the dust on her shoes. She kicked them off, put on her track suit trousers and tucked them into her socks. Then she put a headscarf over her hair so that the flying dirt and crawling mites couldn't reach her hair. She told Gary she had an earache. As she lay in bed shivering with disgust, he said, 'Maybe it's flu.'

She didn't tell him about the marauding beasts and the filth which he, one of the dirty people, couldn't see. She thought he might really get her sent to some institution; the only way to avoid this was either to pretend to go along with his stupidity or leave the flat. She couldn't bear to abandon the flat, so she suffered him to take her shopping, to the pub on Sunday lunchtimes, dancing on Saturday nights, walking on the common after tea. They went to bed each night at ten and Gary made frantic love to her while she closed her eyes and thought of smooth polished wood and clear glass. Gary smelled permanently of grease, oil and sweat, though he showered every night.

She could only keep up with the housework by creeping out of bed after he'd fallen asleep and doing the less noisy and more controversial jobs; changing the wardrobe paper and polishing the windows. The vacuuming was done in the evenings before Gary came in from work. In this way, she managed to keep the dirt and the ravening mites at bay.

Joyce watched from behind her pink ruched blinds as Zoe went out to work each morning. Zoe knew Gary had been to see Joyce and told her to stay away from his wife; it seemed cruel, when Joyce had been the one to warn her about the need to fight dirt. And when she'd taught her about proper cleaning.

Week after week Zoe led her double life, pretending acquiescence but cleaning through the night, going to work and then returning to the flat for more cleaning. Each evening, the air in her home was so thick with creatures and detritus that she went into a surplus store and bought herself a zip-fronted one-piece camouflage suit, goggles and a face mask. Safe in this protective gear, she could dust, polish, vacuum and scrub until she heard Gary's key turn in the lock. Then she'd rush into the bathroom, hide her outfit and get under the shower. Sometimes she fantasised about killing Gary, or pretended he'd crashed his car.

One morning, she went out to find Joyce scrubbing the front steps. She tried to sidle past Joyce's hand as it whizzed round, pushing the scrubbing brush in hectic circles. But Joyce put out a soft, damp hand to grasp Zoe's. Pulling herself to her feet, she leaned against the railings and looked at Zoe with her large, sad eyes. 'Zoe, I should have told you before. We're supposed to take turns each doing these steps. Can you do them next week? Fourteen steps. It's a lot for me on my own.'

Zoe blushed. 'I didn't know, Joyce. I'll start Saturday.'

'Good girl. Can you whitestone the edges like I do, and the paving stone just in front of the gate? It gives it that finished look.'

Zoe promised. At work, she locked herself in the ladies and cried. She cried because she was tired, and because although she kept down the number of house-dust mites, the survivors seemed to be getting larger. As big as small crabs, some of them, with gaping mouths full of rotten teeth and vicious claws. Sometimes, the larger ones got stuck in the pipe of the vacuum cleaner and she had to poke a stick up the pipe. She'd feel the stick strain against the creature's shell, then a splintering and the end of the stick would be touching softness, all resistance gone. Although she loathed the creatures, killing them this way made her retch. She cried because Gary smelled awful, looked permanently soiled as though he could do with a good bleaching and wanted to touch her all the time.

That Friday, Gary said he'd booked tickets for a coach outing from the pub the next day. Zoe smiled and planned to get up at six in the morning to clean the steps before he woke up. At six o'clock, she slipped out of bed, got dressed in the kitchen and picked up her bucket of soapy water, scrubbing brush and cloth. She remembered with a pang that she'd forgotten to buy a whitestone, and a particularly repulsive house-dust mite peered from behind the fridge, sneered at her and scuttled away.

Zoe opened the front door and started scrubbing the steps with a whish and a whizz of the brush and a slap and whoosh of the floorcloth. She'd only scrubbed three steps when Gary's feet appeared, standing on her work. She said furiously, 'Get off, Gary.'

Instead, he kicked the bucket and brush into the basement area, grabbed Zoe by the wrist and dragged her upstairs.

He said, 'She's been getting at you again, hasn't she? I'll sort that cow out, once and for all.'

He ran downstairs and banged on Joyce's door. Zoe heard the door open and Gary shouting, though his words were indistinct. She heard Joyce shuting back, then Gary got louder and Joyce's door slammed shut. Gary came upstairs and tried to cuddle Zoe. 'She won't bother you again, love. Let's go back to bed, sod the outing.'

There was practically a whole teaspoonful of grease and grime behind Gary's ear. She pushed him away and went into the sitting room.

Later, she said, 'You don't understand, Gary. It's all right when I'm outside, or at work. It's when I'm in the flat. I see lumps of dust falling on the furniture and the floor. They make a plopping noise, like fireworks bursting.'

Gary said he'd take her to the doctor.

The doctor looked into Zoe's eyes with his light. He said he couldn't see anything wrong but she'd better have an appointment for the eye hospital.

'It's not my eyes,' Zoe said stubbornly. 'I see dust mites as well.

They have big mouths with horrible jagged teeth, and they pick up all the dirt and stuff with their pincers, and they eat it.'

The doctor didn't look up. 'If you don't hear in a month, come back to me.'

That night, Ted came upstairs. He stood looking sheepishly at his feet, not noticing a huge lump of soot falling from his sleeve into Zoe's chips. She pushed her plate away.

Ted said, 'I've come about the steps. Joyce is in a right state. She's always had the steps cleaned every week, ever since we came here in 1941. The people who used to live here never minded taking their turn. She's driving me up the wall. Couldn't you see your way to doing them, Zoe? I'll pay if you like.' He put his hand in his trouser pocket and produced some coins covered in chunks of grey fluff.

Zoe said, 'It's Gary. He won't let me.'

'Too bloody right I won't,' Gary said. 'She's off her marbles as it is, told the doctor she can see all these little animals walking about. And your Joyce should be put away, Ted. You told me yourself she's cracked. No way am I going to let Zoe scrub the steps, it's not right.'

'I could swill them down every week,' Zoe offered. 'I don't mind.'

'No,' Ted said sadly. 'She wouldn't have that.'

'That's it,' Gary said, standing up. 'That's enough about steps.'

'Well, no harm in asking,' Ted said, smiling wistfully. 'I'll see you down the pub, Gaz.'

The next night, and every night afterwards for four months, Joyce could be heard scrubbing the steps long after Zoe and Gary had gone to bed. The noise kept Gary awake, so Zoe couldn't get up to do her cleaning.

Gary said, 'Ignore the silly cow, she'll soon get fed up.'

Not only did Joyce not get fed up but she started to incorporate the cleaning of the hallway into her nocturnal scrubbing. Every night, she scrubbed and swished and whooshed her way up the steps and along the hall, then up the stairs to Zoe's front door. She banged her brush against the door itself, chipping the paint.

Gary spoke to Ted in the pub, and Ted said Joyce now insisted that the steps and the hall had got to be done daily, and she couldn't spare the time from her other cleaning to do them at a sociable hour. Once or twice (Ted said) he'd been phoned in the middle of the night by irate neighbours; this didn't matter, he said stoically – he couldn't get to sleep anyway.

Zoe lay in bed beside Gary, listening to Joyce's hurt feelings propelling her up the steps and across the floor of the hallway. Listening to the hiss and plop of falling dirt, the scrambling of dust mites towards the site of the fall (she was sure they were blind) and the constant sound of munching. While Gary swore, Zoe fretted about falling behind with her own housework, thanks to Joyce. Sometimes there was so much mess in the flat, so many dust mites creeping and feasting, she had to phone in sick so she could stay home and catch up.

Gary was talking about going to see Jake at the housing association, or to a solicitor, when Joyce died on the basement stairs. Zoe said she'd heard Ted shout at Joyce, then a thumping noise, then silence. Gary looked away and said, 'Poor old Ted wouldn't hurt a fly. You're imagining things again.'

Zoe didn't think so.

Joyce's daughter organised the funeral. Afterwards, she took Ted away to live in Hammersmith, leaving Joyce buried miles from anyone in Wimbledon.

It took Zoe hours to get to Wimbledon and back on a bus. She left the building society because she had to visit Joyce every day. She had to make sure nothing interfered with Joyce's white marble headstone or the white chippings that covered her grave. Every day, she cleaned Joyce's white marble with special cleaning mixture she made from bicarbonate of soda, a squeeze of lemon juice, water and salt; averting her eyes from the dirty, unenlightened people who cleaned their loved one's headstones with thick bleach, straight from the bottle. Then she tidied the graves nearest to Joyce's so that Joyce wouldn't be affronted by scruffy neighbours. When everything was done, Zoe put her cleaning mixture, water bottle, trowel, dustpan and brush into a plastic bin liner and went home to scrub the steps and the passage.

After she started with the psychiatrist, Gary left her alone. Zoe was pleased when he started ostracising her, she hoped he'd meet someone and leave.

She stopped seeing the dust mites and the swooping, floating dirt in her home; then she realised they'd migrated to Joyce's flat, which her daughter had locked up and left without so much as taking an ornament or lace doily as a keepsake, let alone those beautiful ruched blinds. Just in time, Zoe had seen her floorboards begin to bulge as the mites, having filled every room of Joyce's flat from floor to ceiling, tried to burst through.

Travelling to the cemetery, cleaning her own flat and Joyce's and then telling lies to the bored psychiatrist each week, kept Zoe busy. He'd ask how she was, she'd answer 'Fine.' Keeping her cracked, worktorn hands out of sight. She had to do the steps and the hallway every day; if she missed, she'd hear Joyce all night through, whirring, whooshing, sloshing and slapping away with her scrubbing brush and floorcloth. She couldn't tell Gary, in case he told the psychiatrist. The only thing to do was keep up, keep up no matter how tired she felt and even if she never slept for the rest of her life.

She managed to save some time by eating only invalid food and a little honey, and discovered she could keep this food completely germ-free by screwing the lids on tight and boiling the jars. Even Joyce hadn't thought of that, Zoe thought.

After a time, she even hit on the idea of starving the house-dust mites by catching and eating falling pieces of dust before they could settle.

THE OWNER

Michael Marshall Smith

In a remarkably short time, Michael Marshall Smith has established himself as the owner of a singularly compelling voice in the field of unsettling fiction.

His story 'The Dark Land' – an everyday tale of two men carrying an old bicycle – appeared in Nick Royle's excellent *Darklands* collection (1991) winning the British Fantasy Society's best short story award for 1992. The previous year Michael won the same award for 'The Man Who Drew Cats' plus the Icarus Award for best newcomer. At one stage he may well have worried that he could soon have more awards than he had stories published.

Michael was born in 1965 in Cheshire but spent most of his childhood in the United States, South Africa and Australia, returning to the United Kingdom when he was ten years old. Recent projects include working on screenplays, short stories and a new novel. His eagerly awaited first novel, *Only Forward*, is due from Grafton in March 1994.

He doesn't really have any superstitions . . . although he has been known to have the same problems with locks as the hapless protagonist in this tale.

When she noticed that she'd been staring at the flame from her lighter for more than five minutes, spinning the wheel time and time again in a mindless daze, Jane realised it was time to go to bed.

She looked across at her clock on the filing cabinet. 12.35 a.m. Letting her head loll back she heard the bones crack in her neck and gazed upwards for a moment, summoning up the energy to move. For reasons best known to himself the owner had wallpapered the ceiling, and it was coming apart in a thin line down the middle. When she tilted her head back upright she could see the crack in the plaster of the wall by the window, a crack that was the baby sister of one running down the wall by the kitchen. Compared to the carpet or the upholstery on the uncomfortable sofa the paintwork was in reasonably good nick, but it was still far from perfect.

One hundred and thirty pounds a week. Seventy-seven pence an hour. Jesus Christ.

While she waited for the computer to finish juggling 0s and 1s she stood with her mug at the window, looking down into the garden of the first floor flat. In the thin moonlight the few pieces of heavy iron furniture were picked out in soft glints. One of the white chairs had been half painted black in a desultory way, making it look like a frozen Dalmatian in the half-light. The set looked like some odd tableau, the kind of thing the self-proclaimed avant garde at college would have celebrated as unconscious art.

In the week since she'd moved into 51 St Augustine's Road Jane hadn't spoken to the young couple who owned the ground floor flat, and her most frequent thought concerning them was a desire that they muzzle their two children to put a stop to their regular screaming competitions. In fact, she hadn't spoken to anyone in the building. They never seemed to be in. Mail came and went from the downstairs hallway, and she sometimes heard voices and thumps at night from the flats above and opposite. That was all. It was like living in the *Marie Celeste*.

The computer pinged to signify that it had finished closing down, and Jane reached behind to turn it off. As she walked across to the tiny kitchen to rinse her mug the floorboards creaked massively as they always did. The boards in the living room and hallway were right at the top of the list of things which irritated the hell out of her about her new flat, and the tiny kitchen full of hideous seventies cutlery was up there on the list too. Her mug was the only thing in there which was hers.

When she walked back out of the kitchen the floorboards in the centre of the living room squealed extravagantly again.

'At least I don't live underneath,' she muttered quietly to herself, and grinned for a moment, suddenly feeling a little better. Time to go to bed. If she kept staying up so late she was bound to get tired, and if she was tired she was bound to feel grumbly. And there was no point doing that. Upwards and onwards.

In the hallway she clicked the catch down, then pushed it again as hard as she could, counting quickly to eight out loud. It was a source of more than a little irritation to her that she seemed to feel compelled to do this. She wasn't especially concerned about the prospect of intruders, and the house's main door was double-locked. So why this big thing over the lock?

She pushed down on the catch once more, and counted to eight again twice, maintaining the pressure throughout. Then she twisted the knob hard, reassuring herself that the door was indeed locked. It was, unsurprisingly, but she twisted it again, counting to eight three times to make sure.

In the bedroom she undressed quickly and hopped beneath the duvet. She smoked her customary final cigarette propped up on one elbow, looking round the room. She hadn't got round to moving any of the furniture in the bedroom, had simply stowed her clothes and left it at that. It was actually the biggest room in the small flat, unhelpfully; as all she was likely to be doing in it in the immediate future was going to sleep, she would have preferred an extra couple of feet on the living room. A large bedroom seemed too much like a taunt.

Catching yet another negative thought romping through her head, Jane stuck out a mental foot and tripped it up. Christ, she thought, what a wingebag. Forget it. In fact, shut up and go to sleep. Turning the light off she rolled on to her side and snuggled up into the duvet. At least the pillows were good and thick.

A few minutes later she was on the edge of sleep when there was a creaking sound. When it came again, louder, her eyes flicked wide open, staring at the wall. The creak sounded as if it was coming from the hallway.

Then voices boomed from the hallway outside the door, and the light in the corridor flicked on, sending shadows through the pane of glass over her front door and into the bedroom.

The boards obviously stretched out from her hallway into the corridor. The people returning to the flat opposite had set them off. That was all.

Jane closed her eyes and headed back towards sleep.

She felt much better when she got up the next morning. It was genuinely pointless, she realised, dwelling on things. There was no problem in the world that could be solved by feeling depressed about it, and the world was a much drabber and more dangerous place when you were feeling down.

Her state of Genial Positiveness took a bit of a lurch when she discovered that there was no hot water. Again. Swearing vigorously she twisted the tap off and stalked into the kitchen to boil the kettle.

Before leaving the flat she stood on the creaking floorboards in the hallway for a moment, checking the lock. Her ritual had ended up loosening the lock in her previous front door, and she didn't want to do the same here. It seemed fine though, reassuringly sturdy.

A man in overalls was touching up the paint on the steps outside the house. She wondered briefly who'd hired him, and then dismissed the thought.

When she walked into reception at QQCA, Whitehead was standing in the middle of the main office area, smugly surveying his empire. On seeing Jane he stared theatrically at his watch.

'Bright and early this morning,' he said, surprising Jane, who'd been expecting a dose of his running joke about part-timers sneaking in at the last moment. She glanced at the clock to see that it was only 9.50, and that she was ten minutes ahead of schedule.

'Keep forgetting I don't have to leave so early,' she smiled.

'How is the new flat? Compact and bijou?'

'Compact, mainly. Compact and expensive.' As Jane started to walk down the corridor towards her office Whitehead joined her, heading towards his own spacious lair at the far end.

'Ought to buy, you know,' he opined unhelpfully. 'Buying's the thing.'

'So everyone tells me,' said Jane. They did, and it was beginning to piss her off. They paused briefly outside the door to Jane's room.

'I'll pop in a bit later,' said Whitehead, 'See how you're getting on.' Then he ducked into his own office, where his phone was ringing. He seemed to spend most of the day on the phone, reassuring people that the association he ran really did have a purpose. Up until recently Jane had been his right-hand person in that endeavour, and it wasn't something she missed.

Walking into her room she took her Filofax out and got straight to phoning Klass 1 Accommodation. It was only as she sat listening to the phone ringing that she noticed something had happened to the office.

A desk had been placed along the wall with the window in it, and a computer terminal sat squarely on its empty surface. Not only that, but one of her shelves had been unceremoniously cleared, its contents stuffed into crevices in the shelf above. As she waited for an answer Jane reached out and pulled one of her software manuals from where it had been wedged. The cover was crumpled and torn.

When Victor, the tall and elegant Indian half of Klass 1's double act, eventually answered the phone Jane was too distracted to be properly cross about the hot water. The letting agent expressed fulsome sympathy, tutted, and promised to get something done about the boiler that very day. Smiling a little, she replaced the phone, and then went back to frowning as she took in the room once more.

As she stood in the kitchen area, waiting for the kettle to boil and smoking her third cigarette of the day, she was joined by Egerton. Her heart sank, as it always did.

'Morning!' he sang, face beaming with rosy-cheeked and idiot good humour, 'And how are you!'

Jane had tried long and hard to work out quite why Egerton irritated her so much. Her provisional conclusion was that it was partly his continual chirping banter, partly the fact that he swanned about the place as if he owned it, partly that he had a ten-word job title and yet seemed to do damn all, and partly that his hair was so bloody curly. But mainly it was just that he was incredibly irritating.

Egerton yanked the lid off the kettle and peered into it, checking the amount of water inside. He looked like he was appearing in a pantomime for mentally handicapped children. Satisfied, he nodded curtly, slammed the lid back on, and went back to beaming at Jane.

'How was your weekend?' he half shouted.

'Fine,' she replied, dismissing a conversational sally that had palled for her after the first fifty or so Monday mornings she'd spent at QQCA. 'I couldn't help noticing that there appears to be another desk in my office.'

'That's right,' Egerton confirmed cheerily, nodding several times, as if she'd complimented him on something. After a pause in which Jane realised that he really didn't understand the subtext of her observation, she continued.

'Why?'

'You're going to have company. Didn't Whitehead tell you?'

'No.'

Egerton waggled his eyebrows at her, still beaming, and then, coffee in hand, sailed off down the corridor just as Whitehead emerged from his office.

'I gather I'm going to be sharing my office,' she said.

'That's right,' Whitehead nodded. 'Bit of a reshuffle after the staff meeting on Friday. Decided to reorganise things a little. Getting a bit crowded in the main office, so . . .'

He trailed off smoothly, as if there was no more to be said. As far as he was concerned, there obviously wasn't, but making an effort to speak as conversationally as possible, Jane pressed him.

'But why my office? It's not the largest.'

'True, but you are only here three days a week now, and not really a member of staff any more, so . . .'

Jane nodded, to show she understood. She understood all right. After three years of doing half of Whitehead's job for him she was now just a freelancer, and bought labour sat where it was put and did what it was told.

'I see. So who . . .?'

'Camilla.'

'*Camilla*? But she's only been with us, with you, for three months.'

'I know, but she's coming on very well. And she's used a machine like yours before, so . . .'

'Isn't she mainly a secretary though?' Mainly an ambitious, flirtatious and smug little smart arse was what she meant, but tried not to let it show. Whitehead finished manufacturing his coffee and floated back in the direction of his office, where the phone was once more ringing.

'Won't do any harm to have someone else who knows how to use the beast. Can't have all our eggs in one basket, can we?'

Jane stared after him for a moment, and then went into her office to work.

By the time she was standing on the Northern Line platform, waiting to go home, Jane had calmed down slightly. The buzzing irritation that had built up in her during the day had burst the moment she left QQCA, leaving her feeling empty and tired.

Sodding Camilla. Minutes after her conversation with Whitehead, the secretary/flavour of the month employee had slipped into Jane's office and settled herself at the new desk. She had then spent the rest of the day alternating between hammering out typing at rock concert volume and looking over Jane's shoulder as she finished the layout for the inside of the QQCA's new brochure. At one point she had asked Jane if there wasn't an easier way of doing what she was currently engaged in. The politeness of Jane's reply, Jane felt, should have shut the girl up for the rest of the day. But it didn't.

As she stood on the tube, buffeted by meaty bodies and smothered by lank hair, Jane tried to rationalise her feelings about the girl. She was nineteen. She wanted to get on. There was nothing wrong with that. The fact that her star was in the ascendant at the same time as Jane's took a nose dive was not her fault. Jane closed her eyes and tried to tune out the people around her, tried to grope once more for Genial Positiveness.

When she opened them the tube was stationary at Mornington Crescent, and on impulse she got out.

Walking down the road she fought hard against the feeling that this probably wasn't a good idea. After all, they were supposed to be friends, and friends called on each other, didn't they? She stopped at the flower-seller at the corner and bought a small bunch of irises.

Standing at the entryphone she pushed down another surge of doubt and pressed Chris's bell. After a pause Chris's voice said, 'Hello,' accompanied by the familiar whine of feedback.

'Hi,' she said brightly, her heart beating irritatingly hard, 'It's me.' There was a pause. 'Jane,' she added, less brightly.

'Oh, right, hi.'

'Are you going to let me in then?'

'Yeah . . . yeah, sorry.'

The door buzzed and she pushed it open.

The door was open when she reached the top of the stairs and she walked straight in.

'I picked up some flowers,' she said, smiling, 'because I know you never bother . . .'

She trailed off. Chris was standing awkwardly by the door, hands thrust deep into his pockets. Sitting on the sofa was a tall and deeply tanned girl, power-dressed in a deep green suit that went perfectly with carelessly beautiful blonde hair. Jane faltered, and came to a halt a couple of feet into the room.

'Well,' said Chris heartily, 'Jane, Nikki, Nikki, Jane.'

'Hello,' the girl said, and before she dropped her head Jane noticed just how perfect her cheekbones were.

'Nikki was just passing,' volunteered Chris with elaborate blandness. Jane nodded, not looking at either of them. She was looking at the table under the window. On it stood Chris's large vase, filled with a huge bunch of uncut flowers, still in their paper. The same paper that was wrapped around hers.

'Well,' Nikki said into the silence. 'I must be off.'

When Chris returned from seeing her to the door he went to some lengths to convince Jane that Nikki really had just dropped in. He needn't have bothered: Jane believed him. Her shock had simply been that of seeing her for the first time, seeing the girl who previously had only been the shadowy cause of thirty different kinds of hurt. Now that she didn't have Chris either it didn't seem to matter so much.

Yes it did. And he'd lied, another one. Nikki *was* more attractive than her.

The conversation limped along for a while, each turning seeming to lead down a blind alley, each dead end showing how few roads were left between them. At first she said her flat was fine, then admitted how much she hated it, how tired she was of living between someone else's walls surrounded by someone else's furniture, of hiring her life. When Chris asked her why she didn't buy somewhere she couldn't help reminding him that she'd wanted to. She'd wanted to buy somewhere with him.

Each time she said something like that he sat back, a patient expression on his face, a face that said he was trying in the face of difficult odds. And each time she brought herself to say something that wasn't small talk she felt a twist of resentment. He didn't deserve to have her talking about her feelings to him. He wasn't close enough to her any more.

In the end she stood up.

'This was a mistake,' she said firmly, and shook her head at him when he halfheartedly disagreed. 'I'm obviously not ready for friendship yet. I'll try again later.'

It wasn't until she was at the door that she noticed she was still clutching her bunch of irises. She thrust them at him.

'Here,' she said. 'To add to your collection.'

She spent the evening on the sofa trying to read, but really just trying not to think. Whenever her mind drifted from the words in front of her, her head was suddenly full of pictures, fragments of scenes. Nikki, laughing naturally and beautifully, seen in profile against the white wall of Chris's flat. Nikki, holding something playfully out of reach, and just Chris's hand and wrist as he stretched for it. Each time she shook herself away from the images her eyes searched around the room for something to hold them, something to bring her back into herself.

But there was nothing there. Her books, her objects were like moss on a pavement, toys in an empty playground. All they did was accentuate how much the place wasn't hers, how much it was the owner's. It was as if he'd seeped into the walls.

The phone rang, surprising her so much she cried out. She leapt across to it, heart thumping. It was for Mr Gillack. The owner. She gave the caller Klass 1's number and clunked the phone bad-temperedly back down.

It took her five goes at the lock before she was satisfied that evening. She pushed down the catch and counted ploddingly to eight, leaning down on every number. She did it again, and then once more, twisting the knob. She got as far as the bedroom door and then had to go back again. She undid the lock, showed herself it was open, and then pushed the catch down, watching the bolt slide through the crack between the door and the frame. Then she pushed it down hard for two more counts of eight. She knew it was no good asking herself why she did this. It was better just to get on with it.

When she opened the wardrobe to hang up her blouse something at the back made her start. Then she realised it was just Mr Gillack's most hideous possession, a large champagne bottle with a huge frond of pampas grass sticking out of it, which she'd thrust at the back of the large walk-in wardrobe within ten minutes of moving in. She moved one of her coats to hide it more thoroughly.

In the morning she spent a good fifteen minutes under the shower, braising her skin, waking herself up.

She felt better. As she roughly swept the soap she cuffed herself around the psyche, pushing and prodding in the way she knew sometimes worked. It was time to accept that Chris was history, water under the bridge. He wasn't even going out with the girl he'd been unfaithful to her with. It was all over. Finished.

She was squeezing the soap so hard in her hand that on one particularly dramatic sweep up her arm it squirted out and ricocheted off the tiles on the wall to smack her in the chest. For a moment she felt like a hurt child, as if the world had unexpectedly slapped her, and then she burst out laughing.

By the time she was finishing her tea and simultaneously slipping on her shoes, she felt positive enough to even wonder if her lock ritual was something to do with the last year. She could remember the night Chris had told her about Nikki, could recall clearly her feeling of complete and utter shock in the face of something so unexpected, so surprising, something so much at odds with the way she thought things had been. When you thought you knew your world and suddenly found out that you didn't know anything at all, maybe you came to doubt your own perception, to distrust your memory. Maybe you had to keep suspecting things just for your own peace of mind, keep reassuring yourself again and again in rituals of self-protection.

Remembering for once that she lived closer to the centre now, Jane glanced towards the filing cabinet to check the time. The clock wasn't there. Puzzled, she slowly panned round the room until she found it. It was on the bookshelf. Shaking her head at her own absent-mindedness she returned it to its proper place and left for work.

When she arrived at QQCA Jane went straight to the kitchen to make her first cup of coffee. The Northern Line had pulled off one of its occasional bouts of suspicious efficiency and she was both early and feeling relaxed. Perhaps today she would be able to make an effort, get Camilla on her side.

These feelings drained instantaneously out of her when she passed her office. Her machine was on, and Camilla, a model of bright young ambition, was sitting at it, manual in hand.

Jaw clenched, Jane made her coffee and walked into the office with it. She stood over Camilla for almost a minute before the girl noticed, so absorbed was she in invading someone else's territory. When she eventually noticed she smiled without a trace of guilt and moved, rather than retreated, back to her own desk. Jane sat down, turned her back on her, and started work to a soundtrack of incessant typing.

The morning passed slowly in a low monotone of boredom and irritation. Halfway through the phone rang, and Jane reached out for it without looking. When her hand reached the cradle the sound of typing had stopped, and the phone was no longer there.

'QQCA,' sang Camilla. 'Certainly. May I say who's calling? One moment.' She held the call and said, unnecessarily loudly, 'It's for you, Jane. A *personal* call.'

Jane took the phone. She unheld the call and found that it was Sue on the line before she noticed that the din of typing had not recommenced. She turned to Camilla, who was covertly watching her, and the girl started to type immediately.

She wanted to talk to Sue, who was an old friend and someone who might understand the way she was feeling, but not with Camilla in the background. It made her too conscious of the fact that this was office time.

Instead she arranged to call her in the evening and settled back once more to her screen. The new QQCA brochure was still at least a day's work away from completion, and each time she looked at it she felt an increasing sense of dull frustration, bored beyond belief at the task of designing yet another leaflet saying the same things in the same way for the same organisation. If she did anything unconventional it would be rejected by one of the innumerable committees, but if it looked the same as last time it would seem that anyone could do her job. She couldn't afford for it to look that way, escpecially now.

Egerton popped his head in during the afternoon. Grinning inanely he asked Camilla if she'd like a cup of tea.

'Hmm, lovely,' she replied, turning and favouring him with a winning smile. Egerton disappeared and then a beat later his head reappeared, less energetically this time.

'Jane?' he said.

She stopped at Sainsbury's on the way home, and struggled

back up Agar Grove and St Augustine's Road with a heavy bag in each hand, sure that her arms were actually lengthening. The bags were full of things she liked to eat, including a tray of fresh brownies, and standing at the checkout she'd been filled with a complex mixture of feelings: guilt at buying so much fattening food, and a sad defiance. She could afford to put on a few pounds and, after all, who was there to give a shit. If no one else was going to spoil her, she'd do it herself.

Some ghost or phantom that inhabited the house liked to sort the mail in the morning, and when she stood outside the door to her flat, fumbling for her keys, she saw that a pile of letters had been propped up against her door. It was all for the owner, apart from a Barclaycard bill.

There was a message on her answering machine. It was for Mr Gillack.

Jane had purposefully not brought a copy of the brochure file home with her, feeling that she ought to get into the habit of only working the time she was paid for. But as she sat on the grubby sofa letting banal television wash in front of her, she wished she had some work to do, anything to inject some purpose into the wasteland of the flat.

Instead she ate three brownies, swearing each was to be the last, and tried moving the furniture in the bedroom around. But no new arrangement seemed any better, and the pieces of heavy pine furniture seemed to feel a pull from their original positions, as if the owner's arrangement was the only one they would accept. In the end, hot and irritable, she left them as they had been.

Mid-evening she called Sue back, but had barely time to tell her about the way things were going at work before she heard a doorbell down the line. Sue's boyfriend Steve had turned up unexpectedly to take her out. As she signed off Sue sounded delighted and alive, and Jane wondered if Chris had ever had the same effect on her. Without thinking she picked the phone up again and her finger was millimetres from the programmed button that would dial his number before she stopped herself.

At eleven she realised that there wasn't any point staying up any longer. She did quite well on the lock, only checking it three times. Then she went to bed.

Half an hour later she found herself suddenly awake without knowing why. Then there was another creak, and another, even louder. Turning very slowly in her bed, feeling her heart beating heavily in her ears, Jane held her breath. There was another creak from the hallway, this one quieter. It was followed by three more, each soft and at regular intervals, as if someone was walking in her hallway. Then they stopped.

There was no sound of the door of the flat opposite being opened this time, and Jane remained poised, lying tense as a board. In the end she knew she wouldn't be able to sleep unless she checked it out, and quietly slid out of bed.

Peering into the hallway she saw a light in the bathroom, a kind of blue glow. Keeping her feet at the edges of the corridor, where the boards creaked less, she crept towards it and pushed the door open tentatively.

The light was just that of a streetlight seeping through the blind. Sighing out heavily with a relief that made her feel silly, she went back to bed.

'What the *hell* . . .'

'Profanity, Jane?' said Whitehead's voice from the doorway.

Jane looked up from her screen. She was early again, and still had the office to herself, as Camilla usually got in at ten on the dot. Somehow for her that was punctuality, not 'sloping in at the last moment' as it would have been for Jane.

'Someone's been messing around with the file.'

'Messing around?' asked Whitehead airily, coming closer, hands held behind his back.

Struggling to keep her voice steady Jane gestured at the screen.

'There's lines all over the place, the rest of the copy's been typed in, it's . . . Christ: the graphics have all been shifted around . . .'

'It's been finished, you mean.'

Jane turned to stare at him.

'Finished?'

'Yes,' said Whitehead, and then expanded with patronising clarity, 'those things which remained to be done have been done.'

'You knew about this?'

'Well.'

'Camilla, yes?' Finally furious, Jane turned back to the screen.

'She stayed late last night, decided to have a go. I think she's done rather well, don't you?'

Jane took a deep breath, and decided to let herself be angry.

'Two things. Everyone here works on computers. They have *their* files on *their* computers. Now if *I* hung around late at night messing around with their work, I'd get the sack. Camilla does it, and she gets a brownie point.'

'She wasn't "messing around". She asked permission.'

'And you *gave* it?'

'Yes.' Whitehead looked calmly back down at her. 'And the second thing?'

'These lines aren't aligned properly. I'm going to have to redo all of them. This text isn't locked to the baseline, so redo that. Moving that graphic has skewed the whole layout, which will have to be put back. Tidying all that up will take me three times as long as it would have taken me to do it in the first place. I can't even go back to the way I left it last night, because she's made the changes to the master copy. Yes,' Jane spat, feeling dangerously light-headed, 'she's done *really* well.'

'Jane.'

'Doing this isn't as easy as it looks, you know.'

'I *know* it isn't,' said Whitehead, abruptly and transparently switching into conciliatory mode. 'Look. She's obviously got a bit to learn, and she shouldn't have altered the master. I'll tell her off for that, okay? She's *learning*.' He smiled meaninglessly at her and left.

'Yeah,' said Jane, to his back.

Later, as she stood waiting for the kettle to boil, Egerton wheeled up with her cheque for the month.

'Re: your invoice of the twenty-eighth!' he warbled and then, though he'd written the cheque himself, took a long unnecessary look at what it said before handing it over, as if the sum on it caused him actual physical pain. As he strode off again, fingers clicking on the end of arms swinging like a demented toy soldier's, Jane noticed that Whitehead was standing talking to Camilla in the main office area at the other end of the corridor. As she watched he made a comically cross face and mimed angry speech. Camilla laughed, her head thrown back, pretty in profile against the white wall.

When she left at five Jane was feeling marginally better, purely because her three days were up and she was almost done with QQCA for the week.

'Have a nice weekend,' howled Egerton from his position at the fax machine. He seemed to like standing there, watching the incoming tedium as if it was crucial news from some distant battlefront.

'I'm back in on Friday,' she said, managing a smile for him. 'Board presentation.'

'All set, are we?' said Whitehead, looming up as she put on her coat. 'All our lines in the right place?'

Jane looked at him, recognising this kind of joke, and for a moment it was as if she was still an employee there, still Whitehead's valued aide.

'I think so.'

'Good,' he smiled, 'see you Friday.'

She smiled back and headed for the door.

'Wait for me!' called Camilla.

In the lift Jane kept silent for a moment, then realised it would be rude not to speak. She didn't care in the least about hurting Camilla's feelings, but she didn't want to allow herself to be churlish. The most harm people can do to you, she realised, is making you behave in ways you can't respect.

'Bit early for you, isn't it?' she said, which seemed a good compromise between remaining silent and not giving an inch.

'Yes I know. My boyfriend's got us tickets to see *Les Mis*.' The door opened and they walked across the foyer. 'Have you seen it?'

'No,' said Jane. Camilla smiled smugly, not realising that wild horses couldn't have dragged Jane anywhere near bloody *Les Misérables*.

Outside Jane was about to walk off when Camilla stopped.

'I'm sorry if I messed up your work,' she said, 'I'm a butterfingers really. Don't know what I'm doing.'

The insincerity with which she spoke was almost a taunt, and Jane thought, Right: I don't have to put up with that.

'I think you know *exactly* what you're doing,' she replied, and walked away.

As she hurriedly squeezed the teabag in her mug Jane reached across for a brownie, humming. A programme Sue had worked on was about to start, and she didn't want to miss the opening sequence, which was apparently one of the best. She was looking forward to the programme, and still feeling chipper at having called Camilla's bluff. Best of all, she didn't have to go to QQCA the next day.

With the brownie an inch from her lips, she stopped. There was a bite missing. Surprised, she stared at it, trying to remember when she might have done that. Last night she'd eaten three, but finished them all. Not this morning, surely: she couldn't face chocolate before lunchtime.

Still pondering, a small frown on her face, Jane settled on to the sofa. The adverts finished and a programme started, but it wasn't Sue's. Confused, she looked up at the filing cabinet to check the time.

The clock wasn't there.

Still chewing slowly, Jane looked around the room, and found it. The clock was back on the bookcase. She stared at it for a long time. She couldn't remember putting it there, and thought she remembered putting it back on the filing cabinet.

Suddenly she felt frightened, in a vague, formless way, as if some infinitely deep bedrock had shifted. On impulse she quickly got up and sat at the desk. She pressed a button on the phone and waited for it to connect.

'Oh, hi . . .' she said, unsure of what to say, just needing some contact, something to tie her back down.

'. . . sorry but I'm not here at the moment. If you leave a message I'll . . .' – here there was a pause, as if Chris had been distracted by something – 'I'll get back to you. It's going to beep any second.'

Jane pressed the pips down and dialled again. This time she was listening for it, and heard it more clearly. Chris had paused because someone was making him laugh. If you listened carefully you could hear him saying 'Shh,' and the sound of female laughter.

In the hallway she reached out for the lock, preparing herself to go through the ritual again and seal herself safely in, but then stopped. No, she thought, I'm not going to do that. I know what's done this to me, and I'm not going to let it. She reached out and simply pushed the catch down.

As she lay in bed, drowsily awakened once more, Jane heard creaking from the hallway again. She closed her eyes, determined to ignore it, but the creak sounded again, much louder this time. Then there was a series of quieter creaks, as there had been the night before. Jane breathed deeply, vowing irritably not to get out into the cold to check it.

Then there was another creak, and her eyes swivelled quickly. That creak hadn't come from the hallway. It sounded as if it came from the boards in the living room. Through the noise of rushing in her ears she heard the sound once more, and this time there was no doubt. It was a board in the living room that had creaked. Moving quietly, Jane, slipped out of bed.

The hallway looked the same as it had the night before, dark with blue light seeping out from the bathroom doorway, but tonight there was something else, a slight flickering. Feeling silly, but knowing she had to check for her own peace of mind, she padded silently down the hall towards the bathroom. Just before she got there she realised that the flickering was reflected on the wall opposite the living room door, and she turned to glance in.

Her televison was on. Her computer was also on, and there was a man sitting at her desk.

He wasn't looking at the computer but sitting side on, legs outstretched, watching the television with the sound turned down. He was drinking coffee out of one of the flat's mugs.

Feeling the tiny hairs on the back of her neck rise in swathes, Jane stared at him. She swallowed, too astounded to be more than very, very frightened.

'Er, hello?' she croaked. There was no response. 'What do you think you're doing?'

The man turned slowly to face her. In his late thirties, he was of medium build and had short dark hair slicked back. There was something odd about his face.

'Watching television,' he said, and then turned back to the screen. Jane took a small step into the living room.

'Who the fuck *are* you?' she said, and was glad to hear that her voice carried anger as well as fear. The man turned his head back towards her, but kept his eyes negligently on the screen.

'The owner,' he said.

'*What?*'

He flicked his eyes lazily towards her. They were calm, unremarkable.

'The owner,' he repeated.

'The hell you are. The owne . . . Mr Gillack is in Belgium. On business. This is *not* your flat.' The man shrugged, and went back to watching the television. 'How did you get in?'

'Through the door,' he said. Jane was trying to remember if she'd put the catch down when suddenly she noticed something by the side of the desk. It was the champagne bottle with the pampas grass in it.

'What the fuck is that doing there?'

'I put it there,' said the man, reaching for something on the desk. He picked it up and took a bite. 'Good brownies.'

Suddenly anger surged to the front of Jane's mind. She was still partly asleep, and confused, and afraid, but the brownies gave her something to hold on to. Whoever he was, those were her brownies and he had no right to be eating them.

'Get out!' she shouted.

'I'm the owner,' the man said. Jane took another step into the room.

'I don't give a toss. Neither you or anyone else has any right to come in here without my permission.' The man simply looked at her mildly, sipping his coffee. 'Get out! GET OUT!'

After a pause he raised his eyebrows and got up slowly. Jane stepped backwards into the hall, and shrank into the bathroom as he passed. The man reached out and slid the catch up before opening the door. He took one step out and then turned, standing facing back in, hands behind his back.

Jane leaped to the door and slammed it in his face. She pushed the catch back down and then feverishly lunged for the small bookcase in the hall, pulling it round to wedge it against the door, spilling books that were not hers all over the floor.

Sobbing quietly she slid down the wall to land in a heap by the door, her leg poked painfully by a hardback book. She snatched the book up and ripped it, pulling the covers off and mangling it, and then hurled it at the wall. She toppled slowly over to the floor to tuck herself up into a foetal position, hugging her legs and crying.

Next morning found her striding up the Pentonville Road at ten o'clock. It was light, it was daytime, and she was furious.

Andrew, the second half of Klass 1 Accommodation, stood up with some trepidation when she swept into their office. He was much shorter than the pony-tailed Victor, and Greek rather than Indian, but just as courtly.

'Er,' he said, 'Oh, Jane, isn't it? St Augustine's Road?'

'Yes,' she said curtly.

'Is there a problem?'

'Yes. There is a problem.'

'Some coffee, I think,' said Victor, rising to assume command. Looking concerned, Andrew set about wielding the kettle. 'What exactly—' started Victor, but Jane cut him off.

'I want to know what the *hell* the owner was doing in my flat last night.' Victor and Andrew looked at each other, and then both looked at Jane.

'I'm sorry?' they said, simultaneously.

'I woke up,' she continued, 'to find Mr Gillack in my living room.'

'What was he doing?' asked Andrew.

'Watching television,' Jane snapped, and Victor held out his hand to Andrew to forestall further questions from him.

'Jane, Mr Gillack is in Belgium at the moment, on business. He isn't due to return until two weeks after your lease runs out.'

'He was in my living room!'

'Victor, is it possible that Mr Gillack might have returned early without informing us?' asked Andrew, handing out coffee.

'He has no right to come into the flat. Not without my permission, and certainly not in the middle of the night.'

'Absolutely not,' said Victor. 'You're sure this, uh, person, was Mr Gillack?'

'Yes. He said he was the owner. He said it several times. The only way he could have got in was with a key.'

'True. Well, this is very irregular. Andrew, do we have a number for Mr Gillack?'

'In Belgium? I think so,' his colleague said, turning to hunt through a chaotic filebox.

'He's not *in* Belgium. He's *here*.'

'Jane,' said Victor calmly and seriously, 'the only means Andrew and I have of contacting Mr Gillack is at his office in Belgium. So we must try that first.' Andrew triumphantly produced the right card, and Jane watched stonily as Victor dialled the number.

'Good morning,' he said after a while, enunciating clearly, 'could I speak with Mr Gillack please?'

'Is he there?' asked Andrew in the pause, and Victor shrugged.

'Is that Mr Gillack? It is. Ah. This is Victor here, from Klass 1. Oh no, everything's fine.' Eyes wide, Victor looked around for inspiration, and caught sight of a Post-it note. 'Just a message. American Express rang for you. Could you call them? No problem. Goodbye.' He put the phone down. 'That was Mr Gillack. He is in Belgium.'

'He was in my flat last night eating my brownies.' Jane felt confused, but adamant. 'Belgium isn't exactly Mars,' she added. 'He could have gone back this morning, or last night. You didn't ask him if he'd been there all the time, did you.'

'It would have been rather difficult.'

'Great. So what am I supposed to do?'

'Well, if it happens again . . .'

'What, if I wake up in the middle of the night to find a man in my flat *again*, you mean?'

'Yes, call the police. Make sure you lock up securely at night.'

'I *do*,' Jane shouted. If they only knew how bloody securely she locked up. Then she stopped short. Had she checked the lock last night? She couldn't remember. She remembered thinking about her ritual earlier on in the evening, but what had she done when she went to bed?

'Also,' concluded Victor, 'you have our number. Call us if there is the slightest cause for concern.'

'I should have spoken to him,' she said, her mind elsewhere. Maybe she hadn't checked it. But she had definitely pushed the catch down. Hadn't she? 'I would have recognised his voice.'

'The fact that he said he was the owner,' offered Andrew, 'that could have been untrue.'

'No. He sat there as if he owned the place, and,' suddenly she went cold, putting something together that she should have realised some time ago, should have known immediately. He'd been in her room. 'The bloody champagne bottle was back in the living room, and it was in my cupboard.'

Victor and Andrew looked at her, like a pair of bemused cats. They had no idea what she was talking about.

'Why would anyone except the owner do that, hm?'

'Jane . . .'

'I know, I know. He was in Belgium. Well, thank you anyway. And yes, you can rest assured that if it happens again you'll know all about it.'

The two men watched her sweep out, and then breathed a sigh of relief.

'What a strange morning,' said Victor.

'Some coffee, I think.'

Jane was still fuming when she got to St Augustine's Road. She was glad to be still angry. If she stopped feeling angry she might have to think about the logistics of what had happened, and she didn't want to do that. She knew what she'd seen. She could remember it clearly. She didn't want to call her memory into question again.

The man in overalls was back, fiddling with a fusebox or something attached to the side of the building's stairs. In the house hallway was a pile of mail, sorted into flats. All the mail for Flat 8 was for Mr Gillack. Jane grabbed it furiously and spun it out into the street, slamming the door after it. She stomped upstairs and opened the door as viciously as she could. The light on the answering machine was on again and she slapped the button.

'Could Mr Gillack call . . .'

'Fuck OFF!' she shouted. A little frightened at herself she put her hands to her ears to blot out the sound of the message and walked jerkily out of the room. Suddenly a thought struck her, and she trotted back outside the house and leaned out over the stairs.

'Do you do locks, by any chance?' she said.

An hour and a half of loud banging later, the man stuck his head into Jane's living room, where she was supergluing the clock to the filing cabinet and humming.

'Miss, I've finished,' he said.

In the hallway she inspected the lock. It looked even more solid than the last one, and the catch went down with an irrevocable clunk. She flicked it up again, and then pushed it down.

'That's your set of keys, and the spares,' the man said, jangling them at her, and then nodded approvingly at the door. 'Good lock that. British.'

'Have you got the old one?' Jane asked, flicking the catch up again. The man nodded out into the hallway. 'Do you mind if I keep it?'

Slightly surprised, he picked it up and gave it to her.

'Nope,' he said. 'It's your lock.'

'No,' she replied, pushing the catch down again, counting to

'Hm? Please what?' Back against the wall, Jane sidled towards the door. 'Please . . . and thank you?' He took a step towards her, blocking the way to the door. 'Please? Please?'

'Please, go away . . .' Jane shrank back as he took another step, staring at his blank, anonymous face. Her neck spasmed wildly and her mouth opened. Her face wanted to cry but she was too frightened.

'Oh I don't think so,' the man said mildly. 'I don't have to go away. I'm the owner.'

Jane's teeth crashed together as her face responded to anger from somewhere inside her. She leant forward from the wall and shouted at him.

'Get out! Get out! GET OUT!!'

'No,' he said, with a winning pout. He took another step towards her and before he could get any closer Jane lunged to the side and got round him. As she ran to the door he turned elegantly and made a swipe for her, tearing her blouse, but she made it past him and into the hallway. She was halfway to the living room before realising that was stupid, and instead swerved towards the door. She grabbed at the chair and yanked at it but it wouldn't budge. The wood from the chair had flowed into the wood of the door, jamming it shut.

As she tugged uselessly at it the owner watched her from the bedroom, smiling indulgently. Just as he started to move towards her she realised she was pulling the chair the wrong way. She pushed it aside and pulled at the door but it wouldn't budge. The owner stepped into the hallway and she grabbed the chair and flung it at him. She tugged frenziedly at the door again and then realised that the catch was down. She flicked it and swung it open just as a hand fell down towards her shoulder.

She moaned as she stumbled out on to the tiny landing, and leapt straight for the stairs. Her heel caught and she fell most of the way down the flight, banging her face against the railing and tearing the nails out of one hand, but she got up as soon as she hit the bottom and careered out into the street.

She found a phone booth and rang a number. As soon as Klass 1's answering machine message started she began to scream at it.

'He's in my flat! He's in my flat! HE'S IN MY FLAT!'

She kept screaming until even she couldn't hear the whisper of her voice.

Camilla reached out and took the brochure proofs from the printer.

'There,' she said. 'And it does look better than hers.'

Whitehead nodded and smiled.

'Good,' he said. 'Now all we need is Jane.'

Camilla looked at her watch. It was ten to four.

'She's cutting it a bit fine, isn't she?'

'She'll be here,' said Whitehead. 'Whatever her faults, she's reliable.'

Jane stepped out of the lift and opened the door to QQCA. As she walked into reception she shook her head slightly. Her hearing appeared to be slightly deadened, and there was a buzzing sound. The office seemed very still, calm with quiet business. People came and went, passing paper. Egerton plucked a piece of paper from the fax machine and marched across the room to drop it heartily on someone's desk. People answered the phones though they weren't ringing, and looked as if they were talking into them. She took a step towards the corridor. Egerton plucked a piece of paper from the fax machine and marched across the room to drop it heartily on someone's desk. Jane blinked at him, watching him stop to answer a phone, his whole body declaring buoyant stupidity. Then he was at the fax machine again and she turned away.

Slowly she walked down the corridor. Behind her she thought she heard the ghost of a voice call her name, call it as a question.

When she looked into the office Whitehead and Camilla turned to smile at her. There was a new plant on Camilla's desk and a poster for Les Misérables on the white wall. Suddenly the buzzing stopped as their faces dropped.

'Jane, what's happened?' Whitehead asked, the lying bastard trying to look concerned as he stared at the blood under her nose and her torn clothes, the bruise on her cheek and her ragged hair. She ignored him.

'Get OUT!' she screamed at Camilla, and swept her arm along the desk. The plant sailed along the surface and flew straight out of the window. As Whitehead lunged with a cry to look out after it Jane ripped the poster from the wall and began tearing it to pieces, arms flailing.

'Jane, please,' Camilla stuttered, cowering.

'Please WHAT?' Jane leant over until her face was right up against hers, until she could see the mascara glistening on her lashes and smell the foundation makeup, and screamed, 'Please can I have EVERYTHING?'

She stuffed a piece of the poster into her mouth and hummed. Whitehead stepped warily towards her.

'Er, Jane . . .'

'*What?*' she said, blowing the pieces out of her mouth at him.

'Perhaps you'd better go home . . .'

She fell towards the door, laughing weakly.

'Go *home*? Go HOME?'

Egerton was in the doorway, staring at her with childish surprise.

'Yes?' she shouted, 'What the fuck do *you* want?' He stumbled backwards, hands held up, and she turned to look once more at the room, at the shelves, at the machine, at the acres of white wall with so many things in front of it and none of them hers. Before she could cry she ran out into the corridor.

The door to Flat 8 was still ajar. She walked in and shut it behind her. The buzzing in her ears was back, and louder, a loud bass hum.

The furniture was back where it had been when she moved in, the champagne bottle in position, his pictures back up on the walls. Her things had disappeared from the bathroom, and shaving foam and aftershave had materialised in its place. The fragments of her mug were gone from the kitchen sink. The bedroom seemed least altered because it had been least changed by her, but her clothes and the photo of Chris were gone.

She walked back into the living room and looked out of the window. It was coming dark outside, and someone had taken the garden furniture and placed it on top of each other so it stood like a sculpture. When she turned the owner stood behind her, hands behind his back like a solicitous waiter.

'Yes?' he smiled.

'I'm going,' she said dully. He looked disappointed with her, and spoke with a slow mocking kindness.

'You *can't* go.'

'I am,' she replied, feeling about four years old.

'Where?' he asked. 'Where are you going to go?'

'I'll find somewhere.'

'You won't. There isn't anywhere.' He started to walk towards her and suddenly her breath was hitching, uneven, because it hurt and she wanted to cry again. She backed away.

'Please . . .'

'Please what? What do you *have*, Jane?' he asked quietly, cocking his head like a robotic dog. 'Some have, some . . . haven't.' Still advancing, he threw his hands out expansively. 'You haven't. Everywhere's somebody's. There's nowhere *to* go.'

Then suddenly he shouted terrifyingly loudly, and Jane flinched as she had just before Chris slapped her the night he left.

'WHERE'S THERE TO GO, JANE?'

She broke and tried to run for the door, but he intercepted her. She darted the other way along the wall, but he got there first. As she slid back and forth along the wall he tracked her and backed her into the corner.

'WHAT DO YOU HAVE, JANE?'

He slammed her against the wall and she fell as the breath punched out of her. He grabbed at her and she rolled and tried to stand but he slammed her over again and leant down towards her, mouth hanging open as he reached to choke her. She fumbled out with her hand and found something and swung it round to smash it on his head.

The champagne bottle didn't break, but bounced out of her hand as he fell with a grunt on top of her. She squirmed away and stumbled towards the door but his hand whipped out and grabbed her ankle, tripping her so that she fell on to the sofa. She tried to pull free but his hand was too strong and snatched up her leg, tugging at her. Scrabbling out with her hand she found the bookcase. The old lock was on it and she grabbed it as his hand wrenched her thigh, turning her round to face him. Blood was seeping down his neck out of his matted hair but he wasn't going to lie down.

'Mine,' he said.

She smashed the lock down into his face, feeling his nose momentarily resist and then spread like butter across his face. For a second his head remained upright, and then he toppled over on to his front.

Jane staggered up, leaning against the wall, watching him. His hands were flapping up and down lightly, like a damaged bird. She stared round the room and could see nothing that was hers, so she grabbed a picture off the wall and threw it at him. The owner's hands started flapping more wildly, beating against the carpet, and he began to make a humming sound that got louder and louder as his whole body began to vibrate violently.

He wasn't going to die. People like him never did.

Scrabbling in her pocket she pulled out her lighter and held it next to the curtain.

'Own this!' she shrieked and spun the wheel. The thin cheap curtains caught fire very quickly, flames pouring up towards the ceiling. Through the billowing smoke Jane limped coughing towards the door, stumbling round the owner, whose whole body was whipping back and forth with an insectile violence that must be tearing every tendon.

She ran out into the hallway and as she wrenched the door open she heard his voice shouting to her from the depths of the fire.

'Where, Jane?'

Victor braked hurriedly. He and Andrew leaped straight out of the doors of the car, but Mr Gillack beat them to it. They'd all been inclined to treat the whole thing as a joke, but to be on the safe side Mr Gillack had come back from Belgium. Suddenly it didn't seem very funny any more.

'I think our commission may have gone down the pan,'

muttered Andrew as they trotted after Mr Gillack towards the blaze.

A policeman brusquely stopped them from getting too close. His manner changed when he heard Mr Gillack was the owner, but still wouldn't let them go any nearer. Mr Gillack just stood and stared, running his hands wildly through his long blond hair, watching his flat burn down.

Jane sat in the back of a police car, her legs outside. She felt cold, even though a blanket was wrapped around her. The inspector snapped his pad shut.

'Well, madam, we're going to have to ask you a few more questions later, but for now . . .'

He stopped and glanced at the constable who'd just returned from talking to the fireman. Out of sight of Jane, the constable mouthed the news. There was no one else in the flat.

'Ah,' said the inspector, very slowly nodding and turning to look warily at the woman in the back of his car. 'But for now,' he concluded, 'I think we'd better get you down to the station.'

He gently lifted Jane's legs and swung them round into the car. Quietly shutting the door he looked at the constable over the roof of the car and they both breathed out heavily, shaking their heads.

Jane stared at nothing as the car pulled away past the knots of bystanders. She still felt cold, but it was nice to have the blanket.

She looked out at the passing pavement. Standing there neatly, smiling and waving like a child as they passed, was the owner. He was on fire.

She turned back and looked down at the blanket for a while. The pattern was unfamiliar. It didn't look like one of hers.

THE WOODS BE DARK

Bentley Little

A former newspaper reporter and an accomplished jazz musician, Bentley writes very formal letters, excellent novels – check out *The Mailman* or the Bram Stoker Award-winning *The Revelation* and see for yourself – and virtually unclassifiable short stories.

He sent two of these for consideration in *Touch Wood* and this is the one that made it. The other, 'Monteith', has prayed on my mind ever since I turned it down. But then it would have been the same other way around. All I can say is keep your eyes peeled for 'Monteith' and, wherever it appears, buy the book. It'll be money well spent.

Bentley falls asleep each night on his stomach, his head facing to the left, because he believes that if he does not do so he will choke to death in his sleep. 'Bizarre as it may seem,' he says, 'this is something I actually do each evening – I've always felt that I would die either by choking to death or suffocating. It's not a shared superstition . . . just my own personal ritual. But I think it counts for your purposes.'

To the woods, to the woods . . . and bring a torch!

Momma let the dishes set after supper instead of washing them and came out on the porch with us. She kicked Junior off of the rocker and took it for herself, just sitting there rocking and staring out at Old Man Crawford's trawler out there on the lake. It was one of them humid July nights and the dragonflies and the bloodsuckers was all hanging around the porchlight looking for a good arm to land on. Petey was up with a magazine, running around trying to kill all the bugs he could.

Momma was out on the porch with us because Robert hadn't come home before dark like he'd promised and she was waiting for him. She pretended it wasn't no big deal. She sat there and talked to us, laughing and joking and telling stories about when she was our age, but I could tell from the expression on her face that she was thinking about Daddy.

I was standing off by the side of the railing, away from the door, by myself, trying to loosen my dress from where it'd caught on a nail. I was listening to Momma tell about the time the brakes went out on her at Cook's Trail and she had to swerve into the river to keep from smashing into a tree when I heard a low kind of rustling sound coming from the path on the side of the house. I scooted next to Momma on the rocker. 'What is it, Beth?' she said.

I didn't say nothing. Then I heard the sound again, only this time all of them heard it. Momma stood up. Her face was white. She walked to the railing where I'd been standing and looked off toward the path. We stood around her, holding on to parts of her skirt.

Petey saw it first. 'It's Robert!' he called. He pointed off to where the path met the woods.

Sure enough, Robert was coming out of the woods across the clearing carrying a whole line full of fish. I heard Momma's breath start to relax when she saw it was Robert, but then she pulled it all in like someone'd hit her. Robert was kind of staggering across the clearing, weaving like he was drunk or something.

But we all knew he wasn't drunk.

'Get the shotgun,' Momma said quietly.

I ran into the house and grabbed the gun out of Daddy's closet. I ran back out and gave it to Momma. She loaded it up and pointed it at Robert without no hesitation.

We could see him pretty clear now. He was halfway across the clearing and the lights from the house sort of lit up his face. He was still staggering around and walking like he was drunk and he was still carrying his line of fish. His face looked real white, like Daddy's face, and he didn't seem to even see us standing there on the porch. Petey was calling out to him – Petey was too young, he didn't really know what was going on – and Junior was holding him back.

Robert stopped about ten yards away from the house and waved. His wave was real slow, real strange. 'Hey, Momma!' he said, and his voice was strange too. 'Look what I got.'

Momma kept the gun trained on him. 'Don't you come any closer,' she said.

He shook his head. 'Momma . . .'

'If I'm still your momma you'll wait there for me til dawn. If you're still there come morning you'll be welcome back. But until then you just stop and wait right there.'

He took a step forward. 'Aw, Momma—'

The gunshot blew his head clean off. His face just exploded in on itself and little pieces of blood and bone and eye went flying every which way. Petey started screaming and the rest of us watched while Robert fell on to the meadow grass. His hand was still holding on to the fish line. Momma reloaded the gun and aimed it at the center of his body just in case, but he didn't move. His body just lay there, the mash of skin that used to be his head bleeding into the grass.

We stayed on the porch all night. Petey, Junior and Sissy fell asleep a little while later and I fell asleep about halfway through the night, but Momma stayed awake the whole time.

After the sun came up, we all went out in the clearing to look.

There was nothing there. His body was gone.

Momma spent that morning explaining things to Petey.

We waited on the porch again that night, eating supper early and standing out there before it started to get dark. Sure enough, he started staggering up the path about the same time he had last night. There was nothing we could do this time, so we just stood there huddled together and watched.

'Robert Paul's come home,' he said, and his voice sounded like it was coming from the bottom of a well. 'Robert Paul's come home again.' We could see his grin even from this far away.

When he got to the spot where Momma'd shot him, he stopped.

And his head exploded.

He fell on to the ground just like before, and in the morning he was gone.

We went out to the spot. The grass was trampled and brown and looked like it'd been burned. 'That's all,' Momma said, kicking the spot with her shoe. 'It's over now.'

But I knew it wasn't. I could tell. I could feel it in my bones. I knew that we'd have to do the same thing we did for Daddy. And I was scared.

Scared bad.

That was one of them weird days when everything was backwards and all the directions was wrong. Our house was suddenly facing south when it'd always faced west, and I stayed close to home. I knew that if I lost sight of the house I wouldn't never get back to it.

It was overcast the whole day, and in the kitchen things broke for no reason. Momma'd walk out to the living room for a minute to talk to one of us kids and when she'd go back into the kitchen all the silverware would be poured out on the floor or one of her good dishes would be smashed or something. She tried to ignore all this, but one time I caught her saying the Prayer to herself when she thought no one was looking.

I said the Prayer too. I knew what was happening.

After supper we all just sat around and waited for night to fall. We didn't sit on the porch this time. We stayed inside. Sissy closed all the windows and drapes and Junior turned on all the lights.

I was almost asleep when something huge crashed against the north wall of the house. I jerked awake. It sounded like a cannon. Everyone else was wide awake too and Petey was crying. Momma held us all tight. 'Stay here,' she said. 'Don't go near the windows.' She didn't say nothing after that and I looked up at her. Her eyes was shut and it looked like she was praying to herself.

Something crashed hard against the wall again, making the whole house shake.

Outside, I could hear voices. It sounded like there was at least six or seven of them out there. Their words was all running together and I couldn't understand what they were saying. I plugged my ears and closed my eyes but I could still hear the voices talking inside my head.

And I could feel it when the thing crashed against the wall again.

I fell asleep plugging my ears.

I dreamed about Daddy.

We went to see Mrs Caffrey the next day. All of us. We went into her little trailer out there by the edge of the lake and waited in the tiny waiting room out front. When she came out she was all dressed up. Momma told her what happened and Mrs Caffrey prayed over her small bag of bones and threw a handful of sticks on to the table. When she was through she nodded. She held her head in her hands, closed her eyes and sort of hummed to herself. When she looked up she was staring at me.

I tried to look away but I couldn't.

Mrs Caffrey reached over and grabbed my arm and I could feel her sharp nails digging into my skin. 'You must go to the bad place,' she said. 'You must go through the ritual.' Her voice got real low. 'But be careful. There are many dangers. The woods be dark.'

She let go of me and I ran out of the trailer. I was crying bad. I knew this would happen and I didn't know if I could go through the ritual again.

Mrs Caffrey came outside a few minutes later and put her arm around me. She opened up her bible, closed her eyes, put her finger down and made me read. 'Walk while you have the light,' I read, 'lest the darkness overtake you.'

She closed the bible, smiled at me and patted my head. 'It'll be all right, child,' she said. She went back inside to talk to Momma.

No one said nothing on the way home.

It was noon by the time we got back to the house and Momma said there wasn't enough time to do it today, I would have to wait til tomorrow.

I was glad.

They came back that night, pounding on the walls and talking in our heads.. All us kids sat on the couch together, holding on to each other. Momma pretended like she didn't hear a thing, and she worked on a big sack for me to carry the next day.

I fell asleep listening to the pounding and the voices.

Momma woke me up before it was even light and told me I had to take a bath before I went out. 'You must cleanse yourself,' she said. I took my bath real quietly, but everyone was up by the time I got out of the tub. It was already starting to get light out.

Momma gave me the sack and told me to be careful, and I said goodbye to everyone just in case. I didn't spend too long on goodbyes though because I couldn't afford to waste no time. I had to get back before dark.

It was overcast again and the sky was covered with solid grey clouds and I couldn't see the sun. I walked down the path through the clearing, past the spot where Momma'd shot Robert, into the woods. Momma packed me a flashlight in my sack and I got it out. I needed it. The woods was dark, real dark, darker even than when I went in for Daddy, and it was completely silent. Usually you can hear the sounds of the lake or someone's car or people talking out by the boat launch, but I couldn't hear nothing. Even the birds was quiet. My footsteps sounded real loud, and I had a headache from my heart pounding and thumping the blood in my head.

I was scared.

It took me about a half an hour to get to the shack. I could feel it before I saw it and I looked in the other direction as I ran past. I didn't want to see them open windows and that black doorway. I didn't want to know what was inside. I made that mistake the last time and I almost didn't get no farther than that, so this time I just looked the other way and ran by.

There was something inside the shack, though.

I could feel it.

And I thought I heard it when I ran by.

I slowed down when I was out of breath, a good ways from the shack. It was hidden way back behind the trees now, so I didn't have nothing to worry about. The shack was about halfway to the bad place, I knew, maybe a little less, but the second half of the trip was a lot tougher and took a lot longer. The path ended a little ways up ahead, I remembered, and I'd have to find the rest of the way myself.

No path led to the bad place.

Sure enough, the path just sort of petered out. It got smaller and smaller and harder to see and after a while I realized it had ended some ways back and I hadn't noticed.

I was on my own.

It was real dark here and it kept getting darker the deeper I went into the woods. I saw shadows of things moving through the trees out of the corners of my eyes, but I ignored them and pretended they wasn't there. I said the Prayer to myself.

I didn't really know where I was going but I knew I was headed in the right direction. Tons of moss was hanging from the tops of the trees and it kept brushing my face and my blouse as I went past. I climbed over old dead logs and through thickets of sticker bushes. I started getting hungry, and I pulled out one of the sandwiches Momma made for me. I didn't sit down and eat, though. I kept walking.

Finally I came to the ruins and I knew I was getting close.

I remember Momma used to scare us when we was little by telling us that she'd take us out to the ruins and leave us there if we didn't behave, but I'm the only person I know that's actually seen them. They used to be part of an old stone fort during the war. A bunch of soldiers was stationed there to protect the county, but something happened to all the soldiers. All kinds of government people came down to check on the fort afterward, but none of them could figure out what happened.

The people around here knew what happened, though.

They built the fort too close to the bad place.

Now the ruins was just old piles of stone block and pieces of wall with plants and ivy growing all over them. A few buildings were still left, but I got the same feeling from them that I got from the shack and I just ran by.

After the ruins the trees started to grow weird and the directions got all lost again. I was going south then all of a sudden I was going west and I hadn't even changed my course. The trees became all gnarly and twisted, and the moss started to grow into shapes. Strange shapes that I knew what they were but I didn't want to admit it.

It got even darker.

And then I was there.

The bad place looked just like I remembered it. The leaves of all the trees was all black and brown and they twisted together to make a roof over the clearing and completely blocked out the sky. It was always night here. On the sides, small trees grew in between the big trees and made a solid wall except for the entrance where I was coming in. The middle of the clearing was covered with bones and skulls and the teeth of rats, all laid out in little rows, like crops. Dead possum skeletons hung from frayed old ropes in the trees, and they was swinging but there wasn't no breeze.

Nothing grew in the center of the clearing. It was all dust. Even the plants was afraid to grow here.

In the very center was the open grave.

I swallowed hard and took Momma's bible out of my sack. I was scared, even more scared than I'd been with Daddy, and all of a sudden I wanted to run, to run back home to Momma. The noises at night, the voices and pounding, didn't seem so bad now. Not compared to this. I could live with them.

But I couldn't run. I had to go through the ritual.

I walked slowly into the middle of the clearing toward the open grave holding tight to my bible. The little white wood cross at the head of the grave was tilted and almost falling over. I kept my eyes on that and didn't look into the hole. Finally I reached the grave and stood at its foot, trying to calm down. My heart was pounding a mile a minute and I couldn't hardly get no breath.

I stood like that for a few minutes, staring at the cross, trying to be brave. Then finally I looked into the hole.

Robert lay on the bottom. His skin was pure white and glowing and his face was smooth and perfect and I couldn't tell where Momma'd shot him. He was holding his hands up in the air toward me and they was moving a little, twirling in strange little circles.

Then his eyes jerked open and he smiled. His eyes was pure red and evil and I started to shake. 'Robert Paul's come home,' he said. 'Robert Paul's come home again.' It was all he said. It was all he could say.

His voice was just a whisper.

I reached around to my sack and took out the page with the Words written on it. The grave was deep, I was thinking. It was deeper than last time. The sides went down maybe ten feet to Robert at the bottom. I put the Words on the bible. 'Lord protect me in this ritual,' I read. 'Keep me safe from harm. See my motives not my actions. Keep me safe from harm. Give this tortured soul his rest. Keep me safe from harm. Guide me through this and preserve me. Keep me safe from harm. Amen.'

I folded the paper and put the Words into the bible.

At the bottom of the grave Robert was moving even more now. His head was rolling from side to side and his arms was still twirling in the air and he was grinning even worse. I could see all of his teeth. They was glowing.

I took a deep breath, said the Prayer, held the bible to my chest and jumped into the open grave.

I fell, fell and landed with a soft thud on Robert's body. His grin got bigger and his eyes got redder and I could see them right next to my face.

He started laughing and his voice changed.

He was no longer Robert.

And he took me.

I woke up by the ruins. My sack was gone and the bible was gone and my clothes was all torn up and half hanging off me. I still felt kind of dopey or sleepy or whatever it was, but I knew I had to get out of the woods before dark. I didn't know what time it was so I just started running. I ran past the ruins and somehow found the path again.

Something was standing in the doorway of the shack when I ran by but I didn't look at it. I kept running.

It was broad daylight when I came out of the woods. The clouds had all burnt off and the sun was shining. Everything was okay. Momma was waiting for me and she ran up and hugged me as I came down the path. I could see she was crying. 'You went through the ritual?' she asked.

I nodded and told her I did.

She led me back to the house where I slept for two full days.

Two weeks later my belly started growing.

It was just a little bit at first. But a month later it was obvious.

People didn't bother me none about it though. Folks around here understand about the bad place. A lot of women around here've got pregnant the same way when they was my age. No one talked to me about it or paid me no never mind.

Two months later I was ready to give birth.

Momma took me to Mrs Caffrey's. She didn't tell none of the other kids about it, she just said that we were going into town for the day and for Junior to keep an eye on everyone else and not let them leave the house.

It was just like before. The thing was all slimy and pink and wormy. It made horrible squawking noises and tried to claw up Mrs Caffrey as she held it.

It had Robert's face.

'Do you want to see it first?' Mrs Caffrey asked me.

I shook my head. I could see it good enough as it was, and I didn't want to see no more of it. I sure didn't want to touch it.

'I'll take it outside then.'

'No,' I said. 'Wait a minute. Let me do it.'

Momma shook her head. 'No. You're too weak.'

'It's all right,' Mrs Caffrey said.

Momma helped me up out of the bed, and Mrs Caffrey took the baby outside. She put it on the ground outside the trailer and it started squawking and twirling its arms in circles.

I searched the ground and picked up a boulder. I held it up as high as I could and the creature looked up at me and spat.

I smashed its head.

It lay there twitching for a minute, a small trickle of black blood flowing out from beneath the boulder, then it was still.

I watched as Mrs Caffrey took the dead thing into her trailer. She cut it up and burned it and put the ashes into a stew. I ate a bite of the stew and said the Prayer.

Momma drove me home.

That night, Momma was inside washing the dishes and all us kids was out on the porch. Petey was trying to kill bugs and Junior and Sissy was fighting on the rocker and I was standing by the railing looking out at the woods when all of a sudden I heard a rustling sound coming from the meadow. I looked back quickly at the other kids but none them'd heard it. I held my breath and looked closer, leaning over the rail to see better, saying the Prayer to myself.

But it was just a scared little jackrabbit, and it stopped and stared at me and then ran across the path and disappeared into the bushes and meadow grass at the side of the house.

TRAFFIC

Simon Ings

Simon Ings's first novel, *Hothead*, a science fiction thriller, appeared from HarperCollins in May 1992. His shorter work has appeared in several anthologies and magazines, including Holdstock and Evans's *Other Edens III* – with the quite superb 'Blessed Fields' – and *Omni*.

In response to the inevitable question regarding personal superstitions, Simon professes to have always had a 'healthy admiration' for werewolves. 'As a child,' he writes, 'I did whatever I understood was necessary to effect my own transformation. Some of my earliest auto-erotic experiences consist of lying naked under a full moon somewhere secluded in the Home Counties. I had somehow repressed all memory of these events until last year, when I read Susy McKee Charnas's excellent werewolf story "Boobs". I think it strange that my unconscious ever felt such repressions necessary.'

If you live in the Bow Area of London, consider yourself warned.

WIFE

At noon she sweeps the porch. She has a new brush; her husband bought it for her. It has a wooden handle, painted yellow, and red plastic bristles. She likes it because it shines in the hazy midday light, as if it were wet. The porch is dusty, and sweeping it makes her cough. There is litter, too: sweet wrappers. There are brands she has never heard of; there are brands she remembers from when she was a girl. Sometimes she stoops to pick up the ones she recognises. She unravels them and reads them. Sometimes she smiles.

She sweeps the path. The concrete is broken, so weeds grow in the cracks. Sometimes she washes the weeds, to make them shine. There is fresh litter on the path each day. She likes the way it changes, week by week. Sometimes she finds bits of newspaper, and she picks them up and reads them, but the print is a language foreign to her. Undeterred, she reads it aloud; foreign words stutter out of her dry mouth.

She sweeps the yard. It is hot here. She wants to undress. She unbuttons her blouse. The hazy sun catches her breasts. People can see her breasts swing as she sweeps the yard. Sometimes boys come and watch her. Sometimes they shout and laugh. She does not let them come into the yard. If they come in, she shoos them out with her broom. She does not smile at them. Her father-in-law saw her smiling at them, once. She has bruises now, and the bruises remind her not to smile.

There is litter here, too. Tin cans clatter when she hits them with her broom. Sunlight flashes from the dented cans as they roll about the yard. They make dry, hot sounds. When she picks them up they scald her fingers.

She sweeps the drive, because her father-in-law likes a clean drive. He has a big blue car, and he does not like the sound a can makes when he crushes it under his tyres. She sweeps the drive for a long time. Dust billows from her broom and settles on the road. The road is grey with dust.

She puts the papers and wrappers and cans into plastic shopping bags. She carries the bags to the big hopper on the other side of the road. She opens the hopper and drops the bags inside. She does not like the smell of the hopper.

She tried to clean it once. She pulled out all the rubbish the women in the road had thrown into it, then she carried a big pail of hot, soapy water to the hopper. Two women came out and shouted at her. They pointed to the rubbish. Some bags had broken. Litter blew all about the road. They made her sweep it up and bundle it in fresh bags, then helped her put it back in the hopper. Afterwards one of them hit her across the face.

Perhaps someone else will clean the hopper. She does not like the smell.

She surveys the drive, the yard, the path, the porch. There is a can on the porch step. She carries her broom up to the porch and hits the can.

She dents it. It does not move. She bends down and takes hold of it. She plucks it out of the cement and looks at it. She laughs.

It is evening. She has swept and cooked and cleaned, and she has washed herself. She waits for her father-in-law. He has been working late this week. He is a busy man, and very worried. She does not know what he is worried about, and he will not tell her. Her father-in-law says she is not capable of understanding his worries.

His son, her husband, is a policeman. He works late as a matter of course, but maybe, just this once, he will arrive before his father. It has been a long time since she was alone with her husband. She misses those times alone with him.

She said so, once.

Her daughter is at school. She has extra classes. She is a bright girl and she stays late, because, she says, they ask her to. She used to come home early every day. Sometimes they argued, but it was still nice, to be alone with her.

Her father-in-law says she holds her daughter back. She does not want to hold her daughter back. She even said so, once.

She sits by the window.

She looks out over the houses. The Conflux is silhouetted against a misty, ochre sky. Many important roads meet and swirl there. There are flyovers, underpasses, turnoffs, roundabouts, bridges, feedlanes and much else she has no words for. When they married, her husband said he would teach her to drive. If she drove, she would know all the words.

They do not have a car.

Something sparks. It is a tin can, reflecting the light from a street lamp. She watches the can roll into the yard. A little while later, paper blows up the path. Something glimmers in the air, flutters against the window; it is a sweet wrapper.

The drive, though, stays clean. There is no litter on the drive. Litter will fill the drive tomorrow, early in the morning, once her father-in-law has left for work in his big blue car.

She smiles indulgently as litter fills the yard.

It tries to be friendly.

HUSBAND

He is sitting on a plastic chair. He is uncomfortable; he cannot sit still. His movements make a pain in his side. He finds it difficult to concentrate, because his side hurts a great deal.

A long time ago he was shot. He was patrolling the Baixa. A pusher shot him. He was very ill for a long time. He still gets the pain.

'There are black spots.'

The chief gestures to the video screens. They line the wall behind them, three deep. The husband wonders how he will ever survey them all.

The chief laughs. He understands. 'It's not so difficult. You'll pick it up.'

'Yes, sir.'

'There are black spots.'

The chief presses some buttons. Some screens zoom in on the roads they watch. Other screens flash and hiss. When they settle, they display a new road, or a new angle of the same road; he cannot tell which.

'There are many accidents in the Conflux. You probably know that.'

'Yes, sir.'

'You must learn where the black spots are, what makes them dangerous, and how we make them safe.'

'Yes, sir.'

'You will learn how to change signals, display warning messages on the boards by the side of each road, change the timing of traffic lights, and much else besides.'

'Yes, sir.'

The chief does not say anything for some time.

The policeman wonders whether he should ask the chief a pertinent question. He cannot think of one.

The chief coughs. When he looks up, there is something in his eyes that wasn't there before. Amusement? Not quite. It is a look growing common in the city. A look that says, 'Slowly, a pattern emerges.' A look that says, 'These things are known, now, that before were merely glimpses.'

'Let me show you something.' He points to a large screen in the centre of the wall. The image dissolves and resolves to a stretch of straight three-lane.

Beyond the road, in the distance, smoke rises from bare grey hills. White slashes mark exhausted strip mines. When his father was a boy, the hills were swamped and swathed in rainforest.

'Can you see why this is a black spot?'

The policeman looks back to the road, studies it, and shakes his head.

'Here is a map.' The chief shows him a map. He unfolds it quickly and stabs repeatedly at the relevant spot. The policeman notices that the chief is flushed. He looks back at the map. He scratches his head.

'Here is a table of streetlamp timing.'

The chief crashes the book on to the table, over the map. He jabs at the page.

The policeman's side hurts a lot now. He makes what sense he can of the figures. He shakes his head. 'I don't know how—'

'Here is a timetable of different warning messages we display each day, depending on weather conditions and traffic density.' The chief throws the handbook in the policeman's lap. The policeman looks at him. The chief is grinning. Sweat glistens on his brow. It reflects the grey fluorescent which is the room's only proper light source. The policeman looks at the chief and thinks of his father. His side is burning. 'I don't get it, chief,' he says.

The chief takes a deep breath. He is trying to calm himself. 'Nor do we,' he says. 'Drivers just – crash.'

The two men stare at the screen. Cars cross from right to left in a regular, hypnotic rhythm.

The chief runs his fingers through his thin, close-cropped hair. 'Most crashes happen here. We have interviewed survivors from those cars which came to grief first. They are very confused about the accidents they caused. There is, however, a common thread to their stories.'

The chief waits to be prompted.

The policeman is in too much pain to speak evenly, and he says nothing.

The chief says, 'They claim they swerved to avoid a person. A suicide.'

The pain lessens a little. The policeman says, 'These claims are untrue.'

'They are untrue. We have found no bodies. It is as if they had boiled away to corruption within seconds of their deaths, leaving nothing but a smear on the tarmac, perhaps a cloud of flies.' He shakes his head, smiling. 'We have found no bodies,' he repeats. 'Underneath the Conflux there are many prostitutes. They have seen nothing to support the drivers' stories about—' The chief breaks off.

'About the suicides.' The policeman finishes the sentence.

The chief smiles at him. The humour-that-is-not-humour shines behind his eyes again. 'The *suicide*,' he corrects.

The policeman is non-plussed.

'Every driver sees the same suicide.' The chief leans towards him. 'A woman in a black dress.'

The policeman smiles. Beneath this polite exterior, however, he is angered. He is irritated by such stories. It is not the chief's fault, he tells himself. It is merely the fashion.

Even his father tells him ghost stories, now, and he is a bullish, unimaginative man. And even that look – that look of mystic recognition – he has seen it on his father's face.

It is the look that says: 'These things, these old women's tales: how potent have they become!'

DAUGHTER

She is a good girl, a bright girl, and she has learnt well from older girls what is expected of her. She wants a new dress – a silk dress, dark, well cut – the kind the older girls wear. She wants a new home. The kind of home you can bring friends to. The kind of home you can party in. The kind of home the older girls rent.

She never wants to see her grandfather again, or hear her mother's laughter. After school, she walks past the bus stops and under the Conflux. There is no need to change her school clothes. Men like her dressed the way she is. They make believe that they are corrupting her. She has learned to weep afterwards. They like that very much.

She leaves the path. The ground is a mulch of crushed cans, newspapers, beads, glass, wood splinters, oily rag, used prophylactics, cardboard and tyre rubber. The air is full of flies.

Behind the concrete pile, hidden from the path, she pulls up her skirt. She pulls aside her pants and relieves herself.

Flies fill the space between her arched legs. She watches them settle upon the puddle at her feet.

She looks at the flies, feeding upon her urine. They are brightly coloured – red and dun and black with yellow flashes. Their hides glisten wetly. Their wings catch the hazy, smoke-screened sunlight.

The flies are beautiful.

She remembers what she has been told. These are the last creatures of the jungle. These are the foundation of what once grew here. These things do not forget.

She waits for trade. Her third man wants to do something she has not heard of before. He offers money, more and more money, more money than she has ever seen before. At last she lets him do it.

She takes her clothes off first, and afterwards lets the sun dry her damp skin.

Flies settle on her, feeding. She sits amid the rubbish and enjoys the tickle of their legs.

She smiles. The heat makes her drowsy. Through half-closed lids she looks about her. An abandoned fridge, packing cases, old shoes, plastic bags filled with rubbish, bits from gutted automobiles, a magazine, an old radio, a length of rubber tubing and the damp trash at her feet take on strange shapes behind her eyes.

The flies rise from her flesh and dance before her.

They swirl around each other, lending outline and shadow to the new shapes.

She imagines a bowl of green earth, a tree, the crawling things which inhabit it, a bird.

She stirs herself. Now she sees that the bird is made of light. It is a mass of fly-wing reflections. The flies disperse and the illusion is broken.

She thinks: from filth and from refuse comes the rebirth of the world.

She abandons her clothes and walks naked among the pillars of the flyover. She has often walked naked here, and has seen strange things amid the filth – toadstools, grasses, the droppings of strange birds.

She stops. At her feet there is a heap of flies. She bends down and scoops them up in her hands. They are alive. They are copulating. Smiling, she lets them fall through her fingers, then brushes them aside. She uncovers a dress. She snatches it up. The cotton is fresh, unfaded by dust or sun.

She shakes it. Flies rain from folds in the material.

She puts on the dress and looks about her.

There is a great river of fresh water in the distance. She hears it roar.

FATHER

An important man in business drives through the Conflux to his son's home in the poorest part of the city.

His son needs him. He was shot on patrol. He is ill. He needs someone strong to run things. That stupid mad whore he married is of no use to him. He has a daughter, too, and it takes a firm hand to bring up children here.

He is an important man in business and he has many burdens. The mines are dead. The cattle are sick. Sometimes he thinks the city itself is crumbling. He is not alone. All around him, at the office and in the bars, his fellows wallow in superstition and fear.

Today his business partner said, I bought a whore, under the Conflux. She was every lonely journey I have ever taken, every unloved place I have ever visited, every pang of guilt I have ever felt. What does this mean?

The important man laughed at him, but he is sure, in some small uncontrolled part of himself, that something terrible is going to happen.

It is less what is said on these occasions that unnerves him; it is more the look which accompanies these tales. He sees that look all around him. It is the look of superstitious men whose absurd beliefs have, against all probability, been borne out by the world. And sometimes he thinks that this city, this acme of the man-made, this minute-hand urging the mere world's midnight, must somehow have been balanced somewhere by some darker twin, so that the further it strove towards the proofed and the repeatable, the stranger and more magical its ghostly twin became. And if every victory of its enchromed reason was balanced, somewhere, by a manifestation of something weird, mouldy, riotous, was it any wonder that yesterday his son's wife – more a slut than a wife – was it any wonder that she'd said what she had said? That she'd plucked a Coke can up by the root?

He remembers he'd slapped her for this nonsense; slapped her, because she spoke for the dark – had, in her stupid way, expressed its power – had, especially, told the truth. And with this thought, not previously admitted, comes the look – he feels it spread like a contagion over his face.

The truth!

He remembers, too, that his son leaped to his feet to stop him slapping her, stop him slapping the darkness out of her, leaped up and fell down in agony. His son wept with pain.

His son wept.

His son!

The rear suspension is squeaking again. He cannot afford a new car. He has his son's hospital bill to pay. Anger fills him. Why didn't his son join the business? They have proper ways of doing things there. Proper insurance! No guns! He may not be able to meet this month's payment on time. He wonders whether they could sell the slut for spare parts. He grins.

The grin freezes.

There is trouble ahead. He senses the shunt before it happens. He grips the wheel and foots the brake. He is a good driver. He is proud of his driving. He does not skid.

In the distance, cars collide. For a split second he sees an opening, a way to avoid the wall of tangled metal approaching him. He lifts his foot from the brake. The car guns into the gap.

Metal screams and tears. He is wedged in. The car is crushed by neighbouring vehicles but he is safe. The whole tangled mess, his car and others, skitter to the edge of the flyover and crush the barricade.

The car jolts. One wheel slips over the edge.

The important man in business grits his teeth. He stares into the frosted windscreen and thinks, don't push me further. Don't let any bastard crash and push me further.

There is a corner of the windscreen which has not shattered. There is a dot of blood there.

He looks at it: his vision is unusually acute at this moment. It takes him only a fraction of a second to realise that the droplet rests upon the outer surface of the glass. He draws comfort from this.

It is not his blood.

Something jolts him from behind.

Another wheel goes over the edge. The car rocks – and then it is still.

The man laughs. When he has finished laughing he looks again at the corner of the windscreen.

He has been mistaken.

It is not a drop of blood. It is a fly, its chitinous shell shining ruddily in the evening light.

It squats, feeding upon the glass, then it flies away.

THE MOUSE

Neil Gaiman

Following on from the vanguard British foothold established in the American comicbook medium by Allan Moore, with his interpretation of DC Comics' *Swamp Thing* character, Neil Gaiman has secured a place for himself as the doyen of the graphic novel with his own 'version' of a DC character, *The Sandman*.

Eloquent and enigmatic, depressing and depraved, scary and even occasionally scatalogical, the adventures of Gaiman's King of Dreams and his baroque family have captivated a newly literate generation of fans of the word-ballooned panel. His characters live and breathe, and they die and regret; his plots continue to stagger the imagination; and his scripting style belies the once-common criticism of comics being only for kids. His offbeat (even potentially litigious, if the Bard were alive today) treatment of *A Midsummer Night's Dream* (illustrated by the excellent Charles Vess) won the prestigious World Fantasy Award (1991) in the Best Short Story category – the first time a comicbook story was nominated for a non-comicbook award. Of the comicbook awards themselves, Gaiman has won them all – many more than once.

He also moonlights.

Among his many projects – which goes some way to explaining the scarcity value of a new Gaiman short story – the collaborative (with Terry Pratchett) novel *Good Omens* made it

on to the *Sunday Times* bestseller list . . . but the bad portents in
that particular cookie is that the book has been optioned (along
with *The Sandman*) by Hollywood. And if you like horror stories,
get Neil to tell you a little bit about *that!*

As for personal details and beliefs, how about:

'Born 1960 – still alive.

'Superstitions . . . I always believed that you were safe, as long
as you had a book with you.'

1

They had a number of devices that would kill a mouse fast,
others that would kill it more slowly. There were a dozen
variants on the traditional mousetrap, the one Regan thought of
as the Tom and Jerry trap – a metal spring trap that would slam
down at a touch, breaking the mouse's back. There were still
other devices that suffocated the mouse, others that drowned it,
or electrocuted it.

'These weren't quite what I was looking for,' said Regan.

'Well, that's all we got in the way of traps,' said the woman,
who wore a name-tag that said her name was BECKY and that
she Loved Working FOR YOU at MacRea's Specialty and
Animal Feed Store. 'Now, over here—'

She pointed to a display of HUN-GREE-CAT MOUSE
POISON sachets. A little rubber mouse lay on the top of the
display, his legs in the air.

Regan experienced a sudden memory flash: Gwen, extending a
hand, her fingers curled upward. 'What's that?' she said. It was
the week before he was due to leave for America.

'I don't know,' said Regan. They were in the bar of a small
hotel in the West Country, burgundy carpets, fawn-coloured
wallpaper. He was nursing a gin and tonic, she was sipping her
second glass of chablis.

Gwen had once told Regan that blondes should only drink white wine; it looked better. He laughed, until he realised she meant it.

'A dead one of these,' she said, turning her hand over, so the fingers hung like the legs of a slow pink animal. He laughed. Later he paid the bill, and they went upstairs to bed . . .

'I don't want to kill it,' he told the saleswoman, Becky.

She looked at him curiously, as if he had just begun to speak in a foreign tongue. 'But you wanted mousetraps . . .?'

'Look, what I want is a humane trap. It's like a corridor. The mouse goes in, the door shuts behind it, it can't get out.'

'So how do you kill it?'

'You don't kill it. You drive a few miles away and let it go. And it doesn't come back to bother you.'

Becky was smiling now, examining him as if he were just the most darling thing, just the sweetest, dumbest little thing. 'You stay here,' she said. 'I'll check out back.'

She walked through a door marked Employees Only. She had a nice bottom, thought Regan, and was almost attractive, in a dull, mid-western sort of way.

He glanced out the window. Janice was sitting in the car, reading her magazine: a red-haired woman in a dowdy housecoat. He waved at her, but she wasn't looking at him.

Becky put her head back through the doorway. 'Jackpot,' she said. 'How many you want?'

'Two?'

'No problem.' She was gone again, and returned with two small green plastic containers. She rang them up on the till, and as he fumbled through his notes and coins, trying to assemble the correct change, she examined them, smiling, turning the packets over in her hands.

'My lord,' she said, 'whatever will they think of next?'

The heat slammed Regan as he stepped out of the store.

He hurried over to the car. The metal door handle was hot in his hand.

He climbed in. 'I got two,' he said. The air-conditioning in the car was cool and pleasant.

'Seatbelt on,' said Janice. 'You really got to learn to drive over here.'

'I will,' he said. 'Eventually.'

Regan was scared of driving in America: it was like driving on the other side of a mirror.

They said nothing else, and Regan read the instructions on the back of the mousetrap boxes. It seemed the main attraction of this type of trap was that you never needed to see, touch, or handle the mouse. The door would close behind it, and that would be that. The instructions said nothing about not killing the mouse.

When they got home he took the traps out of the boxes, put a little peanut butter in one, down at the far end, a lump of cooking chocolate in the other, and placed them in the pantry, one against the wall, the other near the hole that the mice seemed to be using to gain access to the pantry.

The traps were only corridors. A door at one end, a wall at the other.

2

In bed that night, Regan reached out and touched Janice's breasts as she slept: gently, not wishing to wake her. They were perceptibly fuller. He wished he found large breasts erotic. He found himself wondering what it must be like to suck a woman's breasts while she was lactating. He could imagine sweetness, but no specific taste.

Janice was sound asleep, but still she moved towards him.

He turned away; lay there in the dark, trying to remember how to sleep, hunting through alternatives in his mind.

There was a sharp scream from the garden, then. Janice stirred and rolled away from him. It had sounded almost human. Foxes can sound like small children in pain – Regan's mind called this up from some long ago wildlife programme. Or perhaps it was a cat. Or a nightbird of some kind.

Something had died, anyway, in the night. Of that there was no doubt at all.

3

The next morning one of the traps had been sprung, although when Regan opened it, carefully, it proved to be empty. The chocolate bait had been nibbled. He opened the door and replaced the trap by the wall.

Janice was crying to herself in the lounge. Regan stood beside her; she reached out her hand, and he held it, tightly. Her fingers were cold.

Later, she made a telephone call.

A package arrived for Regan just before noon, Federal Express, containing a dozen floppy disks, each filled with numbers for Regan to inspect and sort and classify.

He worked until six, sitting in front of a small metal fan which whirred and rattled, and moved the hot air around.

4

He turned on the radio that evening, while he cooked.

'. . . what my book tells everyone. What the liberals don't want us to know.' The voice was high, nervous, arrogant.

'Yeah. Some of it was, well, kinda hard to believe.' The host was encouraging; a radio voice, reassuring and easy.

'Of *course* it's hard to believe. It runs against everything they want you to believe. The liberals and the how-mo-sexuals in the media, they don't tell you the truth.'

'Of course they don't. We'll be right back after this song.'

It was a country and western song. Regan kept the radio tuned to the local National Public Radio station; sometimes they broadcast the BBC World Service news. Someone must have retuned it, he supposed.

He had a sharp knife, and he cut through the chicken breast with care, parting the pink flesh, slicing it into strips all ready to stir-fry.

Somebody's heart was broken; somebody no longer cared. Then the song ended.

'Thing is, nobody believes it at first. But I got the documents. I got the photographs. You read my book. You'll see. It's the unholy alliance, and I do mean unholy, between the so called pro-choice lobby, the medical community and the how-mo-sexuals. The how-mos need these murders because that's where they get the little children they use to experiment with to find a cure for AIDS.

'I mean, they talk about Nazi atrocities, but nothing those Nazis did comes in even close to what they do. They take human foetuses and they graft them on to little mice, to create these human-mouse hybrid creatures. Then they inject them with AIDS . . .'

Regan found himself thinking of Mengele's wall of strung eyeballs. Blue eyes and brown eyes and hazel—

'Shit!' He'd sliced into his thumb. He pushed it into his mouth, bit down on it to stop the bleeding, ran into the bathroom and began to hunt for a Band-aid.

'Remember, I'll need to be out by ten tomorrow.' Janice was standing behind him. He looked at her blue eyes in the bathroom mirror. She looked calm.

'Fine.' He slid the Band-aid over his thumb, hiding and binding the wound, and turned to face her.

'I saw a cat in the garden today,' she said. 'A big grey one. Maybe it's a stray.'

'Maybe.'

'Did you think any more about getting a pet?'

'Not really. It'd just be something else to worry about. I thought we agreed, no pets.'

She shrugged.

They went back into the kitchen. He poured oil into the frying pan, and lit the gas. He dropped the strips of pink flesh into the pan and watched them shrink and discolour and change.

5

Janice drove herself to the bus station early the next morning. It was a long drive into the city, and she'd be in no condition to drive when she was ready to return. She took five hundred dollars with her, in cash.

Regan checked the traps. Neither had been touched. Then he prowled the corridors of the house.

Eventually, he phoned Gwen. The first time, he misdialled, his fingers slipping on the buttons of the phone, the long string of digits confusing him. He tried again.

A ringing; then her voice on the line. 'Allied Accountancy Associates. Good afternoon.'

'Gwenny? It's me.'

'Regan? I was hoping you'd call eventually. I missed you.' Her voice was distant; transatlantic crackle and hum taking her further away from him.

'It's expensive.'

'Any more thoughts about coming back?'

'I don't know.'

'So how's wifeykins?'

'Janice is . . .' he paused. Sighed. 'Janice is just fine.'

'I've started fucking our sales director,' said Gwen. 'You've been gone for six months now. I mean, what's a girl to do?'

It occurred then to Regan that that was what he hated most about women; their practicality. Gwen had made him use a condom, although he disliked condoms, while she had also used a diaphragm and a spermicide. Regan felt that somewhere in all there a level of spontaneity, of romance, was lost. He liked sex to be something that just happened, half in his head, half out of it. Something sudden and dirty and powerful.

His forehead began to throb.

'So what's the weather like out there?' Gwen asked, brightly.

'It's hot,' said Regan.

'Wish it was here.'

He said something about it being lovely to hear her voice again. Then he put the phone down.

6

Regan checked the traps. Still empty.

He wandered into his office, and flipped on the TV.

'. . . this is a little one. That's what *foetus* means. And one day she'll grow up to be a big one. She's got little fingers, little toes – she's even got little toenails.'

A picture on the screen: red and pulsing and indistinct.

It cut to a woman with a huge smile, cuddling a baby.

'Some little ones like her will grow up to be nurses, or teachers, or musicians. One day one of them may even be president.

'But *this* little one will never grow up to be a big one. She's going to be killed tomorrow. And her mother says it isn't murder.'

He flipped channels until he found *I Love Lucy*, the perfect background nothing, then he turned on the computer and got down to work.

After two hours chasing through columns of figures his head began to ache. He got up and walked into the garden.

He missed having a lawn; missed a proper English lawn, with proper English grass. The grass out here was withered, brown and sparse. He followed the track out into the woods. Something grey and sleek slipped from behind one tree to another.

'Here, kitty, kitty,' called Regan. 'Here, kitty, kitty.'

He walked over to the tree and looked behind it. The cat – or whatever it had been – was gone.

He went back into the kitchen, and poured himself a cup of coffee. He missed tea, but it just didn't taste the same out here.

7

Janice got home about six.

'How was it?'

She shrugged. 'Fine.'

'Yeah?'

'Yeah.'

'I have to go back next week,' she said. 'For a check-up.'

'Make sure they didn't leave any instruments inside you?'

'Whatever,' she said.

'I've made a spaghetti bolognese,' said Regan.

'I'm not hungry,' said Janice. 'I'm going to bed.'

She went upstairs.

Regan worked until the numbers no longer added up. He went upstairs then, and walked quietly into the darkened bedroom. He slipped off his clothes in the moonlight, dropped them on to the carpet and slid between the sheets.

He could feel Janice next to him. Her body was shaking, and the pillow was wet.

'Janice?'

She had her back to him.

'It was horrible,' she whispered. 'It hurt so much. And they wouldn't give me a proper anaesthetic or anything. They said I could have a shot of Valium if I wanted one, but they didn't have an anaesthetic there any more. The lady said he couldn't stand the pressure and anyway it would have cost another two hundred dollars and nobody wanted to pay . . .

'It hurt so much.' She was sobbing now, gasping the words as if they were being tugged out of her. 'So much.'

Regan got out of bed.

'Where are you going?'

'I don't have to listen to this,' said Regan. 'I really don't have to listen to this.'

8

It was still too hot in the house. Regan walked downstairs in only his underpants.

One of the mousetrap doors was closed.

He picked up the trap. It seemed a trifle heavier than before. He opened the door carefully, a little way. Two beady black eyes stared up at him. He pushed the door shut again.

He couldn't kill it. He couldn't kill anything.

The trap smelled acrid, and the bottom of it was sticky with mouse-piss. Regan carried it out into the garden.

Outside the house a gentle breeze had sprung up. The moon was almost full. He knelt on the ground, placed the trap carefully on the earth.

He opened the door of the little trap.

'Run away,' he whispered, feeling embarrassed at the sound of his voice in the open air. 'Run away, little mouse.'

The mouse didn't move. He could see its nose at the door of the trap.

'Come on,' said Regan. Bright moonlight; he could see everything, sharply lit and shadowed, if lacking in colour.

He nudged the trap with his foot.

The mouse made a dash for it, then. It ran out from the trap, then stopped, turned, and began to hop into the woods.

Then it stopped again. The mouse looked up in Regan's direction. Regan was convinced that it was staring at him. It had tiny hands. Regan felt almost paternal, then. He smiled, wanly.

A streak of grey in the night, and the mouse hung, struggling desperately, from the mouth of a large grey cat, its eyes burning green in the night. Then the cat bounded into the undergrowth.

He thought briefly of pursuing the cat, of freeing the mouse from its jaws . . .

There was a sharp scream from the woods; just a night-sound, but for a moment Regan thought it sounded almost human, like a woman in pain.

He threw the little plastic mousetrap as far from him as he could. He was hoping for a satisfying crash as it hit something, but it fell soundlessly in the bushes. Then he went back inside the house, and the door closed quietly behind him.

THE GHOST AND THE SOLDIER

William Relling Jr

William Relling was born in St Louis in 1954.

Before becoming a full-time professional writer he spent time as a carnival ride operator, supermarket clerk, produce truck driver, summer camp counsellor, street crew worker, bus boy, janitor, purveyor of fine wines and spirits, musician, hospital orderly, patio furniture salesman, magazine editor, high school teacher and college instructor.

During 1976-77 he lived on the Pine Ridge Indian Reservation – 'probably the strangest eleven months of my life' – and moved to Los Angeles in 1978 . . . with the Colin Sphinctor Band. He's been there ever since and now lives in an area called Silver Lake (see Jackson Browne's first album) with his wife Ann and young son Tommy. His heroes – apart from Ann and Tommy – include Groucho Marx, Albert Schweitzer, Pete Townshend and the Lone Ranger.

Three novels have already appeared and a fourth – *The Darkness and the Light* – is due any time. His short stories have appeared in various anthologies and virtually every magazine from *Omni* to *Cavalier*: a collection – *The Infinite Man* – is scheduled for release soon. He recently broke into TV and movie writing and he is also working on the book and lyrics for an original stage musical, 'Rainbow Pie', with composer Timothy Bruneau.

Like many others, Relling does not consider himself to be

superstitious . . . but there have been occasional exceptions.

'When I was playing team sports I'd always put on my uniform in precisely the same way . . . and before taking exams I'd pray to every deity I could think of to help me do well. I also ate the same candy bar – a Nestlé's Crunch – before taking an exam . . . but in the back of my mind, I was aware it was more for the sugar-rush than for good luck.'

※

If a man loses anything and goes back and looks carefully for it, he will find it.
Tatanka Yotanka (Sitting Bull)

1

The first time Richard Battles dreamed about the Dance of the Ghosts, he was seven years old.

It was in mid-July of the year 1953, one week after Richard's birthday. The dream occurred on the night of the day that his mother received a telegram informing her that her husband was dead. Richard's father, Sam Battles, was a gunnery sergeant in the United States Marine Corps. He'd been killed in combat in Korea.

Mother did not tell Richard right away that his father was dead. She waited until the following day to explain why the sad-faced white man in the dark suit had driven all the way from Rapid City in his dusty, black automobile to see her. After the man had left, Richard's mother said nothing. She went about her chores, preparing supper for Richard and his grandfather, mending their clothes, waiting until sundown to water the parched vegetables in the small garden behind the house.

That night, in a dream, Richard saw his father.

The next day Richard's mother told him the reason why she was dressed in her best dress and leaving him for the day with his grandfather – her father, Gaylord Kills Buffalo. Grandfather would look after the boy while she drove one hundred miles to Rapid City in their battered DeSoto to meet with the man from the government and arrange to have the body of her husband shipped home. Richard didn't tell his mother about the dream. He waited until after she'd gone, and then went to find his grandfather.

For the rest of his life Richard would remember the afternoon he told Grandfather about the dream, and how afterward the old man told him the story of the Ghost Dance. He would remember the blazing, yellow-white sun that beat down relentlessly, causing the dry road and the brown hills beyond their rocky driveway to shimmer, as if the land that lay before his young eyes were part of a vision.

The boy and the old man sat on the porch beneath an overhang that gave them shade but did little to assuage the fierce summer heat. Richard listened intently to his grandfather, who had been, at one time, a medicine man of their Oglala Sioux tribe. As the boy listened, he watched the shimmering in the distance. He imagined that he could see what his grandfather described, out there on the land.

Grandfather's face was as seamed and brown as the parched earth, his voice as scorched as the summer air. 'You're certain you saw your father last night?' the old man asked. 'In your dream?'

'Yes, sir,' answered Richard.

'And in the dream he was alive?'

Richard nodded.

'He came to speak to you of the Dance of the Ghosts,' Grandfather said.

Richard frowned, perplexed. ' "Dance of the Ghosts"?'

Grandfather nodded. 'I'm going to tell you about something that happened long ago. I was alive at the time myself, though I was a very small boy. Younger than you are now. Some of this I have been told, but some of it I saw with my own eyes. Though it was only much later, after I'd become a man, that I understood what my eyes had seen.'

Richard waited.

Grandfather said, 'Once there was a man named Kicking Bear, who was from Cheyenne River. He came to see the great chief Sitting Bull. This was when Sitting Bull was living at the Standing Rock agency. Kicking Bear had gone with another man named Short Bull to see a man from the Piute tribe that lived far away, near California. The man they went to see was a holy man named Wokova. At the time there were some who said that Wokova was Jesus Christ come again, only this time as an Indian.

'Wokova met Kicking Bear and Short Bull at a pow-wow, and he said to them, "My children, I am going to talk to you about your relatives who are dead. I will teach you how to dance a dance, and when the dance is over, the earth will roll up like a blanket, and all the bad things the white man has brought – all the fences and railroads and telegraph poles – will disappear. Underneath will be our old Indian earth, with all our relatives come to life again." Then Wokova began to dance and sing, and Kicking Bear and Short Bull and all the others from many different tribes who had come to see this holy man began to dance and sing with him. They danced the Dance of the Ghosts late into the night, until Wokova told them they had danced long enough.

'Kicking Bear and Short Bull came back to teach all the Sioux people the Dance of the Ghosts, telling them that soon the day would come when the earth would be covered with new soil which would bury all the white men. The new land would be covered with sweet grass, and the buffalo and the wild horses would return. And all the people who danced the Dance of the Ghosts would be taken high into the air while the wave of the new earth passed over. Then they would be set down again among the ghosts of their ancestors on this new land, where only Indians would live.

'I saw them dancing myself,' Grandfather continued. He'd turned away from Richard to stare over his shoulder, as if he were trying to look into the past. 'I saw them holding on to each other. They would dance and dance until they fell to the ground, and then they'd lie there as if dead. After a while, they would wake up. "We saw our dead mothers and our dead fathers," they would say. The leaders of the dance would tell them not to be afraid of white men who hated the Dance of the Ghosts. The leaders gave the people Ghost Shirts to wear. On the shirts were magic symbols which would protect the dancers from the white man's bullets.

'For months everyone danced. Then one day that winter the news came that Chief Sitting Bull had been shot to death at Standing Rock. "What shall we do?" the people asked our chief, Big Foot. And Big Foot said, "Let's go to Pine Ridge and see Chief Red Cloud. He'll protect us from the soldiers."

'We got into our wagon and drove toward Pine Ridge. The day was very cold and snowing, and it was not a happy ride because the grownups were all so worried. We got as far as Chankpeopi Wakpala, Wounded Knee Creek, which is where the soldiers stopped us and told us to make camp. We did as they said. The soldiers made a ring around us and would let no one leave.

'I remember that night very well. It was so cold that I had to sleep between my mother and my father to keep from freezing to death. In the morning the soldiers came and woke us up and took us outside. They fed us hardtack biscuits for breakfast, but that was all.

'Then more soldiers came. "We're here to take away your weapons," they said. Many of the people went to get their rifles and their knives and their axes, and they made a big pile in the middle of the camp. But the soldiers weren't satisfied, so they decided to search the tents. Then they ordered the warriors to remove their blankets. You could tell that the warriors were angry, but only Yellow Bird, the medicine man, protested. He began to dance the Dance of the Ghosts. He sang to the warriors that they were wearing their Ghost Shirts, so the soldiers couldn't harm them. He chanted in the old language, "Don't be afraid. Their bullets cannot hurt you. Their bullets cannot hurt you."

'The soldiers found only two rifles, but one belonged to a bad Indian named Black Coyote. They grabbed him and tried to take his rifle away. Black Coyote fired the first shot. After that the soldiers started to shoot back.'

Richard looked into his grandfather's dark, glittering eyes. 'I remember hearing a noise,' Grandfather said, his voice distant and hollow. 'Like a thousand claps of thunder, all at once. My father burst into tears, and I could hear my mother wailing. Everybody was acting crazy, and there was blood on the snow. So many people, Indians and soldiers, lying dead. Three hundred people, all dead . . .'

The old man's voice trailed off. It seemed to Richard that Grandfather had gone some place very far away, had willed himself back in time. When the old man spoke again, his voice had grown soft. 'This is what I remember,' Grandfather said. 'The people danced the dance, but the earth never rolled up, and the buffalo and the wild horses never returned, and the dead never came back to us. It was the soldiers who came. They didn't know that the dance was a peaceful one. They must've thought it was something else.'

For a time the old man was quiet, until at last he said, 'That is why your father came to you last night. He was trying to tell you about the Dance of the Ghosts. He was trying to tell you not to be afraid, and that someday you'll see him again.'

After that, Richard and his grandfather sat on the porch, neither one speaking until long after the sun had gone down, and Richard's mother had returned home.

2

The second time Richard Battles dreamed about the Dance of the Ghosts, he was in a military hospital in Vietnam.

In 1964, he graduated from Red Cloud Indian School at the Holy Rosary Mission, four miles north of the village of Pine Ridge, where he and his mother had moved following his grandfather's death in 1960. After graduating, Richard spent a year and a half driving a tow truck for his mother's cousin, Joe Kills Buffalo, who owned a Sunoco service station in the village. Working for his uncle, Richard knew, was simply marking time, especially after President Johnson announced in April 1965 that the government would be increasing the number of military personnel in Vietnam. In February of the following year Richard received a notice to report for his draft physical. The next morning he drove the tow truck to Rapid City and enlisted in the United States Army.

He completed basic training that spring at Fort Leonard Wood, in southern Missouri, the first time in his life he'd been more than three hundred miles from his home. After a month's leave, which he spent in Pine Ridge, he reported to Fort Bragg for Advanced Infantry Training. For a few months he was stationed in Washington DC, until March 1967, when he was sent to Vietnam. On the day he stepped off a transport plane at a place called Tan Son Nhut, Richard was four months shy of his twenty-first birthday. Having been trained as a rifleman, he reported to Company B, Third Brigade, Twenty-Fifth Infantry Division.

One morning in February 1968, a few weeks into the Tet Offensive and less than a month before his tour of duty in Vietnam was to expire, Richard's platoon was helicoptered to a landing zone near Chu Lai. The LZ was hot. NVA regulars hidden in the surrounding jungle opened fire on the lead slick – the one in which Richard was riding – as soon as it reached treetop level. The chopper's gunner shouted, 'Hit it!' to the infantrymen, commanding them tò jump.

Richard was the second man out. He tumbled to the ground, somersaulted to his feet, and managed a half dozen zigzagging steps toward cover before a heavy blow struck the side of his helmet. The blow knocked the helmet away, and Richard staggered, falling to his knees. Oblivious to the cyclone of activity swirling around him, he reached up to pull his soft cap from his head. The cap was soaked with blood.

A second blow slammed into his left shoulder, spinning him around. He collapsed to the ground. The burning agony in his shoulder throbbed with each rapid beat of his heart. Dimly he became aware of the *whip-whip-whip* of helicopter blades over-head, like the beating of wings. A cocoon of blackness, tinged with red at the edges, enveloped him. Gradually the burning pain receded, the blackness smothering him, and he thought: *So this is what it feels like to die.*

He came to in the medevac that was transporting him from the LZ to the hospital. 'I'm not dead?' he whispered hoarsely to the corpsman bending over him. The corpsman shook his head and grunted sardonically, 'Sorry to disappoint you, buddy.' Richard immediately passed out again.

His head injury turned out to be a relatively minor scalp laceration, the helmet having protected him from a fatal wound. The other injury was more serious. A round from an AK-47 had smashed into the upper portion of his left humerus, shattering the ball-and-socket joint of his shoulder. By the time he was being prepped for surgery, Richard had lost nearly three pints of blood and was in a state of hemorrhagic shock.

That night, while in the recovery room following the emergency operation and still feeling the effects of the anaesthesia he'd been given, Richard dreamed of the Dance of the Ghosts. This time, however, his father was not alone in the dream. Gaylord Kills Buffalo, Richard's grandfather, was there as well.

In the dream, Grandfather spoke first. 'You weren't wearing your Ghost Shirt, were you?' he castigated Richard. 'That's why the bullets could harm you.'

Richard asked, 'Am I going to die?'

'Yes,' Grandfather answered. 'But not today.'

'It's not your time yet, son,' said Sam Battles. 'There is still something you must do.'

'What's that?' Richard asked.

'You must decide,' replied Grandfather. 'You must choose which is it that you are to be. The ghost or the soldier.'

Richard turned to his father. 'I don't understand.'

'No man who is divided against himself can ever understand,' said Sam Battles.

'It is only when the separate pieces are brought together into a whole that understanding comes,' said Grandfather. 'Only then can you truly learn the Dance of the Ghosts.'

As Richard watched, the figures of his father and grandfather began to dissolve, swallowed up by dream-mists. He called to them vainly, begging them to return, but they ignored him.

There followed almost immediately a second dream. In it, Richard saw himself back on the battlefield where he'd been wounded. It was as if he were a disembodied spirit hovering over the scene. He watched himself – Richard-in-the-dream – leaping from the helicopter, tumbling, coming to his feet, dashing toward the jungle. At the precise instant his dream-self was struck by gunfire, there came a brilliant sunburst-flash. Suddenly there were *two* Richards-in-the-dream: the one who lay on the ground bleeding; and another, uninjured, who was hurrying into the jungle, seeking cover with the rest of his fellow soldiers.

In his mind, Richard screamed: *No!* At which point he awoke, shivering with terror.

Neither dream recurred during his period of recuperation, nor following his release from the hospital. He was soon to discover that while the emergency operation had saved his life, there was little the surgeons could do to repair his ruined shoulder. For the rest of his days, Richard's left arm would be all but useless, its motion so restricted that he could not raise his hand higher than his chest. He was awarded a Bronze Star for bravery and a Purple Heart, and given an honorable discharge from the service and a disability pension. In July 1968, he went home.

3

The third and final time Richard Battles dreamed of the Dance of the Ghosts was in 1973, at Wounded Knee.

He returned to Pine Ridge in the summer of 1968 to find that little had changed during the time he'd been in the army. His bedroom at his mother's house looked the same as it did the day he left for boot camp. His Uncle Joe had his old job waiting for him. The reservation was as hot and dusty as ever. There were still poor people everywhere.

Over the next four years, Richard's existence fell into a numbing routine. He worked for his uncle six days a week, helping out in the station's garage when he wasn't driving the tow truck. On Saturday nights, he invariably went out with the same group of friends, all of whom had been buddies in high school; half of whom – as adults – were unemployed and had families and children on welfare. They would pile into the tow truck and make the short drive across the state border into Nebraska. As it was illegal to buy or sell alcohol on the reservation, they would fill the truck with cases of beer and drive back to Pine Ridge, where they would go to one or another's house and drink themselves into a stupor. Unfailingly hungover on Sundays, Richard would nevertheless drive his mother to Holy Rosary for mass. His mother was a devout Catholic. Richard had stopped believing in God many years before.

It was in 1972, at a Christmas party at his Uncle Joe's house, that Richard's life began its inexorable progress toward the night of his last dream of the Dance of the Ghosts. At the party, he was drawn aside by Kate Mesteth, one of his cousins. Kate was a year younger than Richard. They had been close as children, but they hadn't seen one another in six years. Richard was already in the army when Kate moved from Pine Ridge to Vermilion, on the other side of the state, to attend the University of South Dakota. She'd stayed in Vermilion after earning her Bachelor's Degree and had gone to work for the militant American Indian Movement.

Richard had heard of Kate's group and was acquainted with two of the better-known local figures associated with AIM, Russell Mix and Eddie Pourier. Earlier that summer, Mix himself had asked Richard to join the group. The movement especially welcomed vets, Mix had told him. Richard declined, but Mix assured him that the invitation would remain open.

At Joe Kills Buffalo's Christmas party, Kate intended to repeat Mix's invitation to her cousin to join AIM. By the time she was able to get him alone, however, Richard had been at the party for an hour and a half and was already drunk. His sorry condition infuriated her. Instead of speaking about AIM, she accosted him. 'I've been wanting to ask you something for a long time, cousin,' she challenged. 'I've always wondered if you appreciated the irony of your situation while you were over in Vietnam. Here you were working for the very same government that slaughtered your own people, not a hundred years ago, and you're personally doing the very same thing to the native people of another country. Did you ever think about that when you were over there? Do you ever think about it now?'

Seething with resentment, Richard attempted to draw himself from his cousin. She clutched him by the arm to restrain him. He focused his bleary eyes on Kate's, which were ablaze with fury and indignation. He jerked his arm free. 'No,' he lied sullenly. 'I don't ever think about it. I never have.' Then he stormed away.

For two months, the memory of their confrontation skulked in the back of Richard's mind. Until the morning of 28 February 1973, when a group of two hundred Indians led by AIM overran the town of Wounded Knee, twenty-five miles east of Pine Ridge. The town – though it could barely be called such – consisted of only four structures: a trading post, a post office, a Church of God, and the Sacred Heart Catholic Church. The group that took over the town on the morning of the twenty-eighth captured eleven hostages, all of them citizens of Wounded Knee and all of them white. AIM – under the direction of Russ Mix and his associates Dennis Banks, Carter Camp, and Clyde Bellecourt – set up a command post in the Sacred Heart Church. The church stood on the same grounds as Wounded Knee Cemetery, where the victims of the infamous 1890 massacre were buried.

While watching a network news show the following evening, 1 March, Richard Battles witnessed what millions of other Americans were seeing at the same time: a force of several hundred FBI agents, US marshals, and BIA policemen organized by the Justice Department to surround Wounded Knee. An FBI agent speaking for the authorities explained that the deployment of so many men was for the sake of the hostages – even though all, except for the ones who'd asked to stay, had been set free already. When a television camera panned the faces of the Indians occupying the town, Richard recognized several. Among them was Kate Mesteth.

That night after supper, Richard told his mother he was going to Wounded Knee in the morning to join the occupying group. She regarded him with dismay and concern. He argued calmly, 'A lot of people are probably already sure I'm AIM, so I may as well be there, don't you think?'

When he arrived at Wounded Knee on the morning of 2 March, he was astounded by the size of the counterforce that had been assembled by the government. It reminded him eerily of Vietnam: deputy marshals carrying M-16s; ·50-caliber machine guns mounted on armored personnel carriers; enough ammunition to wipe out every Indian in South Dakota; helicopters whirling overhead. He was able to make his way around the roadblocks and barricades being set up by the makeshift federal army without difficulty. As he walked up the hill to the Sacred Heart Church, Kate Mesteth and Russ Mix emerged from the front door of the building, opening their arms to welcome him.

The occupying Indians were as shocked as Richard was by the size of the force assembling against them. 'I thought we'd be here two or three days at the most,' Kate said ominously to her cousin as she took him around to meet the others in the command post. 'Now I'm not so sure any more.'

Richard was one of several vets who were part of the AIM group. He shared their skill in constructing trenches and bunkers and handling weaponry, none of which the majority of the group occupying Wounded Knee knew much about. Within days, perimeters had been established around both the church and the trading post. Armed with a meager supply of dynamite, a few handguns and rifles, and several dozen Molotov cocktails made from empty bottles of soda pop, the AIM forces hunkered behind their makeshift barricades. And waited.

On 7 March, the government issued an ultimatum to the AIM forces: be out of Wounded Knee by sundown on 8 March, or face the consequences. When the deadline arrived and the Indians hadn't budged, both sides opened fire.

The firefights continued sporadically for three days and nights, until a ceasefire was called on 10 March, and the government announced that it was lifting the siege. For the first time in nearly a week, the battle lines were freely crossed. Richard left the compound to visit his mother. When he returned to Wounded Knee on the morning of 11 March, the cheerful mood of the day before had evaporated. The gloom was as palpable as the winter storm that swelled the heavy, lead-colored sky. Richard discovered that on the previous afternoon an FBI agent had been shot during an exchange of gunfire between him and a van full of Indians who were returning to Wounded Knee from a nearby village. By the evening of the eleventh, the barricades were up once more. The truce was broken. The firefights resumed.

Four days later, on the morning of 15 March, the fighting stopped again. The blizzard that had been threatening for days struck at last. By noon, a bitter cold wind was whipping stinging sheets of snow across the plains and hills, making it impossible for anyone to see anything more than a few yards in front of him. Another ceasefire settled over the battleground, this one imposed by Nature herself.

By nightfall, a foot of snow had fallen on Wounded Knee. The storm had blown eastward, leaving behind a clear, onyx sky dotted with stars like diamond pinpricks. The temperature of the evening air grew bone-chillingly cold.

At ten thirty p.m. on the night of 15 March, Richard was sleeping on a cot in the sacristy behind the altar of the Sacred Heart Church. He'd been asleep since the AIM forces hiding in the church had shared their evening meal. He'd hoped to rest until midnight, when he was to go outside to relieve the guard watching the perimeter that surrounded the rear of the command post.

Asleep, he dreamed of the Ghost Dance one final time.

The dream startled him awake. He sat up abruptly, groggy and disoriented. He was shivering – not so much from the cold, though the church was poorly heated, but from a vague sense of terror that was the residue of the dream. He shook his head, forcing the unpleasant sensation from him. He looked at his wristwatch and saw that his guard did not begin for another hour and a half. He sighed, aware that trying to go back to sleep would be futile.

He got off the cot, dressed himself, and went out into the church. The huge interior space was dimly lit by Coleman lanterns and candles. Richard could make out the dark shapes of dozens of his comrades sleeping on the pews, bundled in coarse blankets, huddling with each other to fight the chill. He saw two people standing near a table set up in the vestibule at the rear of the church. He smelled freshly brewed coffee, the aroma beckoning him like a siren's call.

As he neared the table, Richard recognized the voice of his cousin Kate. She was speaking in low tones to Eddie Pourier, who was standing beside her. She turned at the sound of Richard's approaching footsteps, greeted him with a smile, then filled a mug of coffee for him. He accepted the mug and nodded thanks. 'How're things outside?' he asked.

'Quiet,' answered Kate. 'Very quiet.'

Pourier smiled. 'Just like in them old western movies. You know, where the cavalry's hiding behind the walls of the fort, waiting for the Indians to attack, and the one soldier says, "Quiet, ain't it?" Then the other soldier says, "Yeah. *Too* quiet." '

Richard and Kate chuckled. He sipped his coffee, wrapping his hands around the mug to warm them. Then, without preamble, he said to Pourier, 'You don't happen to know how to make a Ghost Shirt, do you, Eddie?'

Pourier regarded him with curiosity. Kate asked, 'What's a Ghost Shirt?'

Richard looked to Pourier. 'You know what I'm talking about, don't you?'

Pourier nodded. 'Yeah. I know.'

'I don't,' said Kate. 'What's a Ghost Shirt?'

'Something from the old days,' Pourier answered guardedly. He turned back to Richard. 'Why are you asking me if I know how to make one of those?'

Richard shrugged. 'No reason. I just . . . I had a dream, that's all.'

Pourier's eyes narrowed with concern. 'A dream?'

Richard shook his head and smiled disarmingly. 'It's nothing. Don't worry about it.'

Pourier continued to watch him with care. 'Hey,' Kate challenged. 'Is somebody going to tell me what you two're talking about, or what?'

'Eddie will,' Richard said mildly. Having finished his coffee, he handed the mug back to Kate, then gave her and Pourier a small wave of farewell. He went back to the sacristy to retrieve his overcoat, hat, gloves, and rifle. After bundling himself, he went outside through the rear door of the church.

Richard made his way cautiously to the barricade that marked the perimeter of the outpost and began his watch. The night sky was the color of anthracite, the stars like tiny chips of ice. Staring up into the vast blackness, he felt a chill deep in his bones, deeper than any that could have been caused by the bitterly cold air. Wrapping his arms around himself, he could feel the moisture in his nostrils beginning to crystallize. *Don't think about how cold it is*, he ordered himself.

He stood motionless for a time, aware of the eerie silence that enveloped him. Gradually he began to hear an unbidden voice in his mind. He recognized the voice – it was the same one he'd heard in his dream less than an hour before. Now, as then, the voice was singing:

'He yoho ho! He yoho ho!
The spirit host is advancing, they say,
They are coming with the buffalo, they say,
They are coming with the new earth, they say.
He yoho ho! He yoho ho!'

Richard shuddered. *Don't think about that either.* The words were from the song of the Ghost Dance that his grandfather had taught him nearly twenty years before. *This would for sure be a night for ghosts, if ever there was one.*

The stillness was unexpectedly broken by a distant sound of surreptitious footsteps crunching through the hardened crust of snow. The sound made Richard's hair stand on end. A frozen hand clutched at his insides. He dropped into a crouch, whirling around in the direction of the footsteps. Ignoring the ache in his left shoulder, he unslung his rifle and held it ready. He could feel the muscles in his legs and arms tightening.

From behind the barricade, Richard studied the silver-shadowed landscape before him. The rises and declines of the land around Wounded Knee Creek lay blanketed by the fresh snow. He listened hard for the footsteps, aware of the sound of his own inhalation and exhalation of breath. He blew small clouds of vapor in the sharp, cold air.

There. The footsteps were coming from the direction of a darkened depression behind a short, sloping hill fifty yards to his right. He peered intently at the shadows. He saw nothing at first – until he noticed a man-shaped figure vaguely outlined in the gloom. The footsteps had stopped. The man was standing still, his back to Richard, who could read the white letters emblazoned on the back of the man's dark jacket: 'US MARSHAL'. Richard scowled.

Steeling himself, he crept forward. Crouching, he walked on tiptoes, moving as silently as he could, trying to keep his boots from scraping the crusted snow. He held his breath as he approached the man from behind. Stealthily he closed the distance between them, until he was less than a half dozen yards away. He could see the outline of the M-16 the man was carrying. Leveling his own rifle at the man's back, Richard uttered in a low voice, 'Turn around, asshole. Nice and easy.'

The man stiffened at the sound of Richard's voice. Then, slowly, he did as he was told.

They looked into each other's faces simultaneously, their eyes widening, their mouths dropping open. And Richard Battles – Vietnam veteran, tow truck driver, borderline alcoholic, fringe member of the American Indian Movement – found himself staring into the face of Richard Battles.

Awareness flooded over each of them in a blinding blaze of satori – the awareness that each was seeing *himself*, as if he were looking into a mirror. The man with 'U.S. MARSHAL' stenciled on his jacket was a Richard Battles who had *not* been wounded in Vietnam; who after completing his army enlistment had continued to work for the government that had cared for him; who had never returned to the reservation but instead had taken a job with the Department of Justice; who was to the man he now faced the Richard-of-his dream, the dream he'd had while lying in the military hospital, the dream *after* his dream of the Dance of the Ghosts. The dream of death.

Each could read the other's life history – *the Richard-I-might-have-been* – in one another's eyes. Each of them suddenly and with absolute certainty – *knew*. Each raised his weapon and fired.

4

Richard Battles stood between his father and grandfather, watching from atop a steep rise. They saw Kate Mesteth and Eddie Pourier, the first ones to dash from the church at the sounds of gunfire. Kate and Eddie ran to the barricade where they could see a group of deputy marshals gathered in a small circle fifty yards away. The marshals were shining flashlights upon something that lay on the ground in the center of the circle. Kate and Eddie hesitantly crossed the barricade and made their way toward the group.

One of the deputies spun around, brandishing his M-16. The deputy standing adjacent to him placed a restraining hand on the barrel of the weapon. The circle opened before Kate. She looked down at the body of her cousin, Richard Battles. His solitary figure lay illuminated by cones of light. Blood seeped from a wound in the center of his chest, staining the snow. His rifle lay on the ground beside him.

Richard turned to his father and said in a hushed voice, 'I'm dead?'

'Listen,' commanded Sam Battles.

'We don't have any idea who shot him,' one of the deputies was saying to Kate. 'We heard the shots, and we ran right over here, but all we found was him. He was dead when we got here.'

Richard frowned, bewildered. 'What happened to me?' he whispered. 'I mean, the *other* me?'

'There is no other,' replied his grandfather. 'Not any more.'

'He doesn't exist,' said Sam Battles. 'There will be no record of him, no memory, no evidence that he ever was.' Richard's frown deepened. 'You remember what I told you once before?' continued his father. 'How no man who is divided against himself can ever understand?'

'Do you understand now?' Grandfather asked.

Richard could feel his frown shifting into another expression. He nodded. 'I think so. Yes.'

Sam Battles lay a hand on his son's left shoulder. Richard pulled away reflexively, then was startled to realize that the pain in his shoulder had vanished. He allowed his father to turn him around.

He blinked his eyes. The cold night had disappeared. Before him lay rolling hills covered with sweet grass. The sun was shining brightly. The air was warm and fragrant, redolent of early summer. The hills were dotted with huge, dark, shaggy shapes that grazed contentedly.

'There's a pow-wow tonight,' his father said to Richard. 'You're welcome to dance with us, if you like. Your grandfather and me.'

Richard replied, 'I'd like that very much.'

He looked from one man to the other and smiled. Then the three of them fell into a single-file line – grandfather, father, and son – and began to make their way down the hill.

This story is dedicated to the memory of Buddy LaMont,
an American Soldier

ORACLE BONES

Garry Kilworth

Garry Kilworth was born in York in 1941 and has spent most of his life travelling the globe, living and working in such places as Hong Kong, Singapore, Kenya, Cyprus, the Caribbean, much of the Middle East – where he spent his childhood – Malaysia and rural Essex . . . where he now resides.

He has an honours degree in English from King's College, London, and describes himself as a storyteller, producing science fiction, fantasy, thrillers, ghost stories and general fiction for both adults and children. 'I believe the storyteller is the priest of fiction,' he says.

Before becoming a full-time writer in 1981, Garry worked in cryptography and satellite communications. He now travels with his wife, Annette, an artist and itinerant social worker.

HarperCollins published his animal fantasy novel *Frost Dancers* in 1992 as well as *In The Country of Tattooed Men*, a new collection of his short stories, in 1993.

'Superstitions? Only that animals have an insight to the spirit world which we have lost through civilisation.'

Read on . . .

When the youth reached the hill village, the elders were in the Happy Hut, locked in a debate concerning the nature of heavenly bodies and their effect on regional game. The old men were of course smoking opium in order to keep their heads clear during the argument and to increase their skill at presentation. There was nothing the tribespeople enjoyed more than a lively contest of words. It was at the height of this serious discussion that the runner arrived, bristling with urgency. He was told to wait.

One shrivelled husk with a hollow, rattling chest stated emphatically that each time a bird was caught in a snare, or a squirrel was shot with a musket, a new star appeared in the night sky. There was an impatient murmur of agreement. This fact was not in dispute. That a tally of the hunters' kills was maintained by the gods was a truism. In the time of the first ancestors, far back, the heavens had been black and almost empty. The point that was contested was whether each star was a permanent replacement for each separate kill, because certainly the game had decreased dramatically in number over the centuries. It was a fact that the wild pigs had all but disappeared. The deer, which had once been as numerous as the termites which the tribe were now forced to eat, were now impossible to find.

The young messenger, who was from the same tribe but from a different village, waited outside the Happy Hut in frustrated silence for the debate to finish. Though the women had immediately taken care of his thirst, his bare feet were hot from the three-day run, and he longed to bathe in the cool stream. He sighed and scratched his insect bites, his heart full of things other than the carrying of urgent messages.

The boy's own people lived three valleys away in the direction of the sun and his long run was not yet over. There was the return journey to make. When he had been asked to deliver the message he had been halfway through a careful but hasty erection of his bridal hut. Fifteen years old, he had been wed just over seven days, but had yet to consummate the marriage. The living-hut which he had inherited from his father was not a fit place for the sexual act, since the spirits of his ancestors hovered around the corners and flickered on the support poles, and they would be shocked if he and his bride performed in their view. So, like all young men, he had to build a separate little bridal hut of bamboo roofed with banana leaves. This post-nuptial dwelling had to be at least a body-length from the living-hut. There, he and his new wife could reveal themselves to each other, away from the eyes of family ghosts. He had to build *carefully* since it had to be strong enough to withstand youthful athletics, yet *swiftly* because he was eager to experiment with procreation.

The youth looked up at the sky and sighed again. Dark clouds were buffeting each other across invisible terraces. He could make out the shapes of dogs amongst them, and wondered what that meant. A rain-wind was coming in low, through the treetops. He could see the shape of this broad wind running like a river over the foliage. Perhaps that was all it was? Rain coming?

Amongst the creased and withered elders, who puffed on their clay pipes creating a dense fog in the debating hut, was a man of great standing. He was the most ancient of any of the tribal dignitaries, having survived disease, accident and the rigours of opium for an unprecedented half century, though a recent respiratory problem indicated that it was doubtful he would make his fifty-first birthday. Though this particular village was one of the poorest of a poor nation, this man was their most powerful shaman. It was to him that the youth had come running.

The village was on a tall place, the peak of long ridge, and the youth hopped from one foot to the other, staring out over the hardwood forests below thinking of the beauty of his bride. She was plump and round-faced, with large dark eyes, and when he had first taken her to the courting garden and offered to push her on the swing made of vines, she had accepted without hesitation. There had been problems with her father of course, who had not approved of the youth as a suitable husband, but the boy had obtained a magic egg and had enticed the girl into the jungle. Once they had cooked and eaten the egg together, without interruption, the father naturally had to consent to the marriage. The egg had cost the youth two piglets, but she was worth it. Her cheeks were like ripe fruits and she had strong fat thighs. The youth's feet itched when he thought about those thighs.

Finally, though the debate was not yet at an end, the elders left the hut to perform their individual toilets. Clearly the exercise and fresh air was not good for them, because as soon as they were on their feet and out of the smoke they began to stagger. The messenger went immediately to the shaman, who was leaning on a portal attempting to catch his breath.

'Great one,' cried the boy, 'messengers have come from the big river to warn us of a coming!'

Red-veined eyes regarded the youth with little interest.

'Coming?' wheezed the old man. 'Who is coming?'

'Men. Men clad in clothes stained brown and green, and they have weapons which belch plumes of fire. They are as numerous as marching ants, and some of them come from the sky in whirling things which spit exploding balls. We are afraid they are coming to kill us all.'

'What do you want me to do?' whispered the shaman, coughing red flecks into the palm of his hand.

'You must tell us what course of action to take. The headman of my village has sent me here to ask your advice. This is an evil which threatens our whole nation and you, as our greatest shaman, have been given the authority to consult the oracle bones.'

A light came into the shaman's red-rimmed eyes.

'The oracle bones?' he breathed. 'Aaahhh!'

The elders were recalled from their functions in the forest and told of the news. It was universally agreed that the shaman *should* consult the oracle bones and a woman was despatched to fetch the last two bulls owned by the village headman. The corral where the cattle were kept was much closer than the village from which the young man had made his run, and the domestic beasts were in the hands of the shaman by nightfall. A ritual killing took place, then the flesh was stripped from the bulls and roasted over log fires. The old men put aside their pipes and feasted on the meat, which since the bulls had been slaughtered by the shaman in secret ceremony, was sacred and could therefore only pass the lips of an elder. All this was only right and proper.

The smell of the roasted bulls drove the young man mad and he went off into the forest to sleep. There under the moon-green roof of the world, he lay and dreamed of his fourteen-year-old bride. He had seen some of the girls in this village, as he had passed the spring where they filled their gourds, and none of them were as pretty as his own puff-cheeked wife. They had giggled as he ran swiftly past them, a stranger in their midst. It was true that there were probably several in the courting gardens that evening, waiting to see if he would appear, for there is no one more likely to cause turmoil in the hearts of local maidens than a youth from foreign climes. In his own village he might cause little excitement amongst the girls he had grown up with (his beloved being the one exception), but here he was a slim young god from exotic regions. There would be much speculation amongst older married women of seventeen or more about what his loincloth shielded, and concerning the tight roundness of his buttocks. The thoughts of the maidens, less direct, would be dwelling on his sinewy arms and thighs, and on the clarity of his eyes. Altogether, there would be little of his anatomy left untouched by the minds of the female population of this high village.

He slept fitfully, bothered less by the bark beetles and the spiders than by his own mental agitation. He went once to the spring for water, and interrupted an illicit meeting between a couple, married, but not to each other. The sounds of the elders feasting were disturbing the whole community, and there were few people in their beds. At dawn the women rose and began to pound the rice with footworked beam-hammers, and even the demons deep in the earth had their teeth rattled. The young man went and performed his ablutions, passing cleansed under the gate with the dogs' skulls and wooden figures that guarded the village. Elders had told him that once he was old enough to smoke opium and be privy to the *true* nature of the universe, he would see those wooden figures dance on the ends of their poles. The young man was not certain he was looking forward to this privilege.

The elders rose at noon and found their instructions for scraping clean the bulls' sternums had been duly carried out. A charcoal oven which had been built beyond the village perimeter was consecrated, and the two large bones were heated in this makeshift kiln. The young man knew that the shaman would retrieve the bones, once they had been allowed to cool, and inspect the cracks caused by the intense heat. Reading these symbols, sent by the gods through the fire into the bones, the shaman could divine the future. One sternum bone represented *peace* and the other *war*, and by this method would he know how the tribe should treat with the hordes now crossing the big river.

The youth waited in an agony of loneliness and homesickness while this ceremony took place. He wondered what his beloved was thinking right at that moment, as she worked out in the fields under the blazing sun. Was she dreaming of him? Of course, she must be. And the hut, still only half finished! Perhaps if he had made it smaller, it might be nearer completion, but then they had little enough room in which to romp as it was. Like most youths he wanted it large enough for her to be able to hold herself temporarily aloof, so that the eventual coming together would be that much sweeter. They needed to find each other in the darkness, not too soon, or the pleasure would be common and earthly. He anticipated going out on his first hunt, after their first union, and bringing home a tree squirrel or a fish for the pot. How her delighted cheeks would shine for him! He had been told by the elders that the pleasure of satisfying boy-girl desires was secondary to the wonders of the pipe, which he would be allowed to discover after his twenty-fifth birthday, but he could not believe such a tale. That was old men's talk, for those whose loins had since dried like seedpods under the sun. That was talk from those who could enjoy only dreams, whose passion had moved to their heads.

The following day he was summoned to the hut of the elders and the shaman gave him double-edged news.

The oracle bones had emerged from the charcoal without a crack on either of them. Such a thing had never happened before in the history of the tribe.

'It means,' said the shaman, 'either the tribe has no future to record on the bones, or the invaders will pass over us without disturbing us.'

'Should we risk it? Why don't we all hide?' said the youth. 'Why don't we run up into higher country still, where I have heard there are caves? We could stay there until these invaders have left our country, and then return and rebuild our villages. They would never find us up there.'

The shaman pursed his lips.

'Would you have us defy the gods?' he said.

'Is it possible,' asked the youth, 'that the fire was not hot enough? Or the bones too fresh? I have seen hotter fires, bones that were drier.'

'Leave us,' said the shaman. 'Go back to your village.'

The youth left readily enough and ran for three days, pausing only to drink from some broad-leafed plants that had formed basins for the rainwater during the last downpour. He arrived back at his home just as news reached his own elders that a village further down the valleys was in flames. The elders took his message and fell immediately into grave debate, while the young people crowded round the youth and asked questions of one that had travelled the world outside, had journeyed to the unknown regions of another village.

The boy ate then slept after that and awoke to the sound of rapid gunfire. He snatched his own long-barrelled musket, powder and ball, and ran outside. His young bride was running towards him, having raced from the fields. Her round face was bright with fear.

'The enemy are coming,' she gasped. 'They are shooting and burning.'

The youth waited no longer. He grabbed her by the wrist and led her towards the first ridge. He would take her to the next village and try to persuade the elders there that they should take action, prepare to resist the foe, or escape into the mountains. As he ran, pulling his frightened bride behind him, he called to his brothers, sisters and cousins to join him, but they merely stopped and stared as if he were mad, then turned their bemused eyes in the direction of the forest from which plumes of flame emerged with crackling roars. The sound of whirling clatter came from the distant sky.

This time the youth took four days to reach the village where the great shaman lived, due to the weariness of his own body and the slowness of his new wife. On the way he stopped to shoot a domestic pig with his long rifle. The pig had not belonged to him but the young man argued with his bride that now the end of the world had arrived, private property had become public.

When the pair arrived at the great shaman's village they found that the elders had just emerged from a long debate concerning the blankness on the oracle bones. These grave and pious elders took their duties extremely seriously. The opium was their link with their ancestors and it was the work of the elders to extract opinions from their hallowed forebears and impart it to their fellow debatees. Unfortunately, there were as many divine dead as there were men to question them. The fact that the old men could hardly stand when they left the Happy Hut, and frequently toppled over, indicated how long and hard the discussion had been.

They had finally come to the conclusion that 'blank bones' meant the tribe had no future. The invaders, said the elders, would kill every man, woman and child in the tribe.

'That's true, that's true,' cried the excited young man, 'they have already destroyed my village. Look, you can see the smoke from here . . . ' and pointed to the black vertical column which rose from beyond the southern ridges. There were other pillars of dark smoke behind the one indicated.

The great shaman ignored the youth. The old man's face was full of light and wisdom. He lifted his ancient hand, extended a bony finger and pointed dramatically towards the smoke in the south.

'It was when we saw *that* sign from the gods,' he told his people, 'that we knew the tribe had no future.'

The young man nodded vigorously, and was about to remonstrate with the elders, to spur them to some kind of action, when they retired to the debating hut once more to decide whether their particular village had no future because of the presence of the invaders – who might indeed be satisfied with their conquest of the lower villages and come no further – or because the elders had killed its last two bulls and could not survive without breeding stock.

The youth was disgusted with the old people. He and his young wife set out for the caves in the distant mountains, he explaining to her that there was no need for a bridal hut now, because their ancestors had been left back there in the village of their birth. She, not without a little pique, was explaining to him that if he loved her as much as he said he did, he would not forego her traditional rights just because they had been forced away from their roots. He was supposed to build her a pretty hut of bamboo poles and banana leaves. *If* he loved her, he would still do this little thing.

A healthy discussion ensued, as they hurried onwards.

When they reached a mountain pass, they came across more of the enemy emerging from huts with whirling arms that had come down from the gathering rainclouds. The green and brown warriors carried guns the boy had never seen before and looked more like wooden figures from a sacred gate come to life than they did flesh and blood men. Clearly the enemy were not interested in debate, for they swooped on the village in a silence interrupted only by the roar of their weapons.

The youth and his bride hid in a cave and they stayed there for two days before venturing out again.

At the time of the attack the great shaman had been caught in the middle of some wonderful rhetoric, for his blackened jaw was still wide open. When the youth sorted through his smouldering bones, in the haze of a smokey afternoon, he found they were cracked in many places. Although he had never smoked opium, the boy was able to read these divine messages easily, and predict the future of the tribe.

In the evening, it rained, sizzling upon the hot earth.

BORDERLANDS

Christopher Evans

Christopher Evans was born in South Wales in 1951 and works as a teacher in a South London comprehensive school.

His novels include *Capella's Golden Eyes*, *The Insider* and *In Limbo* and he has also produced a non-fiction guidebook, *Writing Science Fiction*. He is also responsible – along with co-editor Robert Holdstock – for the excellent *Other Edens* anthology series of a few years back. His latest books are *Chimeras* and a new science fiction novel – *Aztec Century* – published by Gollancz in May 1993.

'I'm not going to be much help to you on the subject of my own little rituals to appease the gods of entropy,' he writes. 'I don't think I'm especially superstitious, though I never walk under black cats and always try to avoid stirring tea or coffee exactly thirteen times . . . I find it tends to make the milk go sour.'

One winter morning when Alcia was six, her mother took her out across the fallow fields while her father sat at breakfast. The Myriads still shone in the paling skies, and a solitary caterwauler was greeting the dawn with its mournful screech. Their well had frozen overnight, and they were going to fetch water from the river.

It was the farthest Alcia had ever been from the farmhouse. As the sky lightened, she saw that frost had dusted the swathe of the valley, jupiter trees and tanglethorn standing stark against the grey. Her tiny breaths plumed in the still air as her mother hurried her along.

The river was smaller than Alcia had imagined, a shallow rock-filled band that coiled away to both horizons. The water was locked under a milky skein of ice, though she could still hear a trickling.

Her mother was beating a hole in the ice with the bottom of her bucket when the mist enveloped them. Winter mists were common, but this one came in without warning, cloaking everything in grey. Alcia wandered along the bank, tossing stones on to the ice and stamping her feet against the cold. It was then that the figure materialized on the opposite bank.

It was human-shaped, but its outlines seemed to shift as the mist coiled about it. Its face was as white as flour, eyes black shadows under a heavy brow. Alcia stood frozen, terrified.

The figure did not move or speak. It was wrapped in a tattered cloth. Alcia knew it was staring at her. She wanted to flee, but she knew she dared not move, or look away. Then her mother's fist closed tight around her wrist.

'Go away from here!' her mother shouted in a frightened voice. 'This is our land!'

The figure made no reply. It seemed to retreat without moving, but as the fog thinned around it, Alcia saw that its position had not changed.

Water slopped from the bucket as her mother gestured angrily.

'Go, I say! You're not wanted here!'

But it was she who withdrew, dragging Alcia with her.

Her mother's nails dug into her wrist as they hurried across the fields towards the farmhouse.

'Who was it?' Alcia asked, straining to peer back over her shoulder. The figure had been swallowed up again by the mist.

'It won't cross the river,' her mother said ardently. 'The river's the border that marks us off from them.'

Alcia struggled to avoid being splashed by the icy water in the bucket. 'Was it a man?'

'A Demon,' her mother replied.

From then on, her mother told her stories about the Demons at bedtime, sometimes reluctantly but always with a fearful relish. The Demons were pale-skinned, they hated the sun and drank human blood. Some said they were shape-changers who could take on any form to lure true people into their clutches. They used magic potions and unholy plants to assist them in their aims. Once they had lived everywhere but had been driven out by true people, confined to the borderlands where they could be watched, spurned for their mischief and evil.

All this was horrible and fascinating to Alcia.

'What do they do to you?' she would ask.

'They steal your mind away. Take it over. You become a shell. They eat you.'

'Eat you?'

'Not in the usual way. They eat your thoughts. All of them, until there are none left. Until you're empty. Then one of them takes over your body.'

'How?'

Her mother would show signs of impatience whenever she was pressed on details. 'Nobody knows how. That's why you must stay away from them.'

Alcia would ponder deeply, staring at the waxlamp, the only pool of brightness in the dark of her bedroom.

'How will I know if I meet one? If they can change shape?'

'You'll know. They aren't like us.'

As she grew older, Alcia would sometimes steal away to the meremeadow at the edge of their land. She would trace the path of the river from one end of the valley to the other. The Demon land beyond the river looked exactly like the land on their side with its bindreed marshes, jupiter and briarbush, its flowering summer grasses. She always nurtured the fearful hope of glimpsing a Demon again, but never did: there were no buildings in sight, only rampant scrub and grassland. Gossamerhawks and blackdaws found perches and nesting places on both banks, heedless of the divide. Emboldened, Alcia would sometimes wade across the river and stand on the far bank, expecting something, though she did not know what. The sun shone down on her as before, while nectarflies droned among musky passionweed. No Demon ever came out of the undergrowth, though one sultry afternoon she disturbed a wereworm, which promptly bit her in the ankle before slithering away into the reeds. She fled back across the river, convinced the creature was a Demon in disguise. The ankle swelled up, and she spent the next three days confined to bed in a delirium, certain that a Demon had claimed her but determined not to tell her mother that she had acquired the bite on their land. Afterwards, chastened, she had a greater respect for the river as a boundary, an invisible barrier protecting true folk from the dangers of the unknown.

While Alcia helped her mother with the poultry and swinehogs, her father worked from dawn to dusk in the fields, growing groundapples, corn and nylonea. He had a crossbow and would sometimes bring home leatherjacks and piebald snakes whose pelts her mother fashioned into hats or mufflers on long winter evenings. One spring day her mother went off in the carthorse, its great bowed back piled with provisions for the market fair. Alcia accompanied her father out to the whoreshorn hedge which separated their land from that of their neighbours, the Lortons.

It was the first time she had been left alone with her father, a sign to Alcia that she was now grown up. Her father was soon busy pruning the hedge and planting cuttings in the gaps. The sun was hot on her head, and she quickly grew bored with pleating grass and playing duck-and-run through the twisted arches of the nylonea vines.

'You won't keep the ferals out,' she told her father. Last winter they had lost four chickens after a raid on the coops which her mother said was due to ferals. There had been scarlet feathers everywhere.

Her father did not reply; he had few words, and was always occupied with his work.

She decided to demonstrate. Seeing a gap further along the hedge, she promptly scuttled towards it, intending to crawl through.

She was just about to do so when her father's gloved hands grasped her roughly about the waist. He hoisted her into the air and held her out in front of him.

'Don't go near them,' he said sternly.

She was puzzled. 'Near what?'

She followed his gaze and saw a cluster of black flowers growing in the shade of an elder bush next to the gap. The flowers were bowl-shaped, darkest purple, she saw now, with a wrinkled scarlet egg at their centre.

'What are they?' she asked.

'Demon's Cup,' her father said. 'You stay away from them.'

'Why? Did the Demons plant them?'

Her father lowered her to the ground and picked up a cutting.

'Did they?' Alcia persisted.

'Some say so.'

'Are they poisonous?'

He pushed his sharpened stick into the ground to make a hole for the cutting.

'You brush against them,' he said, 'and you'll get a fiery rash. The pollen'll give you fevers, drive you mad.'

She looked at the flowers. They were beautiful and horrible.

'Why don't you chop them down?'

'They'd grow back just as strong.'

She thought about this. 'You could dig them up.'

He took another whoreshorn cutting. 'Their roots go everywhere. Like cobwebs. You can never get them all out. Disturbing the earth just spreads them.'

Alcia was fascinated – as much by the fact that her father was actually engaging her in conversation.

'Will they invade our fields?'

'Not as long as I'm here.'

He did not elaborate. She crawled in front of him, forcing him to meet her eyes.

'How do you stop them?'

He gave a sigh of impatience. Then he straightened.

'Make me up a fire,' he said.

Alcia immediately scurried about, gathering up twigs and pulling fistfuls of dry grass from the hedgerow bank. She piled them up until her father told her she had enough. Then he struck a match and set fire to it.

Alcia watched as he carefully approached the Devil's Cup. He put a gloved hand under the largest flower, then snipped the stalk with his pruner. He held the purple blossom up like an offering.

Its petals shimmered with rainbow hues in the sunlight.

'It's the flowers that hold the seeds and the pollen,' he explained to Alcia. 'The trick is to burn them before they're ready to burst.'

He dropped the flower into the centre of the fire.

Black smoke began to coil up as the petals withered and burst into flame. The smoke was peppery, spicy – an attractive yet dangerous aroma.

'Stand clear,' her father cautioned, pulling her back a step.

The egg-like centre began to bulge. It blistered and finally popped. A dark red liquid oozed from it, sizzling in the flames like blood. Alcia was repulsed: in the liquid she was certain she had glimpsed tiny creatures like maggots squirming before they burst.

Her father was regarding her with a hint of grisly satisfaction, eyes large in his dark face. He held out the glove and pruner.

'Now fetch me the rest,' he told her.

Twice a year a travelling reverend would visit their farm and they would kneel together saying prayers which always ended with the earnest plea that Demons would never lighten their door. Her mother was very religious, Alcia knew that, but mostly she was too busy with her chores to make a ceremony of it. Alcia's father never attended these 'prayer meetings', preferring to muck out the swinepens or repair an outbuilding roof. 'Pious platitudes,' was the only explanation he ever gave to Alcia, and it was no explanation at all.

Every autumn a harvest festival was held at the farm of Mr Milkham, who was said to be the richest man in all the borderlands. His farmstead included a huge barn which was a sweeping curve of dull metal, overgrown with ivyberry and blotched with the sulphur and rust of lichens. The children were allowed to play inside it while the adults pursued their own entertainments.

On the way to the festival when she was thirteen, perched in the carthorse's hollow with their produce, Alcia began her bleeding. She was now a woman, her mother told her, and must beware the temptations that all women face.

Big nylonea tents had been set up in Mr Milkham's farmyard, and there were stalls and barrowbeasts holding goods brought by families from all the farms in the district and merchants from the town of Chipstone far to the south. Acrobats and fire-eaters entertained the crowd, their skins emblazoned with pearly tattooes.

Her father went off with the other men to inspect the livestock; he would come back later smelling of ciderwine and pipesmoke. Alcia helped her mother set out the jars of pickled eggs and fireberry jam on their stall; their speciality was preserves. They exchanged these for clothing or utensils, or they would accept worn coins that bore the faded portraits of men and women from long ago, inscriptions that spoke in a lost tongue of ancient times and ways.

Mr Milkham strolled about, overseeing everything, a stout bald man with a walking stick and two russethounds who followed him everywhere. He wore a smart chequered oversuit which Alcia's mother told her had been tailored for him in Chipstone. The sunlight gleamed on his mahogany head.

Towards evening, Alcia's mother released her so that she could join her friends in the shadowy interior of the barn. Its pitted metal ledges and alcoves were ideal for hide-and-find. Far below them, in the gaping entrance of the barn, the adults were dancing to the music of an arcadian. Rows of square metal openings were at the perfect height for leaping down into the cushioning clusters of pillowfern.

As dusk gathered, braziers were lit and the air thickened with the smell of woodsmoke and roasting haunches of swinehog. The creamy shards of the Myriads formed a ragged band across the sky. Then abruptly the arcadian music fell silent. Those who had been dancing stopped.

From her vantage point in one of the barn's windows, Alcia saw two strangers walk into a brazier's light. The taller figure was a woman, the shorter, a boy. Both wore ragged clothes, and both had skins as pale as uncooked meat.

Brazier smoke kept obscuring the scene, but Alcia saw the woman moving around the circle of people, talking to everyone in a strange tongue, holding out her arms, then gesturing to the child at her side. She was pleading with them, Alcia was sure. No one moved or spoke.

Then Mr Milkham burst into the light. His hounds were snarling, and he held them tight against their leashes. Approaching the woman, he thrust a small sack into her hand, vegetables spilling from its top.

'Here!' he cried. 'Take it and go!'

For a moment the woman did not move. The silence was unbearable. Then she stooped to pick up the marshmarrows and corncobs that had fallen from the sack. Her child began a gentle crying. Clutching her sack to her breast, the woman seized the child's hand and led him away into the darkness.

It seemed a long time before anyone moved. Alcia heard Mr Milkham tell three of his men to take the hounds out and ensure that the woman and her son were gone from his lands. He did not call them Demons, but 'Aboriginals'.

On the way home that night, she sat in the wagon with her father while her mother squatted in the carthorse, poring over their acquisitions. Her father was relaxed with the wine he had drunk, and Alcia decided to broach the subject of the woman and her child.

'Were they Demons?' she asked her father.

He was silent for so long she thought he wasn't going to answer her.

'Maybe they were and maybe they weren't,' he said finally.

'But Mr Milkham called them something else. *Aboriginals*.'

She had memorized the word so she could say it properly. Was there the hint of a smile on her father's lips?

'They have all sorts of names,' he told her. 'Your mother calls them Demons because that's her cast of mind. Others call them aliens, natives, chalkfaces. They all mean the same thing.'

'Do they always speak a different language?'

He continued as if she hadn't spoken. 'Go any distance and you'll find people using words you've never heard of.'

'Why did she come? The woman? Was it for food?'

Her father cleared his throat and spat out of the wagon.

'She was hungry all right.'

'Don't they grow their own food?'

He pinched her cheeks between his thumb and forefinger. 'Curiosity killed the caterwauler. Stay away from them, that's all I'm telling you. Your mother and me are one on that.'

The winter which followed was the fiercest in living memory. Frosts burned the vines, the river froze solid, and blizzards swept the land. With the start of the spring thaw, matters did not improve, because her father began coughing blood and shivering uncontrollably. One afternoon Alcia's mother found him collapsed in the barn, and Alcia had to help carry him indoors. She felt frightened and helpless as she struggled to support his dead weight.

They made up a bed beside the fire, and then her mother went off to fetch Mrs Lorton. Alcia did her best to keep the blankets on her father as he flailed about in his fever. She sat at his side all afternoon while wind and icy rain battered the shutters. Her father had always been a symbol of strength and endurance, and she was terrified he might die before help arrived.

Finally her mother returned with Mrs Lorton, a plump, smiling woman with a halo of frizzy grey hair. She was a herbalist, Alcia knew, clever at treating sickness in animals and humans alike. Alcia was ushered away and left to sit in fearful anticipation in the stultifying silence of her bedroom.

At length her mother came and told her what she knew already:

'Your father's very ill. It may be some time before he's well again.'

She sat down on the bed and took Alcia's hands. 'You'll have to go away for a while. To be looked after.'

Alcia was indignant. 'I can help! I can look after myself!'

Her mother was firm. 'You're going to your grandmother's house. In Chipstone. Mr Lorton'll take you in the carthorse.'

Alcia was astounded. 'I didn't know I had a grandmother.'

'Well, you have. She's your father's mother. Her mind's a bit addled with age, but you'll come to no harm with her.'

'I don't want to go away.'

'It'll only be for a while. Until your father's better.' She leaned close and said confidentially, 'There won't be enough food to feed all three of us this year. Your father's going to need what we have so he can recover his strength.' She produced a folded scrap of paper. 'I've written your grandmother a letter to explain things.'

Numbly, Alcia took the paper and unfolded it. She hadn't even known that her mother could write. The marks on the paper were meaningless to her.

'Is he going to die?' she asked.

'God will preserve him. But I can't have you under my feet while I'm tending to him. When he's better I'll come and fetch you.'

Alcia shook her head adamantly. 'I won't go.'

Her mother gave a great sigh of forbearance and resolution. 'You have to. These things are sent to try us.'

The journey to Chipstone took three days. Mr Lorton followed the river, through farmland and marsh, down lonely valleys where ferals hissed in the dusk, along a broad raised trackway, glutinous with mud, the carthorse snorting and steaming, obdurate and relentless in the face of all adversities, the river always in sight. They slept the first night with a family of five in their tiny farmhouse; the second night they huddled in the ruins of a long-abandoned settlement, its smooth-walled buildings clotted with creepers and vines, stained with algae and faded markings that might have been writing. Her mother had always warned her to avoid ruins, where she claimed poisons lingered in the very air and Demon-plants abounded. But Mr Lorton showed no such fears, and he was, after all, her guardian on their journey. She slept peacefully in the carthorse's hollow, and before they moved on next morning found a shard of shiny stone as pale as a Demon's face.

The third night they spent sheltering under a big broken pillar that had once been a bridge where another raised trackway joined the one they were following. Mr Lorton told her of the legend that the Myriads had once been a single heavenly body, a shining disc of light, until it was shattered in the great wars between the true humans and the Demons. Did he believe that the Demons ate your soul and could take on any shape? Mr Lorton sucked on his empty pipe and told her that true people had every reason to fear them, that he had once known a young man bewitched and driven mad by a Demon woman.

'What happened to him?' Alcia was eager to know.

'One day he vanished,' Mr Lorton said with grim satisfaction. 'He was never seen again.'

The day dawned bright and warm, and the trackway wound through spring-green woods, traversed a hill, and suddenly, there below them, was Chipstone.

Alcia had never seen so many buildings. They were clustered together, spreading out across both banks of the river, the river itself submerged beneath them. Far beyond, glimmering grey in the distance, was the sea.

Her grandmother lived in a spacious two-storey stone house with a pitched roof of slates and ivy-clad walls. Alcia's mother had described it in detail, and they had no difficulty finding it: in the courtyard opposite the house was an ornate iron whipping post, adorned with a Demon's head, its twisted face the personification of evil, as her mother had promised.

A cadaverous man dressed in black answered their knocks, then retreated in some confusion when Alcia presented the letter and explained why she had come. He took the letter with him, closing the door in their faces and leaving the two of them standing on the doorstep in the chilly evening air.

At length the door opened again. They were admitted and shepherded into the presence of Alcia's grandmother, a venerable lady who sat blanketed in a wheeled chair before a fire of black stones.

'Who are you, child?' the old woman demanded, craning forward to peer at her with milky eyes.

'I'm your granddaughter,' Alcia replied simply. 'Didn't my mother say in the letter?'

The scrap of paper lay in the old woman's lap, along with a reading glass. She picked both up and studied the letter minutely, one eye looming large through the glass, her lips silently mouthing the words. The man who had admitted them stood with his back to the door, gazing at her with disapproval. Mr Lorton warmed his hands at the fire. The house was fusty with age.

'We never saw eye to eye,' her grandmother said at length. 'Did you know that? I never wanted your father to marry her. What's his name, child?'

'His name?'

'Your father. If you're his daughter, you should know his name.'

Alcia told her.

The old woman sat motionless, still intent on her, the letter trembling in her withered hand. Her skin was like old leather, and there was a hairy wart between one nostril and the fold of her cheek.

'Is he dying?'

Alcia swallowed a great lump in her throat. 'It's only till he's better.'

The old woman made a clicking sound. 'I haven't seen him in

years. Since he married. You'll have to earn your keep, you understand that?'

Not knowing what else to do, Alcia nodded.

'Prout,' her grandmother said to the man in black, 'we'll have some sweetmint tea.' And then, as an afterthought, 'And some cakes for our guests.'

She fell to talking to Mr Lorton, asking him the precise details of Alcia's father's sickness. Prout returned with the tea and cakes, still eyeing Alcia with unmistakable disapproval.

Alcia bit into a yellow tart with a dusty topping.

'Whorlnut and marzipan,' the old woman informed her. 'You may call me Grandmother.'

Alcia slept the night in a bedroom at the back of the house which looked out over a long walled garden, overgrown with briars and vines. Beyond, there were more houses, and as darkness fell a reddish glow filled the horizon, a glow that emanated from somewhere in the town itself.

When she rose next morning, she found that Mr Lorton had already left. Her grandmother announced that Alcia was to wheel her to market.

Chipstoné was aptly named, for it was grey – grey stone houses, grey slate roofs, grey cobbled streets that wound and twisted between the jostling buildings.

The market occupied a cobbled square at the centre of the town, a bustling place selling all manner of goods, many of them unfamiliar to Alcia. A stallholder showed her how an umbrella worked, another gave her an aniseed stick to taste, a third demonstrated a wind-up metal carriage that scurried along the countertop on four wheels. It was clear that her grandmother was an important person in the town, respected and deferred to by everyone she met. The people wore patterned tunics, skirts and shawls; their perfumes intermingled with the smells of herbs and the elusive aromas of exotic fruits. Wide-eyed, Alcia manoeuvred her grandmother through the crowds.

The old woman was inspecting a bolt of indigo cloth when Alcia saw the Demons. There were two of them, man and woman, exchanging coins with a stallholder for a bag of flour. They were dressed just like everyone else, but their skins were unearthly pale under wide-brimmed hats. Alcia froze in surprise and fright.

Old though she was, her grandmother was alert, and she immediately noticed Alcia's unease.

'What's the matter, child?'

Alcia pointed.

The old woman stared, straining her pale eyes.

'Demons,' Alcia blurted in a whisper.

The rest of the crowd kept their distance from the two, and the stallholder concluded his business with them as swiftly as possible. Then the two went off and were lost in the crowd.

Her grandmother twisted the chair around to face her.

'That's what you call them, is it? One of your mother's words, I suppose.'

'Two of them came once to our harvest fair. A woman and her child. They steal your minds away.'

The old woman made a clicking sound that might have indicated disapproval or disbelief, Alcia wasn't sure.

'Do they live here?'

'They have their own quarter, on the other bank. They're iron-smelters. Now, child, take me home.'

Alcia struggled to comprehend the arrangement as she wheeled the chair back through the streets.

'Aren't people afraid? Of having them so close?'

Her grandmother was dismissive. 'People here tolerate them. For their usefulness. For their knives and scissors.'

'But they're shape-changers.'

More clicks. 'Superstitious nonsense!'

Now Alcia was thoroughly confused. 'Aren't they dangerous? Different from us?'

'Everyone's different, child. See?'

The old woman reached into her mouth and pulled out her teeth. They sat on her hand, pink and white, made of hard nylonea. Her mouth had collapsed to a pucker.

'We fear anyone that's not like ourselves,' she said gummily, chuckling at Alcia's surprise.

Her grandmother proved maddeningly elusive on the whole subject of the Demons, though as the days passed Alcia gradually learned more of their place and status in the town. Here they were known as Smiths, their quarter studded with forges and foundries. Trade was conducted with them out of necessity, but otherwise they kept to themselves, knowing they were feared, though the reasons for those fears remained obscure. Apparently people here did not credit them as shape-changers, but they weren't trusted. The previous summer, a child had gone missing and a mob had attacked their quarter, killing several. The child was never found, and many people still believed it had been taken, perhaps eaten, by the Smiths. Her grandmother's only verdict on the whole episode was that there was no end to people's foolishness.

In the room where they sat in the evenings was a tall glass-fronted cabinet, entirely filled with books.

'Have you read all those?' Alcia asked her grandmother one day. 'All those books?'

Her grandmother slurped tea from a china bowl.

'Once upon a time,' she replied.

The books were old, with faded bindings of charcoal and burgundy and blue. Their spines were frayed, silver and gold lettering cracked, the pages browned through the glass. The cabinet door was always locked.

'Will you teach me to read?' she asked.

'I haven't got the eyes for it, child. If your mother hadn't been so wooden-headed, *you'd* be able to read to *me*.'

Every night Alcia said prayers for her father's recovery, but by day there was much to occupy her mind in her new surroundings. She took her grandmother shopping most mornings, and sat with her beside the fire in the evenings after dinner, learning needlework or playing find-the-jester, her grandmother's favourite card game. In the afternoons the old woman took a nap, and Alcia was free to do as she pleased. Prout, her grandmother's houseman, resented her arrival, she knew, but her presence in the house enabled him to escape for a few hours each afternoon. He always returned more cheerful, smelling of spirits, with the overbearing manner of someone satisfied that a debt owed him has been repaid – or at least an installment on that debt.

On afternoons when Prout remained in the house, Alcia found time to explore the town on her own. The river intrigued her. It was still a border, the Smiths' quarter on the far bank, but the town itself sprawled without pause over bridges and arches so clustered together that they often blended into a continuous procession of houses and streets so that it was impossible to say where the territory of the townsfolk ended and that of the Smiths began. Did this wall, or that line of railings, or this prickpeach hedge mark the divide? Did the border run along this line of cobblestones, down that gutter, across this square? Were borders fixed or hazy? How would you establish one in the absence of rivers, along grassland or through woods? By painting lines or digging channels in the very earth?

On the rare occasions when she saw Smiths in the street, she would stop and watch from a distance. To all appearances they behaved just like ordinary people, though there was always a certain hesitancy or guardedness in their manner, as if they knew suspicious eyes were on them at all times. She listened to their voices – softer, but no different from anyone else's, using the same words as her. They wore sober clothing, hiding from the sun under hats or umbrellas. She always imagined that at any moment they might transmute themselves into ferals or werebeasts and would come snarling after her, to eat her alive.

The weather turned hot, hanging cream candles on the whoreschest trees and filling the air with the scent of blossom. Alcia lay naked on her balcony window, letting the afternoon sun warm her.

On Sabbathdays, everyone who was not in church gathered on the green for sports. Alcia liked the tugs-of-war and archery tournaments, the galloper races and coffee-apple stalls. One afternoon a group of men in white tunics spread out around another who stood guarding three sticks with a flat bat. One of the men then began rolling a wooden ball which the man with the bat hit.

Alcia lay on the buttercupped bank, watching the sport with the remote fascination of one who is wholly ignorant of its rules. Presently a voice at her shoulder said, 'Hello.'

She turned. A boy no older than herself was crouched at her shoulder, a white grin dividing his nut brown face.

'I'm Jay,' he announced. 'I've seen you around. You live with the old witch, don't you?'

She sat up indignantly. 'She's not a witch. She's my grandmother.'

His grin only widened. 'When I was younger, we used to throw pebbles at her window.'

'We?'

'Me and my friends. She'd send her servant out to chase us. We always thought that if she caught us, she'd turn us into toads.'

'That's silly. She's just a harmlesss old woman, and you were mean.'

'I was young then.' He sat down cross-legged beside her. 'What's your name?'

She told him.

'You aren't from around here, are you?'

She told him about the farm and her father's illness. Her grandmother had sent medicines by posthorse, but there was still no news of him.

Jay had the most startling blue eyes. He listened with perfect seriousness, which was all she could have asked for, coiling grass-stalks around his fingers all the while. He didn't try to offer sympathy, and Alcia was somehow glad.

'Did you know we're neighbours?' he said.

'Neighbours?'

'My house is back to back with the old w— with your grandmother's.'

'Then perhaps I'll remind her about you and tell her where you live.'

'Next time you see me I might be a toad.'

'It might be an improvement.'

He went into a crouch and began croaking. Alcia laughed.

'Do you come here every day?' he asked.

'Why?'

He was on his feet. 'I've got to go. Errands to run. See you here tomorrow.'

With this he ran off across the green, leaving Alcia surprised and somewhat disappointed by the abruptness of his departure.

That evening her grandmother opened the French windows so that the living room filled up with the rich scent of latex vine flowers. She told Alcia she had once been wealthy, trading in all manner of horses before the collapse of the business following an epidemic of hoofrot. Her husband had died, and she had never forgiven Alcia's mother for taking her only son away to live on a distant farm rather than remain in the town to help rescue the family's fortunes. All this had happened before Alcia was born. Now only Prout remained of a dozen servants, and there would be nothing left except the house when she died.

Next day, to Alcia's frustration, Prout went out that afternoon, leaving her to mope frustratedly about the house, unable to keep her rendezvous with Jay. She was certain Prout had done it deliberately to spite her. Through the tangle of the garden, she could see a single window in Jay's house, but the shutters were drawn.

The following afternoon, she went to the green, but Jay was not there. She sat on the riverbank, dangling her feet in the water and watching a coalhauler move downstream. The coal was dug out of the hills, according to her grandmother, used in domestic fireplaces and the forges of the Smiths.

She was daydreaming when someone tapped her on the shoulder. She whirled around. It was Jay.

'Do you always sneak up on people?' she said with studied irritation. 'I almost fell in.'

'Just be thankful I didn't decide to *push* you in.'

Not to be outdone, she reached up and grabbed him by the tunic, pulling him towards the edge. She only intended to scare him, but he overbalanced and went tumbling into the water.

Alcia couldn't help laughing as he surfaced, spluttering. She reached down to help him out, and was not entirely surprised when he pulled her in.

The river was shallow here, and they splashed one another merrily before finally clambering out.

It was another hot afternoon, and they flopped on the grass.

'What happened to you yesterday?' Jay asked.

She explained. Jay seemed to find the very mention of Prout's name amusing. He giggled and referred to him as 'the witch's apprentice'.

'Have you lived here all your life?' she asked him.

He nodded, kicking off his sandals. 'It's the only place I know.'

He looked perfectly bedraggled. Then his expression turned mischievous as he studied her.

'Your clothes would dry out faster if you took them off.'

'Would they?' Alcia was incensed at his presumption.

'No one can see you here.'

'Except you.'

Again the grin. 'It's nothing I haven't seen before.'

'What do you mean?'

'I've seen you. On your balcony. From my bedroom.'

So it *was* his window. Alcia could feel the heat rushing to her face. At the same time she was enraged.

'You were watching me?'

His grin became even more infuriating. 'It's the best fun I've had in ages.'

Instantly she was on her feet, ready to storm off. But he leapt up, too, and grabbed her.

'Let me go!'

She strained against him, but he held on to her.

'I'm sorry,' he said. 'I didn't mean to offend you. There's no shame in it, you know.'

'Isn't there? Then why don't *you* strip off?'

It was a challenge she did not expect him to rise to. He nibbled his bottom lip, then, to her surprise, began peeling off his tunic.

Within seconds he stood naked, his sodden clothes in a heap at his feet. Alcia was embarrassed, amused – and even a little delighted. Not knowing what to do with this confusion of emotions, she simply acted, snatching up his clothes and hurling them into the river. Then she was off, running, laughing, leaving him to flounder once again into the shallows to retrieve each garment before the river carried them away.

Alcia could not persuade her grandmother to read to her, but she did begin to tell her stories of long ago. The tales were muddled, she freely admitted, but most told of ancient days when people had changed the very world in which they lived. They had powers that enabled them to fashion new plants and animals, build huge flying wagons and boxes that held luminous worlds. Then there had been a war, a war fought not only with killing machines but also with terrible diseases that had slaughtered uncountable numbers, bred grotesques and led to great movements of peoples. She believed that the fear and hatred of the Smiths was a relic of those days.

Alcia was still puzzled, unable to see any connection. 'But why? Did they cause the war?'

'No one knows. It's just as likely they were victims of it. No one escaped the terrible suffering then. But people believe that some, like the Smiths, still carry malignancies and sicknesses that they can pass on to others.'

Alcia found all this hard to digest.

'Do you believe they can?' she asked.

Her grandmother clicked her false teeth. 'Child, I believe they've got more reason to fear us than we them.'

Whenever she could escape in the afternoons, she would meet up with Jay, seeking him out at the green or the river. He took her exploring, through the ruins of the Old Town in the woods; to the coast, chasing sandskitterers along the dunes; under the town bridges dank with moss and dripping stone needles, the roosting places of shrikers and fishbats. Sometimes a few of Jay's friends would accompany them, but Alcia liked it best when they were alone.

A letter arrived from her mother. Her grandmother read it out, clicking with disapproval at the poor spelling and choice of words. Her father was recovering but still weak. The warmer weather was sure to bring a further improvement in his condition. By the end of summer he would almost certainly be well enough for her to come home.

'Can I send a letter back?' Alcia asked. 'You could write it for me.'

'With these hands?' her grandmother said. The joints were swollen, fingers too stiff to hold a pen.

'Perhaps Prout would do it for me.'

'He doesn't read or write. But there's plenty of clerks in town that'll do it for you. For a fee.'

Alcia was sure her grandmother would pay the fee if she insisted, but it wasn't what she wanted. In any case, she wasn't certain what to say in a letter. It seemed a sin to be enjoying herself so much while her father was still sick. Instead she asked the posthorse rider to tell her parents that she was well, loved them and missed them, and hoped to see them soon.

It was a summer of green and gold and depthless blue. Jay taught her to swim, to ride a rubber-wheeled bicycle, and he even kissed her in an unguarded moment when the two of them were alone beside the waterwheel that worked one of the town's many mills. It was a kiss he repeated when Alcia did not protest, a kiss that she relished and feared as much as she relished and feared his arms closing around her, their breaths growing more rapid the longer it went on, a kiss that abruptly ended when a shadow fell across them.

It was Prout. He looked down at them with the rigid blankness of disapproval. How had he found them? How had he known where to look?

'Your grandmother wants you,' he announced to Alcia.

'There's news from your mother.'

Instantly she knew that the news was bad. Her father had died, and now all the happiness in her life would cease.

She found Jay sitting alone in the bandstand by the green.

'Your father?' he said immediately.

'Yes. But it's not what I thought. He's better. Well enough for me to go home. My mother's arriving tomorrow to take me back.'

He held her out at arm's length, examining her face with great seriousness.

'I'm going to miss you,' he said at length.

'I don't want to go.'

They hugged one another, holding on as hard as they could. After a long time, Jay said, 'At least we've got this afternoon.'

It seemed such meagre compensation that she couldn't say anything. But he was determined to be cheerful. 'Let's make the most of it. Do whatever we please. Come on!'

He took her wrist, dragged her out into the sunlight, made her run to keep up with him, across the green, through the streets and out of the town, running faster and faster, until she began to laugh with the madness of it all and was still laughing when they finally collapsed into a mass of pillowfern in the dappled woods.

They lay there for a long while, chests heaving. Then Jay sat up and said, 'I think it's time we had an adventure.'

He took her hand again and led her through the woods to a clearing where the ridged grass was festooned with clusters of ragged milky trumpets.

'They come out at the end of every summer,' Jay told her. 'Watch.'

He crouched and broke off several trumpets before smearing their juice over his cheeks and forehead.

The pale liquid soon coated his face, making it look white. The effect was scary and funny.

'You look like a Demon,' Alcia said, a little nervously.

He grinned, rubbing the juice over his hands and neck. 'That's the idea.'

She knew he wanted her to try it, too. And because it was their last day together, because she might never see him again, she, too, began plucking the trumpets and rubbing them into her skin.

The fungi smelt meaty, and as the juices covered her, her cheeks began to tingle. Soon, with Jay's help, all the exposed surfaces of her skin were covered. They both looked like ghosts.

'Come on,' said Jay, taking her hand once more and leading her back towards the town.

The sunlight speared her eyes as they emerged from the woods. Alcia began to feel as if she were floating, contentedly at the mercy of her whims. The meaty taste of the fungus was on her lips – a meatiness spiced with a sharper, giddying flavour. The sunlight danced, and Jay's form blurred as he leapt and skipped ahead of her, a beautiful phantom she was happy to follow anywhere.

They entered the town, and were enveloped in grey. Jay took her down unfamiliar streets, and it was a matter of remote amazement to her when she finally realized they were in the Smiths' quarter. Fires burned bright in open furnaces and forges, while greasy black smoke billowed into air. There were smells of sulphur and soot, a taste of metal on her tongue, and all around her moved pale, silent people – Demons, Smiths, hammering radiant bars of metal, shoeing horses, wraith-like children wallowing silently in the filth and heat, in the noise and black-stained clutter of their miserable ramshackle houses.

The quarter was an inferno, like Hell itself, and every hammerblow, every clang of metal or hiss of steam, pierced Alcia's brain like a knife. None of the Demons paid them any attention because she and Jay were now white-skinned and moved amongst them as if they were Demons themselves. Even so, Alcia began to grow nervous in case their subterfuge were discovered and the Demons fell upon them and carried them away. She began to plead with Jay to leave. At first he seemed to pay her no heed, but presently she became aware that they had finally left the heat and smoke and noise behind. They were walking down a quiet street, towards the doorway of a tall house that she knew must be his.

Jay led her not to the front door, but down a narrow alley at the side of the house and through a latched wooden gate. They were in his garden, a high-walled, overgrown garden like her grandmother's. She heard him saying that they were quite safe, his parents had gone out for the day. He was laying her down on a big mossy stone like an ancient tomb, putting his arms around her, kissing her.

But her fear had not gone away, and now it flowered. She lurched upright. All around her were plants unlike any she had ever seen before – scarlet vines with leaves like withered hands, crimson blooms that seemed to pulse like human hearts, creepers with purple chasmed flowers of sexual allure. The air was intoxicating with scents, thick with pollen.

Jay tried to hold her again, and now he was naked. Naked, and white-skinned all over. His eyes blazed like fire.

Alcia struggled to free herself from his embrace. She was trapped, lured and seduced by the creatures she feared most. He was saying soothing words, but all the time he was changing, now a werebeast with a sleek sable coat, now a feral with striped fur and slitted eyes, now her father with his jaw set hard and his eyes merciless. Then he was Jay again, looming over her, holding something in his hands, trying to press it into her mouth.

A Demon's Cup, its ripe red egg straining with life, pulsing to burst.

She wrenched herself free and fled to the back of the garden, plunging into the tangle of climbers, hoping despairingly to find a doorway that would lead to escape. But now the plants themselves were trying to stop her, tendrils coiling themselves around her limbs, furry blossoms stroking her face, black thorns lacerating her flesh. But she plunged in even deeper, knowing that Jay was still pursuing her with the evil flower that would make her utterly his.

Then, through the curtain of briars and vines, she saw a doorway set in the wall. A doorway to her grandmother's garden. A doorway across the border, back to the world of the true people. She hurled herself forward, felt something lash her face and clutch at her ankles as she plunged down into darkness.

It was Prout who found her at dusk, crouched and whimpering at the bottom of her grandmother's garden. She could not explain how she had got there, and was mystified when a mirror showed no trace of the juice she had rubbed into her skin. She had no memory of getting through the doorway, remembered nothing after her final headlong flight. As soon as she was able, she fled to the bathroom and retched until her stomach was empty.

It was late, and after she had bathed, she was allowed to go straight to bed. Though she feared a night of terrors, she quickly lapsed into sleep. When she woke, morning was well advanced, and her mother was sitting at the foot of her bed.

'Tell me what happened,' was the first thing she said.

Alcia sat up stiffly. The briar scratches were scarcely noticeable.

'I ate some mushrooms,' she said.

Her mother was silent for a while, scrutinizing her face.

'I warned you,' she said finally.

'They made me sick. I didn't know where I was.'

'Where did this happen?'

'In the woods.'

Another silence, then, 'Were you alone?'

'Yes.'

She did her best to meet her mother's eyes, determined to brazen it out. She could not possibly tell her the truth.

'You're sure there was no one else involved?'

'No one.'

More silence. 'What about this friend of yours?'

How much had Prout told her? How much did he know?

'He was just a friend. Nothing happened with him.'

More scrutiny, a longer silence. Her mother seemed to be weighing things up, and Alcia had the feeling that she really didn't want any awful truths. She would prefer a comforting lie if – if what?

'Promise me you'll never do anything like that again.'

So that was it, that was all she wanted. To wipe it clean, reject it so it would go away. Alcia felt like a whore, beyond redemption.

'I promise.'

'Swear in God's name.'

'I swear.'

Her mother exhaled a sigh that she seemed to have been holding in ever since Alcia had woken.

The day was cloudy, and rain began to fall as the last of Alcia's belongings was loaded into the carthorse. While her mother fussed with the horse, Alcia shook hands with Prout – cordial at last now that she was leaving – and embraced her grandmother.

'I'm sorry about yesterday,' she whispered. 'I let you down.'

The old woman fixed her with a gaze that always managed to be penetrating, despite her cataracts. Was it possible she knew everything? What Alcia feared most was the possibility that Jay had caught up with her and filled her with Demon's Cup before she was rescued. If so, vile creatures might be multiplying inside her even now. It was too horrible to contemplate, and she dared not ask her grandmother anything in case her worst fears were confirmed.

The old woman thrust out a big black umbrella.

'Take this,' she said. 'Bring it back next time you come. And get your mother to teach you to read. There's nothing worse than needless ignorance.'

They embraced again, Alcia holding on tight to her frail, musty body.

'Go on,' the old woman urged her finally. 'She's waiting.'

Alcia clambered up alongside her mother on the carthorse. Then she saw a figure standing across the square, leaning against the whipping post. He gave a distant smile and raised his arm in a wave.

Alcia went rigid.

'Who's that?' her mother said. 'Is that your boy friend?'

She separated both words as if they might contaminate one another.

'No,' Alcia said, turning her gaze from Jay to her mother. 'No. I hardly know him. Can we go now?'

Her mother tweaked the reins. The rain began to come down more heavily as the carthorse lumbered off.

'Get that umbrella up,' her mother said in her protective way of old. 'It's time we got you home, child.'

Alcia suppressed a shiver. She did not look back.

THE WAGER

Thomas F. Monteleone

Tom Monteleone made a name for himself at a UK Fantasycon a few years back when his predilection for British beer – which he lists in his biographical details – rendered him completely incapable of delivering his Guest of Honour speech on the Saturday evening.

On a more sober note, Tom is the author of more than eighty short stories – including the masterful 'Love Letters' in Richard Chizmar's *Cold Blood* – and some twenty novels, the most recent being the critically acclaimed thriller *The Blood of The Lamb* for which he won the Bram Stoker Award for best novel. He is also the editor of the prestigious *Borderlands* anthology series, now in its fourth volume.

In addition to books and writing, he spends his time playing with his computer, watching and playing baseball, travelling to exotic locales and driving his sports car on back country roads. He lives in Baltimore, Maryland, with his Lady Elizabeth and sons Brandon and Damon.

With his characteristically infectious chuckle, Monteleone freely admits to his superstitions. 'I'm scared to death about self-fulfilling prophesies,' he says. 'Like when you make an excuse to someone as to why you can't be somewhere – "Oh, hey, I'd like to but, you know, my father's had an accident." That kind of stuff. It's always bothered me using someone else's imaginary misfortune.

'I also had a problem with rituals – particularly the worry that not keeping them going might result in the worst. Checking on the kids at bedtime was always a nightmare for me. You know, had I checked them already? Maybe not . . . I'll check them again anyway. Seems to me that once you start something, you've got to keep it going.'

And, talking of which, meet Henry Pearce Huntington and Gordon Kingsley . . .

For an instant, Gordon Kingsley had forgotten where he was.

Had he drifted off to sleep? Impossible! After what he'd just experienced . . . no, it was plainly impossible.

And yet he'd felt himself blink, felt his entire body spasm, as though he'd been abruptly awakened, as though from a trance.

The darkness held him like a fist, and although he had not reached out to touch the walls of the coffin, he knew the prison of its wood loomed terribly close. He wished he had his watch with its luminous dial, just to check the time. But that would be against the rules.

The bastards, he thought with amusement. They're all probably jowl-deep in their *Wall Street Journals* by now, but Gordon knew at least one of them would be monitoring the simple control panel Huntington had designed for this particular little adventure.

That was one of the conditions – someone would always be monitoring both of them in case there was either (a) an emergency, or (b) capitulation.

Gordon Kingsley cleared his throat, wondering if the sound was loud enough to arouse whoever might be listening. No, that's right; they couldn't hear him unless he flicked on the mike. He thought about turning on the light, but that would enact one of the other conditions – for every minute you kept your light on, one was subtracted from your total time.

No, he thought. For now, I'll just lie here in the dark and think about why I'm here . . .

Murder is always murder. So is theft.

Gambling, however, is one of those fascinatingly odd pastimes that wears the clothes of its practitioner. If you're tuxedoed to the nines at Barclay's Casino in SoHo, playing roulette and baccarat all night, you're the jaunty gentleman. But if you're throwing dice behind the YMCA or getting toasted at Aqueduct's two-dollar window, you're the biggest scumbag in Manhattan. There is something elegant about betting with bankers and industrialists, but altogether tatty when you do it with steamfitters and housepainters. Gambling carries both its own social stigmata and imprimatur. It's not what you do; it's *whom* you do it with.

And so it was with the members of the Colonial Club – the oldest men's club in New York, dating back to the earliest days of New York's inclusion into the original thirteen colonies. Gambling among its brethren was as natural as hand-rolled cigars or imported sherry. To hear a wager being offered or taken in the Club's drawing room was as acceptable as a market price being quoted. Topics ranged from the most mundane of sporting events to personal boasts of prowess to the outcomes of political and financial futures. Amounts ranged from paltry dinner tabs to portfolio items. In all, the Colonial Club found gambling to be a delightful pastime.

But sometimes, a wager could take on a new level of meaning, of competition, and perhaps an even sinister nature.

This kind of bet was rare, and usually only witnessed between men who were sworn adversaries. There are certain types of men who *require* a personal nemesis to give them the energy needed to live life most fully. Men such as these are resolutely bored with the usual challenges in life; they have met these impediments and have vanquished them. In other words, they have made their fortunes, raised their children, divested themselves of sour marriages, travelled the world, and proved their manhood in all the other customary ways.

Truly to enjoy their jaded lives, men such as these need a

personal demon, someone to *hate*, someone they can *best at all costs, someone whose misfortune will make them feel good.*

The Colonial Club stabled men such as these, T. Gordon Kingsley and Henry Pearce Huntington being the most notorious.

Gordon had taken an instant disliking to Huntington the moment he'd met him. The Huntington family had only come into their wealth during the thirties. Before that, they'd been a loose circle of laborers and railroad louts. The worst part of this history was that Huntington continually blared out his nouveau riche status, as though he were proud of the fact that his grandfather swung from the back of a caboose. He may as well have declared that his ancestors swung from trees. Gordon was certain that if he searched through the Huntington genealogical record, he would find more than one Irishman in the woodpile, and that would more than account for Henry Pearce's lack of manners and general sense of decorum.

At fifty-five, Henry Pearce Huntington was in remarkably good shape, boasting at the amount of exercise in which he indulged. Despite his suspected mongrel status, Huntington sported the finely chiseled features of true nobility. This too irritated Gordon Kingsley, who had allowed himself to grow soft and weak as time and gravity stepped up their assaults. Indeed, *everything* about Huntington grossly annoyed Gordon Kingsley. Gordon found himself actually studying the man, watching his every move and hanging on his every word, searching for ever *more* reasons to loathe this *poseur* to true American aristocracy.

And so, Gordon Kingsley never let an opportunity pass wherein he might embarrass, chide, or challenge Henry Huntington. Not that the latter had any trouble carrying on his end of the unspoken agreement; it seemed that Huntington found Kingsley's new-Tory arrogance and his corpulent presence an equally hated target. If these men had lived in the age of dueling, they would have both carried more slugs than an Uzi's magazine. Neither man could hurl enough insults at the other. They were the Ford and Chevy of their social set; the oil and water; the yin and the yang.

Tensions between them became the norm at the Colonial Club, and their tête-à-têtes became legendary sources of interest and amusement. A wager between the two men invariably meant bravado, guile, and a certain amount of spectacle.

The latest engagement, however, had no equal.

Huntington had been sitting in the lounge sipping, contemplating the onion in the depths of his Martini, when Gordon had entered the room. Feeling flushed from the victory of their last showdown – a marathon poker game in which one or the other would clean out his opponent's $100,000 table stakes – Gordon had let loose on Huntington.

'So, Henry Pearce, how's it feel to be a hundred thousand lighter these days?'

Huntington forced a smile to his lips, enacted a shrug dripping with ennui. 'A straight flush beats a full house every time, Gordon. I can live with that.'

'What's that supposed to mean?'

'Only that any baboon can draw cards to his hairy belly,' said Huntington, warming to the call to combat.

'I'm not sure I follow you, old man,' said Gordon.

Huntington smiled. 'Really? Well, follow this: don't start bragging about *luck*. Your winning hand had *nothing* to do with your skills or abilities – unless you've got a talent for *legerdemain*?'

'Are you accusing me of cheating?' Gordon Kingsley's voice ascended the octave range.

Once could almost *hear* the collective attention of everyone in the lounge shift to the molten core of their conversation.

'How declassé,' said Huntington. 'Of course not, enemy mine. What I mean is this: a reliance on luck cheapens the contest, don't you think?'

'Cheapens!?'

'Just so. However, I've been considering a wager that depends upon nothing but the sheer, tensile strength of our wills, Kingsley.'

'How's that?'

'Have you ever read Poe's "Premature Burial"?'

'It's been a long time – at Andover – but yes, of course. Why?'

'Ever think about what it must have been like for any of those poor bastards who woke up in their coffins, sunk six feet in black dirt?'

'What's the game, Huntington?'

'Ever think about what it would be like if *you* woke up in your coffin?'

Gordon paused, hesitant to say something, *anything*, he might later regret. He didn't like the gist of their conversation. Something lurked beneath its polished surface. Something dark and slippery. Something dangerous. What the hell was his nemesis getting at?

'Earth to Kingsley . . . are you there, Gordy?'

'Yes,' he said softly. 'Yes, I've thought about it. Haven't we all?'

'I would think so,' said Huntington. He sipped his Martini with a measured precision, then stared at his adversary.

This made Gordon uncomfortable but he forced himself to look directly into Huntington's eyes. Something was going on behind them, dark and slick as Timkin bearings, and he had to fathom it out. He couldn't let his sworn enemy think he might be getting the best of him.

'Is that it, then?' asked Gordon. 'I mean, come on now, Henry – what's the point of all this? All this talk of the dead and their coffins . . .?'

Huntington smiled. 'Hold on! No one said anything about the *dead* . . .'

'No, I suppose you didn't. But what of it? What's the game, Huntington?'

Henry Pearce Huntington, that living monument to the nouveau riche, grinned like a Cheshire Cat. 'Simply this: do you think you could, *one* stand to be buried in a coffin wide awake, and, *two* stay down there longer than me?'

The silence that punctuated his question hung heavy in their midst. The eavesdroppers seemed to hold their breath as one. Could he be serious? Had he gone too far this time? What kind of a mind could even *conceive* of such a proposition?

Gordon scratched his nose, cleared his throat. A quick glance about the room confirmed the stolid gazes of his fellow Colonials – each one trying to seem less interested than the next, but attentive as hungry dogs none the less.

'What kind of a question is that?' he said, his words seeming to actually *boom* throughout the room.

'Just what it sounds like,' said Huntington. 'I've offered you the terms of a wager, Gordy. Are you man enough?'

'You're insane,' said Gordon.

'Most likely. But I've got another hundred thousand that says I can stay down longer than you.'

'What?'

A soft murmur colored the room.

'If we both stay down for thirty days, we call it a draw.' Huntington smiled. 'What do you say?'

Again, the weighty silence enclosed as the room itself seemed to take anxious pause. They were all listening, all waiting to see what kind of a man he was. Kingsley had agreed to the sky-diving and the bungy-jumping and even the William Tell re-enactment, but this latest escapade – this one danced upon the wall of true madness. Gordon had always believed he was a touch claustrophobic, and just the thought of being in that kind of tight space made him shudder.

'Well, what's your answer, old sport? Have I finally called your game, or what?'

'Can I assume that you've already worked out all the details? And that you've put together a set of conditions?'

Huntington grinned. 'After all this time, all the wagering we've done, how could you even ask such a question? But yes, I thought I might call them *ground* rules, eh?' He laughed at his small pun.

Gordon nodded, swallowed hard. 'All right then . . . let's hear them.'

'Does this mean you're on?'

Gordon hesitated only for an instant. 'I'm game. One hundred thousand.'

Someone coughed; the tension in the room spidered and cracked like an old windshield. Exclamations of shock and encouragement, salted with the odd deprecation, filled in the empty spaces between his thoughts. What the hell had he just agreed to? What came next?

Huntington smiled broadly, bringing together his hands in a steeple. 'All right, Gordy. Here's the way I envision it. If something offends you terribly or strikes you as unworkable, just raise your hand and stop me. We can talk about it, okay?'

'Go on . . .'

Huntington hunched closer across the bar, warming to the subject. His eyes grew brighter, the voltage of his imagination having been stepped up a few notches. 'Okay, here's the way I see it. Two coffins, buried side by side, you in one, me in the other. I have a game preserve in Hansford, Connecticut. Plenty of land, we can do what we want there without any interference or prying of the locals. Anyway, we outfit them with some special equipment and supply lines.'

Gordon raised a hand, feeling foolish for acting so obediently. 'What *kind* of special equipment?'

'I think we'd want an intercom, and maybe a lamp of some sort. Then there's air, food, water, getting rid of waste. A system of buried tubes and cables should do it just fine.'

Gordon shuddered again. The thought of being down there long enough to want to eat, to have to take a piss . . . who could last that long?

'And you solved these problems?'

Huntington nodded. 'I'd say so. Studies confirm we could live on nutrient-enriched liquids for *months* if necessary. And we don't have to worry past thirty days, right? A catheter and a simple pump will take care of liquid waste, and there wouldn't be any solids – a good nutritionist could see to that.'

Again the image of actually being *in* the coffin slammed into his thoughts like a left jab to his jaw. It was madness! No one could go through with it, he thought. And perhaps that was the rub – this was an elaborate joke on Huntington's part. An attempt to show him up, make Gordon look silly.

'What's the matter, Kingsley? Having second thoughts? I know what you're thinking, and I had a hard time getting used to the idea myself. All that dark earth on top of you, all around you, and that little tight, dark space for a home. The Brits have a name for coffins, you know – narrow houses! I'd say they're right, eh?' Huntington laughed, tossing back his head dramatically like the villain in a bad thirties film. Gordon watched him, thinking he looked more than a little mad. 'No light, no sound. Just the hammerfall of your own pulse in your ears, and of course the faint burrowing of the worms, trying to get through to you!'

Again a murmur suffused the lounge. The Club members were getting their money's worth this day.

'Yes, I've thought about it,' said Gordon, running his fingers through his pale, thinning hair, 'and as bad as it sounds, I know I can outlast a loud-mouthed showman like you.'

'Well, we're going to see about that,' said Huntington. 'Any last questions?'

'Only one,' said Gordon. 'When do we start?'

. . . and so went the preamble to what now transpired.

Gordon stared upward in the darkness, noticing for the first time how he was already losing sense of spatial orientation. Were it not for the insistence of gravity, he wouldn't know which end was up. It made him think of a study he'd read somewhere – the *Smithsonian* or some other pop-science magazine – about subjects who underwent sensory deprivation tests. Seems that when you put someone in a special chamber that canceled all sense of smell, taste, hearing, feeling, or seeing, you were pretty well sure of pushing them off the edge of rational thought and experience. What usually happened, the researchers discovered, was that when a person cannot receive any sensory input from outside himself, he will create his own. Subjects reported seeing strange creatures, hearing bizarre music, and so on.

Would that eventually happen to him?

And what of Huntington? If he went mad, how would he know Gordon had bested him?

Stop thinking about it. Just lie here and take it like a man. Right. Easy to say. Gordon had kept reminding himself that the best way to handle the situation was to try not to *think* about where you really were. Yes, of course, but that would be—

'*I say, old sport, are you there?*'

The voice was canned, electronically flavored, but achingly familiar. It poured from a speaker near Gordon's head. What was going on now?

'*Kingsley, are you there? Don't tell me you've had your overdue coronary and we can just leave you down here?*'

'Fuck you, Henry.'

'*Ah . . .! There you are! Good to hear you're your usual self.*'

'Would you mind telling me what the hell's going on?!' Gordon tried to sound most outraged, but honest to tell, he welcomed the human contact, even from a fool like Huntington.

Laughter filtered into the narrow house. '*Did I forget to tell you we'd be connected by the intercom system too?*' Huntington paused for effect. '*Yes, Gordy, just a little extra bonus I thought up at the last minute. And, it's on its own channel, so anybody on the monitoring equipment can't hear us. Just you and me, buddy.*'

'You never cease to amaze me with your boldness, Henry.'

'*Thank you.*'

'I mean, why? What's this for? To irritate me? To amuse yourself? Isn't it a violation of your own rules?'

'*Of course not! No contact with the surface, remember? We're both down here. Nothing said or agreed that we can't talk amongst ourselves . . .*'

'Henry, I've known you too long. What gives?' There was a bad smell to things already. Gordon felt himself tensing up, he fought the urge to push upward on the solid lid just inches from his face. At any moment everything could just collapse *in* on him.

Soft laughter.

Then silence.

Henry Pearce Huntington was obviously going to play psych-warrior. Well, fuck him. Gordon could play too. Don't give him the satisfaction of a reply.

Seconds ticked past him like gnats crawling on his arm.

Finally the speaker crackled. '*You know, Gordy, I'd bet it's never occurred to you that you've been had . . .*'

Don't answer him. Ignore the nonsense he was suggesting.

'*I mean, how do you know, really know that I'm down there with you, old sport? Sure you saw me get sealed in, just like you. But did you see my coffin get lowered into the ground and the dirt piled on . . .?*'

How could that be? Impossible. The Colonials . . . there were witnesses . . .

'*And don't think I'm not beyond paying off a member or two . . . or that there aren't larcenists in our little club that are down on their heels enough to take a bribe or a little blood money . . .*'

'Don't be ridiculous!' The words escaped him like air from a ruptured bellows. He hadn't wanted to sound so out of control.

Again soft laughter. '*Is it, old sport? Well, you'd better hope so . . .*'

Gordon waited for more, but there was only a deadly silence. The closeness of his prison suddenly gripped him, even in the absolute darkness. He thought about the PVC airshaft ever flushing the chamber with fresh oxygen, suddenly realizing what a totally fragile connection to the surface that tube represented. How easily it could be interrupted or sealed off with something as silly as a sock or as intentional as a cupped palm.

Huntington wasn't that crazy. Murder could not be explained away . . .

'*We're an influential lot, we Colonials. A police inspector would be told to listen closely to whatever we said, Gordy. We—*'

'Shut up, you moron!' Gordon stiffened, pushed against the sides of the enclosure. It was like the bastard was reading his mind, anticipating his every thought . . .

'*Oh, yes, Inspector, it was an unfortunate accident. We were engaged in a . . . a contest, if you will. Sort of an initiation into a secret order of the Colonials. Oh yessir, you know about such things. Yes, that's correct, they have them at places like Yale and Harvard, sir. And yessir, I do believe our current President is a member of such a secret club. Well, at any rate, it was a terrible accident when the air compressor failed like it did . . . yessir, it was very tragic, and yes, we at the Colonial Club would certainly appreciate the lack of publicity concerning Mr Kingsley's unfortunate demise . . .*'

'I said shut up, Henry! You're just trying to shake me up,' said Gordon, summoning up what strength remained to him. 'What happened? You get down here and realize you're not going to be able to take it?'

A chuckle fell from the little speakers, clattered all about Gordon's head.

'You underestimate me, old sport. That's why you lose so many of these little wagers.'

'What do you mean?' Gordon fought to keep the panic from his voice.

'Don't you know that if I'd really intended to outlast you, I'd have trained for the event long before wising you to the game! Why, I'd have been sleeping in a casket, with the lid up, then down, then spending a few hours every evening in my little narrow house — building up my endurance, acclimatizing myself to the environment.'

Gordon was stunned by the concept. Of course! That's *exactly* what Huntington would do!

Without thinking, Gordon had put his hand to his mouth. It was an odd uncharacteristic gesture, made more awkward by the cramped area in which he could move his arm. He reached down to the toggle switch on his left and clicked on a soft halogen lamp.

Almost instantly, he wished he hadn't.

The light only served to emphasize the horrible closeness of where he was. The satin lining of the casket, with its sickly pearlescent shine made his stomach lurch.

Is this what it's going to be like?

Forever . . .?

He could see his stockinged feet seemingly so far away. What had it been like actually to bend and touch them?

So close.

Nowhere to move.

Nowhere to go.

Just stay right where you are. Just like this. Forever.

He thumbed the toggle switch; the darkness engulfed him and he welcomed it. The lamp, he realized now, had been another velvet trap set by Huntington. There was no comfort in its hard illumination, only a special kind of horror.

'Earth to Kingsley . . . come in. . .' the speaker crackled, followed by the softest hint of Huntington's sardonic laughter. *'I know you're down there . . .'*

The bastard! Gordon had no idea what to do, much less say. If what Huntington said was true, then no one knew they could converse like this. If his opponent was trying to psych him out and Gordon panicked, pushing the alarm button on the right side of the casket, then he would not only be scammed, but he would lose the wager.

But how could he even think about something so mundane? The primitive forebrain of his consciousness was *screaming* at him to preserve the life essence, to *get out* of this hellish prison at any cost. Fuck the wager! And fuck Huntington!

Surely he could prove that there had been tampering, collusion, or whatever you'd want to call it.

'Earth to Kingsley . . .' His nemesis paused as if savoring the phrase. *'You know that's quite a pun isn't it, under the, shall we say, "gritty" circumstances . . .'*

'Dammit, Huntington,' he said softly, trying to retain control. 'This is a shabby stunt. Trying to trick me into quitting the game. You must be desperate.'

'You mean you still really believe I'm down there with you? Do you actually think I'd be stupid enough to let myself be interred in a bloody coffin!'

More laughter. This time a brutal cascade full of mocking disdain.

'Especially when you consider where you are . . .'

'Why, Huntington? Why all this? Because you're such a sore loser, you had to *cheat* your money back? By conning me into quitting? Because if you think—'

The remainder of his sentence stuck in his throat. Silence held their conversation in a timeless void. Licking his lips, he forced himself to speak.

'. . . Huntington, what did you just say . . .? If I consider *what* where . . .?

'You really are a piece of work, Gordon,' then more of that idiotic chuckling.

'Get to the point, man! What're you talking about?'

'*Just two interesting points of fact. One – that you didn't enquire as to why I selected the particular location for this wager, and two – that you're interred in land once owned by your family. Bought and sold several times before I purchased it, of course.*'

'I'm afraid I don't follow you . . .' Gordon's mind galloped ahead of his words, of Huntington's reply. There was something ominous, something sinister in the man's tone. Even in the tight space, Gordon felt the leathery pouch of his scrotum tighten, contract.

'*Your family is from Connecticut, Kingsley. Originally from the town of Hansford, which is the name of my game preserve. Strange that you didn't comment or make any connection . . . I half expected you might.*'

What in God's name was Huntington getting at? 'Hansford,' said Gordon. 'Should that name mean something to me?'

'*Come on, Gordy, didn't your father ever tell you about the Hansford Sanatorium?*'

'Other than the fact that Grandfather had built it, or that we owned it . . . no, why?'

Huntington clucked his tongue, sighed. '*Did you ever remember hearing or reading about the Great Influenza Epidemic of 1918?*'

'Huntington, cut to the chase, would you!? You can damn well bet I don't know what you're talking about!'

'*It was a terrible thing. More than thirty percent of the population of the cities on the East Coast died in a twelve-month period. A half million dead. People were dying so fast, nobody knew what to do with them. Nobody except your Grandad, that is . . .*'

There was an absence, a distinct void, as Huntington's voice trailed off. Gordon felt himself almost lurch forward in the oppressive darkness. He knew he didn't want to hear what Grandfather might have done. And yet, he must. When he spoke, he sounded hoarse, weak, even puny.

'What did he do . . .?'

Huntington cleared his throat. '*Well, it seems your grandfather had a small army of Irish laborers working in his quarry near*

Wallingford. When the influenza ripped through their ranks like cavalry, the poor micks swelled the Hansford Sanatorium to bursting. When they started dying like blowflies, your grandfather didn't want to be bothered with the details and expense of getting them all back to their Manhattan tenement families . . .'

'What're you talking about? What did he do?' Gordon shifted uneasily on the soft padding of the casket.

'A most ingenious solution, really. He had all those dumb Irishmen's bodies thrown into lorries and hauled off to a big quicklime pit he'd dug just beyond the trees on the Sanatorium grounds.'

'Huntington, you're a lying bastard!'

There came a soft chuckle. *'No, old sport, I'm afraid you're the one who's lying – right in the middle of that nasty old quicklime pit . . .'*

Like a blade, something twisted in the core of his being. He could not keep a silly, melodramatic *gasp* from escaping him.

'Oh, I know it's been a while now, Gordy, but I'd say you're not very far from a big pile of those poor micks' bones.'

The confines of the casket were suddenly smaller, the air staler. His entire world reduced to a six-foot wooden hull embarked upon a journey into madness. His skin felt dry, itchy. Places he couldn't reach had started tingling with histaminic urgency. Although clutched in darkness, Gordon's eyes remained tightly shut. He didn't want to think about what lay beyond the thin wood of his cell.

Just get out. Just open your mouth and start screaming and push the button and get yourself out of this fucking pit.

. . . No, wait, stay calm.

'As a matter of fact, being a betting man, I'd wager there's more than one angry Irish ghost twisted up in the dirt and the bones that're wrapped around you like a fist.'

Stay calm. Talk it out. Get a grip.

'Is this what it's all about, Henry? All this business about the *Irishmen* – Let's see if I can figure this out. Let me tell you what happened: my grandfather threw yours in the quicklime, right? I always thought that crap about railroads was just crap. Your grandfather was nothing but a common laborer, and his son made his money bootlegging with Joe Kennedy's bunch!'

'Ah, Gordy, you make me proud, me boy! You're smarter than I ever gave you credit for. But did you ever imagine that all the years and all the wagering has been nothing but a setup?'

'What's that? What're you talking about?'

'Revenge, old sport. Someone said it's served best when served cold, and I have to agree with that.'

'You're a madman! A fucking looney!'

Huntington chuckled. It was a lilting, almost musical sound. 'But not as crazy as you're going to be before you ever get out of there. By the time they get to your fat ass, you won't even know it.'

'I'm sounding the alarm,' said Gordon, summoning up the most authoritative voice he could find. Fumbling for the switch at his right hip, he massaged the button, but didn't push it.

'Kiss your money goodbye, Gordy . . .'

Caressing the button, his fingers tapped it lightly, but not enough actually to depress it.

This was exactly what Huntington had wanted all along: he had been manipulating everything to get things to this point. The slick son-of-a-bitch thought he was going to con him out of the money, but Gordon Kingsley would show—

The sound was so subtle, so soft, he almost missed it . . .

'So, where's the alarm, Kingsley? I'm sitting here waiting for you.'

'Shut up, you blathering idiot! Shut-up-shut-up-shut-up!'

Huntington chuckled softly, but Gordon was listening to another sound – the barely audible sound of something scrabbling through dirt, pawing, scraping, clawing . . .

He was suddenly aware of grinding his teeth together. The muscles in his jaws felt like piano wire, stretched to its limits. He tried to open his mouth, but couldn't. Something was wrong here. Something not right, and—

A new sound.

Not a scrape as much as a tick! along the side of the casket.

Along the outside.

Holding his breath, Gordon listened. The sound repeated itself. A rhythmic series of tappings, as though something were signalling him in Morse code.

He had no idea how long he listened to the sound.

In the darkness, it was everything. There was nothing but the tapping on the wood. Time lost its sense, its measure. Gordon lay in the thrall of the sound and nothing else. Inanely, the notion that knocking on wood brought good luck passed through him, the shock of conscious thought released him from the hypnagogia.

He pressed his hand against the left wall of the casket, felt the vibration of the impact. Something was *out* there.

But that was ridiculous.

Impossible.

Out there.

As he struggled to rein in his panic, he realized the tapping had ceased.

But only for an instant.

To be replaced by a scraping sound. A deliberate *gouging* of the wood as if by some sharp tool, like an engraver's awl, or maybe even a . . .

. . . fingernail, or a

. . . *finger-bone.*

He must have cried out, but had no memory of doing so. His mind full of white noise static, a radio-burst of pure terror. A muffled voice spoke to him that could have been Huntington, but he was beyond the comprehension that accompanies hearing. The measured pace of the gouging and scraping had increased, faster and faster until it sounded like the machine-like digging of a dog for his bone. Kingsley, in fact, had begun his own gouging and scraping, having torn away the satin celing of his narrow house, and his own fingernails as he clawed at the wood just inches from his face. Maple has a sturdy grain and he'd made little progress, but he was beyond notice.

The thing that so furiously worked the wood at his left shoulder had fared far better.

When Gordon toggled his lamp and sounded the alarm, the last thing he saw was the splintered wood collapsing in . . . towards him.

'Oh yes, Inspector, most tragic,' said Henry Pearce Huntington.

'How could any of us have known old Kingsley's ticker was bad?'

He stood in the four-car garage of his Greenwich, Connecticut estate. In addition to the police inspector, there were two uniforms and the county medical examiner, who was inspecting a body in a casket. The casket rested on a large table, trailing several tendrils of electric wire and plastic tubing.

The inspector shook his head gravely. 'Of course not, Mr Huntington. I mean, who could know?'

Huntington nodded gravely. 'And of course, I'm sure you're in agreement that there should be no publicity. Some of our most respected institutions have secret societies and initiation rites . . .'

The inspector grinned. 'Hey, what're you kiddin'? I heard the President was in one of these secret clubs when he was at Yale!'

'That is correct, sir,' said Huntington, as he followed the inspector to the side of the casket.

The medical examiner looked up, away from the slack-jawed, sunken-eyed corpse of Gordon Kingsley. His hair a dead white, Einsteinian nimbus.

'Something scared the shit outta this guy,' said the M.E.

One of the uniforms chuckled. 'Guy must've been a flake,' he said. 'I mean, if he'd been buried in the ground, hey, that would be one thing . . . but this guy, I mean, he was just lyin' here in his buddy's garage.'

MYSTERIES OF THE WORD
A Dark Fable

Stanley Wiater

Illustrated by Gahan Wilson

Apart from the fact that he possesses the biggest Roladex in the world, Stanley Wiater's claim to fame is that he has interviewed more horror authors, film-makers and artists than any other writers. His articles and interviews have appeared in the long-gone and much-missed *Twilight Zone* and *Fear* as well as in the likes of *Prevue* and *Writer's Digest*. Stanley has also been a contributing editor to *Fangoria*, *New Blood* and *Fear* so it's reasonable to assume that, by now, he should know the secret of how to write horror fiction. And he does.

His first published short story was the winner of a competition judged by Stephen King: others have appeared in *Castle Rock*, *Twilight Zone*, *Cavalier* and *Mike Shayne*, and in anthologies such as *Masques*, *Obsessions* and *Borderlands*.

In 1989 he edited the anthology *Night Visions 7* (*Dark Harvest*) and his second (*After the Darkness*) appeared this past spring. Wiater's first collection of interviews, *Dark Dreamers: Conversations with the Masters of Horror* (Avon), won the Horror Writers of America's Bram Stoker Award and his 1992 collection, *Dark Visions: Conversations with the Masters of the Horror Film* (Avon), was a Bram Stoker Award nominee.

Always expanding his own visions, Wiater has teamed up with Stephen R. Bisette to produce a new volume of interviews, *Comic Book Rebels: Conversations with the Creators of the New Comics.* And, in terms of fiction, he is clearly on the cutting edge of the genre by recently exploring the new technology of CD-Interactive media with the creation of a haunted art museum game.

'Alas,' he says, 'I have no personal superstitions to share.' Then he goes on to say how he grew up with two older sisters and used to think that if he ventured into their room at night their doll collections would come to life and attack him.

He lives with his wife and daughter in rural western Massachusetts with not a doll in sight!

Gahan Wilson is descended from such authentic American folk heroes as circus and freak king P.T. Barnum, and the silver-voiced orator William Jennings Bryan.

He was officially born dead by the attending physician in Evanston, Illinois, but, rescued by another medic who dipped him alternately in bowls of hot and cold water, he survived to become the first student in the Art Institute of Chicago to admit he was actually going there to learn how to become a cartoonist.

Wilson's work is known chiefly because of its association with *Playboy* but he has shown up in periodicals as diverse as *The New Yorker, Weird Tales, Gourmet, Punch* and *Paris Match.* Selections from this accumulation have appeared in some fifteen cartoon collections so far, and a big retrospective, *Still Weird,* is due out next year.

He has also written a number of children's books, including a series on *Harry, the Fat Bear Spy,* and authored and published an uncounted number of spooky stories for grown-ups which have appeared in *Playboy, Omni, Fantasy and Science Fiction* and numerous anthologies. He has also authored two mystery novels, *Eddy Deco's Last Caper,* a bizarre tough private eye story told in words and pictures, and *Everybody's Favorite Duck,* which features thinly disguised versions of Moriarty and Fu Manchu.

Experiments in two new fields are currently underway: the

comicbook form with a book on Poe, another on Ambrose Bierce and an upcoming third on Howard Phillips Lovecraft, and he has just completed his first animated movie, a gruesome cartoon short for 20th-Century Fox called *Gahan Wilson's Diner*.

When he's decided to use a cartoon idea, Wilson likes to draw a little circle deosil about it. 'And when I've finished doing the drawing,' he adds, 'I'm always careful to give the initial note eternal peace by tearing it gently in twain.' Outside of that he is totally free from any superstitions, 'except, of course, to take the usual reasonable and sensible precautions whenever I sense the presence of vampires, werewolves and other suchlike nuisances.'

DEDICATION

To anyone who ever asked 'why' at the improper
time to the wrong adult.

1

Early one morning, for reasons known only to him, Paul Henkin snuck inside the Girls' Room at school. He had never been inside a girls' restroom before. Much of what went on in there was still a mystery to him and most other boys his age.

Before anyone came in and caught him, he needed to see everything he could. Anything he could find that was supposed to be a big secret might gain him respect with the few students he knew in his fourth grade class.

And maybe even gain him some friends if he was able to explain to other curious boys what had once been forbidden knowledge.

2

Paul went through the entire Girls' Room as quickly and quietly as a skinny, hungry rat through a wet drainpipe. He was shocked but not surprised by some of the things that he saw. He was an only child, which was one of the reasons why he was so ignorant about girls as well as boys. He was also at an age when he had to be careful what questions he asked of any grown-ups.

As the young intruder was about to leave, he saw something else he had never seen before. It was printed on the wall right above the closed entrance and seemed almost to glow, as if the letters had been applied with some special kind of reflective paint. But from another angle, it was nearly invisible.

It was a single word. One which was not meant to be easily noticed or memorized or pronounced by just anyone.

Paul was soon to learn it was *the* Word.

3

Stimulated but confused by what he had seen, Paul went back and joined his fellow students as they entered their homeroom class. No one appeared aware of what he had done; what highly dangerous mission he had just successfully completed. Yet as the first set of lessons began, he could concentrate on nothing but that highly unusual Word.

The morning crawled by like a worm cut in half. Paul began to wonder if this was a word which everyone already knew about, and that he was alone – as usual – in his ignorance. Maybe his not knowing about so many neat things was one of the reasons why he had no real friends.

When it came time to go to lunch, Paul mustered his courage and went to the teacher, Mrs Crindle. Maybe she could tell him what the Word meant, just to set his mind at ease if nothing else. He didn't want to look like a jerk by asking one of the guys until he knew for sure.

He spoke, as best as he could pronounce, the unusual Word.

4

But instead of giving him answer, Mrs Crindle was instantly revolted. 'What did you say?' she demanded, a look of utter disgust unfolding across her already unattractive features.

Paul innocently repeated the Word, hoping he had been only misunderstood in his first attempt at pronunciation. But Mrs Crindle only became more angry, the blood draining from her face like a sliced tomato tossed out on a hot summer sidewalk.

'You are going to the principal's office this minute and repeat to Mr Stiles precisely what you've said to me! And give him this note to make sure he knows what you said.'

Paul started to protest, but the intense look on her face quickly convinced him it was useless further to declare his innocence. He looked down at the floor as the woman scribbled furiously on a notepad, not believing this could be happening.

What had he said that was so awful?

Worse than that, it looked like he was going to miss lunch, and he had already skipped breakfast so he could arrive at school before any of the other students. Still avoiding her face, Paul silently took the note and left the room, confused and angry.

He had no idea that this was a day he was going to remember for the rest of his life.

5

Paul walked down the long, empty hallways towards the office of the school principal, Mr Stiles. (Nobody knew if he had a first name other than 'mister.') Head hung low, he felt like a prisoner going to the warden to plead for his innocence before being sent to Death Row – or something even worse.

With all the other students already in the cafeteria, he felt more alone than when he had arrived early to privately check out the stupid Girls' Room. Just as bad, he had seen so much and never had a chance to tell the guys in his class about what he had discovered!

For whatever it was worth, he even carried proof of the mysterious Word in the folded note he was carrying so nervously in his hand.

6

Miss Atkinson, the very overweight school secretary, told him where to sit while she informed Mr Stiles that he was here.

Paul had to wait only a few minutes, but it seemed like hours to him. His palms were beginning to sweat. And his feet were starting to itch. Anyone who came by the front lobby could see him squirming there on the hard wooden bench – guilty before proving himself innocent.

After being directed inside his private office, Paul took a deep breath and gave Mr Stiles the note that Mrs Crindle had made him deliver. Mr Stiles never smiled, and nobody at school – not even the other teachers probably – liked him very much. He never laughed either. Mr Stiles read the note to himself, touching it with only the tips of his fingers as if Paul might have infected the damp paper with his nervousness.

The principal definitely wasn't laughing as he asked, 'Mr Henkin, is this supposed to be some kind of a gross joke?'

Paul just shrugged his shoulders and tried to hide the fact that he was shivering at the same time he was sweating.

'Do you know what this filthy word means?' the tall and cold-blooded principal demanded. '*Do you know*, boy?'

7

'No,' Paul said, and out of fear foolishly repeated the Word. 'I *don't* know what that means. Why don't you just tell me?'

Mr Stiles did not laugh at all at what he thought he heard Paul say. Instead he frowned so hard it looked like his thin and brittle lips were going to break off at the edges from the strain of containing his anger inside his mouth. His sharp nose actually twitched as if the air in the room was now polluted.

The principal of Hooker School suddenly leaned forward over the top of his barren desk.

Paul could only lean back an inch or two in his chair, suddenly thinking in turn how a King Cobra strikes at the live food – the baby mice or rats – given to it at the zoo.

8

'I'm going to call your mother and have her pick you up immediately. You will not be allowed into this school again until your parents can explain where you picked up this sort of language. This is a good school. I thought you were a good student. I realize now that I must have been wrong.'

Paul stared helplessly at the note that Mr Stiles was still holding and wondered if the Word was going to be repeated to his mother over the telephone. The young boy didn't get a chance to find out, because he then was ordered to wait outside the school building itself until she arrived.

Simply because of saying the Word, he was not welcome here anymore.

Paul was very confused, and becoming more than a little worried at how people were reacting to him. He wasn't sure what this terrible Word meant, but it didn't seem right that he should be guilty of doing something wrong when nobody would even *tell* him. Tell him exactly what it was that he was saying which every grown-up obviously believed was very plainly and clearly wrong.

How could a single word be so scary to adults?

9

Returning to the main lobby, Paul was instructed by Miss Atkinson to go outside and sit on a bench located near the entrance to the school. She and the bald security guard glared at him like he was an unwanted visitor from another planet.

He was more concerned as to what Mr Stiles was going to tell his mother about his encounter with the Word. He still didn't know what the Word meant, and so was more determined than ever to find out. *What could he possibly lose?*

More importantly, Paul felt that if he could discover what the Word meant, it would gain him some special respect among the other boys. So much so that even telling them what else he had seen in the Girls' Room would be pretty dull in comparison.

If he explained the problem correctly, maybe – just maybe – his mother would help him out and calmly explain everything.

Paul looked up to see a huge dark cloud block out the warming rays of the sun. There had been no clouds in the sky five minutes ago when he first glanced outside. The boy shivered. He didn't recall the weatherman saying anything about rain today. Paul also couldn't recall ever seeing such a strange, odd-looking cloud before.

The boy shivered again.

10

On the ride home, Paul immediately tried to explain to his mother what had happened to him. She was already visibly upset by what the school principal had told her, but appeared willing to let her son tell his side of the story.

However, the final comment Paul had to make was simply to ask her if she knew the meaning of this supposedly awful word. She shook her head, saying she hoped it wasn't the awful word Mr Stiles had hinted at.

Smiling bravely, Paul then spoke the Word as politely and sincerely as he could.

His mother nearly drove off the road in shock and anger.

'Just you wait until your father gets home!' was all she would say after that, and the rest of the ride back to his parents' house was endured in a nerve-wracking silence. Paul didn't dare look at the tearful woman once.

Gazing forlornly out the car window, he noticed instead how the noonday sun was nowhere to be seen. There seemed to be nothing but darkness on the horizon as more and more ugly clouds blotted out the blue of the sky like a rotting batch of dirty gray mushrooms.

11

Back at his parents' house, Paul sat alone in his room.

It never had seemed so small and confining before. His mother had forbidden him from listening to any music, watching television, or playing any video games until his father came home. His room was to be his cell in the meantime. Even the posters on the wall seemed to turn away from his gaze.

Try as he might Paul still couldn't understand why a single word could upset so many people. He had never encountered such a terrible mystery before.

It just didn't make sense!

The silence surrounding him was louder than any music he had ever played to forget his troubles.

12

He read sixteen comic books before he heard his father's car pulling into the yard. They lived on the very edge of the city, and Paul's room was directly over the garage. Located at the very beginning of the city's decaying suburbs, the small houses of their neighbors were only seventy-five feet away from either side of the borders of their tiny, rarely used lawn.

As far as Paul was concerned the city's sidewalks were wider and more functional than their backyard. A car door opened and slammed shut somewhere below.

Putting down the last comic book, he waited in silence for his father to come upstairs so they could at last discuss the Word.

13

His heart thumping, Paul thought he heard the front door downstairs open and close. Leaning against the bedroom door, he could just barely hear his mother speaking excitedly to his father. What was said exactly was not clear, but the sounds which carried through the closed door of his room were harsh and jarring to his ear. It didn't sound good at all.

Paul felt like an innocent bystander to a bad accident for which he nevertheless would still be blamed.

Pacing around his room, Paul looked forlornly through the window. Outside, what remained of the late afternoon sun was drowning in a wave of darkening clouds rising up against the horizon. The temperature outside was dropping more rapidly than normal.

It didn't look good either.

14

The door to Paul's cell flew open.

His father charged into the room, his angry face bright red as if he had somehow embarrassed himself in public.

In foolish desperation, Paul defended himself by demanding to know the definition of the Word. He spoke the Word repeatedly, trying a slightly different pronunciation each time to prove his curiosity was innocent, his intent sincere.

His father's face only got redder. Downstairs, they could both hear a woman sobbing loudly like a baby.

'Shut your filthy mouth! You're no son of mine!' he shouted at his only son. 'You can pack your bags and get out if you think you can talk to me or your mother like that!'

The man suddenly turned around and slammed the bedroom door behind him – his final reply to the questioning look on Paul's face.

A long shadow fell across Paul's open mouth like a closing shroud.

Outside, nearly two hours early, it was starting to get dark.

15

The entire house became uncomfortably quiet, like the place where dead people are put on display for their friends and relatives to gawk at and later count their blessings over.

Fighting back tears, Paul went to his bottom dresser drawer and collected whatever money he had hidden there. He then went to the closet and put on a heavy woolen shirt and a blue pullover sweater over that garment. He didn't know really what he was doing, except that it was up to him to prove that everybody was wrong about his wanting to know the true meaning of the Word.

Looking around his room, he realized how queer and foreign everything appeared in the lengthening shadows. The model kits which he suddenly couldn't remember building. The posters of sports cars and famous athletes he probably would never encounter. Even the furniture appeared to belong to someone else.

Shaking his head back and forth, Paul packed a small brown suitcase that was as old as his parents. He had no idea where he was headed. He only knew he had to go.

Now.

Paul looked around the stranger's room one last time.

16

Paul went to the only window in the room and quietly opened it. He took a deep breath and then stepped out on to the sloping roof of the garage. He next carefully dropped the small suitcase to the ground, hoping it wouldn't pop open when it hit. With a little more caution, he was able to climb safely down the wooden latticework held there by a clinging ivy which grew thickly against one side of the garage.

Crazy as it sounded even to him, Paul knew that unless he learned the answer to the mystery of the Word, he could never show his face to anyone – not even his foolish parents – again.

Yet no one seemed to care he was leaving as he stepped on to the front sidewalk and walked slowly away into the cold waiting arms of the early October evening.

17

Paul had never walked so far away from home by himself.

And especially never as the night took over the sky.

The rising moon was full and bloated, the pale color and

texture of a sickly man's pock-marked skin. Meanwhile, fewer and fewer cars or trucks passed by on the long and empty street.

For reasons known only him, he was heading toward a poor section of the city which was occupied mostly by some truly rundown houses and a lot of deserted buildings. It was not a good place for children or young people to be after dark.

Actually, it was not a good place for anyone to be caught.

In the blink of an eye, something was flying wildly in the air, momentarily staining the ugly face of the moon even further.

Bats, Paul instantly surmised. Then they were gone as quickly as he was able to recognize what they were.

What he hoped they were.

18

Paul nervously noticed how there were very few reassuring lights in the windows of the houses and tenement buildings as he walked further downtown. He also told himself that because it was suppertime, and the end of the workday, no one happened to be traveling along the sidewalk in that direction except himself.

The rows of silent houses and decaying apartment buildings seemed to be asking him: *Where do you think you are going, you foolish little boy?*

All alone.

All alone.

Alone.

Even now, Paul Henkin wasn't sure himself. He only knew he *had* to find the answer, no matter what the risk.

The few lights visible in the windows seemed to stare at him like big hungry eyes.

19

Several blocks closer to the stilled heart of the city, Paul saw a small fire burning in a steel drum.

There were no longer any inhabited dwellings in this section, only deserted businesses and shops. Even the streetlamps were few and far inbetween, the majority having had their bulbs either repeatedly broken or shot out.

The young runaway knew he should be terribly afraid, but weirdly enough, Paul no longer felt he had anything to fear at this point. Ever since he had first encountered it, the Word had been playing over and over in his mind like a haunting theme or lyric from a forbidden rap song. And he had kept repeating it to himself whenever he felt that the courage to go any further had also burnt itself out.

No matter what happened, Paul had to know that what he had said and done this morning was not wrong. Maybe not right, exactly. But certainly not so wrong as to have him thrown out of school and his own home. In fact, he now firmly believed the Word was the only weapon he had to protect himself with as he approached the burning steel drum on an empty street corner in the worst part of the city.

20

Paul came upon the old man sitting on the other side of the burning trash can. The rough and ragged appearance of this homeless person startled him, as the old man's features were further distorted by the flickering flames. For a few seconds he didn't seem even to notice Paul was there.

Unable to keep from staring, Paul noticed the man had a scarred face which looked like it might have been burnt by passing out beside too many open flames. Like a statue coming to life, the man turned his head slowly and began to stare back at Paul, his half-closed eyes glazed and unblinking. The boy was ready to run away if he came any closer, but meanwhile stood his ground, realizing that he didn't have a clue as to where he had ended up.

Suddenly realizing he was hopelessly caught in the web of the city.

21

'Well, what do you want, kid?' the scarred man asked bluntly. He sat on the sidewalk, apparently resting on a cushion of rags stored in a dirty plastic bag. In the poor light of the trashcan fire, Paul couldn't honestly tell if the man was forty or eighty years old. The man looked and smelled like someone who hadn't taken a bath in almost as many years.

The young runaway continued to stare at him unashamedly, trying to find the necessary courage to speak.

And dare to ask the question about the Word.

22

'I . . . I need to find someone who can tell me what a certain word means. I know it sounds crazy, but everybody I've asked has hated me for asking. That's . . . it.'

'And what word is that?' asked the old man. Smiling in an unpleasant way, he added, 'Come on – I've heard them all before. Said most of them, too.'

The rapidly burning fire cast long, shaky shadows on the cracked and littered sidewalk. The fire had to be fed soon or it would be in danger of going out completely. And when it did, both of them would be left in the darkness. Together.

Paul took a deep breath, then rapidly whispered.

The Word.

23

The old man said nothing for a long time. He spat at the fire, missing it completely and not seeming to care. Finally, he looked directly at Paul and appeared to grin a little more cruelly than before through his dirty and broken teeth.

Paul shuddered, but not from the cold. He watched the man slowly wipe his mouth and chin dry as if from kissing someone too hard and without their permission.

'So. You'd like to know where to go to find out what that means, huh?'

24

Paul cautiously regarded the old man, all the while wondering what he was doing out here – or why he should even believe this creepy guy. While probably lost in a part of the city where nobody in their right mind should be after dark. Talking about some crazy word he never knew existed before this terrible day had started. And searching for an answer to something that maybe should never have been questioned.

A sudden gust of wind blew his brown hair across his left eye, temporarily blinding him.

'Yes, sir,' was all Paul could say.

25

Chuckling to himself, the stranger gave explicit directions as to where Paul should go next on his special mission. Paul listened very intently, his heart beating swiftly. He was scared to go further into the inner city, but was also thrilled that someone had listened to him speak the Word and then been willing to help. Maybe he had been too rash in judging all adults the same way – even if they had been so rash to condemn him.

The boy grasped his one piece of luggage in his trembling hands, wondering next if the old man would demand some kind of payment in return for the secret information.

But the old man said nothing else after finishing with the directions.

Not a word.

26

Stuttering out his thanks, Paul left the comforting warmth of the fire and went off into the semi-darkness in the direction he had been told to go. Empty buildings loomed over him on either side like gigantic dead trees, with only the occasional street lamp struggling to keep back the black cloak of the night.

As frightened as he was, Paul took comfort in knowing that the question which had troubled him since the beginning of this incredible day would finally be answered in less than four blocks.

Even so, Paul angrily bit his lower lip and blinked back a tear that was trying to escape. There was nothing more hurtful than seeking to learn something new and being told time and time again that it was forbidden knowledge.

That it was not for you.

That you were too young to know the truth.

By keeping this anger burning in his heart, Paul kept his feet moving along the sidewalk long after the old man and his flames had disappeared from view.

27

Cautiously looking all around him, Paul walked as fast as he could toward his ultimate destination. The only sounds he could hear were the pounding of his heart in his chest and his sneakers crackling lightly against the dead leaves and scattered debris on the pavement.

Way off in the distance, the wailing of police sirens and ambulances could be heard very faintly, like the sounds deep-sea creatures might make moving about aimlessly beneath the shifting waves of the unknown parts of the ocean.

Paul became a shadow lost among the other shadows.

28

At last, Paul reached the four-way intersection the homeless man had described to him. The intersection was of course deserted, and the only cars visible were abandoned wrecks, seemingly cast up on shore like the hulks of dead things tossed out of some unknown sea. Still clutching his suitcase, Paul thought it so unnerving not to see anyone around the area. No homeless people. Not even a roaming street gang. He was actually glad of that, and yet, could feel the cold stillness and the emptiness growing all around him like an oncoming tidal wave not yet visible.

A brief gust of wind sent dirty scraps of a newspaper up against his face. Paul awkwardly tore it away, remembering what had happened when he had walked blindly into a huge spiderweb while sneaking into his grandparents' attic one hot summer day.

What had he accomplished by going up there to explore? He tried to remember the events of the day without success.

He shook his head, not knowing what mattered anymore. All he knew now was that it was time to get *this* mission completed. Paul looked up towards the clear night sky and swallowed hard.

Searching for the full moon to show him the way.

29

Realizing there was no turning back, Paul did as the scarred man had instructed. Trembling, he shouted out the Word as loudly as he could. The few stars that were visible above the deserted buildings seemed to ignore him.

For in spite of his cries, absolutely nothing happened.

Paul clenched his fists and raised his arms to the sky. He was *so* angry that he had to be out here; that nobody else could claim to make sense of this weirdness except some nameless bum!

It wasn't fair!

And he shouted the Word even louder.

30

'*Cthulhu!*' He yelled the Word again at the top of his lungs.

He turned toward the full moon as it quickly rose into the night sky behind a section of the deserted buildings. It seemed to have crept around the tallest building and floated into view right upon hearing Paul's speaking of the Word.

His throat began to hurt from the force of his shouting.

'*Cthulhu!*' he screamed one more time at the scarred and uncaring face of the moon.

31

Something abruptly soared across the pale yellow face of the harvest moon.

And it wasn't bats.

32

Yet it had gigantic wings!

Still repeating the Word, Paul couldn't begin to comprehend what was happening as the air beat around him with the flapping sound of great leathery wings. Flapping in the motion of a thousand bats somehow fused into one awful mass of hairy flesh.

As it rapidly descended, Paul thought he could see the faces of hundreds of young boys imprinted upon the thing's massive body and wings. Questioning faces that seemed frozen forever in the middle of a scream.

33

Not that it was going to make any difference; Paul was still foolishly shouting the Word as the clawed feet reached out and grabbed him. In a second he was completely enveloped by the foul-smelling mixture of wet fur and cold flesh and hollow bones.

Fortunately, the curious young man never got a look at the creature's awful face as its dripping mouth swiftly opened wide to keep him from saying the Word ever again.

It swallowed most of Paul whole with the first bite.

Cutting him off right in mid-scream.

34

As the eldritch thing flew away into the night, all that remained of Paul's existence was his tattered little suitcase. It fell to the ground in the middle of the empty intersection, covered with a terrible smelling slime.

Wisely or not, Paul had written down the Word on a piece of paper which he'd locked inside the suitcase before leaving his parents' house. He had no further use for the Word anymore.

Finally, the night passed away into morning.

Even then, nobody came looking for a young runaway or his battered suitcase. Not even the scarred man who slept only a few blocks away seemed to care if its contents might be of any lasting value. Apparently people tended to mind their own business as they got older and wiser.

If they lived long enough to get any wiser.

35

Not surprisingly, by the next morning, some curious person had claimed the suitcase. Sooner or later, they would wash off the

slime and unlock it to see what they could take of its meager contents. Perhaps they would find and read the slip of paper that Paul Henkin had written on—

Or maybe they would wonder what had made the huge, deep scratch in the side of the suitcase and be smart enough just to throw it away unopened.

Otherwise, someone else might want to try to solve another one of the mysteries of the Word. Other mysteries such as: What the Word truly meant, where it had originated, and why it was perhaps better not to know the answer to everything there is to question in the universe.

36

Anyone chancing to look up at one of the gargoyles in the tallest building at this intersection would find, however, a very important clue to one of the mysteries of the Word. Especially if they spotted the gargoyle with the very young-looking face and most surprised expression.

Wiser for knowing it or not, Paul Henkin at last possessed the final answer to his particular mystery of the Word.

And, for reasons known only to him, could silently treasure that useless bit of knowledge forever and ever and ever.

And ever.

37

Keeping it to himself, that is, until some other curious boy came along.

AUTHOR'S NOTE

'Mysteries of the Word' is my retelling of an 'urban legend' collected by folklorist William E. Koch. For anyone who is interested in reading more about contemporary folklore and legends, I heartily recommend *The Headless Roommate and other Tales of Terror* by Daniel Cohen, and *Scary Stories to Tell in the Dark* by Alvin Schwartz.

SPLINTS

D.F. Lewis

He's been called 'brilliant' and 'the new Lovecraft', both of which appellations he has survived magnificently.

He has been cited as one of the acclaimed *Gothic Light* journal's four favourite fantasy authors – along with Harlan Ellison, Ray Bradbury and Lewis Carroll.

He has been praised by the likes of Ramsey Campbell, Thomas Ligotti and Karl Edward Wagner. And since 1987 he has published more than 500 stories in the United Kingdom and the United States, including appearances in *Signals*, *Best New Horror* (volumes I and II), *Year's Best Horror Stories* (volumes XVIII, XIX and XX – with volume XXI coming up), *The Ultimate Zombie* and *Darklands 2*.

He is, of course, Des Lewis.

Des Lewis was born in 1948 in Walton-on-Naze, Essex, and has two children, one of whom – his daughter Berenice – was named after the story by Edgar Allan Poe. Last year, he lost his job as a company pensions expert causing friends to fear that he may become a prolific writer.

His main superstition is an obsession with writing stories – *oh, really?* – and he believes he'll never write another unless he writes one every twenty-four hours. Other than that, he deliberately tempts fate by such acts as walking under ladders – he's easy to spot because he's always covered in paint.

The superstition in 'Splints' is one told to Des by his

grandmother – that being left-handed or associating with a left-handed person is unlucky. 'After all,' he points out, 'the Latin for "left" is "sinister".'

QED.

Watkins examined the matchbox. When he was a small boy, they sold toy lorries in matchboxes, and racing cars, and family saloons, and bright red tractors. Recently the world had become a boring place for Watkins. Matchboxes contained only matches. And cigarette packets had only cigarettes: no attractive cards to flip bearing pictures of footballers, tropical birds, Second World War aeroplanes and, yes, even bright red tractors.

The matchbox sat in the palm of his hand. Life was usually too busy for such minutiae. The last time he stopped to breathe was when his mother died. Even when he was supposed to be relaxing, his mind raced with this or that project. Yet today was different. The world had suddenly hushed, as if the act of impending was its raison d'être – and Watkins was flagrante delicto: about to take a sneaky smoke, a habit which his better self had officially given up yonks ago.

With the unaccustomed intake of breath that would not re-emerge until his lungs started flapping like dying fish, he pored over the crumpleable cuboid of the matchbox. The larger geometry of the cigarette packet nearby – which he had originally intended to plunder with the more surreptitious fingers of his left hand – did not belong to him. Nor did the matchbox, for that matter. In fact, their owner was a mystery – especially as Watkins lived alone, expected no imminent visitors (nor, even, any just departed ones), and had in fact not unlocked his front door since Emily left in a huff a fortnight ago. The artefacts could not possibly have belonged to Emily, to sweet sweet Emily. She was so green, he thought she must come from Mars. Recycling, for her, was not necessarily living on a déjà vu biking holiday.

And you could say that again.

No, the presence of the smoking equipment was decidedly an enigma, which, in many ways, was a better word than mystery and also obviated a boring repetition. Watkins shook his head. Could he, of all people, be thinking such thoughts? On top of which, he had just spotted a man's pipe resting upon a shelf of the bookcase within the bay window alcove. He may have succumbed to fags in his chequered past – but never a pretentious pipe! Men who smoked pipes had the personality of a car exhaust or worse.

The matchbox just moved, a barely perceptible budge in the palm! A horrible feeling. As if he were a boy again with a trapped wasp. Except this was more a wriggle than a buzzing bounce. A slither, not a head-bashing. Yet quieter than Watkins's resumed breathing.

Emily wasn't ever coming back. He knew that. He and Emily were usually chalk and cheese, but not necessarily in that order. She a schoolteacher with a degree in method acting – he, well, he had smelly feet, didn't he? And his mother had never properly house-trained him. Now it was too late. An old dog could never learn new tricks.

Yet he did remember a trick he once knew as a boy. One with a matchbox. Two live matches were needed. And a penny (an old penny in those days). One match was positioned vertically head-up at one end of the empty matchbox's label-side by means of a punctured hole. The other leaned head-up against it with the white stem creating a hypotenuse, its end resting on the label with the penny between. You then asked someone how you could get the penny without touching the matches . . .

Also, there were those cotton-reel tractors, with a stub of candle, elastic band and one matchstick, which his father used to make for him. Memories were flooding back.

But all this was before the matchbox seemed to move in his palm.

Yet how could it? Certainly without the presence of an independent motive force. Tricks were never *that* prestidigitatious. So, he speculated upon sliding out the tiny drawer, to gauge what was what – until the interruption of the door-bell going. Surely not Emily. But if not, who?

He had expected no imminent visitors.

The last time Watkins had unexpected visitors was the occasion he had suffered a chimney fire and one of the neighbours had called the fire brigade. Nosey-parkers, all of them!

He pushed gently on the fragile tray with his nose to reveal the most surreptitious of his own left hand's fingers (the little one) lying in its narrow coffin. Slightly slithering between the corners of its fingerhouse. Brown-stained at one end and bright red-stumped at the other. It looked to be in a torture of traction.

He tried to snap it shut before calling the snoop-police, worried that he might get Emily the whale-lover and part-time RSCPA ambulance-driver instead. But none of the number-pads worked. And the door-bell had indeed gone. Only the squeaking of Watkins's lungs remained. The fingermouse? It had dropped out with a crumply plop and died – touch wood.

Warner Books now offers an exciting range of quality titles by both established and new authors. All of the books in this series are available from:

Little, Brown and Company (UK),
P.O. Box 11,
Falmouth,
Cornwall TR10 9EN.

Alternatively you may fax your order to the above address. Fax No. 0326 376423.

Payments can be made as follows: cheque, postal order (payable to Little, Brown and Company) or by credit cards, Visa/Access. Do not send cash or currency. UK customers and B.F.P.O. please allow £1.00 for postage and packing for the first book, plus 50p for the second book, plus 30p for each additional book up to a maximum charge of £3.00 (7 books plus).

Overseas customers including Ireland, please allow £2.00 for the first book plus £1.00 for the second book, plus 50p for each additional book.

NAME (Block Letters) ....

....

ADDRESS ....

....

....

☐ I enclose my remittance for _____

☐ I wish to pay by Access/Visa Card

Number ☐☐☐☐☐☐☐☐☐☐☐☐☐☐☐☐

Card Expiry Date ☐☐☐☐